June 24, 2010
Carrie,
Enjoy the adventure!
Lloyd Gordon

THE

MONEY
TRAP

First edition, 2010.

www.thedirtymoneytrap.com

ISBN: 1450558275
ISBN-13: 9781450558273

The life of every man is a diary in which he means to write one story, and writes another.

~James Matthew Barrie

CHAPTER 1

Vancouver, British Columbia, June 2009.

A LOW CEILING of heavy cloud hung over the coastal city, alternately precipitating everything from a soupy, soggy fog, to a light drizzle, on to steady, hard rain as a wet weather system from the Pacific crossed the region. Street level neon signs of every description ambitiously shouted their '*Look here, Look here!*' messages through the air, murky and grey. Traffic snaked its way endlessly on dreary downtown streets and made a constant *wsshh, wsshh* wet sound as the tires of vehicles cut through the water on soaked, asphalt pavement. One of those vehicles was driven by Mathew Crawford as it rounded the corner of Robson onto Burrard Street, his destination just ahead.

The agreed time and place for the meeting was 1:00 o'clock at The Sutton Place Hotel Vancouver in the back of the bar by the lobby. Mathew had completed the task of depositing $500,000 into several accounts in the Philippines where bank secrecy laws allow for virtually anonymous banking. It would be manipulated through many transactions and converted by multiple financial instruments in several countries, before being wired back to Canada as money to purchase an upscale condominium in Burnaby, BC. Start to finish, the placement of funds into a financial institution, the completion of several transactions to disrupt the possibility of an audit trail, and the transferring of the funds back into *legitimate* currency took nearly a month, starting at the beginning of June and ending June 28th, 2009.

The legal term is *money laundering*, and Mathew Crawford was among the best in the business of converting proceeds derived from crime back into lawful capital. As a specialist, and one constantly exposed to legal prosecution, his usual fee for service was twenty percent of the gross dollar amount. This transaction, which took twenty-eight days, paid him $100,000, which he skimmed off the top before wiring the money to buy the condo. His customer, Mario Sorentino, a diamond broker, would keep the condo one season before selling it at the same price, if not more than what he paid. His only real cost would be real estate commissions and, of course, Mathew's fee.

Mat and Mario had been introduced through one of Mat's underworld contacts, when it came to light that Mario had found a means of embezzling product from his diamond supplier in Africa. On a shipment of around $5 million worth of stones, Mario could funnel off about ten percent to sell privately and illegally. Mat didn't have privilege to the information as to exactly how this was being done, and he didn't particularly care. His only job was to manipulate the $500,000 from dirty money back into mainstream capital.

Pulling off a heist in the hundreds of thousands of dollars, or more was only part of the problem for an operator like Mario Sorentino. What is he going to do with the ill-gotten funds? Put it in the bank? Canadian banking laws stipulate detailed reporting to the government of deposits and withdrawals. He could try and make a cash purchase of one or more luxury items like an exotic car or yacht, but any vendor might be suspicious of that and may report it to the police.

Every scheme he imagined had a flaw or weak point which could result in his exposure. It's one thing to steal the money. It's quite another to put it to use somehow. After rolling it around in his head over and over, Mario decided the best thing to do was distance himself from the money until it could be legitimized somehow. The safest thing was to place the money with a proven specialist, for a fee, who would have the experience and knowledge of how to launder the booty back into lawful money.

Then there was the issue of having his supplier find out that he'd been bilked out of $.5 million worth of product. African diamond miners don't take kindly to that sort of thing. Chances are Mario could end up at the bottom of The Strait of Georgia handcuffed to a manhole cover, or find himself in bed with a deadly black mamba, flown in just for the job of sending a message to other diamond brokers who might get a little too ambitious. Africans hack off people's heads with machetes for less than Mario's crime.

Mat had been contacted by Jack Kincaid, another specialist in his own right an intermediary who could line up interested parties to virtually any transaction, legal or otherwise. At an unnaturally lean, six foot four inches, he was a long limbed, conniving sort of ectomorphic schemer who had a knack for finding shady deals and opportunities to make a quick buck. This guy was a serpent and operated on the fringes of mainstream business, orchestrating deals set mainly to avoid disclosure to the government and, of course, taxation. Jack rarely participated directly in such arrangements. He just found one party with a need, then contacted another party who could fulfill that need, and he'd clip a coupon as the middle man for introducing the two. In this case, arranging a meeting between Mat and Mario earned him $10,000, tax free, which Mario gladly paid. Hence, Mario needed to turn $.5 million of criminal proceeds into above board, legal capital. Mathew Crawford was the man.

What security did he have that Mat wouldn't just take the $.5 mil and disappear? Clearly, there was an element of trust at play, but if Mat vanished with the *package*, as it was called, he could be a marked man for life, and that could invite the kind of company he didn't want to have… hired assassins – *hit men,* in the vernacular. And Jack Kincaid would be happy to arrange the contract on Mat's life, for a fee, if it came to that.

Now Mat and Mario were meeting again so that Mario could present another envelope, this one containing some $700,000 to be transformed into legal capital again. The prospect of his $140,000 fee lured Mat into accepting this meeting, though, as always, he was wary that something could go wrong. *Accidents never happen because of something you're expecting*, he had told himself.

Mat entered the ornate bar and noticed Mario sitting at a table in a dimly lit corner. He approached the man.

"Mr. Crawford," Mario said, rising from his chair. "Good to see you again." He stood and reached forward, and the two men shook hands. Mathew unconsciously wiped his hand on the leg of his pants. Mario continued, "I have to tell you though, the last month has been one of many sleepless nights for me. This business is nerve wracking." He sipped his scotch from a crystal rock glass. "Thank you for your services."

"Glad to help out, my friend. No need to lose sleep over it. I'm always careful to insulate my client from any connection to the funds. Now you're the proud owner of a condo in Burnaby as part of your compensation package from a shell company in France that will be your employer. Congratulations!"

"Well done, indeed. But we have some more business to carry out. It's *more* money this time, and I'm curious as to how you're going to clean it up and get it back to me promptly. I can't keep buying real estate," Mario said.

"Oh, there're many ways to disguise the funds and cover up the trail of where they've come from. By the time I get it back to you, there won't be an auditor in the world who could prove that this isn't legal tender. And best of all, the question will never come up," Mat said with confidence.

"Well, I pay you well for your services, you'll agree. You can understand my apprehension that something, shall we say unanticipated, might arise. I need to be certain all the details are covered. Let's go someplace we can go over the fine print. I have a room booked upstairs. We can discuss it privately there."

This didn't feel quite right to Mat. His inner voice was warning that there was something odd about Mario's hasty proposal to go to a private hotel room to talk about their next deal. What was there to discuss? *Hand over the envelope under the table and we can finish our drinks and go through the same process as last time,* he thought. In a month Mario will have $560,000 in one form or another that could not be traced to anything suspicious.

Mario smiled broadly in a genuine and courteous manner as he made his request. Mat decided that he was probably just being careful since this sort of thing was obviously new and exciting to him. The first deal went down smoothly and garnered Mat an easy hundred thousand. Mario gained a new condo that he could sell for liquid, instant, and legal cash, all from stolen diamonds.

Another hundred and forty thousand bucks would put Mat and Foley on easy street for several months, so he said, "My friend, there's lots of ways of laundering money. Rest assured, you'll get your funds, and it won't leave a trail to anything nasty you might have done to acquire this money. All right, let's go, but you go first and I'll follow so we aren't seen together. I can't be long. An associate is waiting for me and he's not a patient man. Shall we?"

As they walked to the elevator, first one, and then the other, Foley watched discreetly from his bar stool. He had worn a big brimmed safari hat to keep dry from the intense rain and it hung on the back of the barstool beside him to drip dry. He flipped the hat onto his head and followed, with a newspaper tucked under his arm like any other hotel guest. Mario Sorentino had no inkling until now that Mat had anyone waiting for him, and he certainly didn't suspect any of the other guests in the elevator, including Foley. Mat and Foley made no eye contact and gave no indication that they knew each other. On the eighteenth floor the elevator dinged and the doors parted from the middle with a *pssshhh* of compressed air. As Mario and Mat exited to the right, Foley stepped out also and proceeded down the hall to the left.

The two men walked casually down the corridor to room 1874, and Mat still had an oddly uncomfortable sensation.

Mario seemed a little too tense, despite his convivial demeanor. His forehead glistened with an oily sweat. Mat noticed Mario undid the center button of his jacket as he placed the card key into the reader in the door. As they entered the room, Mario made a point of allowing Mat to go in first and, as Mat glanced backward over his shoulder, Mario clearly reached inside his jacket for something. Mat's fears were confirmed. As the hotel room door closed, Mario was pulling a hand gun on him. But why? The possibilities flashed through his mind. The fee could not be recovered by Mario. It was well hidden in a Libyan shell company account, so robbery was out. Was Mario a federal authority of some sort now making an arrest?

Immediately beside the door inside the room was a small table with an accent lamp on it. Before Mario could raise the gun, Mat grabbed the lamp and swung it full force directly at his face. Although the lamp did little damage as a weapon, it did hit him and succeeded in momentarily distracting him.

Mat grabbed Mario's gun hand with both of his and pushed it into the wall with all his might. The men struggled for control of the weapon and Mat called out, "No! No! Son of a bitch!" In their brawling, Mario's trigger finger squeezed, and the gun went off twice with the *whump, whump* noise of a sound suppressor attached to its muzzle. Mario swung Mat around toward the door and slammed his head into the wall with his elbows. Stunned by the blow, Mat loosened his grip, giving Mario the advantage.

Mario was the larger and stronger of the two men, and the gun was being muscled downward toward his opponent's head. Mat was horrified that he was about to be shot by this madman and fought back with all his strength, but it was no use. Mario moved the gun closer and closer to Mat's ear. In desperation, Mat eased his resistance long enough to turn his head toward Mario's hands, now pushing the gun to his face. With animal ferocity, Mat opened his mouth and bit Mario's left hand, right behind the thumb, with all the strength of his jaw and grabbed again at the weapon trying to wrestle it away.

Mario screamed out in pain as Mat felt the bones in Mario's hand crunch between his teeth. With brutal force, Mat then kicked his knee into Mario's groin at least three times. In agony, Mario at last dropped the gun to the floor. Now both men, still grappling, fell to the ground and seeing the gun near his feet, Mat kicked it across the room and out of reach of his assailant. Mario, on top of Mat now, brought his forehead down on Mat's face like a skilled street fighter in a head butt, with punishing cruelty. Mat was stunned, and his nose streamed blood freely from both sides. Mario now freed himself, stood up and crossed the room to retrieve the gun. Knowing that this was likely the end, Mat pulled himself to his feet and feebly pushed down the door handle, releasing the catch. What else could he do now but attempt to run?

As the door swung open, there in the hall before the two combatants, stood Karl Folkestad, every bit the Norwegian Viking that his ancestry and disposition had made him. Six feet three inches, two hundred thirty pounds, with broad shoulders and long thick limbs. High cheek bones, strong jaw and blonde hair, now graying at the temples. He was dressed in casual slacks, an open collared shirt and a leather bomber jacket. He didn't say a word, but the look on his face left no question that he meant business and was accustomed to handling trouble. No man in his right mind would go willingly toe to toe with this guy. Mat took one look at him and uttered, "Foley!"

With a decisive sweep of his right hand, Foley reached into the room, grabbed Mat by the collar and yanked him into the hall like a rag doll. Mario ran towards the door, gun in hand. In a move surprisingly swift for a big man, Foley pulled a metal knife from his belt and threw it overhand, impaling Mario right through his throat before he could get a shot away. Both Mario's hands went to his neck, and blood sputtered from his lips and gullet as he dropped to his knees, eyes bulging in terror. The blade of Foley's knife protruded three inches out the back of Mario's neck and he fell forward, gasping desperately. A moment later the blood stopped pumping from his carotid artery and he was dead.

"I think we should scoot now," Foley said casually to Mathew, who was sitting in disbelief against the far wall of the hallway, where he had been hurtled only moments ago. His face was a bloody pulp. The front of his shirt was soaked crimson red. Astonishingly, in all the commotion, no onlookers had gathered, and though it seemed like forever, the actual fight had lasted only a minute or two. If anyone should see them now, however, especially Mat, they would know that an assault had taken place and would want to call for help. Seeing Foley, it would be assumed he was the attacker and they'd probably find themselves in a discussion they wouldn't want to be having. And when they discovered the body inside room 1874 it would be disaster for both of them.

Mat said, "Wait. I'll have to clean up a bit. Let's go back inside."

Foley got his drift. "Okay, pal, you're right. You'd have a better chance of winnin' Miss Canada than getting outta here lookin' like that. Get that bloody shirt off and you can wear my jacket till we leave the hotel. It don't fit ya, but it'll draw a lot less attention than a blood soaked shirt."

The two men went back into the room where Mat washed up and stuffed the bloody shirt into the plastic liner of the bathroom garbage can. A wad of toilet paper was stuffed up each of his nostrils to try and stem the flow of blood. Mat was very careful to clean up all traces of his blood, knowing that it contained DNA which he didn't want to leave as his calling card. He wiped up everywhere the fight had taken place and everything he touched.

Foley withdrew his knife from dead Mario's throat, and rinsed it thoroughly under the tap. Mat checked inside Mario's coat to see if the envelope with the money was there. Nope. Nothing. Then he looked in his wallet to see if he might have been some kind of federal agent. All his ID indicated he was Mario Sorentino, of Diamond Brokers International, Inc.

"Foley," asked Mat, "How did you know which room we were in? We lost you when we got off the elevator." Mat dabbed around his injured nose with a wash cloth at the mirror.

"Those bullet holes in the top of the door gave me the notion that somethin' no good was goin' on in there," Foley replied. "I was comin' down the hall listening for clues as to where you might be, when *crack, crack* – two shots come through the door a few feet in front of me. I was just figurin' on how to get in when the door opened, and there you were. And quite a sight at that, I might add."

"I'm done here. Open the door and check," said Mat, pulling Foley's size 46 jacket over his 40 Frame. "Make sure the coast is clear and we'll get the hell outta here right now."

With three strides across the hotel room, he kicked the limp Mario hard in his ribs with a *thud*. "Bastard!"

In a matter of minutes, they were behind the wheel of their rented Ford Explorer and driving away from the nightmare that could have ended Mat's life, and probably ruined Foley's.

Moments later in the car, an exhausted Mathew Crawford, holding a blood soaked towel to his face said, "What the hell just happened?"

"Jesus H. Christ. You look like a victim from a bad car crash. If you were a cat, I'd say you're down to about four lives," Foley replied.

Thirty minutes earlier, Mat Crawford had been a relatively attractive young man in his mid-thirties, with wavy, medium brown hair; the kind of average guy, attractive features you might see on a male model in a department store flyer. At five-eleven, and a trim one hundred eighty pounds, he looked fit, though neither tall nor short by most standards. This was a man in his prime – no one would call him a kid, but he wasn't yet middle-aged either. Now, he looked like a graphic photo in *Sports Illustrated* of a prize fighter, still standing after a twelve round bout with Evander Holyfield.

"Why was he trying to kill me?" Mat wondered aloud. "He couldn't get his money back. I did that son of a bitch a favor, and he tries to kill me!"

"You know, Buck, for bein' such a slippery little bugger when it comes to movin' money around, you sure ain't got much sense when it comes to figuring out people's motives," said Foley.

"What do you mean?"

"Well, think about it. If he didn't want to rob you, and he wasn't a cop or federal agent trying to bust your ass, then why else would he want you dead?" Foley asked.

The rain was lifting now and sunshine beamed through the clouds, accenting the full spectrum of color in the environment and flora all around them. Mat paused and looked into the distance towards the luxuriant, green landscape of the Rocky Mountains of British Columbia, a magnificent rainbow crowning the scene below.

Thinking out loud, he said, "Because I know who he is, and what he does, and what he *did*. He stole from the Baken Diamond Mine in South Africa, and I am the only link between him and $.5 million worth of missing diamonds. I could have held him hostage and blackmailed him on that information. I could have made him pay, and pay, and pay." The light finally came on for Mat. Mario was simply trying to cover his tracks by eliminating Mat, once and for all.

"Bingo!" said Foley. "God almighty – if anything ever happens to me, you won't last a month out here in the world on your own."

"Ya," said Mat, "Nothing's gonna happen to you, Rambo. By the way, *Thanks*. But did ya have to throw me against the wall like that? I think I cracked my shoulder."

"Well, I didn't exactly have time to discuss the matter. As you may recall, he was going for a gun and I had to get you outta harm's way, fast," replied Foley.

"I was just warming up. I had him right where I wanted him. One more second and he would have been fuckin' toast," Matt continued in a weak attempt at levity.

Foley just looked at him. "Well, that towel looks like you just received a heart transplant. We'll have to get rid of it, and that shirt in the bag, once you quit bleedin'. Better have that nose looked at. I'd say it's busted. And you better start rehearsin' the story you're going to tell Christine. She ain't gonna be too impressed with your face, I'll predict. God knows, I'll get the blame one way or another."

The two men drove off with a narrow escape from disaster behind them; Mathew Crawford, money launderer and international financier, and Karl Folkestad, his body guard, buddy, and associate. Both men, Buck and Foley, more brothers than business partners – life long pals and comrades, completely and inseparably entrusted to each other. And the adventure of their lives was only just beginning.

CHAPTER 2

CHRISTINE ROTH HAD met Mathew while they were attending the University of British Columbia in Vancouver. They graduated together in 1994 with bachelor's degrees, his in business, and hers in early childhood education. Mathew, at twenty-three, was a year older than Christine. Throughout the last two years of their attendance at UBC they had been exclusive to each other and their fiery romance had been pretty much destined for the alter from the start. As new graduates each went on to start careers after their marriage in 1995. Mathew got a job as a loans officer in a bank and Christine became a teacher with the local School Board. Over time, Mathew advanced in title and responsibility within the banking circles, and by the year 2000 he was promoted to Branch Manager of one of the big five Canadian banks. Christine's career was less disposed to any meteoric rise through the ranks, but she held down her job as a teacher reliably and enjoyed her work. They bought a nice house in the suburbs and adopted a dog from the SPCA. The picture was evolving nicely and they had everything they needed to make a good start in life.

Mat loved Christine and always felt like she was his version of winning the lottery. She'd been an undisputed beauty among the college students and had an air of aloofness about her, even with Mat. But that only contributed to her mystery as a woman for him. He'd talk to her about something routine and she'd smile coyly at him like she knew a secret or had a naughty plan that she was withholding. She had a natural ability of being a subtle tease, a flirt, in everything about her manner with Mat, and he loved it. Undeniably, he was a lucky guy to have landed her, as there had been a long line of other suitors at the ready, if he hadn't.

Following a typical day early in their marriage, night fell, and after tending to everyday chores like cleaning up the supper dishes, and watching some light entertainment on TV together, Mat and Christine retired to their bedroom. Tired from a long day, Mat fell into bed and rolled over on his side. Christine changed into her satin nightwear and snuggled up to his back, spooning her body contours with his.

"Tired tonight, Sweetie?" Christine whispered, hotly in his ear.

"Ya, today was brutal. Five client meetings, and we started at seven this morning."

"Ah, poor baby. Maybe I can make you feel better,"

"I always feel better when I'm with you, Mrs. Crawford."

"How about feeling some of this," She coaxed, rolling Mat over and placing his hand under her night gown and over her warm, plump breast. "Does that ease your suffering at all, lover?"

"*Mmmm...* Now that does feel nice."

Christine responded to her husband's caress and arched her head back, closing her eyes and smiling. With a swing of her leg, Christine was on top of Mat now, straddling him lustily, looking down at him in the pale moon glow coming through their bedroom window. Moments later, after sensually moving her hips over his, Mat responded as expected. He ran his hand now from her breast to her tummy, to the downy, slick mound between her thighs and her pearly lips engulfed his fingers in a slippery, female warmth. She whimpered a joyful little sigh, and he responded by easing himself into her until she murmured *"Uhhh..."*, and he felt like he was in heaven. Then they gazed amorously into each other's eyes, and climbed passionately together to a climax of ecstasy.

"Not so tired after all, huh? Mat? *Helloooo...* You in there?"

Mat's breathing was heavy and he lay still, satisfied beyond measure. Within seconds, he was snoring softly, blissfully asleep. Christine fluffed her pillow and nuzzled herself at his side. Time now for slumber, and off they drifted together.

Nine months later, in 1999, a darling little girl was born to them with blonde hair and blue eyes, just like her mom. She had her dad's facial features, and looked like a little pink, new improved version of both parents. She couldn't have been loved or cherished more by anyone, and Mat and Christine must have considered every name in the English language for her – Roxanne, Chelsea, Ashley, Chloe, Emily, Madison, Olivia, Delilah – on and on. Finally, they settled on *Hannah,* a name with roots in English, Hebrew, French, German and Dutch. It meant 'favor' or 'grace' in Hebrew, had a pleasant ring to it, and seemed to suit her perfectly. They were indeed, *graced* with her birth, and she came to them like a *favor* from heaven. And with that, they became not just a couple, but a *family,* and Mat's chest swelled with pride and love for his two girls.

On the change table while Mat was putting on a fresh diaper, he'd hold her chubby little feet in his hands and kiss her soles, saying, "These feet will carry you down the long road of life, my darling, and bring you adventure and trials you would never have imagined possible. May your journey bring happiness and good things!" A parent's wish for their children's success in life is nearly universal.

Growing up, Mat had never really experienced love within his family, and now, with Christine, he felt things so strongly that it seemed like he was making up for lost time. Sometimes in the evening he would place his head in her lap on the sofa and she would stroke his hair and temples. It was comforting to know that she loved him, would never hurt or leave him. In fact, her love for him was undoubted. It felt like this was the love that had been denied him during childhood. Here was a man who could dance with the devil when it came to his livelihood, but who still had the capacity for real love when he looked upon this woman.

As a young boy, Mathew had only known a household filled with discipline and disapproval. His father, Frank Crawford, had been an investigator with the RCMP of commercial crimes and narcotics, and an authoritarian who cast a patriotic shadow over everyone else in the family, especially Mathew.

"Boy," he used to say, "Get out there and dust off that driveway. Hurry now," if it had snowed the night before.

Mat would comply without question or complaint because he wanted to please his father, always at a loss to understand why he never seemed to be able to do so. Never did Frank call Mathew "Son" or "Lad" or any other endearing term commonly heard between fathers and sons, not even "Mat" for that matter. Always "Mathew" or "Boy", even until he was seventeen years old, when Frank died of a mysterious illness.

In these early years, within the Crawford household there had been a continual air of tension and unhappiness. His mother and father had not loved each other and both Mat and his little brother Jason had felt it. Kids know some things intuitively. Their mother, Helen, would complain that theirs was not a normal family and that she never expected or deserved to be treated like an staff subordinate or a dependent.

"God in heaven, Frank, can you stop being inspector Crawford for five minutes and just be my husband for once?" she'd complain. "I never thought I got married to be a cook and a cleaner. You leave early and come home late every night and we never spend time as a normal family. And all I do is housework and cook for you and the boys, then you order us around like we're new recruits at the detachment."

"What are you squawkin' about now, woman?" he'd fire back. Rarely did he address her by her name – Helen. "Isn't it enough that I work sixty hours a week for you bunch of ingrates? I put food on the table, clothes on your backs and a roof over your heads, and all I hear is how rough you all have it. Anyways, what would you have me do? Quit the force and get a job selling cars? You knew what you were getting into."

"I *wish I* only had to work sixty hours to do my part to prop up your career. Do you ever take time to realize that your family should come before your work on the grand scale of your priorities? We're not your assistants. We're your wife and sons and we need a hus-band and father, not just a provider of the essential ingredients to support life. I'd like, just once, to have you walk through the door, see you smile and tell me what a great day you had at work today, and use the word *Honey* somewhere in the sentence. Instead, you tell me. What's on your mind right now, tonight?

"I can't talk about ongoing criminal investigations. You know that. Don't ask!" he'd curtly retort.

"And you know that we need more than food and clothes. Where's the love, Frank?"

"God damn it!" he would holler, "Will you give it a rest, wife? No wonder this kid is so mixed up he doesn't know right from left without checking with his mother," gesturing towards Mat. "Mathew has spent his whole boyhood hiding behind his mommy's skirt instead of learning to be a man. Where's the love? Don't talk to me about love. Love doesn't pay the bills. Love doesn't turn a boy into a man. They don't preach love at the military academy. The RCMP didn't turn me into an under-cover officer by putting me through a *love in* during my training. How could I have spawned a pathetic little '*May Fly*' like this, who spends all of his time watching cartoons or wandering by himself in the woods by the river? I'll tell you how. Because while I'm at work catching the bad guys, you're here at home teaching him how to be a *girly boy*. You've turned him into mush. The boy needs to learn discipline and respect, by God! It's never too early and I'm afraid, thanks to you, now it might be too late."

By some point during these all too common arguments, Mathew and his brother would most likely be crying in their room or hiding downstairs, ashamed of their weakness, because men don't cry, even if they're only eight and six like Mat and Jason were.

As time went on, Mat's mother grew increasingly distant and the boys sensed that her dissatisfaction with the marriage had turned to resignation. She was trapped. She had two boys that needed care. They needed to have food and shelter and she couldn't work at anything on her own that would provide well enough for them. She never gained the upper hand in these continual confrontations with her husband, and as time moved on, he became more abusive to all of them. She just sort of gave up, didn't bother complaining, didn't bother fighting, and hardly ever smiled or laughed. By the time Mat was eleven his parents had taken separate bedrooms. Everyone in the family became room mates more than family members. Mat, especially, was alienated. His brother Jason was born into and grew up in this atmosphere and he seemed to just accept it over time. So Mat became branded as 'the sensitive one', another insult to his manhood. In the end, there was just an awkward silence around the dinner table, unless Mat or Jason made some critical blunder to arouse their father's ire, like putting their elbows on the table, or dropping a utensil to the floor. No one dared make eye contact with him and no one initiated a conversation with him because it always ended in an argument and a full scale personal attack on their inadequacies.

Still, Mat was a boy who wanted his father's approval at a visceral level. Every normal little boy wants to see his daddy smile and feel that he is proud of him for who he is. On the one hand, Mat wanted his dad's acceptance and to hear his say-so. Oftentimes, however, he would find himself under attack just for being a normal little boy, and his natural reaction was to fight back, though he always lost, and he didn't want to fight with his dad. He wanted to hang out and be friends like normal fathers and sons and it made him feel confused and miserable. Mat's formative years lacked the guidance and love that only a father can give to a son.

But he did have Foley.

Foley was as close to a male mentor, or big brother that Mathew Crawford would ever have. He had been hired when Mat was ten to protect the family because Frank was involved in so many dangerous investigations. Foley, then, was a strapping young lad of twenty two who had distinguished himself in the military and had migrated to the world of private security after his discharge. He was licensed to carry a fire arm and he had an assortment of surveillance equipment, pepper sprays, hand cuffs, two way radios, tape recorders, knives and the like that you might expect of a trained body guard. In the army he learned how to kill a man with a variety of weapons, or with his bare hands, how to assemble and detonate explosives, track a man through the wilderness or the city, and how to wire-tap a phone to pick up private conversations. He was well qualified and well equipped to do the job, and his mandate, quite simply, was to watch over and ensure the safety of Frank's family at all times.

Frank Crawford had participated in many, many investigations into illegal activities involving the criminal world's lowest operators. Drug trafficking, counterfeiting, prostitution, kidnappings, contract murder, embezzlement, fraud, extortion, bootleg tobacco and alcohol, car theft rings. You name it, Frank had been assigned to it, and most times he got to the bottom of it. Drugs were seized, arrests were made, charges were laid, people were jailed, illegal operations were broken up. As a result, he had developed a few enemies over the years, and if he was hard on his family he was even worse on criminals. In the seediest corners of Vancouver's underworld, criminals of every ilk knew that if Inspector Frank Crawford got onto your trail, you'd better leave town. Either that or, when a fly is buzzing around your head, you swat it and squash it dead. Inspector Crawford was messing with some very powerful criminal organizations, so it had become evident that he and his family needed protection from that potential swat, and Foley had been assigned the job.

Not long after taking up his position as family security guard, Karl Folkestad picked up the nick name, "Foley" from the boys. At twenty-two, he was twelve years older than Mat, but still young enough to be naturally inclined towards fun things, tom foolery, and devilment in general. To Mat, this was a welcome addition to the family and the two of them spent many hours together in jovial conversation. Foley asked questions of Mat about his opinions or his school work or sports and he listened with genuine interest to his answers. Never before had Mat come across one who took an interest in him as a real person – and Foley never, ever, belittled or criticized him.

Even at an early age, Foley was a *man's man* and Mat watched his every act and listen to his every word with fixed attention. On his time off, Foley even took the boys fishing, or to the go carts or to a movie about James Bond, Batman, Indiana Jones or some such action hero.

He taught Mat and Jason the basics of self defense and gave them practical instruction on what to do in every type of emergency imaginable. Through his coaching the boys learned the philosophy and practice of martial arts, and how to kill a man in seconds with something called a commando choke hold. They learned how to disarm and disable an assailant with either a hammer lock or half nelson when countering a knife attack.

He educated them about military ordnance and incendiaries and showed them how to make and throw a Molotov cocktail. They were given personal tutoring on all sorts of military protocol and taught how army battles, as well as covert operations, were carried out.

He helped them with homework, watched them play soccer, and even counseled Mat on his first awkward encounter with a girl. At school one day, the boys and girls were placed together in gym class to learn the waltz because grade nine graduation was approaching. Mat was coupled up with a girl named Lily Anne Sexsmith. Her provocative name was fitting because even at fourteen years of age she had developed a lovely full bosom that you would expect of a girl much older, and she was proud of her figure and flaunted it coyly for the appreciative boys. She and her best friend, Wanda Ravine, were the objects of much male adolescent jocularity and endless ribald jokes about their respective last names, compounded by the fact that their doting boyfriends were named Wally Rimmer and Dewey Shortreed.

As Johnny Rivers sang *Slow Dancing* and the teacher guided the dancers to a cadence, "One two, One two" Lily Ann pressed her breasts into Mat, seductively. Mat turned and looked at her, face to face, and she smiled sweetly up at him. Then she discreetly but distinctly nudged his pelvis with hers, just once, but enough to send fireworks into Mat's burgeoning male instincts.

Now – what happens when a healthy young man is placed in a romantic embrace with a busty, fragrant, and flirtatious young girl? Predictably, roughly fifty percent of the blood volume in his body immediately rushed to his loins, and Mat instantly got a love Jones. Lily Anne noticed it through Mat's satin gym shorts and went "*Oh my Gawd!* What's that?" Then she giggled hysterically with one hand covering her mouth and the other pointing at his distended shorts. Mat was made a laughing stock in front of the whole class.

At home that night Mat was despondent and Foley picked up on his buddy's sullen mood. "What's eatin' at you, Gilligan? It don't take a psychologist to figure out that something's on your mind."

"Oh, nothin'… just something that happened today at school."

"Well, then, out with it. Let's talk about it or you'll brood about it all night. C'mon, that's what friends are for."

Reluctantly, Mat said "We were taking dance lessons today at school."

"And what? You weren't exactly Fred Astaire?"

"No. More like Johnny Wadd," Mat replied.

"You mean the old porn star?"

"You got it. Lily Anne Sexsmith was my waltz partner and she teased me – on purpose. She's got killer hooters. You can even see them jiggle from behind. We were dancing and she pushed her pussy-snatch into me and I sprung wood, right there on the dance floor. I couldn't help it. Everyone saw, and they all laughed at me. Now I have to kill her," Mat explained, quite seriously.

Foley laughed out loud and said, "Well, that might be over-reacting just a little, but if she humiliated you deliberately, there are *ways* of getting even."

"Like what?"

"I dunno, maybe a double dose of ex-lax discreetly slipped into her food on hot-lunch day. How about putting a big, ugly spider from the pet store in her tote bag? There's something about her, or something she does that makes her a sittin' duck for payback... What is it? You just have to get creative."

The two rascals smiled conspiratorially at each other.

Foley had said, "Dog-gone it, nothin' on earth can provoke or tease a man like a woman. They're genetically programmed to torment us fourteen ways to Sunday – and about thirteen of them will involve your pecker, one way or another. It comes as natural to them as crying or shopping. They can't help it... it's in their *hormozones*. And us boys are made up to be suckers for punishment. You're a young buck now and I'd like to tell ya that it's goin' to get easier with time, but one thing I ain't is a liar. *Man up*, Buck. If its got tires or tits, it's gonna give ya trouble. Best advice? Keep the lumber in your pants 'til the right one comes along. You'll thank me for it one day," then Mat and Foley laughed raucously.

From that moment on, Mat's nickname became *Buck*. A special connection between the body guard and the boys, especially Mat, had clearly taken root. In short, these guys liked each other and were destined to grow together for years to come.

☆ ☆ ☆

Later that week, Lily Anne reached into her back pack at lunch and removed the bottle of Lipton ice tea that she routinely carried around with her. She unscrewed the lid and took a long gulp of it in the lunch room, swallowed once, then spewed the rest out like it was boiling hot poison, which drinking someone else's urine might well be. Instantly, the room went silent. Dozens of students around her stopped eating and talking and stared at her in shock. Then her friend, *Wanda's Ravine*, as the boys called her, took the bottle from Lilly Anne's hand and smelled it. Her face contorted instantly in disgust and she exclaimed, "It's piss!"

Hysterical laughter erupted among her classmates as Lily Anne fiercely wiped at her mouth with a napkin and labored for an explanation to such a mean, sadistic prank. As she glanced all around the room looking for the perpetrator of this outrage her gaze fixed like missile-lock radar upon Mat. Her eyes widened and the expression on her face screamed, *YOU!*

He was standing at the doorway, ready to leave the room. Mat smiled, winked, and gave a subtle forward thrust with his hips, like she had done to him in the gym. Not long after, Mat became something of a local hero amongst the other students as the rumors (never confirmed, nor denied by him), circulated about how his revenge was exacted upon the conceited, snobby, flirtatious Lily Anne Sexsmith.

Justice had been served and Mat's self esteem and capacity for survival had changed forever.

CHAPTER 3

ONE THING THAT did not change, however, was the icy relationship between Frank and Helen. In fact, they avoided each other; or more aptly, she avoided him. Authoritarian and stubborn as he was, this made his attitude and behavior even more repugnant over time. In turn, his constant disapproval and criticism drove her inward, and she became an introverted, isolated and lonely woman. She hated him. He wouldn't leave because this was *his* house. She wouldn't leave because she couldn't. The boys and Foley spent an increasing amount of time away from the home together due in large part to avoid the tension.

Mat was seventeen and in grade twelve, and one day his father became ill. He had lied down on the couch and complained of a pounding headache. He needed to rest. He felt nauseous and went to bed early complaining that he must have the flu. The family took it in stride and not much was made of it. By the next day he was worse. His pallor turned a ghastly bluish grey and he could hardly stand up. Without delay, he was taken to the hospital and admitted to emergency with suspected ptomaine poisoning.

The boys and Foley went about their business with the expectation that the cause of father's sickness would be determined and he would be treated and released in due course. Helen stood vigil by the phone for any news from the doctors. At the hospital in the intensive care unit, tests were run, I.V. lines were inserted, urine and blood were analyzed, monitors went going *beep, beep, beep,* and all the standard diagnostic measures were put into play. But the medical staff was baffled. There were no obvious symptoms of food or blood poisoning. It wasn't any known disease that indicators pointed to. He didn't have a discernable tumor anywhere, and his blood cells showed no sign of cancer. There were no ulcers anywhere in his G.I. tract that made him sick. He hadn't been bitten by a bug, so it wasn't an allergic reaction. And he was getting worse by the hour.

By the end of day three, Frank had lost consciousness. The family was called to his bedside and told that, unless something concrete could be determined about his illness, his chances of survival were declining fast.

"If you can't identify the cause, you can't apply a treatment," the doctor had told Helen. Tests for every possible source of the illness continued at a feverish pace.

Mat stood at his bedside and looked down at him while doctors, and nurses, and his mother, and other hospital specialists talked in medical lingo that amounted to '*We just don't bloody know!*' as far as Mat was concerned. He noticed how small his dad now looked. He felt sorry for him because, despite his overbearing manner all his life, he was now reduced to a sick little man on death's doorstep. No one could help him. He had been a hard man on his sons, and wife, and Mat still loved him if only because, good or bad, this was the only father he would ever have. Mat had never given up hope of pleasing his dad and rising to the standards expected of him. Thinking about how hard he had tried and failed to earn his dad's love and make him proud, his eyes welled up with tears and he stood there feeling utterly helpless and useless, just like his dad had often said. Words escaped him and all he could mutter under his breath was *"Dad..."*

An attractive nurse, working diligently in the room noticed and without comment pulled a tissue from a Kleenex box at his bedside and handed it to Mat compassionately, making him feel self conscious. "Thanks," was all he said.

What he really wanted to say was, *This is not the man you think. This is an Inspector with the RCMP who has brought down more bad dudes than you can imagine. He worked hard all his life to build a career and care for his family and his wife never appreciated his efforts, ever once. All she did was nag and criticize him continually. I love this guy and would be lucky to achieve half of what he's done and I'd do anything to make him proud of me and get well right now. You don't understand. He's my dad... We're blood!* In a few more moments everyone was ushered out of the room so Frank could rest.

"Folks, you might as well go home for tonight," said the attending physician. "We'll keep doing all we can to try and nail down this thing," trying to use optimistic language, "If there's any change, we'll call you immediately." Several other comments were exchanged, laden with pathological terminology and encouragement to not lose hope, but Mat was disheartened and feared the worst.

Helen Crawford was being brave and said, "All right. We know you're doing everything possible, Doctor. He's in God's hands and all we can do keep our faith and wait. Come on, boys, let's go." She, the boys, and Foley walked down the hallway outside unit 144B of Intensive care, leaving Frank to his fate.

It had been Monday when Frank had first laid down with a headache. By Thursday, virtually all of his organs had shut down. Without the fluids from the I.V. line his body would have shriveled like a prune. He lay motionless but for the induced rise and fall of his chest from the respirator attached to his trachea through the front of his neck. His mouth had contorted into a hideous open gape and his head arched back. Ice cubes had been pressed to his lips to keep them moist.

After an eternity of waiting and worrying, Helen and the boys were approached by the lead physician, while they sat at Frank's bedside.

"Come with me, please — I believe we have some news," he said somberly. The family followed him out of the room single file, to the corridor outside.

Helen immediately pressed him for information. "What is it? Have you found a cure?" If the doctor had news, it wasn't necessarily good by the look on his face.

"I'm afraid not, but we think we know what made him sick. It appears to be a highly noxious substance — ricin. It's a poison found naturally in castor beans. It can be reduced to a tasteless powder and mixed with food or water. All symptoms suggest he ingested it somehow."

Young Mat listened to his mom and the doctor discuss the case and finally interrupted, "Are you certain of this diagnosis? Has it been confirmed with some test?"

"I'm sorry, no. There is no reliable medical test to confirm its presence. We can only deduce its presence from the symptoms."

"Then how are you going to cure him?" Mat demanded.

The doctor shifted uncomfortably on his feet, measuring the right words to use. He cleared his throat.

"After this length of time in his system, his chances of recovery are extremely slim. Not impossible, but slim. We can continue to provide intravenous fluids with medications to treat low blood pressure and seizure. We'll try and help him breath. We've already pumped his stomach, but the strategy from here on is to keep him alive long enough for the poison to work itself out of his body. I don't want to instill false hope or unrealistic expectations — he is gravely ill. His chances are very slim, as I say."

Helen had a ghostly pallor and she pursed her lips before saying, "I see. Well then, come boys and we'll go pray for a miracle. Thank you, Doctor," and they slowly walked together away from Frank's room toward the elevators.

The family waited in the hospital chapel. Minutes seemed like hours. The boys were grief stricken, more so than anyone would expect considering how difficult it had been to live with this man. Helen's face was drained of color with worry and she had said very little. She just sat quietly with her hands clasped, looking downward. Colleagues Frank had worked with waited solemnly in the reception area, talking in hushed tones mostly about what a fine, results driven police officer he was. There was an aura of doom and everyone was awaiting the inevitable. At 2:14 p.m. on Thursday, July 10th, 1988, the lead physician entered the chapel and if he had bad news he didn't have to say it. His demeanor said it all.

He shook his head. "I'm so sorry."

Mat walked out of the room and down the sterile, white corridor — and he felt like his chest was going to explode. "This can't be happening. Not now. He wasn't ready. Why did he have to die? Why couldn't those incompetent imbeciles find out what was wrong with him? Dad, I so wanted to have you love me, and Jason, and Mom. Oh God, no!"

Foley was upset too, but he had seen death many times in the service and knew it never comes at a convenient time and it's never good. He felt for young Mat and chased after him down the hallway. "Mat, wait. I'll go with you." He caught up with his young buddy and put his arm around Mat's shoulder as the two of them walked past the main reception and out into a sunny courtyard where luckier patients were sitting in their pajamas and hospital garb with friends and family. Together, they sat down on a wooden bench under a towering weeping willow beside a fish pond with a fountain, gurgling tranquilly.

Mat sobbed into his hands and said, "Foley, you knew Dad. Why didn't he love me? Why wasn't I ever good enough for him? I always tried to do what was right. No matter what, it wasn't enough. Now he's gone and I'll never, ever get to show him that I loved him and only wanted his approval. I could have measured up!" and he wept.

Foley said, "Mat, listen to me. Come on, listen up here." He spoke in a tone that indicated he was counseling Mat and expected his full attention. "It was never *you* that wasn't good enough. It was him. He was a hard man on everybody because he was never satisfied with himself. He couldn't tolerate anything that wasn't perfect or governed by strict black and white rules. He couldn't even live up to his own standards, and he deflected his guilt and frustration on everyone around him, startin' with those he loved most. It's why he ended up doing what he did for a living.

"The police force is not unlike the military, and it's easier to take on a posture of rigid inflexibility against anyone perceived to be weak or undisciplined than it is to show tolerance and patience for people who are still learning or who make the occasional mistake. His twisted ego wouldn't let him admit that he's capable of vulnerability such as love or compassion, even for his own family — *even* for his own son. His own limitations and self doubt made him lash out at the world, like a rabid dog, who's not really himself. He couldn't help it. That's just the way he was. It wasn't you, Mat. It was him, understand? He did love you. He just didn't know how to handle it. And he sure didn't know how to show it."

Mat said, "Foley, was your dad anything like that?"

"No, I had a good dad, and know what? I lost him before I was twenty, just like you. He taught me a lot of things about the world before he went though. We had a lot of laughs together and I think about him and miss him to this very day. Listen Bud, your dad's gone now forever, but I'm not going to let you go this road alone, get it? I got your back and you don't ever have to worry that I won't kick shit outta anyone who tries to harm or cross ya. You and I are partners and I expect you to stand behind me, too, from this day forward. Can I rely on ya?"

This was not a rhetorical question. Foley was looking hard at Mat and he wanted an answer. Saying 'yes' to it meant a gentleman's agreement was in place. Mat answered without hesitation. "You bet you can Foley. You bet."

At seventeen and twenty-nine, Mat and Foley had made a pact of brotherhood and loyalty. They were now officially in the business of being friends and confidants for life. No two brothers-by-blood could ever have been closer.

In the days that followed, an official cause of death had to be pronounced. Frank Crawford's Certificate of Death declared 'Multiple organ failure and uncontrollable fever, likely from the ingestion of ricin, resulting in death,' whatever that actually explained. "Those were the symptoms, but nobody could say with certainty what caused them. Ricin... What the hell is that?" thought Mathew.

The event had matured Mat, and his journey toward manhood had taken a big step forward. He felt responsible now as the senior male in his family, to see that his little brother Jason, and his mother, were taken care of properly. With Foley's support he felt that he would help guide the family through this ordeal and onto whatever lay ahead for them all. In the months after the funeral, he decided that a new plan had to be put in place to focus the family and move forward into a new life.

First things first. What about Foley? With Frank gone the need for a professional security guard to protect them all had been eliminated. The bad guys had no reason to come after any of them now. Still, Foley had become an integral part of their family over the last seven years, and it would be hard to imagine life without him. And Foley had a life of his own and could hardly be expected to linger without concern for where his own career should go from here.

Frank had had life insurance and it had left a tidy sum of $250,000 for his widow, and his pension from work had provided a source of income that she could easily live on. The modest house they lived in had no mortgage as Frank managed to pay it off over the last twenty years. Financially, they were all right, but Helen had fallen into a deep depression and she scarcely communicated with anyone. Mat hoped that she was just going through a natural grieving process and that eventually things would get back to normal. At forty years of age she might even re-marry again some day, he thought. She deserved to be happy.

And what about Jason, that happy-go-lucky little brother of his who hardly ever seemed to be affected by anything? Not his dad's bullying when he was alive, not the constant fighting between his mom and dad, not Foley's big brotherly influence, and not much by his dad's death. He'd been sad for only a few days, and seemed more worried about how the family would cope without Dad's income to provide for everything. Once it surfaced that money was not really an issue, he'd carried on like nothing much had changed.

About three months after the death in the family, at Foley's suggestion, Mat called a meeting to put everything on the table and get things moving forward again. Everyone gathered in the kitchen and looked at Mat. It included his mother, Foley, his brother, and him.

Mat started, "All right everyone. I think it's high time we all got over losing Dad. We have to move on with life. Nothing can bring him back and we each have to carry on. Feeling sorry for ourselves is not helping anything, so let's figure out a plan to get back on our feet."

Foley raised his hand to his mouth to conceal a slight smile. He noted that his guidance of Mat since his father's death had taken hold. Mat was stepping into a role of leadership and being quite the family manager.

"Mom, let's start with you. What are you going to do now? You have to pick yourself up and get outta this damn depression."

"Don't swear at your mother," Foley said.

"Well, now that's a good question. I just don't know, really. I'll have to figure out how to spend my days. I've never worked, but maybe I could find a job at something to keep me busy, and keep my mind off things. Lord knows, it can drive you mad thinking and worrying and thinking and worrying. There's no end to it. Maybe I could volunteer at the church. I could have been a better wife. Frank, I'm *so sorry...*" She placed her hand over her chest and shook her head in heartache.

"You were a good wife, Mom. Nobody blames you for anything," Mat said, now in a more rational frame of mind than during the crisis days of his dad's illness. "Okay, so starting tomorrow, you go on a serious job search. I'll help you. It'll get you out of the house and you'll meet new people and you can start a new life. There's lots you could do to make some money and get out into the community." She didn't look very encouraged, but she acquiesced.

Mat moved on. "Now you, Jason. You seem to be taking everything in stride, little brother. Any comments you'd like to make?"

"I want my own car. I'm turning sixteen in a month and we have the money."

"We'll see. Maybe a clunker that will get you around cheap," Mat replied. "But we're not blowing Dad's life insurance on material things. That's Mom's nest egg and it'll be invested to provide income for her to live on, so get used to it. You want a car? Get a job and buy one, then worry about how you're going to afford insurance." Foley listened without comment, then chuckled.

Jason looked dejected and simply uttered, "That sucks."

Mat carried on. "Jason, in two more years you'll be done high school. The best thing you can do now is apply yourself to your studies to produce the best grades you can coming out of grade twelve. Then you'll have options as to what colleges you can apply to and what you can study. Start now and you will make a success of yourself some day. You put one foot in front of the other and eventually you get there." Mat had delivered his best big-brotherly advice, and as the words were coming out of his mouth he decided that that's exactly what he was going to do, as well. He was just finishing grade twelve, and his grades were pretty good, so he was going to apply to UBC and get all educated up for something, though he didn't know what.

So everyone had a game plan except for Foley. This was different. Foley was part of the family and always would be in a way, but he was not a blood relative. He was a grown man who would probably want to move on now with his own life. Get another job in security, someplace. Maybe find a girl and get married. Have kids of his own.

Mat turned to him. "Foley? We don't have the money to keep paying you, but you've been with us for over seven years, like, and there's lots you could do to, you know, keep involved, and we need you, still." Mat was fumbling over his words a little, but everyone knew he was trying to find a way to keep Foley in the picture. They all looked at Foley expectantly.

Foley looked a little awkward and folding his hands on the kitchen table, said, "Well, now that your dad's gone there's no security threat to the family so you don't really need me like before. I expect I'll keep my security consulting business active and branch off into other markets, but you all know that I won't ever abandon you guys. Helen, between you and the boys, if you'll have me, I'd like to keep my room and help out here and there. Aside from you, I only got two living relatives and they're both back in Oslo and I don't like either one of them, much. Look, we're in a pickle here, but I say that together, we can all build something new out of it. Yesterday's done and gone and who knows what tomorrow will bring, but for my vote, I'd argue that we're stronger together than apart. What d'ya say everyone? I'm still in for the long haul, if you are."

With that, the purpose for the gathering was sealed and everyone felt relieved that a new chapter in life had begun. For the first time, perhaps ever in this house, there was an air of joy and hope for the future in the room.

And that's how it had all started. Mat had miraculously survived a confusing and hurtful childhood with his bully father and had recovered with his self-esteem and hope for the future intact. His brother Jason was off and running as a typical teen-ager in spite of their family difficulties. As for Helen, although she never would have wished it this way, she had been delivered from an abusive, loveless marriage, only to find that she was again depressed, lost, and struggling to find meaning in her life as a widow. Foley had come to their family as if delivered by fate, and he and Mat had struck up a friendship that would endure many more of life's tribulations in years to come. From here, the road map of Mathew's life would have many interesting and unexpected turns, to say the least. There would be surprises, challenges, risks, and rewards, the extent to which Mat himself would never have imagined.

He and Foley set out like eager hikers heading into the woods alone, unaware of the odyssey that lay before them. With youth, camaraderie and foolhardy courage as their principle as-sets, they threw caution to the wind and said to life, "*Bring it on!*"

CHAPTER 4

CHRISTINE WAS IN the house folding a load of laundry that had just gone through when she heard the car pull into the driveway. Mat and Foley had been off on one of their jaunts to see a client about upgrading their security measures at a restaurant and bar downtown, or so they had said.

The two men had long ago established their consulting firm of Bull Dog Security Group, Inc. and had developed a nice list of corporate and private clients that relied on them to advise and install a variety of security systems for protection against burglary and intrusion, for the most part. Business was good and they enjoyed the freedom of working for themselves and being independent.

Now, at thirty seven years of age, and with a wife and ten year old daughter, Mat had paid his dues as an employee at the bank for several years, before being politely let go with a pat on the back and assurances that it had nothing to do with performance or cause on Mat's part. In fact, at the time of his *displacement*, his most recent performance review ranked him in the top two percent of some fifty thousand employees, company wide. It was a consequence of company restructuring and realignment resulting from global changes to the banking industry. So, technically, he wasn't fired — his position had been *eliminated* in the lexicon of corporate speak.

The rhetorical advice and platitudes he heard on the way out from inept managers who remained made Mat shake his head in disgust.

"It's just business. Don't take it personal and don't be bitter."

"Thanks for contributing so much of yourself."

"With your kind of talent, you're bound to land on your feet somewhere better."

"Don't worry. Everything happens for a reason."

They might as well have added, "Here's your hat. What's your hurry?"

After pouring his heart and soul into the job, Mat had felt as if he'd been kicked in the gut by a horse, and he secretly vowed to make it in the world on his own terms from that moment on. He was ready to start settling down and building a life for his family that would be cosmically different from the one in which he grew up. He cherished his wife and daughter and tried to provide all the love and comforts that went into building a solid home and family.

There was one catch. Mat led a double life. He was determined never to be trapped into a monotonous life where he'd work for twenty-five, thirty years for someone else, then die with (maybe) a paid for house and an accumulation of some paltry investments. Although he maintained a portfolio of RRSP's, mutual funds, and similar reserves, he realized that in the end, these financial instruments would never really amount to much. He wouldn't last five years on his nest egg.

With fluctuations in the world economy, how could a regular guy establish any real financial security for his family in the space of one short career and life? He'd wanted to get into the real money. Big money. So he and Foley had set up their company, and they also went to work on the side — as money launderers. It was illegal and it exposed them to some danger, but they were professionals. Foley had the background in security, and Mat knew finance and business from his university education and working experience in the world of banking and investments.

As for the ethical issues of knowingly participating in an illegal activity, Mat had rationalized that, "Governments do it all the time, only under the protection of the laws that they themselves pass. They make the rules, then rob from the citizenry through oppressive taxes and levies of every description, but it's all above board because they say so. Then they recklessly spend money in the billions of dollars on one controversy after another, usually with millions — *or more* unaccounted for in the end.

"Look at the Canadian Gun Registry, introduced by the Jean Chretien liberals, amid howls of protest from citizens and other interest groups in the mid 1990s. It was originally estimated to cost around $1 million to administer. By 2004, nearly $2 billion had been committed or spent on the federal program. I wonder what the cost is by now? If that's not outright robbery of the country's electorate by corrupt, impossibly incompetent politicians, I'd like to know what is. They were only out by *two hundred, thousand percent,* but we were supposed to compliantly pay for it, and vote them back in come next election. *That's* criminal. If anyone in business made an error of that magnitude, they would be summarily fired, and probably face criminal charges. Not politicians.

"And worse, most people wander through life like a bunch of lobotomized, obedient, Stepford wives, hardly ever questioning anything and willing to pay whatever taxes, fees, and levies the bureaucrats demand. Then the government officials give themselves outrageous salary increases, all out of proportion with normal business standards, with taxes paid by regular citizens... and it's *legal.*

"Do you know that Canada Revenue Agency even makes waiters and waitresses keep a log of their tips and they're expected to report income from tips so it can be taxed? You leave a five buck tip on the table after lunch for good service and food and $2 of it goes straight to the government. Christ-all-mighty, those mercenary, petty bastards will stop at nothing to take our money — *tips!*" Mat said in astonishment.

"Examples of unfair and money grabbing tactics by the government upon the general population and corporations are everywhere. Why is there a market for *tax lawyers?* To keep the government out of our back pockets, that's why. Then, what you save in taxes, you pay the lawyer. It's not enough that they tax your income from working. They put a tax on everything you purchase, then they also put a tax on your investments. The government taxes and levies everything conceivable, and it's all legal and non-negotiable. GST, PST, HST, land transfer tax, capital gains tax, gasoline taxes, airline ticket taxes, on and on. It would be preferable doing business with the mafia, I'm certain.

"The government needs a lot of money to run this country, and it all comes from us. Trouble is, they take off on their own little tangents, once they're elected, and the population has no say in how they spend our money. Afghanistan? Where the hell is that? I'll bet you a thousand dollars that if I stopped a hundred people on any downtown street in Vancouver and asked them to point to Afghanistan on a map, they couldn't do it, and for the one that could, it's because he's a refugee *from* there. Take the bet? Didn't think so.

"And if I asked the same hundred why we're sending troops there to fight, or *keep peace,* they couldn't give a clear answer. Disagree? How does defeating the Taliban, who ever they are, have any effect on the security of our country, or the worldwide economy, or prosperity and welfare of my family? The conflict has so far, lost *one hundred and thirty-three* of our soldiers — young men, for the most part, most in their twenties, who should have led productive lives here at home, and contributed to our nation, and there'll be more. And *you and I* are paying for it all through taxes, and when they run out of money, they'll raise our taxes.

"Our government will spend some *$20 billion*, of our money, without our consent, before it's over — *twenty billion!* Do you know how much a billion is? That's *a million, one thousand times…* The numeral 'one', followed by nine zeros. In round numbers, *one billion* minutes ago Jesus was alive. A billion hours ago, our ancestors were living in the stone age, cave men. Our government will spend a *million, times a thousand, times twenty,* of our tax dollars. More money than Oprah has, on waging the *Afghanistan peace keeping* mission! Meanwhile, education, healthcare, infrastructure, trade, the arts, national unity, and how many other real Canadian concerns get shoved to the back burner due to lack of funding.

"Look at it as a business decision. What possible return could we expect to get on an investment like that, never mind the lives of our nation's best young men and women that are being lost over there? Right or wrong, our federal government is stubbornly committed to putting us at the forefront of the Afghanistan movement. Don't worry; I'm sure Afghanistan will pay us back the $20 billion as soon as they're on their feet… In around ten thousand years, or so.

"And here at home, everyone is on the take, from government officials at just about every level, to the bankers who process both legal and shady transactions daily, even to the police who supplement their income with graft from criminals who need them to turn a blind eye to something that has to go down unnoticed. It happens, be assured!

"You don't think Sergeant Moustache doesn't let a hooker off 'Scott free' if she'll agree to a little trade off of the oral variety in the front seat of his cruiser? Are you surprised to learn that Constable Clear Conscience leaves the drug dealers alone if they'll grease his palms with some regular, hard cash? Green dollars, I'm talkin' about," Mat would argue.

"Same with booze and cigarettes. A thirty-eight dollar bottle of Scotch costs about two bucks to produce. I wonder where the other thirty-six dollars goes. Kids are taking up smoking before they're thirteen and adults are dying of lung cancer while the healthcare system is collapsing under its own cost. But that's all legal and good, even though the feds pay lip service to non-support by putting a warning on cigarette packages from the surgeon general.

"Now there's talk about legalizing and regulating other vices, like prostitution, marijuana, crack, and many others, all new markets for taxation and government expansion. Do you know that "escorts" — *A.K.A. prostitutes,* have to apply, *and pay,* for a license from the city to ply their services on their customers? *'There's a step in the right direction',* the beurocrats will say. More revenue from another *sin tax!*

"The big banks turn out profits in the *billions* of dollars every year by charging usurious rates on all money that passes through their systems, and if you want to do something as simple as stopping payment on a cheque through a two minute *telephone* call, they charge your account a $15 transaction fee. Now *there's* customer service at its finest. When they call my private home at supper time offering me a new, better credit card, I should politely say *no,* then send them an invoice for $15. You know what's criminal? Banks that spray those credit cards out to the population at an annual rate of 29 percent then ruin people's credit, for not making the minimum payment of $20 by the due date twice in a year on their balance that's growing almost exponentially due to compound interest.

"When a bank tells you a cheque has *cleared* your account, do you know that legally they can still charge you back for it for six years, if the cheque turns out to be a forgery? They cleared the cheque. They're the *experts.* They endorsed it as good. They gave everything a thumbs up and charged monthly banking fees to your account, but now it's your liability if anything goes wrong long after *their mistake.*

"Examples of this kind of suppression by business and government are in the media every day. McDonald's Restaurants made *$4.3 billion* in profits in 2008, and they pay *minimum wage.* And the reason they pay minimum wage is because that's the law. They'd pay less if they could get away with it. Considering that they're a food service agency, I wonder where else they might be cutting corners, to save money?

"Let's not even *start* talking about insurance companies, cell phone providers, cable and satellite carriers, oil corporations, and many, many others that churn out profits in the billions, and trillions, and gazillions. And the worst, and biggest, and most deceitful, and most diversified and corrupt, and least regulated of all, is the federal government. It amounts to *legalized extortion* and common citizens are coerced into paying fees and taxes on everything they touch and earn for their entire lives.

"How is a common man or woman supposed to work, raise, clothe, and feed a family, own a home and save enough for retirement? They don't want you to retire. They want you to work, and keep on paying them, 'til the day you drop dead', so they can wage wars in places like Afghanistan. Then they tax your estate, if at all possible, and that's when your family better have a good tax lawyer. When it comes to the federal government, the bill is never *paid in full.*

"Mat, you get yourself too worked up," Christine would reply. "You've got a lot of anger in you, do you know that? You must be very bitter to have all that stewing around in your head."

"Good! More people should be angry. Does it sound like I'm preaching? I am! Sorry to ruffle your feathers. The last thing I'd want to do is wake somebody up, make them think, and disrupt their complacent little world. Maybe it's time we all started getting a little more *worked up,* asking more questions and opening our eyes, before it's too late. People don't take action until they've been personally affected by unfairness. It's human nature. There's nothing like a swift kick in the balls to remind you that physical violence is, somehow, just wrong. Before then, you're relatively indifferent to the matter.

"Remember Howard Beale in *Network?* People should stick their heads out the window and yell *'I'm mad as hell and I'm not going to take this any more!'* Get up off your knees and let the system know that you're no longer supporting lies, corruption, stupidity, and sanctioned robbery!"

Having been a model, hard working employee who was rewarded for his efforts by being 'fired', and having observed the proliferation of what amounted to 'sanctioned crime' by government and big business, Mat had bitter resentment eating away at him and he viewed his dalliance in money laundering and tax evasion as trifle by comparison. *What? They can steal, but I can't?*

While working at the bank, Mat was closely mentored for seven years by his manager, Hyman Wexler. Mr. Wexler took a fatherly interest in Mat and they often chatted in his office or over lunch about things outside of routine business. One of the lessons that had a recurring theme from Wexler was that banks were basically just a huge money laundering business on a worldwide scale. For the benefit of appearances, they operated within the letter of the law, but opportunities to cook the books, move money around the globe clandestinely, and siphon off funds for illicit and illegal purposes were plentiful and commonplace. Banks in every corner of the globe worked together in unison and collusion to place money where it could not be exposed to taxation or complete disclosure to the authorities. It is the biggest and oldest conspiracy in the world. Banks and governments make perfect adversaries — Ali and Smokin' Joe.

Wexler had told Mat, "There are advantages to working inside the world's banking system. All businesses have loopholes and ways to skim off extra money and banking is no different. It's like, *Which shell is the pea under?* Trust me, bankers worldwide, know all the tricks to winning that game."

Mr. Wexler had told Mathew, "Money and corruption make the world go 'round, and if you think that it's all legal and within the rules made by self interested governments, think again."

He had said, "Remember Mathew, working at a bank is an opportunity to learn all about money, and I don't mean how to open one account and close another. I mean discovering how to create wealth, move it around, minimize by all means possible its exposure to risk or taxation. Protect the money at all costs and adhere to the first rule of business, *OPM*."

"What's OPM, Mr. Wexler?"

"*Other People's Money.* When it comes to risk and taxation, you never expose your own money," explained Wexler in one of his many lessons to Mathew.

Before Mat left the bank for good, Hyman had called him aside and said, "Mat, I know you're disappointed at losing your job, and you should be. I've heard so many people say to you '*don't take it personally, it's just business...*' Oy, Gevalt — *Oh my gosh!* Well, you know and I know that that's *pure BS.* It's Gevaldikeh Zach — *A terrible, terrible thing!* What could be more personal than robbing a productive, young man with a wife and daughter of his livelihood and future? This is *very personal* and someone at the top is doing you and others a great disservice that should bring shame and ill-fortune upon them.

"I know that you are capable and resourceful and *you will* survive this and resume your career somewhere else, but there may be some rough waters ahead before that happens. Know this, when you are out there in the business world there is a good chance at some point that you, or I, will come across an *extraordinary* opportunity to make money, and it may take extreme caution and some creative accounting to avoid the scrutiny of outsiders. When that happens, if I can be of any service, please feel welcome to contact me at any time. I'll do the same for you. It's a cruel world, Mathew. Be a survivor, not a victim. Are we good?"

"We're always good, you and I, Mr. Wexler. I'll think hard about your advice. I'll miss you, my friend," Mat agreed, and the mentor and his prodigy shook hands warmly, then hugged each other like cherished friends. Mat choked up a bit and Wexler responded by giving him a whack on the back that said, *Smarten up, now... be strong!*

"For gezunterhait — *Bon voyage! Travel in good health,* young man! May your journey bring you adventure and prosperity," and Mr. Wexler bade his young man well wishes and farewell until their paths might cross again under different circumstances.

So it was that through Mr. Wexler's influence, Mat came to the position that he wasn't participating in dirty money. He just acknowledged that basically all money is dirty, and if you can't escape it then why not get in on some of it yourself. *People who see it otherwise are suckers or hypocrites,* he thought.

From the start, Mat's grand plan was to score a few good hits, win enough money to secure an affluent future for his family, and play it safe at all costs. He was fully aware and always cautious in the world of crime and corruption. There were risks, yes — from criminals and the law. There were moral issues, yes. The money he became expert at laundering and reintroducing into the mainstream economy was ill-gotten, one way or another, like nearly all money. But to Mat, the bigger factor was how he would achieve real wealth and independence for his family. He was a practicing *Consequentialist.* As long as he didn't hurt anyone else who didn't deserve it, the ends justified the means in his mind. If the issue was more complicated than that, he wasn't going to lose sleep over it. He was certain of it, almost.

CHAPTER 5

CHRISTINE HEARD THE door to the garage open and she walked through the kitchen to meet the boys and say hello. When they entered the room from the adjoining hall to the garage her eyes widened and she put her hands to her mouth.

"Oh, good God! What happened to you?" she said to Mat. "Was there a car accident?"

"No, I can't talk about it right now," Mat replied. "Can you get me some Tylenol? I'll need to go to the hospital and get this tended to." By now, both his eyes were blackening and had swollen to narrow slits. His nose was still bleeding badly.

Foley added, "Mat had a little mishap. Couple o' days and he'll be good as new. Don't fret. It'll add character to his face. He was too much of a *pretty boy* before, I always thought."

Christine was not to be dismissed quite that easily. "Look. If you guys can joke about this then I want a straight answer. What happened to your face? Right now!" And she wasn't just concerned for Mat. As Mat's wife, she deserved to be answered in an honest and direct manner.

"I got into a fight," Mat said, not lying. "You should see the other guy," he added, not lying again.

"A fight over what?"

"Business. The guy was a jerk and we got into a mix up. It's over now, and I'd like to forget it," Mat went on, trying to pivot the conversation onto something else.

Christine asked, "And Foley, where were you when this happened? Didn't you intervene?"

"Foley looked at Mat, then her and said, "Oh ya. I *intervened*. We need to get cleaned up though and take this piece of hamburger to the hospital to get his beak reset."

Christine snapped back, "Well try not to get into a car accident on the way there, Foley. You seem to attract an awful lot of trouble for being some kind of security expert."

"Told ya I'd get the blame somehow," Foley reminded his pal about his earlier prediction.

As they were leaving the house for the hospital, Christine got in the last word. "We're not through with this. I'm going to want some answers when you get home!"

In the car, rolling down the road to the Vancouver General, Mat said to Foley, "How long do you think we can keep all this secret from her? She's not stupid, and if she finds out anything about our sideline she'll be pissed that I wasn't straight with her from the beginning."

Foley responded, "It's up to you, Bucky. Damned if you do and damned if you don't. Tell her, and she might blow a gasket and hire a lawyer. The kind that specializes in dividing up matrimonial assets, know what I mean? Let her find out on her own, and she could look at you like you're a child molester, finally exposed. You might wind up in the hot seat on *Oprah*, or *Dr. Phil*, explaining yourself on national TV. I'm not married so I'm probably the wrong guy to ask about complete honesty in a marriage. What do you think she'd do if you sat her down and told her the whole story?"

"Starting with Mom?" Mat asked.

Foley pondered the short question. "Ya, I suppose you'd have to go right back to the beginning to make her understand. You don't just wake up one day and decide you'll try your hand at this money laundering thing. It has to come to you like a stork with a baby."

"Cute analogy," Mat replied. "This baby has grown into a rebellious teenager and is getting outta hand."

The men arrived at the Emergency Room where, after a two hour wait and much gawking at by other patients, Mat was taken back to a treatment room and asked the cause of his crushed nose by a disheveled and unlikely looking physician — sort of a medical equivalent of Detective Columbo. His confidence in the health care system waned when he looked at the physician's name badge, *Dr. Jekyll* — a health care professional working the ER with food in his teeth, worn out shoes, and finger nails chewed to the quick. In contrast, his assistant was a younger woman, likely East Indian, with a graceful manner and exquisite, mannequin like features, not unlike Neela on *ER*, the television series. Her name badge, *Abni Ragoonaden, R.N.*

"And what have we here? You get into some kind of altercation?" the doctor asked.

The nurse added, "That looks nasty! *Does it hurt?*"

"Only when I breath," Mat replied with a nasally voice, blood dripping, still, from his nostrils.

Mat explained that he'd been mugged by a trio of thugs and robbed of his wallet while walking through an alley to take a short cut in Gastown. Despite the skepticism on the faces of the physician and nurse, the story must have seemed plausible because no other action was taken, like bringing the police into it. Subsequently, to corroborate his story, he re-applied for all new credit cards, driver's license, and BC health card, a fairly simple procedure for one who could move hundreds of thousands of illegal dollars around the globe in a matter of days, and turn it into legitimate money. Mat was X-rayed to ensure there wasn't more facial or cranial damage than expected. With a local anesthetic, his nasal and vomer bones were set, the bleeding was stopped, and he was released with some antibiotics to prevent infection.

Mat was quiet on the ride back home and Foley sensed that he was brooding over whether, and how much, to tell Christine about the true nature of their business. She meant the world to Mat and he was wrestling with his conscience over keeping a major secret from her for this length of time. The two men had engaged in their side business of moving the proceeds of crime around to make it appear legit for a few years now, ever since Mat's mother had passed on at the age of fifty-five in 2003. It had been fifteen years since the death of her husband. She had never remarried. At the time of her death, Mat was thirty-two. Now he was thirty-eight.

Mat's mind drifted back to those events and he replayed the memories of her in his head. She had been diagnosed with skin cancer — Stage 3, malignant melanoma, after an angry-looking, malevolent patch of boiling, red skin, an inch in diameter, had been discovered on her back, through a routine medical. After extensive treatment involving surgery, radiation, and chemo-therapy, the oncologists thought that her chances of surviving another five years were above seventy percent. The woman had never really recovered from the death of her husband, and her hair had almost immediately turned not just grey, but white, after his death. She had morphed from a relatively young woman into an old, spent senior citizen in a matter of a few short years.

She carried an irrational burden of guilt that she was some-how responsible for his death and nothing Mat or anyone else could say would convince her otherwise. Mat believed that it weakened her at her core, and was a contributing factor to the re-occurrence of the cancer. This time it had metastasized in her lungs, then her liver and pancreas, at which point she was transferred from Oncology to Palliative Care. After a six month battle with the disease, she succumbed.

Near the end, she had called Mat to her bedside and through watery, fading eyes, she said, "Mat. I know, and you know, this cancer is terminal and I don't have long now. I do love you, my boy, and your brother, and I have always tried to be a good mother and do what was right for you both."

Mat said, "I know Mom. We loved you too, and we just..."

"No... no," she interrupted through a whispered voice, as she lay in a bed of stark white hospital sheets. "I'll talk. You listen. There's no time. You were always a headstrong boy, even still, now that you're a grown man. Sometimes Son, we are cast into circumstances that are beyond our control, and we have to go with the flow of events, whether we like them or not.

"We all make mistakes, Mathew — *big ones,* sometimes, and when your turn comes, the next challenge you'll face is how you deal with that mistake, and whether you grow from it, or let it kill you. Some things can't be undone, but they can be managed to a best possible conclusion, and you can march on from there, sometimes with a life long limp. A reality of life is that you can't control everything and you just have to think on your feet and make the best decisions you can in the heat of the moment. I've lived with things that you should know about, and I *want* you to know, because it's the right thing, and I ask you now to finish matters off when I'm gone."

Mat interrupted, "What are you talking about, Mom?"

"Soon, Mat, soon. You'll learn something that will open your eyes to many of the questions that have haunted you, and me, for years." She coughed weakly, her lungs congested with phlegm, and she said, "Please give me some water, there on the table."

Mat obliged and poured his ailing mother a cool drink. He noticed her lips were slightly blue, like she was cold. She sipped on it weakly with two hands. Then she reached into her purse on her night stand and took a small key out.

"Son, when I go, I want you to take this key to the Toronto Dominion Bank at Broadway and Cambie. There is a safety deposit box at the bank and this will open it. There is something in it for you and I want you to have it. You'll know what to do. Make sure you are alone when you open it. Promise me you *will not* do this before I die."

Mat responded, "Mom, what is it? Why do I have to wait?"

"Promise me. It's been a long time, Mathew. You can wait a little longer. You'll understand why later, if you follow my instructions. You're my eldest son and I love you, beyond your dreams. In this life, I've failed you and Jason. I failed your father, and I failed myself. We're all God's children and when we accept His love, we're in His care, now and forever. Through His love, I may find forgiveness."

Mat glanced towards the hallway as a glum looking orderly wheeled a gurney by the door. He stopped to speak with someone in the hallway and the gurney remained clearly in sight. On it lay a despondent male patient, emaciated to near skin over bones with illness, moaning pitifully, dressed in ragged blue hospital wear, stripped long ago of all human dignity, any hope of cure abandoned. His cotton gown hung open, revealing his privates to the world, not that anyone cared, like he was a carcass being delivered for processing at a meat plant. The pathology unit, autopsy, and the morgue were in his near future. They might as well have had the I.D. tag strung around his big toe already. Mat looked on and his mind wandered momentarily.

'What were the events that shaped this unfortunate man's life? In his youth, had he loved, and been loved, by a woman? Did he have children whom he cherished, a circle of friends, a *best* friend? What vocation provided him with a career, colleagues, challenges, opportunities for personal and professional growth? Was he kind and charitable? Did he ever do without, quietly, so that someone else might have more? Would anyone miss him when he's gone? And what creeping, merciless disease brought him here to the hopeless state he was in? Only one end to it possible now. All questions that would never matter. His life's flame was flickering its final embers. Like the last few sands running through an hour glass, the inevitable, unstoppable end was approaching fast. Hours, days, perhaps weeks remained, but it would be soon, *not soon enough, sadly*. Next, he would be summarized in a few paragraphs in the obituaries, and a headstone over a grave, practically anonymous, that some compassionate relative might visit out of guilt or duty every five years or so.

In the end, his life, really, meant nothing. Just another, in the endless procession of people born and deceased throughout history, forgotten to almost everyone a week after he passed. One more lonely soldier marching on to the beat of a drum. Sick as he was, he probably knew all these things, in a mind trapped in a failed body, sliding uncontrollably into the chasm.'

It's just cruel, prolonging his suffering, Mat thought to himself. The harsh clinical lighting cast a fluorescent glow over everything and everyone, making even healthy people look cadaverously pale and morose. *Nothing palliative about this place,* Mat reflected somberly.

Mat's mom gazed out the window by her bed and truly appreciated the beauty of a lovely, autumn scene, suffused with fall colors of gold, and orange, and red, with a fading yellow sun, knowing that her story was almost told. There were children playing noisily, joggers and bikers celebrating their blessed good health, young lovers on the park bench smooching and groping at each other with inappropriate openness, squirrels chasing each other frantically up and down massive trees, song birds chirping on delicate branches, and ducks waddling across the lawn.

There was a certain tranquility in her composure. At last, she was being freed from a life of misery, guilt, and wrong decisions by a fatal disease that was coldly detached of all emotion, fairness, and human compassion. Her journey was almost over, while the rest of the world danced on, indifferent to her concerns. She felt like a hopeless invalid watching a jubilant parade from a wheelchair on the sidelines, scheduled for euthanasia in the very near future. However, her reaction to it all was not bitterness, but relief. Moreover, she had something and wanted to leave it for the enlightenment and benefit of her sons.

Mat watched her almost as an impartial observer and realized that over the last several months he had seen her go through all the phases of grief, as he had himself. Upon her initial diagnosis with the disease her first reaction was one of denial. *This just couldn't be. There must be some mistake. It's been misdiagnosed.* God would never forsake her in such a cruel way. Later she became angry that this fate could have befallen her and she railed at the arbitrary injustice of how she didn't deserve this. *Why did I, of all people, have to get this? Why can't they cure me?* So, too, did she go through the stages of bargaining and depression, pleading with her disease for leniency like it was a judiciary board hearing an appeal from a luckless petty criminal, until she ultimately resigned herself to its inevitable outcome. Now she displayed acceptance, calmly, quietly. Almost agreeably.

Mat nodded reluctantly, "All right, I'll wait. I love you too, Mom." He held her hand tightly, and blinked back a tear. It occurred to him that he would soon have no living parents. His mind raced back to all those years ago when his dad had died and he realized with sadness that soon his mother too would pass on. He momentarily felt the hand of time and pondered his own mortality.

"I need to sleep now," she said. "So, so tired." Her head rested back in a rumpled pillow and she weakly exhaled a raspy, ill-sounding breath.

Mat tucked the key into an inner flap of his wallet and he quietly left room 791B of the palliative care unit. Two weeks later she was gone and finally, Mat hoped, at peace.

She had always been a woman who believed firmly in God and allowed her faith to guide every major decision she faced. "God loves us, and protects us, and welcomes us home when our mission is complete. So we are bound to do His work and follow His word while we are here, but *oh*... what does He really want of us?" she wondered at times.

One of her favorite passages from the bible had been Micah 6:8.

He has showed you, O man, what is good.
And what does the LORD require of you?
To act justly and to love mercy
and to walk humbly with your God.

Mathew recalled that at the funeral a pleasant, young pastor presided over the service and told a fitting story:

"There was a family once who lived in a fine, two story house, and one night, while the family was sleeping the house caught fire. The flames had grown in intensity to an alarming state before the family was awakened and had a chance to react and flee the blaze. Everyone rushed out of the burning structure in an attempt to evacuate the home safely. All managed to escape but for one little girl whose bedroom was on the second floor of the house. In her fear of the flames, she initially took refuge under her bed. By the time her family noticed that she was not among them outside it was too late to re-enter the burning building.

As the fire grew too severe for her to stay under her bed she climbed out of her window and sat on a narrow ledge holding tightly to the window sill.

Her father saw her from below and called out to her, 'Jump, Sarah, jump! I love you, and I'm here, and I'll catch you. I will protect you from harm and I'll save you if you'll place your trust in me.'

Sarah looked down and all she could see were flames and smoke and blackness, and she replied, 'But father, I can't see you. How do I know you'll be there for me?'

Her father said, 'Because I'm your father, and I love you, and that's all that matters.'

It puzzled Mat, always, that the pastor ended the story there, without saying if the little girl placed her trust and faith in her father and jumped to safety or whether she was overcome by doubt, and fearfully clung to the burning building to tragically perish in the fire.

Mat said to himself, "That little girl was you, Mom, and you chose correctly and did the right thing, and now you're in God's hands — safe, loved, and forgiven of all."

Lloyd Gordon

Mat snapped out of his little trip down memory lane. Approaching his house with a bandage covering the bridge of his nose, he said to Foley, "Thanks for waiting with me in the ER. I hope this thing heals quickly."

Foley responded, "What's really on your mind, Buck? If you were brooding any harder, there'd be smoke comin' out your ears."

"Christine,"

"Thought so."

Mat continued, "I'm gonna tell her. The whole story. I think it's time she knew, and I can't keep livin' a lie. Soon as this thing is off my face and I'm feeling better. Right now, I need some rest. Drop me off and I'll call ya tomorrow."

Foley looked concerned. "Okay, but let's talk before you dump the whole truth on her. It could go off like a shit bomb. A second opinion about how to do it might help. You've been livin' it for years but it's gonna be a lot for her to process. You should think carefully about it before you start delivering your testimony. Know what I mean?" He pulled into Mat's driveway.

"I hear ya. Don't worry, I'll do it with kid gloves, and we'll talk before I 'fess up on everything. Get some sleep, yourself. It's been an eventful day. By the way, can you kill a man like that and carry on like you've just dropped off your dry cleaning or something? How did you throw that knife into his neck so accurately?

"Actually, I aimed more or less, at his chest. It was kind of a miss, but it turned out all right, I guess. Must be gettin' old. And no, I don't just kill somebody without feelin' my gut. But it was him or us, plain and simple. I'd never kill for any other reason. Any other questions?"

"No more questions, Hoss. And thanks. I owe you my life."

"*Fugettaboutit...* It's *my job* to protect your life," Foley replied, gesturing theatrically towards his heart with his thumb and fingers pressed together.

"You're a *goodfella,* Foley, but please... You make a bad Italian. You're Norwegian, remember?"

The men parted for the day. Mat stepped out of the car and Foley pulled out of the driveway. Mat walked into the house and wondered how and what he was going to tell his lovely wife Christine about the true nature of his business life, inside the law, and outside. There was quite a story to tell, and it was risky. But he loved and trusted her and felt that she deserved to be let in on the whole truth. Call it a decision of conscience.

CHAPTER 6

NEARLY THREE WEEKS had passed since the incident at the hotel and Mat's nose was looking, and feeling, a lot better. The swelling and bruising around his eyes were nearly gone and he could breath freely though his nostrils again. He and Foley had stuck to their security business and conducted themselves like model citizens. Christine had given up on discovering the details of Mat's injuries, but he did promise her that he would be careful not to get involved with anything potentially violent again.

He knew in the back of his mind that the day was coming when he would sit her down and tell her the long story about his other life, and how it came to be. Mentally, he rehearsed parts of it over and over to try and make it plausible and reasonable. He heeded Foley's warning that she could take it all the wrong way and react badly. He had decided that today was the day. It was warm and sunny, he was feeling healthy and talkative and she was in a good mood. It was just after noon on a Saturday, and Hannah, now ten, was out playing in the park with her friends. A perfect time for some honest, open, spousal communication.

Sitting in deck chairs on their veranda over fresh coffees, Mat said, "Christine, I've been meaning for some time now — actually, a long time now, to talk to you about something."

"What's that, dear? You wanna take me on a second honeymoon?"

"Not exactly, although yes, that's a good idea. I'm serious though. It's… it's not easy for me to go into this, but you are my wife and I'm sorry that I've kept this from you so long. Let me tell you a story, a true story, about how my life has unfolded since you and I were married."

"What are you trying to tell me?" Christine focused intently on Mat now.

"You never knew my dad and trust me, that's not a bad thing. He was wicked and my mother grew to hate him. He was abusive and cruel to all of us, her and me, included."

"I know. You've talked about that before," she said.

"This is something that I've concealed from you since the beginning, first because I wanted to protect you from it, and second, because I was, well, sort of ashamed of it, what my mother did. I could tell you out loud, but I think it's better that you see it first hand yourself. Wait here. I'll be right back, and I want you to read something." He left his chair and went into the house, where he retrieved a concealed envelope from under the broadloom that he gently lifted up where it met a heating register on their bedroom floor. He returned to the veranda and sat down beside Christine again.

"Now Chris, it's taken me a long time and a lot of soul searching to decide to do this. Mom left this for me when she died, in a safety deposit box at a bank. Please read this with an open mind and try to understand the big picture, okay?" he said, and placed the envelope in her hand.

Christine looked perplexed, and for a moment, just looked at the envelope without opening it. "Mat, what is this? Am I going to be upset by this?"

"You'll be surprised, for sure. Upset? I hope not," he replied. "Go ahead, open it." Carefully, she opened the envelope and removed a hand written letter. It read:

June 24th, 2002

My dearest Mathew and Jason,

I write this letter because I have lived with a crime and sin against God and man since the death of your father in 1988. If you're reading it now, it means that I am gone too, for I had vowed to keep this secret to myself for as long as I lived.

Your father was a very competent police officer. You know this. He participated in many, many undercover investigations, and he brought a lot of criminals to justice. Before he died he was working on a case involving an Asian gang in Vancouver. They were importing and distributing cocaine throughout Western Canada, and it was generating sums of money in the millions of dollars. Your father had broken up operations like these by arresting and charging criminal types and he was getting too close to exposing them again. With millions at stake, they had to stop him from continuing his work. He would have identified and arrested the ringleaders and interfered with an enormous drug trafficking operation.

One day, an Asian man approached me in the shopping mall. He said his name was Mr. Shen. He told me that if I didn't cooperate, my boys would be taken and I would never see them again. I was devastated with fear. I could not bear to take a chance on anything happening to you, my sons, so I obeyed his demands.

He gave me a small vile of white powder and told me to put it in Frank's drink or food that night. He promised that it would only make him sick. Long enough for them to make a shipment of drugs out of the city. Frank had known about it, he said, and would have stopped it unless he was paid a huge sum of money. God in heaven, he was committing extortion and it made me ill.

Later that evening, I did as he asked and put the drug into your father's drink. I don't know what it was. I was never told. He did not just get sick. He died. I should have told your dad about the threat. Instead, I killed him.

Mr. Shen also gave me what he called an incentive to cooperate that day in the mall. It was an envelope with fifty, $1,000 bills. I leave this money to you and Jason. I could never touch his blood money for murdering my husband. Mat, please use this cash for something good to help offset something I did that was dreadful. Use it with a clear conscience. You had no part in your father's death and you deserve this.

Please don't think poorly of me, Mat and Jason. What I did was a terrible, terrible mistake by listening to a criminal, and drug dealer. I was wrong and I have borne an agonizing guilt over my actions for the duration of my life since your father's death. I love you, my sons. God be with you, always.

Mother

Holding the letter, Christine's hands dropped into her lap. She looked up and out into the distance reflectively. "My God, Mat. Why didn't you tell me about this before?"

"I just couldn't. It's complicated," he said. "There's more. When I worked at the bank I became familiar with the laws concerning money. You can't just put fifty grand, cash, in the bank. It would be reported to the Government and they would have wanted to know where I got it. You can't even really break it up into smaller deposits. The risk of getting caught is just too great.

And you can't just buy something for that much cash either. It would raise suspicion. I needed to find a way to avoid the kind of attention from the authorities that windfall cash brings. So I had to figure a way to put it into some useable form of currency that appeared legitimate."

"And how on earth would you do that?" Christine asked, with obvious misgivings.

"Well, remember when I worked at the bank and I sometimes talked about Hyman Wexler? He taught me a lot about banking and money in general. He was a confidant of sorts, and he definitely mentored me in the ways of money," Mat explained. "When I got this $50,000, I was scared and under stress. I had to ask someone about it so I went to him discreetly one day and explained that I had come into a large amount of money in the form of cash. I asked him what he thought I should do.

Christine replied, "Why didn't you mention it to me? I'm your wife, remember?"

"I know, Chris. I'm not saying I've made all the right decisions in my life, but I did what I did and it can't be undone, but I'm telling you now. Anyway, Wexler told me that if it was cash and I couldn't reveal its source, then obviously it was from something criminal. I explained to him that it was a payoff given to my deceased mother from fifteen years ago and that I had done nothing wrong. I only wanted to put it into an account somehow," Mat explained.

"Why didn't you go to the police and tell them the story?" Christine asked.

"C'mon, Honey. They would have confiscated the money. It had been locked up in that safety deposit box for years and nobody came looking for it. Why would I give up fifty thousand bucks just because it wasn't legitimate and taxable? If we didn't deserve this money, the cops certainly had no right to it either," Mat replied.

Christine said, "So what was Mr. Wexler's advice?"

"He said that under Canadian baking laws, all transactions of $10,000 or more have to be reported to the Government. It's called Currency Transaction Reporting. Deposits, money transfers, wire transfers, everything. He said if I divided the cash into twelve equal sums less than ten thousand each, they could be wired out of the country to an account in Zurich, Switzerland. Then we could invoice a shell company over seas for consulting work done here, and they could pay us with a cheque drawn from the Swiss Bank. So Foley and I set up a numbered company in Switzerland and we each made six wire transfers to it from different locations here in the city. Everything went down clean and simple. We moved the money overseas, brought it back, and deposited it as fees for service. It was easy, actually." Mat looked at her intently to see if she was getting this.

"So, where is this money now?" Christine went on.

"Foley and I invested it bit by bit into our business account along with regular customer payments. Now it's just shareholder's equity on the balance sheet. And I gave half of it to my brother, as mom had asked me to in this letter," Mat replied. "But, I told you, it's more involved than that. Through my connections at the bank, I came to know some guys who conduct business on the fringes of the law, and sometimes, quite outside the law. They generate money and needed to find someone who could transform it into legitimate capital. Over time, I became somewhat of an expert at laundering money for a fee. Foley and I discovered that we could make a lot more money that way, than by working hard for other people and paying taxes to a government that can never take enough. As it stands now, you and I Christine, have a lot of capital in some overseas accounts. We're rich in relative terms, compared to most families in our neighborhood." Mat looked at her hoping to see some glimmer of approval in her face.

She stared at Mat blankly for several moments. Neither of them spoke. Christine seemed to be processing all the information and its implications in her mind. Then she said, "So all this time you've allowed me to believe that you've been going to work at your business with Foley, you've really been going out to conduct an illegal money laundering scheme and associating with criminals and their ilk?"

"Well, no... I mean yes, sometimes. But we had to run the business too. It's not like we do the laundering thing full time. It was just a diversion to make some extra cash, tax free."

"What you're doing is illegal and criminal. If you get caught you'll go to jail. We'll lose our house. I'll lose my husband. Hannah will lose her father. We'll be disgraced in the community. And you've been keeping this secret from me for years?"

Mat countered, "Yes, it's criminal," his voice raising involuntarily. "Because the people who make the rules to suit their purposes define it as criminal. Money is money, Chris. We're being robbed blind by everyone from the government to the oil companies, the insurance companies, to the very bank that fired me and took away my livelihood when they decided my job and life were expendable. Do you know that the average Canadian has to work until the middle of June, roughly, until their annual income stops going towards taxes and starts going into their own pockets? Do you think we're getting good value for those taxes?

"I've found a way to make us truly wealthy. Not just comfortably middle class, but affluent beyond all doubt. Millionaires. Do you think all the millionaires and billionaires in the world earned their money on the up and up? There's the good guys and there's the bad guys, and sometimes you have to look real close to figure out which one is which. I'm just making money and securing a bright future for our family. I'm not hurting anyone. Let's not get caught up on the fine points of the law and morality."

"Mat, you're participating in criminal activities. You're associating with hoods and felons and gangs and who knows what else. They all get their money through crime, theft, hookers, drugs, and robbery of one sort or another. I'm not stupid — *are you?*"

Mat replied, "No, they're not all like that. You're envisioning the stereotype criminal who is an outlaw, or some bank robber, or a wife beater, or some Mafioso. Most of my clients are just embezzlers, or businessmen who have found a way to skim off enough funds from some account that they need a way to hide it and cover their tracks. I'm really just an accountant with a unique skill set."

"Oh, so it's just white collar crime you specialize in, is it? Well, the law looks more favorably on that sort of activity. Just ask someone like, say, Conrad Black," Christine remarked. "Or Bernard Madoff. He defrauded investors of some $50 billion in a Wall Street Ponzi scheme before he got caught last year, and he'll never see daylight again."

"Ya, they got nabbed and made an example of, but plenty of people have argued that others, especially in the political arena, have pulled off things, sometimes affecting the whole nation that *should* be criminal, and they got off with little more than a bad smell."

"Like who?" Christine asked skeptically.

"There's plenty. Pick just about any of our former Prime Ministers — Trudeau, Jean Chrétien, Paul Martin… all of them, *thick as thieves*. Think about the National Energy Program, the sponsorship scandal, the National Gun Registry, plenty of others. Or, if you want to look south, how about Richard Nixon, Bill Clinton, George W. Bush — what a bunch of role models for our children to learn about in history class. Is it a comedy of errors, or the blind leading the blind?

"One of our country's former leaders, a Conservative prime minster, no less, was implicated a few years back in a scandal you'd expect to see in the movies. You know who I'm talking about, right? This Right Honorable Member of Parliament accepted envelopes on at least three occasions from Karlheinz Schreiber, a German arms dealer, stuffed with thousand dollar bills, amounting to perhaps $300,000, probably more, allegedly for influencing the sale of Airbus jets to Air Canada, a crown corporation at the time."

Christine looked on interestedly. "I heard something about that. So what?"

"He kept it secret in safes and safety deposit boxes and never declared it as income for over six years. When he did, his lawyer negotiated a backroom deal, somehow for him, to pay tax on *only half* of it — a nice, token nod to legality and restitution. Try and figure that one out. You don't think the 'good old boy's club' is alive and functioning in our nation's legal-political system? He gets away with that, but waitresses have to pay income tax on their tips, while they live with roommates in college dorms! Look, when the whole matter was examined by a public inquiry, the accused and his lawyers squirmed and waffled over every part of the story, and finally wiggled out of trouble. Herr Schreiber eventually got extradited back to Germany, where he sits in a jail cell today. Meanwhile, our elder statesman is lounging on his veranda in an ascot and deerskin slippers, sipping Glenfiddich.

"Do you think that's appropriate, or even legal behavior on the part of a prime minister? He fell under suspicion of bribery, tax evasion, abuse of public office, among many other crimes. How does that look on the grand scale of legality, fairness, truth, and justice? Is it appropriate, legal, right? Do you think he really fooled anyone? Why did they let him off? He claimed it was just an *error*, an episode of bad judgment on his part. This guy was a lawyer before he was prime minister. Do you buy that argument?"

"Of course not. And it's obviously not appropriate, or legal, if it's true," Christine replied.

"Oh, and you have complete faith in our legal system to uncover the true and complete facts and deliver justice fairly and promptly? *He got off, 'Scott free'!* And in the face of all this and a thousand other scandals, I'm supposed to have a guilty conscience about my little exploits outside the law?

"If he was a common business man and citizen and not a privileged government official, all *lawyered up*, and connected to the nation's top judiciary, do you think he'd be a free man, like he is now, or sittin' in the Don Jail contemplating the meaning of life, with his backside to the wall and a stolen knife from the mess hall in his boot for protection, sharpened to a razor's edge on the bars of his cell?

"Do you think that money, influence, and high paid lawyers from public funds can manipulate the law and get bold faced criminals off for committing crimes, while employed in the highest offices of politics and business in the land?"

"Yes... I mean, no... I mean, I don't know! What the hell does all that have to do with you engaging in money laundering and associating with criminals?"

"It means that crime and corruption are going on everywhere, every day, and people of high office and otherwise are earning money from it, and if they don't get caught then they're not charged with breaking the law, and if they're not charged, they can't be convicted. Doesn't mean they didn't do it.

"What's against the law *isn't* committing the crime, it's *getting caught, and convicted* of doing the crime. The ones who pull it off and bank the money are resourceful and clever — *and rich.* The ones who get caught are sloppy, or amateurs, or just plain stupid, and they wind up as convicted law-breakers, and I don't fall into any of those categories."

Christine seemed overwhelmed by all the information and the ethical and legal issues at stake. Putting her hands to her forehead, she said, "Oh dear, oh dear... I can't deal with this now. I'm getting a migraine. I have to think. I'm going inside to lie down for a while. Keep an eye on Hannah, please. We'll talk later."

"All right dear. I'll fix dinner tonight. Everything will be fine, don't worry. Foley and I know what we're doing and we're very good at it."

As the screen door slapped shut, Mat sat on the veranda in solitude and looked across the way to the park where Hannah was playing with a group of noisy children. His hands were clasped tightly together in his lap and his pride was stinging from the animated defense he had just put up. Despite his argument to the contrary, he knew, deep down, that Christine wasn't entirely wrong. His actions in the money laundering game placed him in growing danger, as attested by his visit to the hospital three weeks ago.

Watching Hannah playing with the other children, he realized that his unlawful vocation might put her in danger, or Christine, or both, at some point. The criminal types he dealt with would resort to anything to get their way. And then there was the law. If some wise guy cop ever got onto him, he could end up in handcuffs and never see freedom again for a long, long time. He feared a time of reckoning was approaching and for the first time ever, since his involvement in the business, Mathew Crawford felt scared — *very* scared.

CHAPTER 7

MAT'S PHONE RANG at 8:15 the next morning. It was a Monday and he had not slept well, thinking about his discussion with Christine the day before. Having tossed and turned all night, he finally drifted off around 5:00 a.m. and had now slept in later than usual.

"Rise and shine, Buck. We've got work to do today and there's five inquiries on the answering service from over the weekend. Business is boomin'." It was Foley, sounding typically upbeat. He was at the office.

"My head is what's boomin," Mat replied. "I'd just as soon hit the snooze button and roll over for a while."

"Well, you're awake now, so you might as well get up and give 'er hell again. It's light outside, for Christ's sake. You've gotta be restified by now. My daddy used to say, 'Up on your hind legs, son. Too much sleep makes you stupid. You can't make your dreams come true by lying in bed.'"

Mat's little buddy answered, silently, *Really? Mine used to say, 'Get up, you lazy, good-for-nothin' runt. You think you're on vacation? Boy, have I got news for you!'*

"Don't you ever have a bad day?" Mat asked in a groggy voice.

"Hell no, son. I even put a new blade in my razor this mornin'. I feel great, and the Bettys on my trap line always think I *look* great!"

"Wow, do you know how to treat yourself! Do you have to be so damn cheerful, especially on a Monday?"

"Mondays are an opportunity to start all over again. We got a whole week in front of us to make something good happen. You're still between the sheets? God all mighty. I'm not *interruptin'* anything, am I?"

"Christ, no. I should be so lucky. Okay, I'll shower 'n shave and be right down. See you in an hour."

Mat rolled out of bed and his feet hit the cold floor. He stumbled off to the bathroom, placed his palms onto the cool granite vanity, and stuck out his tongue in the mirror. *Oh God, no wonder. Scope, where are you, my friend?* His eyes were weary, with dark circles underneath, and his hair looked like he'd just come off the roller coaster at the PNE. Moments later, hot water from the shower head pounded down on the back of his neck like a soothing massage, slowly returning him to a state of semi-humanity.

After completing the morning rituals involving Aspirin, toothpaste, shampoo, soap, Gillette Foamy, fragrant splashes and roll-ons, he was ready to dress and face the day. He slipped into a pair of dark blue Dockers and tucked in an open collared Eddie Bauer Signature Twill, with matching leather belt and stylish Florsheims. For a brief, twenty minute procedure of grooming and dressing, the end result was quite dashing, actually. *Good enough, let's rock, dude,* summarized his attitude at the end of it all.

Christine was already up and he heard her rustling around in the kitchen. It was mid July and she was off for the summer break from teaching.

Mat finished up and went downstairs into the kitchen. The coffee smelled good and Chris was sitting at the table scanning the morning paper. Hannah was at the table too, swirling her soggy Count Chocula in a bowl of milk. "Morning, love," he said. "Have you had breakfast yet? And How's my little Hannah banana?"

Christine looked up and Mat knew instantly that she wasn't in a good mood. "Hi, no, I'm not hungry. Are you going to the office this morning?" she asked.

"Ya, that was Foley that just called. He says we're gonna be busy this week," Mat replied.

"I can *only imagine*," Christine said with a note of sarcasm. "Hannah, you better go get dressed now, dear," and off the little girl went to her room.

Mat knew what she meant, but he didn't react to it. He felt that what he had exposed her to the day before was a lot to digest and it would probably take some time. Having revealed the whole story to her, it even surprised *him* a little to hear himself admit to a secret, criminal side to his life and the dangers inherent in his activities. It was almost like admitting to an act of infidelity, then expecting your spouse to shrug it off and act as if nothing had changed.

Mat finished his eggs and coffee and pushed away from the table. "Well, I better get to work and tend to business."

He paused before leaving the house. "Darling, I know you're worried about the things I explained to you yesterday, and you've a right to be. But try and understand that when we started this it was only one or two small time transfers of cash and it was no big deal. Over time it grew and grew until one day it wasn't something we could easily walk away from — and we didn't want to, anyways. It became very, very lucrative. It's like a trap that you get willingly drawn into, a day at a time — a drug, almost. See, we are so careful not to get caught and we know all the tricks to avoid detection. Most money launderers operate in large groups involved with organized crime, and there are pitfalls in being part of a big operation. The authorities can set up a sting and bring the whole thing down like a house of cards. Foley and I aren't part of any organized group and we take every precaution we know of to play it safe."

"Keep telling yourself that," she said, tersely. "Go to work and play it safe there — right up until the police show up at your door or some mobster who wants his money puts a gun in your face."

Mat immediately thought of Mario Sorentino and their little incident at the hotel last month, although there's no way he was going to let her in on that story.

"All right. Well, try not to worry about it. I'll call you later and we can make plans for a nice dinner later tonight," Mat said. He kissed her reassuringly on the forehead and left the house. She gave him an icy stare as he walked out. He felt like crap, somehow.

When Mat walked into the office at Bull Dog Security, Foley was sitting at his desk going over paperwork. "'Bout time," he said, glancing at his watch. "Anyone would think you've got a second source of income, or something."

"Very funny," Mat responded. "I'm on the shit list with Christine. I don't need any guff from you, okay?"

"Sheesh, who pissed in your cornflakes?" Foley quipped. "What happened? You tell her about our hobby?"

"Yup. And it went over like a lead balloon. She's acting all pouty and behaving like I admitted to being a serial murderer or something. Shot me a dirty look, times ten, before I left the house."

"I think I might have warned you that might happen," Foley remarked, correctly. "What are you gonna do about it. You'll have to get her settled down or it could escalate into something worse."

"I'm gonna do some head-scratchin' about the situation myself for a bit. I'll deal with it. Don't worry," Mat said. "What's up with all these messages that came in over the weekend?" Mat asked, changing the subject.

"Oh, ya, there's the usual customer inquiries, but there's one here from our old friend, Jack Kincaid. Say's he has an opportunity for you to consider, and it might be the mother lode. Listen to this," and Foley pressed the *message replay* button on the phone.

The message played, and in a whiskey voice the caller said, "Mr. Crawford. Jack Kincaid calling. You know I only call you when I encounter a situation that is suitable to your talents. I don't want to waste your time or mine, but I have come across an opportunity and it's a rare one, indeed. For your usual participation we would make arrangements to compensate you, substantially. It would be in your interests to get back to me without delay. I'll be waiting."

Mat looked at Foley. "Holy shit! It sounds like this low life might have stumbled across something big this time. What do you think it might be?" he asked.

"Not sure," said Foley. "But something about it rubs me the wrong way, already. I don't have to tell you that this guy is not someone you want to place your trust in without safe guards from here to the river. Know what I mean?"

Mat picked up the phone and started dialing.

After speaking with Kincaid, Mat headed out the door to meet with him at his office near the oceanfront. Little more was said on the phone other than where and when to meet. Clearly, there was urgency to the matter because Kincaid had said, "Whatever you're doing, drop it right now and come on down here. You'll want to hear what I have to tell you and trust me, it'll be worth your while. How soon can you get here?"

"Foley, keep your cell phone turned on if you go anywhere in case I need to reach you. I'll go and see what this guy has in the cooker this time and call you as soon as I know anything," Mat had said before leaving.

Driving across town Mat wondered about all the variables that could come into play. He knew that it would involve a sum of money obtained from some illegal activity that they would want him to restore into legitimate currency. That's what he did. But what was the source of the money? Drugs, likely. Probably a few hundred thousand in cash that would attract too much attention from bankers and under cover cops if anyone tried to access it.

Thinking about Christine, he resolved to exercise utmost caution himself in moving the funds into an account and spinning it through a multitude of transactions as a ghost investor so not to tie himself to the funds in any way. He decided that he had been getting careless lately and that even a small mistake could lead to his downfall. *It only takes one small mistake to result in a disaster. Just ask the hapless bug that wanders into a Venus Fly Trap,* he thought silently to himself.

Upon arrival at Kincaid's business, *Evergreen Import Export International,* Mat armed the alarm on his BMW M3 and entered the building. A pretty, mid-thirties blonde in a translucent white blouse covering a lacy, well-filled bra sat at the reception desk. She greeted him. "Mr. Crawford, I presume?"

"Yes, I'm here to see Jack."

"Of course, sir. He's expecting you. Right down the hall to the right." She pointed to Jack's office, like he didn't know where to go.

"Would you like a coffee *or anything else?*" she asked, smiling seductively.

Mat noticed that she was friendly enough, as you'd expect from a receptionist, but moreover, she had that aura about her that men instinctively pick up on that implied *come and get it mister.* This girl was on the make, but Mat was here on business, and besides, he had a good woman at home and wasn't into chasing skirts.

"No thanks. Your offer will be on my mind though." Mat returned the smile as he proceeded down the hall.

Walking in, Mat reached out to shake Jack's hand. "Hello Jack. Good to see you."

"Likewise, my friend." Jack smiled and stood up, unfolding his tall, ungainly frame from the chair to tower over Mathew. He extended his hand, completing the greeting formalities.

"Have a seat. I would like to tell you about some associates of mine that have a little problem they need help with."

"All right. I'm all ears. What's on your mind?"

"Around a week ago, a group of importers brought in a shipment of a pharmaceutical nature from China in a container aboard a cargo ship. It has a street value of $50 million, conservatively speaking." Jack looked intently at Mathew over the top of his glasses.

This was a sum much larger than Mat had ever worked with and his first reaction was to immediately decline any involvement, as it would be too risky. Instead, he remained quiet and listened carefully.

Jack continued, "Now, in the import business, there is always the possibility that a shipment can get diverted from its intended destination, or sometimes, go missing completely. It seems that in this case, the ship had to be re-routed to a terminal other than the one originally scheduled at the Port of Vancouver. You see, the ship's captain is somewhat of a businessman himself, and he had been contacted before leaving the port of origin in China. He had been offered an *enticement*, shall we say, to change the destination terminal at the last possible moment, to deliver the shipment to an alternate buyer, for a considerable fee, of course."

Mat summarized in plain English. "Someone sent a shipment of drugs, likely heroine or cocaine from China to Vancouver and the Captain was bribed, and he agreed to deliver it to another gang at a different port terminal."

"Yes. That would be another way of putting it," Jack agreed.

Mat added, "And let me guess. Now they have fifty million bucks worth of stolen drugs and somebody else wants it back."

"Your astute insight never disappoints me, Mr. Crawford. Now, keep in mind, the *street value* of the shipment is fifty million. The investor had only put up five million, with another five million due upon delivery — still a considerable sum of money. And the vendor, back in China, is an organization of international scope and ability. They want their full payment of ten million, or else someone is going to get eaten alive," Jack explained figuratively – or perhaps literally.

"So I don't quite get it." Mat interjected. "What do you think I can do for this little love triangle? There's no money yet to launder. It's just a shipment of stolen drugs. No cash."

"Ah, but once this product hits the streets *the cash* will start to flow like honey. My client wants us, that is, *you*, to launder the funds on an ongoing basis, until the product is fully liquidated. It should take around three to four months to sell it to the first line of distributors.

"That much product will be in circulation among dealers and users for at least a year. You will be paid a fee of ten percent, plus a million bonus for successfully converting one hundred percent of the proceeds without detection or incident." Jack Kincaid smiled innocuously as he offered up the numbers.

Mathew summed up the salient points of risk. "And in the mean time I've got some Chinese mob trying to find and kill anybody tied to this stolen shipment, there's a gang here who has been ripped off of a $10 million investment, and then there's the cops who may already be tipped off about this caper and may have *under covers* combing the streets for information."

"Six million bucks," Jack summed up the potential profit to Mat.

"And what's in it for you, Jack?" Mat wondered aloud.

"Oh, Lordy, Lordy, don't worry about me. I'll be well taken care of by the end of it all. I'm in business to make a profit, rest assured. *I'll get what I deserve.*"

Mat said, "I'm not going to give you an answer right here and now. This is big and it's dangerous. I need to consider it on my own for a while, weigh the risks. None of the product has been converted to cash yet, anyways."

Jack replied, "Yes, that's true. But we need an answer, fast, because the product will have to move fast to minimize the potential for violence. The quicker the deal goes down, the faster the whole thing will blow over. You know these types. They move from project to project faster than hookers go through Johns in the downtown eastside. Once the deal starts, it will fall like dominoes. All the players need to be in place by this weekend. You have 'til Wednesday to let me know. You're my first choice, Mat, but you're not my only choice."

Mathew studied the man, trying to think of any obvious questions that should be asked. "Okay, I'll let you know by Wednesday. If I'm in, though, I'm gonna need a lot more information. I'm not playing blind at these stakes. Let's go over the whole thing, soup to nuts, right now."

"Understood," replied Jack, and for the next thirty minutes he laid out all that he knew about the hijacked shipment of narcotics and the nefarious parties involved.

The meeting was concluded at that. Mat stood and exited the office. He walked down the hallway and smiled at the comely, young receptionist again. As he left the building, she turned off the intercom on her telephone disconnecting her line to Mr. Kincaid's office. Her eyes widened in astonishment at what she had just overheard.

CHAPTER 8

CONSIDERING IT WAS only 1:15 p.m. on a Monday, Mat had a lot on his mind about new business, legal and otherwise. Moreover, since Christine was now informed and aware of his enterprise, he would have to bring her in on any new ventures he was undertaking, so she would learn to be comfortable with it, and so he wasn't in the difficult position of committing lies of omission by not telling her. Driving back to the office, he would discuss the matter with Foley, assess its potential for risk and reward, and then, if they decided jointly that it was a *go,* he would inform Christine of their plan. He realized that it was past lunch hour and he felt a need to eat something, so he pulled over to a Starbucks and decided to get a coffee and a bite.

Coming out of the coffee shop with an ice coffee and a biscotti he sat down at an out door curbside table. Looking around, it occurred to him that he really didn't need to do this any more. He had over $3 million in overseas accounts and that was like winning the lottery for most people. Here in the city, he had a home in the upscale neighborhood of Deep Cove, North Vancouver, and very little debt. With his lovely wife and daughter, and his security business with Foley, he had enough to work honestly and live out his life like any regular guy. He could just take a salary from the business, pay taxes, work five days a week without risk from criminals or police, take a few weeks holiday annually, and buy a new car every couple of years. Life would be good.

Much better, it occurred to him, than that of the poor soul sitting twenty feet away from him on the curb. A homeless man, maybe fifty, destitute, dressed in rags, unkempt from head to toe. His shoes were bound together with duct tape. He might not make it through one more winter. He stared ahead blankly, like he knew his fate. Mat walked over to him. He looked up at Mat and smiled warmly, despite his condition.

"Down on your luck, partner?" Mat said.

"Good days, bad days. Life goes on. No complaints," he replied. "Spare a dollar?"

Mat knew he'd probably waste it on wine or cigarettes. "I'll do better. How 'bout enough to get yourself pointed in a better direction. Promise you'll try?"

"Sure. Maybe I'll buy a lotto ticket," he replied.

Mat opened his wallet and gave the man five twenties. "I *know* you can pull outta this... Good luck, my friend."

The man looked at the money liked he'd already won the lotto. "*Thank you, my brother!*"

Mat returned to his seat and picked up his ice coffee. *Help one, ignore a thousand,* his inner voice commented. In an instant later, a sickening scene suddenly unfolded before Mat's eyes. There was a screech of tires, a brief *yelp,* and then not ten feet in front of him, a little dog lay, struck by a passing car. Mat rushed to its side and held its head in his hands. The dog stiffened its body momentarily then arched its head back and went limp. Within seconds of the accident, he was dead.

The driver of the car rushed back, realizing too late what had happened.

"Didn't you see it?" Mat called out.

"No. I only saw it just before I hit it. Is it dead?"

"I'm afraid so. The tires went right over the poor little guy," said Mat.

. "Well, it's his own fault. He shouldn't have been on the road."

Mat let that asinine comment go without rebuttal. He turned the dog's collar around and there on a tag it said, *Bandit* with a phone number.

Mat called on his cell phone and a lady answered. "Ma'am, do you own a little dog named Bandit?" he asked.

"Yes, is he out of the yard again?" she replied in an exasperated tone.

"He's out, I'm sorry to tell you, and this is not a call I wanted to be making. He's been hit by a car and killed. I'm sorry." Mat tried to sound compassionate, and he really was. Who wouldn't be upset beyond words by witnessing such an incident?

Mat explained what had happened, and the lady was in obvious grief on the other end of the line. He explained that he would leave the animal's carcass by a nearby fire hydrant on the boulevard for her to retrieve and the call was ended. Mat felt miserable.

The suddenness of this sad event, its awful, cruel outcome, and the finality with which a life can end was on Mat's mind. He returned briefly to his train of thought just before the accident. A few weeks earlier he had witnessed Foley impale a thief and would-be murderer with a Lightning Bolt throwing knife at The Sutton Place Hotel, and he felt little or no compassion for the man.

Somehow, the death of an innocent animal was harder to cope with and Mat reflected on his own life. He realized that life is a fleeting thing, a temporary opportunity in an unforgiving world, and you have to use your time wisely and efficiently to accomplish your goals.

You hear about soldiers getting killed on a peace keeping mission overseas. An innocent child dies of leukemia in a local hospital. A family of four is wiped out instantly in a head on collision on the Coquihalla. A construction worker is killed in a freak accident on a job site. A plane goes down and hundreds of passengers are wiped out in a dreadful crash. Natural disasters occur — tsunamis, earthquakes, wildfires, others... killing hundreds, thousands, more sometimes, of third world people that had practically nothing to begin with, starving nomads by our standards. Homeless bums that were *people* once, die on the streets of Vancouver and get disposed of like garbage. The obituaries in the newspaper contain a litany of deceased souls daily and they all lived a life that may or may not have fulfilled their life's dreams and ambitions — most, had not.

Everyone lives. Everyone dies. And everyone spins the roulette wheel while they're here. There are winners, and there are losers, and worse, there are bystanders who live a meaningless, uninspired existence, then die like worker ants, having only lived in servitude to others, often lesser to themselves on the grand scale. Mat was determined and committed to being a winner, and he had no qualms about bending the rules to do it. *It's not how you play the game, it's whether you win or lose,* he thought privately. He planned on winning. No, he was determined to win.

Mat was who and what he was, a product of his upbringing, education, beliefs and personal experiences and he knew that his own life had a finite period of time in which to carry out its purpose. *In round numbers, my life is already about half over,* he thought, introspectively. He also knew that he had been lured into his life of crime by events and circumstances that were largely beyond his control. Could he just drop the thrill and excitement of his alter ego, involvement with criminality and the underworld, and his ability to make money far beyond what he ever could by playing within the partisan laws of government, main-stream business and the *generally accepted accounting rules?* The question warranted no answer. This was something he just had to do, regardless of the danger and risk involved. And he was aware of the hazards of dealing with criminals and drug dealers. Was he apprehensive and downright scared? *You bet I am,* he said to himself, *but this is something I have to do. I'm driven to it. I feel it.*

He was reminded of the famous quote by Henry David Thoreau: "The mass of men lead lives of quiet desperation and go to the grave with the song still in them." *Not me, my eloquent old friend. I'm going to sing this song loud and clear to a grand finale before I face Saint Peter.*

However, he conceded that the time for taking unnecessary risk was running out and he did resolve one thing. He was getting out of the business as soon as he had enough money to retire with wealth — *real wealth.* The opportunity presented to him by Jack Kincaid could lead him down a perilous road, but it could also provide him with his ticket out of the game, for good.

Having lost his appetite after the dog incident, Mat left his coffee and snack and went back to his car. Whether consciously or not, he drove with extra care and attention, knowing how fast and unexpectedly a fatal accident can happen on the road, or in life in general. Minutes later, he arrived at his office and noticed a dark Ford, Crown Victoria in the parking lot. He paid it little attention, however.

Mat walked back into Bulldog Security, Inc. Foley and another gentleman he had never seen before were talking in a meeting room, and Foley looked up and said, "Mat. This is Inspector Lundgren. He's with the Vancouver police — a detective. He's looking into a death that took place a month or so ago at a hotel downtown."

Mat looked at the Inspector and noted that he was a man likely in his mid forties, with salt and pepper hair, chunky build, conservative grey suit, and piercing blue eyes. He returned Mathew's gaze without a smile and removed a hand sized notebook from the inner pocket of his jacket.

Mat's heart nearly stopped. He did his best not to look panic stricken. He extended his hand, "Glad to meet you, Inspector."

"Likewise. As Karl was saying, we are investigating the death of an individual that took place on July 1ˢᵗ. Would you mind answering a few questions?" replied Lundgren.

"Were you at The Sutton Place Hotel for any reason on that day?" Detective Lundgren got right to the point.

Mat was thinking at a feverish pace. How could he know he was there? What was the tie in? "I'm not sure. I'd have to look back on my schedule. Why do you ask?" He stalled for time.

"Just questions at this point, Mr. Crawford. Do you own a car?" The detective looked up at Mat who was still standing. He tried not to fidget with his hands or show any other outward signs of nervousness.

Now, Mat was good at what he did because he had a quick mind, and right now his mental engine was firing on all eight, in overdrive. It came to him, instantly. The Ford Explorer he had rented when his car was being serviced. It must have been caught on the hotel surveillance camera leaving the parkade. Then they traced the vehicle to the rental company and located the record of who had rented it on that day — Mathew Crawford, address, phone number, driver's license, the works.

"I do indeed," Mat replied.

"And, may I ask, why were you operating a rental vehicle on that day?" asked Lundgren.

"My car was being serviced at Kal-Tire. It was getting a brake job and new tires. I needed transportation. I have the work order if you want to see it," replied Mat.

He then went to his desk and opened his Day-Timer. "Ah, I was at The Sutton Place on the thirty first. I stopped in for a beer. It was a grueling day. We have a number of commercial clients in that part of town."

"Just a beer? But *you did* use the elevators. Can you tell me why?" The detective pressed on.

Now Mat knew that he had been caught on CCTV in the lobby as well. He had to think of an alibi or he would be implicated as a suspect and once that happened, it could only get worse. He looked directly at Mr. Lundgren.

"Inspector, I'm a married man. Occasionally I like to add a little variety to the mix. Monogamy's never come second nature to me. I may have met up with one of our city's escorts for a little *extra...* you understand." Mat tried to look embarrassed like he'd been caught red handed in an obvious indiscretion.

"I see. Then you rented a room, did you?" Lundgren asked.

Mat knew that he could not lie about a room because hotel records would not verify his story. "No, we actually just slipped inside the housekeeping supplies room. It didn't take long. I wasn't trying to impress her. I only needed a quick shoe shine, and she wasn't worth the cost of a room."

"What was her name?" the detective asked, knowing that he was probably wasting his time with this one.

"*Fifi Dubois,*" Mat responded. "I didn't exactly ask her for ID. I hired her off the street on the basis of merit and convenience."

The detective scrutinized Mat like a judge trying to weigh the complications of a case brought against the accused. He scribbled something in his notebook. Then detective Lundgren stared distantly away from Mat and Foley in deep thought for an uncomfortable period of fifteen or twenty seconds.

"Well, I may have some more questions at a later date. I wouldn't make a practice of hiring these girls," Lundgren offered up. "They're usually closely associated with other illegal activities in the underworld. It could place you in the company of criminals faster than you might think. And believe me, once that happens, you're likely to wind up in real hot water, one way or another."

Thanks. I know a little about that subject, Mat thought, straight-faced.

"I'll take that as good advice," he responded. "Can I count on you to keep my little indiscretion confidential?"

"For now," Lundgren replied.

"Inspector, before you go, were there any witnesses to the events surrounding this guy's death?" Mat asked, trying to probe the detective casually.

"Guy? Now, I didn't actually mention the gender of the deceased, did I?" Lundgren replied looking intensely at Mat. "How did you know it was a man? Perhaps you also know his weight, and height, and name?"

"No, of course not. I just assumed we were talking about a man. Was it a man then, or a woman?" Mat asked, trying to cover the blunder of his inquiry.

Foley noticed that if Mat's face had been any whiter, he may have needed a transfusion.

"Can't say at this point, my friend. Let's just say that there were 623 people staying in that hotel on that day, and any of them, or none of them, could be tied to this crime. My colleagues and I have to check into them all. Somebody was killed, and someone else knows why. We mean to find out and get to the bottom of this. We'll be checking out your story, as part of our investigation, Mr. Crawford."

"My *story?*"

"Well let's put it this way. Either you've got a bullet-proof alibi for everything I can think of, or you've got a more fertile imagination for crime stories than James Patterson."

"I assure you, my story's legit," Mat replied.

Lundgren's steely eyes fixed on both men momentarily. "Mr. Crawford, Mr. Folkestad, thank you for your cooperation."

His inquiries complete, Inspector Lundgren smiled unconvincingly, stood and walked directly out the door to his unmarked Crown Vic parked outside. Once he had driven away Foley and Mat looked at each other wide eyed and open mouthed.

"*Jumpin' Jehovah!* If that wasn't the closest call to gettin' busted we've ever come across, I'll eat your shorts," Foley said.

"Mister Folkestad," replied Mat, mimicking the stilted formality of the cop's language, "I'm certain you wouldn't want to be anywhere near my shorts right now." Foley pinched his nose with his thumb and index finger. "How long had he been here before I arrived?" Mat asked.

"Half hour, maybe. I couldn't even phone and tip you off with him sittin' right in front of me. I was tryin' to get rid of him. I told him I didn't know when to expect you, but it would probably be a few hours," Foley said.

"I wasn't sure if you might have said something that might conflict with what I was telling him," Mat said. "One thing I don't understand. How is it that they saw me on the CCTV, but not you?"

Foley pondered the question. "Well, it was raining cats and dogs and I did have a hat on that day, so my face would be covered from the overhead cameras. And, it was your name on the car rental contract so they'd have nothing to tie me to the vehicle."

"You think he'll be back?" asked Mat.

"Not any time soon. He's got around six hundred other leads to follow up on, is what I heard," Foley replied. "And your accounting for yourself had a pretty good ring to it, though I can say with certainty that you've never been within arm's reach of an escort. If I didn't know that, I might have bought your story, like he seemed to. A hooker in the housekeeping supplies room? You've got some head for concocting lies, son. Did you manage to steal some little bottles of shampoo and conditioner?"

"I hope that cop is as gullible as you think," Mat replied "Let's go for a drive. I've got something else to talk about and Danielle can keep shop while we're gone."

"Like usual," Foley commented. "She practically runs this place single handed, you realize."

"I know. We're lucky to have her. She's one in a million, that's for sure," Mat agreed.

Heading out the door the boys said goodbye to Danielle, their office manager, and hopped in the car on their way to talk about Jack Kincaid's proposal.

Once in the car, Foley said, "So what's Kincaid got up his sleeve this time. We gonna get rich quick, somehow?"

Mat replied, "Rich *or dead*, more like it. This one has a big pay day if we can pull it off. Listen to this, and I'll tell you the story.

CHAPTER 9

MAT BEGAN RECOUNTING the details to Foley of the opportunity laid out before him by Jack Kincaid.

"This will be the biggest money laundering project of our careers, my friend, and the one that puts us over Home Plate. It involves two groups who have it in for each other and a Chinese mob that will take all of them out, including us, if they get the slightest chance."

"What's the whole story?" Foley pressed on. "C'mon, cough up."

"Well, a shipment of narcotics, cocaine actually, was sent in a container on a ship from China last week destined for *The Red Sun Boys*, an Asian gang who's been operating on the coast for years. Sometimes, they may also call themselves *Sewer Rats*. They're well established and known for extortion and violence. Unlike most Asian gangs, these are older guys, often in their thirties or more who often have military training and speak Cantonese or Mandarin. They're known to smuggle heroin to the U.S. through Vancouver or Toronto. They've been accused of trafficking arms, and implicated in robberies and kidnapping. They virtually control credit card fraud in Canada. Model citizens, by all accounts.

"Another of their *growth industries* is people smuggling and illegal immigration. They specialize in transporting illegal aliens, a profession they call *Snakeheads*. They're Chinese gangs that smuggle people to other countries. They may use stolen or altered passports, improperly obtained visas, or immigration officials may be bribed or threatened. Millions of dollars change hands yearly on this one. They charge aliens from Asia a king's ransom to bring them over here, usually on refugee status, and then once they arrive, they typically go on welfare."

"Your and my tax dollars hard at work towards building a better and stronger Canada," Foley interjected.

"No kidding. These animals will stop at nothing to extort money from people. They're actually split into two groups. The more senior ones specialize in heroin trafficking from the *golden triangle* of Laos, Burma, and Thailand to North America. The junior ones conduct violent local crimes, including, listen to this... home invasions, at night, where they terrorize whole families, taking jewelry, raping the women, and stealing substantial sums of money that some Chinese keep in their homes, because they don't trust banks." Mat had received quite an education from Mr. Kincaid about who he'd be dealing with, if and when trouble arose.

"Then one of our trusty old, west coast biker gangs, *the Kings Crew,* got in on the act. If it involves money, crime and corruption you know they're going to be drawn to it like flies to shit. If it's illegal, they're probably into it. The bikers and the Red Sun Boys are the number one and two crime organizations in Vancouver, hands down," Mat explained.

"So they're competitors on the streets of crime and drug trafficking, you could say?" Foley asked.

"Exactly," Mat confirmed. "All the gangs in Vancouver compete to profit from drug sales, robbery, identity theft, credit card fraud, gun running, human smuggling, auto theft, extortion, prostitution — you name it. And the Vancouver Port is probably the single most important point of entry for drugs like cocaine, heroine, and crystal meth in North America. There's no doubt that biker gangs have infiltrated the Port Authority at high levels and on the docks. The police are all but powerless to stop it to any meaningful degree."

Foley wondered aloud, "They're just hoods on motor cycles. How hard can it be to track 'em down and put 'em outta business?"

Mat explained, "Trouble is, there's so many different groups of them, and they all compete with one another, and they're violent as hell when it comes to carrying out their activities on the street. There's the Independent Warriors, the Emperors Choice, the Outsiders, the Bandit Bikers, the Devils Drifters, United Front, the Baker Brothers, and of course, the Hells Angels, among others. Each of these groups has distinguishing characteristics, but they all routinely commit crimes and operate well outside the law in the normal course of their activities."

Foley pressed on, "So what happened here? What kinda deal is goin' down?"

"The Kings Crew bribed the ship's captain to divert the cargo to a different port terminal at the last minute. When it docked, they intercepted the drugs and made off with $10 million of wholesale product, and it's worth around fifty million on the street. As you might expect, *The Red Sun Boys* took exception to this and now they're peeved and want their booty back.

"Worse, the biggest and meanest gangs in mainland China, Taiwan and Macau are all part of an organized crime conglomerate collectively called the *Triads*. One in particular is called *Wo Shing Chu*. They made the shipment of drugs to *The Red Sun Boys* for a down payment of five million with another five million due upon docking in Vancouver. And they don't want to hear any excuses about the cargo being hijacked. If the balance owing isn't forwarded right quick, heads are going to roll."

Mat continued, "Kincaid has cut a deal with the hoods for us to launder the money once the product hits market for a fee of ten percent of the gross, with another million bonus for performance when the deal is complete. As usual, we'll skim off our cut before we give them back the clean money with its links to crime all covered up. Kincaid will hold the million bonus as a middle man until the product is sold out. Our potential take would be six million bucks. Not bad chump change, but we'd be in the middle of a bunch of guys who are real bad, real mad, and real mean. And then there's *Johnny Law.* To put it in the BS jargon I used to hear when I worked at the bank, considering the diversity of interests at play here, there is the potential for disharmonious relations between the three gangs, us, and the authorities."

Foley was taking this all in without much comment to this point.

"This might be a little out of our league, Buck. We always weigh the risk carefully in our projects and I'm none too particular about stickin' my neck out just 'cause the stakes are higher than usual. The payoff is huge on this one but it won't do us any good if we're in the Lion's Gate Morgue or locked up in a correctional centre with a bunch of lifers with lover's nuts," he added.

"There ain't much in this world that puts a scare into me, but this one gives me the jitters. Guys like that bunch aren't really members in good standing of the human race. They're not exactly the Philanthropic Society, know what I mean? They'll skin you alive and gut you like a pig if they *even think* you're messing in their territory."

"True enough, and your vivid imagery is reassuring, as usual, Foley. But you know that we always planned on doing this only until we had enough loot on the side to get out comfortably. And we've done this enough times to know how to protect ourselves and keep a low, low profile. This one would be our ticket to freedom and financial independence. It's like the lottery. If you don't play, you don't have a chance of winning. Did we start this to make money, or *by God* make money?"

"I know, I like money as much as you do, but I also value my health and freedom, and don't want to make a foolish error because our judgment's been clouded by greed and a bunch of bloody bull shit about our experience and infallibility. I've spent the better part of my career protecting your skinny ass and I haven't done it so you could keep takin' bigger 'n bigger chances until some prison guard finally leads you away in shackles, and that's if someone else hasn't put a bullet through your head first. One of these days, you're gonna run shit outta luck!"

"Okay... Who are you, exactly, and what have you done with Foley? Just when did you develop an aversion to risk? And it's not greed. It's an opportunity where we calculate all the variables, execute a well-thought-out-plan, and minimize the risk for a substantial payoff."

Foley argued back, "We've never involved ourselves with large criminal groups, or gangs like these before, and there might be too many players and too many conflicting interests to do our jobs properly and keep our heads down. Once they identify us there's no turning back. I don't have to remind you of the importance of secrecy in this particular business. I think we're crossing a line here. I don't like it. You'd have a better chance of selling this as a good idea to a panel of legal experts headed up by Judge Judy and Dr. Phil."

Mat countered, "All we have to do is make it clear that we're the money washers, nothing more, nothing less. And we deal only with one or two regular contacts – Kincaid and maybe one other. When it's all finished, we close up operations and vanish like apparitions. It's no different than before. It's just higher stakes."

Mat's inflection was rising with his temper, as he stood up and paced the room, thinking and talking. "You only run across an opportunity like this, *maybe* once in a lifetime. We can do it. We just need to be organized and careful. It's not like we're new to this game."

Foley wasn't buying it. "No, and we've had enough close calls to know that one of these days our luck is going to run out. What's wrong with your thinking? Did ya bang your head on somethin'? You been drinkin' the bathwater? One little mistake is all it'll take to cook our goose, gooses, geese — forget it. And we'll have either the Chinese mafia, or the Kings Crew, or the Vancouver police or all of them on our tails with revenge in their eyes and fire in their bellies. It's risky and it may not be worth it. Anyways, how long do you think it will be before *we do* get caught if we keep pulling these money laundering gigs. Let's not lose sight of the fact that this is laundering *drug money* — a highly illegal activity, and there are strict counter measures against it at practically every level of law enforcement and corporate policy around the world. We can't sugar coat it, Buck. One thing we have to keep clear in our heads is that this is against the law, big time!"

Mat's patience snapped and he exploded, "Fuck the law, *and* corporate policy! Laws are man-made. Big fish eat little fish... *That's* the law! I know, I was a little fish at the bank and I got eaten. Even my own father, a decorated RCMP officer was on the take, and it cost him his life in the end. It's like war – the victors get to write the history books, only here, the big fish get to write the laws. You're throwing knives through people's throats and your concerned about the law? Sure, he was a diamond thief intent on killing me, and you, and it was self defense but in a court of law, prosecution lawyers would frame the incident so that we looked guilty of something horrible like, say... murder? Do you actually trust our government to administer our legal system, when so many of its officials and practices are corrupt?

"The government claws every dollar they can out of us to run the country, then senior officials of crown corporations are getting paid three, four, five times what regular business managers get. It's legally sanctioned robbery! Do you know I got an invoice and a snarly letter recently from Canada Revenue Agency advising me that I still owe $3.50 from my last year's tax return. The clerk's time who wrote the letter, the paper envelope and letterhead, and the postage were worth more than that.

"Look what happened to the world economy by all the corporations and banks who were allowed to invest our money with pure gluttony and lust for profit. They all followed the laws and policies of the day, and now you and I are worth maybe half of what we were a year ago as a result. And we're the lucky ones, among millions of others. Are they held accountable for our losses? They robbed us of our life's savings, for Christ's sake, and the guys running those very corporations that caused this mess are now getting bonuses in the millions of dollars — legally, while other regular folks are losing their jobs and houses. The rhetoric you hear from politicians and financial experts to explain it all away is sickening. How much have your RRSPs, stocks, mutual funds, and real estate dropped in value? Don't worry, in ten years or so it will all rebound... *maybe*, and we'll be ten years older, and that much closer to the grave.

"We've found a way here to make a hell of a lot of money, and I'll take my chances with the Goddamned law and my own conscience.

"We could have this discussion all night. In the end, the average guy is still gonna get screwed by the law, government, and business. As far as I'm concerned the government has lost its moral authority to impose laws on me and my affairs. If they thought they could tax me on it, they'd probably make money laundering legal.

"This is a rare opportunity to score a bonanza. You jump on the bull and hold on tight until you hear the eight second buzzer. When it's over you jump off, and you're in the prize money. It's *that* complicated. I'm in, with or without you. I thought you had *cojones*. Do you believe we can pull this off, or are you going soft in your old age?

Foley looked mildly offended at first, then his gaze shifted to amusement, and finally to a broad smile.

"Enough already. You had me at *fuck the law*."

"And you watch too many old movies," Mat replied.

"You are a smooth talker kid, and after a speech like that, yes, I *do* believe we can pull this off."

Foley paused and blew a breath into the closed fist of one hand. "All right then. I'm on board, as usual, you little bugger. But we'll have to bring the term *caution* to the level of a fine art form," Foley said relenting to Mat's persuasion.

Mat took his seat again and breathed in, then out heavily, calming himself down, and savoring his triumph in the debate with his partner and pal.

"Okay, old chum," said Mat, feigning a comic British accent. "I'll get back to Kincaid tonight and we'll give it a go then, by gum. Us? Get caught? Not bloody likely! Me bubble's not burst, just yet. C'mon now, keep your pecker up! We're gonna be rich in a jiffy, my jolly, old friend!"

"Indubitably," Foley replied, and the two pals 'high fived' each other.

CHAPTER 10

AFTER A LENGTHY discussion at a restaurant with Foley about all the details of their new assignment, Mat returned home that night and found Christine in their family room. She was sitting quietly, not reading, not watching television, not talking on the phone, not doing anything, really. There was a soft glow in the room from a table lamp, and she was dressed in a favorite satin robe with a night dress underneath. To Mat, she looked as pretty as the first time he met her and he reflected on how much he loved this woman. Mat said, "Honey, I'm sorry I'm late. It's been a long day and I'm tired. Is anything wrong? Why are you sitting here like this?"

Christine looked up at Mat. She had been sipping a glass of German Riesling and she thought contemplatively before speaking. She pressed down the base of the wine goblet with one hand and ran her finger around the rim, producing a low level hum from the crystal glass, vibrating like a haunting note from a melodic violin string. Mat studied her and mused over the musical drone of the delicate wine glass under her willowy finger.

"I was just thinking about things. We really have to talk about this sideline of yours. You and Foley are involving yourselves with hardened criminals, and it scares me. This is something that doesn't just expose you to danger. It affects Hannah and me as well."

Mat said, "I know it's scary, and it's almost over, Chris. I never meant to place you and Hannah in any danger and I take careful precautions to keep us all safe."

"What do you mean, *it's almost over?*" Christine replied.

"Well, we came across an opportunity today that will make us enough money to get out of the business once and for all when it's complete," Mat said. "It's a big one, and yes, there's *some risk,* but we'll take extra care to protect ourselves and finish the job on schedule."

Christine replied, "No. I don't like it, and I don't want money taken from criminals. They'll know who we are and they could come after us, maybe years from now and coerce you into doing it again and again. We'll never, ever be safe and secure again. And worse, you could get caught and arrested. You'd be thrown in jail. Money laundering is a serious, federal offense Mat, and we already have enough money."

"Darling, please, try and understand. We couldn't just walk away from it now if we wanted to. We know too much and it would place us in even greater danger to back out now. I'm afraid the genie is out of the bottle. They might decide to do something rash to ensure we don't go to the authorities with information."

"*Something rash?* Oh my God, this is getting worse by the minute!" Christine said, unnerved and angry. "I wish you had never told me about any of this. I didn't get married to find out that I've been living with a criminal all these years. What about Hannah? You owe it to her to get out of this mess and start leading a respectable, law abiding life, like all the other fathers in our neighborhood." Her face was contorted with fear.

"I know dear. I will do right by both of you, I promise. This involves organized crime, and there is a right way and a wrong way to back away from it. I promise I will get out as soon as possible. Can you just accept that for now?" Mat reasoned with her. He knew that now was not the time to tell her any of the details of their next and hopefully last foray into the world of money laundering.

Christine was rubbing her temples and eyes with her hands, trying to cope with the horror movie she had been thrust into. She was emotionally upset to the point of distraction and her hand trembled as she moved it across her brow. She tried to continue, "I just want... I mean, why don't you tell them? You could just tell them you quit, you're out... Oh, please, *make this stop!*" And she broke down, sobbing. She wept uncontrollably into her open palms, got up to her feet, and walked out of the room.

That night, for the first time in their fifteen year marriage, Mat slept in the guest room, feeling like a shit. What he had told Christine about not really having the option of reneging on Kincaid's deal was not completely untrue. He had called Jack the night before and confirmed that he would participate in the Kings Crew money laundering process, and if Kincaid had told anyone that that part of the puzzle was solved it would be a *real problem* to call again and try to back out. Mat had *a lot* of information. In the circles of organized crime a phone call or a nod of the head is as good as a paper contract drawn up by corporate lawyers in the world of legal business. He was reminded of Foley's analogy of the skinned alive, gutted pig and it made him feel queasy.

Mat had tossed and turned all night and didn't really sleep more than a couple of hours at best. He had risen early and left the house before Hannah or Christine were awake. Knowing that a good night's rest for Christine would help clear her mind, he had planned on coming home over the lunch hour to try and patch things up with her.

It was raining lightly, and the overcast skies closely matched the somber mood he was feeling over their commitment to this risky deal and his wife's growing estrangement from him. As he headed towards downtown, his cell phone rang and Mat wondered who would be calling him so early. It was shortly after 7:00 o'clock. His caller I.D. read, Evergreen Import Export International. *It must be Jack Kincaid.*

"Jack. What's up?" he said, accepting the call.

"Mr. Crawford?" replied a distinctly female voice. "This is Crystal Waters, Mr. Kincaid's secretary."

"Oh, well, good morning, Crystal. How can I help you?"

"I just got a call from Mr. Kincaid. He asked me to call you and to ask if you would meet him at 12:00 noon at an address he gave me. Will that be possible?" She replied.

"Yes. I can arrange that. What's the address?"

"It's Suite 410, 6212 - 146th Street in Surrey. Do you need directions?" Crystal offered.

"No thanks, dear. I'll *Map Quest* it when I get to work. Did he tell you anything else about the meeting?"

"No, sir. He just asked that I call you right away. I tried you at home but your wife said you'd already left the house," she said. "Okay then, I'll let my boss know you'll be there. We'll talk again sometime soon, I'm sure. Bye for now." Crystal disconnected and he snapped shut his cell.

Mat arrived at work and unlocked the front door to let himself in. Right around 8:00 o'clock Foley and Danielle could be expected to arrive. Sitting alone while a fresh pot of coffee was brewing, Mat felt a little uneasy about going to a meeting blind. While there probably wasn't anything overly risky about it, he would have felt better if he had Foley along side. For now, however, he wanted to keep Foley under cover. The less people knew about him, the more effective he would be as a collaborator in their activities. *Caution* was the operative word on this job and if anyone felt threatened by Foley, they might take off his head with a C8 carbine rifle or some other such measure as he left the building. With $50 million of street valued cocaine at stake nothing was beyond imagination.

Right on schedule, Foley walked in the front door. "Mornin', Bud. What happened? You have a bad dream about a Chinese boogieman and shit the sheets?"

"Nope, and what a charming image, you summon, as usual. I wanted to get here first to make sure you're coming to work on time. Your performance review is coming up," Mat scoffed.

"I think I'm due a merit increase, considering the number of times I've saved your bacon," Foley replied.

"Really? I thought you just worked here for all the fun and excitement we have. Right now, for example, I have to fill out a pile of Canada Revenue Agency forms and pay the government around half of what we earned last month. We take the risk, we do the work, and they get the money. Isn't that great?" Mat marched off to his office and worked diligently on Bull Dog Security business until later that morning, and Foley kept busy with customer issues and such.

Later, having finished with the mundane matters of bill paying and government reporting, Mat walked into Foley's office just as he was hanging up the land line from a sales inquiry.

"Hey Fole, can you drop what you're doin' and join me on a little excursion across town?"

"Love to, but I can't. Just bought a new wallet, and I've got to transfer all my credit cards and ID, and the condom that's been in there since 1992."

Mat laughed. "*Forever hopeful.* Seriously, I've got a meeting to go to with Jack Kincaid at noon today, and I feel a little edgy about it. I want you close by, but I don't think you should take a high profile in this, coming out of the gate. I need some way to reach you fast, if anything bad goes down," Mat explained.

"No problem," Foley said opening his desk drawer. "How about this little trinket?" He removed a small device no bigger than the face of a wrist watch.

Mat looked impressed. "What is it?"

"Foley demonstrated its use. "It's *spy technology* from suppliers on the internet. It's a highly sensitive, one way transmitter.

It'll pick up a whisper from ten meters away. Just turn it on and attach it under your lapel with this clip. You insert the SIM card from a cell phone, then I call the number, and listen in. As long as there's cellular coverage, I'll hear the whole conversation and *Bob's your uncle.* If anything goes wrong, I'll hear it loud and clear. But what could go wrong? Who else are you meeting with?"

"I'm not sure. Maybe that's why I'm a little jumpy about it. How do you find all these surveillance and undercover gadgets, anyway?" Mat said, picking up the device to examine it more closely.

"I *get paid* to find ways to cover your back, remember?" Foley reminded Mat with his usual sense of the pragmatic.

"Well it's not very big. You sure it'll work?"

"That's okay, small things work just fine sometimes. You sired Hannah with your sorry little tadpole, after all," Foley remarked.

"Very funny. Does it have a volume switch?"

"Your tadpole? Damned if I know. Don't wanna find out, either."

"No! This bloody thing."

"Ah, don't worry. I got twenty-twenty hearing. If it's transmitting I'll hear every word," and Foley pulled his ears forward like Dumbo for emphasis.

"Geeze, but you're a piece of work, Foley! *Twenty-twenty* refers to one's vision, not hearing, ya dork.*"

"Dork? Sorry if I touched a nerve there, buddy. But the clock's a tickin' and we better get movin'. I don't wanna lose track of ya. Make sure you keep that thing turned on now, Stumpy."

At 11:30 a.m. the two men headed off in separate cars to the meeting with Jack Kincaid. Mat would enter the building alone, and Foley would wait in his car outside. If the conversation started going the wrong direction, Foley could be at Suite 410 in less than a minute. The precaution of the cellular transmitter gave Mat a better sense of security, although he still didn't like being summoned to a meeting without knowing why, or who else might be there.

Pulling up to the address given by Kincaid's secretary, Mat noted that it was a four story, non-descript, brownstone building, probably more than fifty years old. This was a neighborhood that would easily fall into the *undesirable* category for most people. He entered through the front door and boarded the elevator in the lobby. Exiting at the fourth floor he looked down the corridor to find Suite 410.

The building would have seemed deserted but for two large men, well over six feet each, one at each end of the corridor standing by the stairwell doors. They were obviously bikers complete with leather jackets with the pirate's skull and crossbones logo, bandanas, pony tails, jack boots, and facial piercings, including, Mat noticed, three common safety pins poked through the outer edge of one guy's ear. *Class act, all the way,* remarked Mat's little side-kick, inner voice.

Mat saw no one else in the lobby or on the elevator and beside these two patrols, no one else on this floor. The bikers didn't speak or communicate with him or each other in any way, but Mat felt the implied threat of their presence. He had no doubt that they were probably already known to police, if not wanted, and would be armed and ready to kill if the situation deteriorated. There were no sounds behind any of the office doors. Walking down the hall with a tap, tap, tap on the tile floor, he found the suite. He opened the door and stepped inside.

It was a two room office with an old, oversized oak desk out front serving as a reception area. Nobody occupied the desk. From the other office Mat heard voices and footsteps approaching before Jack Kincaid came into the room.

"Mathew. Thanks for coming to our little get together on short notice. We've been going over the details as to how our little caper is going to unfold and we wanted some input from you. We chose this location because the building is vacant. It's scheduled for demolition, so we're assured of privacy."

"Who, exactly, is *we?* You know I like to work alone."

"Right this way. There's someone I'd like you to meet. I'm sure you won't mind bending the rules this time considering the money involved." Jack said, leading Mathew to the office in the back.

When they entered the room there were two other men and a woman sitting at a boardroom table. The men looked to be in their late thirties, early forties, and the woman, a bit younger, perhaps thirty four, thirty five. If these guys were biker-gangsters, it would have taken some convincing because they were well groomed, with no facial hair or piercings, and dressed in *smart casual* business cloths. They stood courteously, when Mat approached the table.

Jack opened the introductions. "Mat, I'd like you to meet my associates, Dominic Hall and Carlos Garcia. Gentlemen?" The men all shook hands courteously.

"And this is Adriana," he continued.

"Adriana Santos," she repeated as she also stood and extended her hand to Mathew, fixing her eyes on his. Mat took her hand and shook it, releasing the pressure of his grip from what he would normally exert with another man.

"Ma'am, nice to meet you," Mat said.

"*Pleasure,*" she replied, looking him in the eye.

First impressions can be everything and in the few seconds that Mat had to assess her he noticed several things. This woman had a compelling presence. She looked at Mat directly, without any sign of intimidation and she had a way about her that was somewhat aloof, though not unfriendly. She was smartly dressed with dark brunette hair falling just beyond her shoulders, penetrating brown eyes, and a strikingly feminine face and figure. Mat found her Latin appearance and female manner attractive at an animal level and he tried not to let her charm upon him be too apparent.

Jack continued to set the tone. "Alright, let's not pussy foot around with conviviality, shall we? There's no pretense about why we're all here, okay? Dominic and Carlos are with the accounting firm of Hall, Garcia and Barlow. They handle the financial side of the Kings Crew's business interests and they do it, quietly and discreetly, so to speak. These gentlemen ensure that the money from operations is properly counted and dispersed to the various accounts. It's a dirty job, but someone has to do it."

Everyone laughed politely.

Jack went on. "Adriana works for me in a consulting role. She's a lawyer specializing in international trade and business. Mat, since you'll likely be moving a lot of money around the world in the next few months, I thought it would be useful to have her participate in an advisory capacity if any questions arise concerning international law."

'An advisory capacity?' Mat thought to himself. He replied, "Really. Well some questions might well arise pertaining to *criminal* law, before we're through. I hope she's versatile."

Mat said nothing further but secretly resented the implication that he might need the advice of some junior lawyer on how to carry out his end of the deal. That would be like him riding along side NASCAR driver Danica Patrick, *in an advisory capacity,* at the Daytona National Speedway. *"Danica, turn left up there, then accelerate. Try not to hit the wall..."*

Jack continued, "Mat has been fully apprised of our situation. He knows that you guys borrowed a shipment of narcotics from the Red Sun Gang, and that the street value of it is in the vicinity of fifty million. If anyone can convert this street money into legitimate capital, Mat here is our man."

Dominic took the floor. "Mr. Crawford, in the interest of knowing where our money will be when it's in your control, we would like to ask just how you plan to put it through this laundering process." He was amicable enough, but the question implied either a degree of mistrust or a lack of faith in Mat's abilities.

Mat replied, "One of my first conditions when I get involved in these matters is complete autonomy concerning the laundering process. I've spent a lot of years learning how to cover my tracks and erase an audit trail to the funds I work with. There're many ways to convert money derived from crime to legal funds. I'll do it as quickly and efficiently and you'll get your money from a legitimate source, in due course. I'm afraid I can't tell you much more than that."

Dominic hesitated momentarily before saying, "Mat, if I may call you that, we don't question your capabilities at your craft, but understand, there's a lot of fuckin' green at stake here — pardon my vernacular," he added, nodding towards Adriana, "And we're accountable to a client who can be downright nasty if things go wrong. They make it worthwhile for us to watch over their proceeds, but if any part of the money should go missing, quite frankly, it would be your ass, and ours that would go in the deep fryer. Do you get my drift?"

Mat observed that despite the gentlemanly façade, these guys were really no better than hoods masquerading in suits. "If you don't trust me, then why am I here?" he responded.

Kincaid interjected. "We all trust you Mat. Don't sweat it. Dom and Cark, I've done business with Mat before. Never once has he done anything unexpected or outside the agreement. I'll vouch for his professionalism."

"Honor among thieves," Mat interjected.

Carlos was watching and listening carefully and now commented, "By saying so, Mr. Kincaid, you're putting your head in a noose if anything goes wrong." His next comment was phrased as a statement of fact.

"You *do* understand that." He fixed a gaze on Jack Kincaid.

Dominic accepted Jack's assurances and said, "If you say so, Jack, we'll put our trust with him but just for our enlightenment, Mat, tell us about the laundering business, when we're dealing in large dollar amounts. We know how to cover our tracks when we're spinning a thousand here, a thousand there, but with this one, we're dealing with *millions*. How do you manage a money laundering project of that magnitude?"

Mat was reluctant to get into it. Discussing trade secrets of this nature could not only be interpreted as interviewing for the job, and by implication, leaving his fee open to negotiation, but it could also put him out of the job altogether if they got the notion that they could do it on their own.

"Quite honestly, it's been too soon since we accepted the job to have a firm plan on how we're going to do it. We'll need some time to assess all the risks and variables, and then we'll decide which avenue of laundering we'll go down," he said.

Carlos persuaded Mat, "Oh, come on, Crawford. Just give us the confidence that you have a working knowledge of your business so we can all leave here feeling right about this partnership. We only want to protect our money, after all. We're the Kings Crew, but we're really just a business, and we need to know that our money will be safe. We've invested and risked a lot to get to this point. We're not going to take chances now, if we think you're anything less than a professional and an expert."

This line of reason appealed to Mat and he decided that a brief discussion on the process was not out of line.

"All right, gentlemen, I'll give you a cook's tour through the process, but understand, I may use some, all, or none of what I'm about to tell you in handling the money that comes in from distributing your stolen drugs. The methods I use to process your funds are not subject to discussion, approval, or disclosure. Understood? Our agreement is that I receive cash taken from the sale of your cocaine and put it through a process to make it pop out the other end as legitimate capital. My fee is ten percent of the gross proceeds and *when*, not *if* the whole shipment is distributed and the cash is converted to legal tender, I get another million dollars, immediately. Are we all clear?"

Jack stepped in, "Yes. That is the arrangement we agreed to, right boys?" Carlos and Dominic both nodded concurrence.

"One other thing," Mat continued, "I've never needed counsel from a lawyer to put these funds through a myriad of transactions and come back clean, so I don't know what you expect me to share with Miss Santos here. If you want her to tag along for the ride, that's probably about all you can expect. No offense, Ma'am."

Adriana was unfazed by the comment and she continued to make notes in her portfolio with the impartiality of a court reporter. Mat noticed she was using an expensive Cross pen. He looked at her and she smiled, not quite perceptibly.

"None taken, I'm sure. I'd love to *tag along*. I'll try not to distract you," she replied, idly playing about her open lips with the pen.

You already have, said Mat's little voice.

Jack came to her defense, "Relax, Mat. I just thought that with a large scale opportunity like this we could use all the talent we can get. Adriana's bright and well connected, both locally and internationally.

"You'll be glad I introduced the two of you before this is done. That's a prediction I'll make." Adriana and Mat looked askance, scrutinizing each other, almost warily.

Mat pulled up closer to the table and gestured with his hands for everyone else to do the same. "Gather round, boys, and girl, or… *woman*. I'm going to tell you about the business of money laundering." Mat had everyone's undivided attention.

Outside, Foley turned up the volume on his earpiece receiver.

CHAPTER 11

"FIRST OF ALL, let's all get a clear picture of what the term 'money laundering' refers to," Mat began the session. "Put simply, if someone comes into a large amount of money, particularly cash, illegally obtained or otherwise, they need to find a way of either putting it to use through a purchase, or they need to deposit it in a bank."

"Yes, I think we all understand why there's an underlying need for the service," Adriana responded, reminding Mat that she, and probably the rest of the parties in the room, were at least, that experienced.

"Allow me to continue, counselor," Mat said, with a smile toward Adriana.

"The need for money laundering services among the bad guys is staggering. Depending on which law enforcement agency is reporting, there is anywhere from five hundred million to well over a trillion dollars that are laundered globally every year. Since it's illegal and covert, there's no way to put an exact number on it, but it's a lot."

Mat looked around the room and began his lecture in earnest. "At an international level it's countered mainly by a set of banking guidelines aimed at offsetting money laundering and terrorist financing through an organization called the FATF, or

Financial Action Task Force. It was established in 1989 in Paris among the G-7 heads of state and by 2004 it had put forth what's now called the *40+9 recommendations* to counter the use of financial systems by criminals. Most nations around the globe have cooperated with these measures, but many still have bank secrecy laws that provide for almost perfectly anonymous banking which can be used to disguise the origin of deposits."

Mat paused for reflection, then continued, "Under Canadian, as well as US law, any single transaction, or any one day's cumulative transactions of $10,000 or more carried out at a bank, has to be reported to the federal government. The agency is called The Financial Transactions and Reports Analysis Centre of Canada, or FINTRAC, for short. They're watching for potentially suspicious financial activity that might be connected to any kind of threat to the security of Canada. So, right from the *get go* we have a problem of placing your money into the financial system. How do we deposit $50 million, cash? There are other agencies of lesser threat like the Canada Border Services Agency or CBSA, the Canadian Security Intelligence Service or CSIS, and of course, the good old RCMP."

"That's the Royal Canadian Mounted Police, right?" Adriana interjected.

For a moment everyone was taken aback by the naïvety of her comment, until she smiled, then the room erupted with laughter at her sarcasm. Mat had made disparaging remarks earlier about not needing counsel from a junior lawyer. Maybe she wasn't going to take it lying down. She was feisty, and bright. He liked that.

Mat continued, "Just trying to be thorough, Adriana. Bear with me, please. Now, the first thing to understand about money laundering is that the essence of it amounts to *sleight of hand*. The more confusing you can make the whole process, the better.

"The classic model of a money laundering operation goes like this. There are three phases to the process of legitimizing funds obtained from criminal activities.

"First, there is the *placement stage.* Let's think about it for a moment. It's one thing to have a suitcase full of hundred dollar bills, but what are you going to do with it without raising suspicion? That's the riskiest part of the whole process because this is where you take the money from crime, usually cash, and *place* it into the financial system. It has to be deposited in sums small enough not to attract attention and in Canada or the US, that means under $10,000. This method of getting the money into the financial system is called *smurfing or structuring deposits.* Consider our situation. We're anticipating proceeds on the order of $50 million, cash. We would have to make over five thousand deposits of just under ten grand to meet that criterion and that's just not possible. We'll have to get the money out of Canada somehow, and deposit it in an offshore account where there's bank secrecy laws that'll veil our activities."

Dominic interrupted, "And where do they allow that sort of thing?"

Mat said, "Well, some examples are Panama, Guatemala, the Philippines, Hong Kong, Singapore, the Cayman Islands, Antilles, Bahrain, the Bahamas. There are others. Developing nations are usually good places to launder money because they're eager for foreign investment and are more willing to turn a blind eye to suspicious transactions. By analogy, if you were starting a business and all the banks turned you down for an operating loan but some independent business man stepped forward and offered to loan you a substantial sum at fair market rates and terms, *no questions asked,* would you be tempted to take it?"

Mat's lecture of sorts made the atmosphere around the table like that of a court room where everyone is hearing the evidence with riveted concentration. He looked around and was a little impressed with himself, that he could have an effect like this on people. Rarely did he actually discuss his trade. He usually only carried out his activities in quiet solitude and secrecy.

"Next we have the *layering stage.* That means the money is moved into and out of numerous complex transactions so that it becomes nearly impossible to build an audit trail as to where it came from. We normally do this by moving the funds through bank-to-bank transfers and wire transfers in different names and accounts from one country to another, until we're satisfied that bankers and the authorities see it as just a normal part of international banking.

"Keep in mind that there are five hundred thousand wire transfers of over a trillion dollars that occur globally every day. The authorities can only scrutinize a very small percentage of them. How many of those transfers do you think involve money laundering?" How much did Bernard Madoff swindle from investors with his Ponzi scheme... billions and billions? Where do you think that money is now? In a suitcase under his bed, or did it just go *poof?*" Mat paused for a moment to let the questions and numbers sink in. Everyone looked a little dumbfounded.

"There are other ways of layering transactions to blur the trail to its true source like complex dealings with stock, commodity and futures brokers. The number of daily transactions is enormous and largely unnamed among the traders and the chance of dirty money being traced is hardly worth mentioning. However, the rules in that arena are changing, as we speak."

Carlos was listening intently and remarked, "But one man can't do all that by himself. You need to have other people cooperating who know when to look the other way, or physically deposit cash in an offshore bank someplace, or collude in some other way."

Mat responded, "Yes, that's correct, and I do have contacts that I have built up over the years in various locales around the world, including right here in Canada. Remember, I'm a specialist and this is my area of expertise. With surprisingly few people, I can process a lot of money through these transactions on a global scale. With e-banking, I can even do much of it from my own laptop.

"I'll continue," Mat said. "The final stage is commonly called *integration*, or re-entry of the funds into the legal economic and financial system of our country. Essentially, the money is assimilated with legitimate funds and it disappears into the financial system. Just as mixing two cups of water makes it impossible to recover each original cup, the dirty money becomes blended with the mainstream capital of the land. We make it look like the money was earned legally, and nobody would question otherwise at this point. Sometimes we set up shell companies in countries where the right to secrecy is guaranteed by law. We invoice them for consulting work or for merchandise supposedly shipped to them and they pay us a fee that looks to be rightfully and legally earned. This is where our job is finished and you guys get your money back, less my fee — *win, win.*

"That's money laundering in its purest and simplest form and definition. Understand that there are lots of other ways of converting dirty money into capital that appears to have been earned legally. Any business that operates primarily on a cash basis is an ideal cover for laundering: casinos, car washes, laundromats, retailers at the mall, even restaurants and nightclubs.

"These types of businesses can readily combine cash from crime with actual sales receipts and inflate their revenues to absorb the dirty money. Trouble is, then it's taxable, and anyways, it's impractical in our project because at fifty million there's too much cash, and we need to turn it into liquid capital that can be delivered to a bank account that someone can write a cheque on tomorrow. And as far as banks are concerned, all we need is one accomplice in an influential position at a major bank and we're across the moat."

"And do you have such an accomplice?" Dominic inquired.

Mathew looked around the room. "What do you think?

"There are many, many other methods and procedures for concealing the source of money and I couldn't begin to tell you about all of them. I don't *know* all of them. I will say that the ease and secrecy of doing business on the internet is the future of the money laundering business. It is absolutely unregulated, there is no audit trail whatsoever from electronic money transfers, and with encryption software nobody can decipher what the heck you're doing.

"Once money is placed into the financial system, cross border and intercontinental movements of large sums can be done instantly. The incidence of e-commerce is increasing geometrically and it's a red carpet for money launderers."

Mat finished up. "Remember, a little knowledge is a dangerous thing. Like most other things that require skill, practice, and experience this only touches the surface of the actual process in the real world. Like the saying goes, *don't try this at home!* Your margin for error is zero, literally. If you get caught *once* they don't exactly let you off with a warning and the guys on the other side are just as skilled as we are.

"You'll have to pay some lawyer your entire net worth to mount a defense, only you won't have any net worth any more. You're going to be fined heavily and you'll go to jail for at least six years, probably more, and they'll confiscate anything that they suspect may have been acquired with dirty money under *proceeds of crime* legislation — your cars, your house, your boat, your furniture, your business, your wife's jewelry, your savings accounts and investments, everything, basically. And once that's all gone and you're in jail, your wife and kids will leave too, if they aren't jailed as accomplices... Well then, any questions?"

Around two seconds later, Mat jumped in again, pre-empting any possibility of questions, "Good! Gentlemen, are we all satisfied that I've got some experience at this? Trust me yet?"

"You seem to be familiar with the fundamentals of the business," Carlos remarked apprehensively. "*Trust* issues aside, it looks like you've got the job. Kincaid, you're right about half the time. Better hope we're not sorry we agreed to this."

"Not so fast," Mat jumped in. "I wanted you to know that I'm qualified and experienced. I understand your offer but I haven't actually said I'm in yet, one hundred percent." Mat thought he might be able to sweeten the deal, or maybe even just take some time to convince himself that this was a good idea. Foley's earlier apprehension about entering into this deal had bothered him more than he let on.

An uncomfortable stillness settled over the room. This was unexpected. Carlos and Dominic exchanged a look that communicated something. Dominic spoke up.

"I will address this." He paused, gathering his thoughts.

"Mr. Crawford, you've conducted this meeting pretty much on your own agenda, haven't you? We appreciate the little gymnastics demonstration you've given us here on money laundering, but you've also learned a lot about our organization and its activities. You've teased us into believing that we're goin' to bed together and now we're standing here naked while you're looking at your finger nails. There's only one way this is going to end, my friend. You're in, like it or not. We don't allow someone to learn *this much* about our affairs, then let them just casually walk away."

Defiantly, Mat went on the defensive. "And if I refuse?"

From under the table, Dominic pulled a Colt .38 Special, snub-nosed revolver. He pointed it at Mathew and said, "You might want to reconsider that position. You can either make a lot of money here – *if* you're as good as you say you are, or you can start planning your introduction to the man upstairs. *One little pull* and we're onto candidate number two." He looked straight at Mat, like he was capable of killing him right here, in cold blood.

Jack Kincaid interrupted forcefully, "Fellas, relax. Dom, put that thing away, Goddamn it!" Dom lowered the gun and set it on the table.

"Mat, what the hell are you doing? I understood you were onside. Are you seriously considering bailing out now, after all we've talked about today, and before?"

Mat had been afraid there was no way out at this point, and he saw little to gain by pressing his luck. "No, I was just having a little fun, boys. I wouldn't have spent the last hour teaching you *Money Laundering 101* if I wasn't planning on jumping on the bandwagon. *I'm in* — lock, stock, and barrel. Let's move on."

Mat had taken the floor earlier in response to the challenge dropped by the two men and proven beyond doubt that he knew his business. He regretted slightly that he had told them as much as he did because they might just decide to do some research and get into the business themselves, which is why he warned them about the consequences of getting caught. They were part of a notorious biker gang after all, and they would stop at nothing to expand their ability to make money and conceal it.

Feeling that he had been placed on the hot seat, he now felt entitled to ask some questions of his own.

"Excuse me for pointing out a rather obvious question, but you two guys don't exactly fit the image most people have of the Kings Crew, unlike your charming associates in the hall."

Carlos smiled and replied, "Ya, we're sort of undercover, in reverse. We have to look like real accountants for the sake of appearances. We're card carrying, full patch members of the club. And the guys in the hall aren't *associates* or *hang arounds*. They're full patch too, and believe me, you don't want to mess with them. You can take our word for it though, we watch the money real carefully and if anything doesn't add up? Well, you finish the sentence." He looked at Mat with a bogus grin worthy of an academy award.

Mat said, "Don't worry. Things will add up all right on my ledger, but I hope you've got more weapons than that pea-shooter, because the Red Sun Boys and Wo Shing Chu are madder than a pack of starving wolves at you guys and they're probably circling Vancouver right now looking for trouble."

"Thank you for that *information*," Carlos said, wryly. "We'll be sure to pass the *Intel* up the line to our brothers at arms."

Jack Kincaid had been listening and looked relieved. He stepped into the conversation again. "Gentlemen, as you can tell, Mat knows his way around the business. I think it's fair to proceed with moving the product without delay, counting and collecting payment, and transferring it to him for conversion to legal funds."

Mat interjected, "I need to have the money available to me in parcels of five million, or less, preferably. Each one will be treated as a separate transaction and you will be returned everything but ten percent to cover my fee. Jack knows how to reach me and I can begin as soon as the money is ready for delivery."

Dominic and Carlos looked at each other and nodded.

Carlos said, "Looks like we're in business. We'll start transferring cash in the next few days, and no more games. You've got your work cut out for you, my friend. We'll be in touch."

"Right. See you at choir practice," Mat replied. The deal was underway and a contract had been verbally agreed upon. Dominic and Carlos excused themselves from the room and only Mat, Jack and Adriana remained.

Jack remarked, "Well, as Sherlock Holmes would say, *'The game is afoot, Watson!'*"

Mat replied, "I'd stick with crime and corruption if I were you, Kincaid. Holmes and Watson were detectives looking to bring down guys like us. Tell me, how did you find out about this caper in the first place?"

"*Elementary,*" Jack replied in an oily voice. "I'm in the import, export business, you see. I have eyes and ears around the globe. One of my sources brought me information about a shipment of cocaine that was due to set sail from China to Vancouver. I made some inquiries among some local business men as to whether they might like to get involved in some small way. Carlos and Dominic came forward and arranged to top up Captain Furlong's retirement fund, in return for docking the ship at a port terminal of their choice. Instead of docking at the Port of Vancouver in the Burrard Inlet, he changed course only an hour from shore and took the ship to a terminal at Roberts Bank in

Delta, thirty five kilometers from the original docking site. Our friends were waiting for them there and assisted in offloading the cargo of interest."

He tilted back his chair, placing one foot on the edge of his desk, managing his lanky six foot four inch frame awkwardly in the balance. Musingly, he placed the corresponding finger tips of each hand together, and studied them in thought. He appeared pleased at his ability to connive such a devious plan. Pulling open the top drawer of his desk he removed a large coffee mug and jettisoned a stream of brown saliva laden with chewing tobacco into it, then wiped his mouth with the back of his hand. Adriana frowned as she tried, poorly, to conceal her disgust.

"So you were behind this, from the start," Mat replied.

Jack smiled, then shifted his gaze towards Mat. "In a manner of speaking, yes. But let's not dwell on the details. The best entrepreneurs don't just wait for opportunities, they create them."

Mat pressed on for information. "And what exactly is in this whole arrangement for you? The hoods get forty five million, I get five million. What do you get?"

"Actually, they get forty-two and a half million. I collect a finder's fee for identifying the deal and for hooking them up with someone who can reliably launder that much cash. You do the math." So Jack Kincaid was taking a cut of two-and-a-half-mil, but unlike Mathew, his part of it was already finished. Suddenly Mat felt a little cheated that he was doing all the work while Kincaid had only to wait patiently for payment.

Adriana joined the conversation, "And then there's me." She smiled.

"You're taking a cut too?" Mat asked.

"Did you think I was working *volunteer*? I get paid out of Jack's share."

Mat replied, "And dare I ask?"

"How much?" Adriana responded. "Not enough, but I'll stay the course, for now. I consider it a learning experience, and one should never pass up an opportunity to indulge in something new and exciting. Do you agree?" She looked at Mat with her chin resting lightly on the knuckle of her index finger. She had exquisite hands, he noticed.

"Oh, I agree whole heartedly," Mat responded reflexively, like a clumsy boy with a crush. He wondered if there was more to her comment than the simple question implied. What was she driving at?

Mat went on, "Well we've worked right through lunch hour and I, for one, am feeling a bit hungry. How about we stop by a nice restaurant for a bite?"

Jack responded, "Not me, thanks. I have a lot to do and I rarely eat lunch anyways. I'm like a dog — I usually eat once a day and puke twice. I'll be at my office if there's anything else to discuss. Otherwise, we wait for the money to start rolling in."

Adriana parted her lips slightly in disgust at Jack's comment, then she casually accepted Mat's offer with, "Yes, a little something to eat would be nice. I'll be happy to join you, if you like."

The meeting ended. Jack left the building first while Mat and Adriana stayed and talked a few moments longer. During their chat they decided where to go for a quick lunch. The two then proceeded to the elevator. On the way down to the main floor, the old lift chugged along slowly. Mat felt a little awkward that Adriana had stood right beside him in the elevator car. On the way out of the building she hooked her hand around his inner elbow for stability going down the stairs to the street. He was simultaneously embarrassed by his juvenile reaction to her and thrilled that he was in personal contact with such a fine woman. Christine was also in the back of his mind. *What would she think of this?* he wondered. *It's only lunch. People have business lunches all the time,* he rationalized.

Business lunch? This was criminal collusion with a beautiful, dirty lawyer — pun intended, to launder millions of dollars of drug money. That's how Christine would respond, he guessed.

Facing away from Adriana, Mat said, "Foley, go back to the office and I'll call you later. Call my cell and let it ring once to let me know you got this."

"What?" Adriana said.

"Nothing, sorry. Just talking to myself," he replied. Foley's twenty-twenty hearing picked up the message, and the cell phone clipped onto Mat's belt rang once.

At the restaurant Mat and Adriana were seated at a table for two. Although the restaurant was still busy with other patrons and servers scurrying about with plates of sizzling food and trays of drinks, Mat saw no one but her. The two made some small talk and were getting more comfortable with each other. There was eye contact, smiling, laughter, and when a point needed to be emphasized they touched hands lightly. This woman ignited all of Mat's senses. She was captivating beyond all measure and even had that female scent that only men can detect.

Mat opened the lunch chatter. "So, Adriana, How long have you lived in Vancouver?"

"Must be about eighteen years now. I attended UBC, then became an articling student, and eventually went right into law practice."

"Eighteen years? Where are you originally from?" he continued.

"Brazil, São Paulo. I still have some family there. My family heritage is Portuguese."

"Ah... The dark hair, the olive skin," Mat observed. *The killer good looks,* he might have added. "And tell me about Brazil. What's it like there?"

Adriana looked upwards, almost troubled, reflecting momentarily. "It's *beautiful beyond imagination* in many parts. Cities like São Paulo and Rio de Janeiro, however, have stark contrasts. Most affluent homes are a virtual fortress of iron bars, bullet proof glass, and protective gates to guard against home invasions and robbery. The poor vastly out number and resent the wealthy throughout Brazil. As a result, there's a thriving underground economy centered around drugs, crime, corruption, and gangs. Even some police are dirty... Many, actually.

"There are over a thousand slums in Rio alone, and virtually all of them have drug trafficking at their core. The dealers and their foot soldiers go by alias names like Bubba-Loo, Cry-Baby, and Scooby. They're well armed with Belgian-made assault rifles, Israeli automatic pistols, bombs and grenades... Even anti aircraft weapons to take out police helicopters. When the police come to a slum, where the criminals have their drugs and weapons, a clash on the order of a full scale war can break out. The police are usually greatly outnumbered and can hardly even put a dent in their operations. It's widely believed that the war on drugs in Brazil, and South America in general, as well as Mexico, cannot be won."

She spoke from experience and obvious knowledge of the subject. She displayed confidence, interest, and guarded opinion about the region, like anyone would, discussing their country of origin as an expatriate. She seemed troubled by the subject, but curiously determined to illuminate the truth. To Mat, it was like watching, and listening to a stunning actress on a Sony HD plasma screen delivering her lines with conviction and passion.

He noticed her dark hair draped around her face, almost messy, and her wish to communicate her message to him, like she was setting the record straight. She obviously cared deeply about what she was discussing, and wanted him to connect with her thoughts on the issue. He was captivated, and he watched, listened, and absorbed her essence intensely. Her affect upon him was akin to the scent of burning incense — aromatic, exotic, musky.

Adriana continued, "Violence and homicides are common — a *hundred times* what you'd see in Vancouver, most always to do with drug traffic. The clash between rich and poor is so pronounced that if you're driving through many parts of the city after around ten at night, you don't *dare* stop for red lights, unless you want to invite a car-jacking, maybe worse."

"That's 'beautiful beyond imagination'?" Mat asked, perplexed.

"Well, it's not *all* like that. Like any third world country, there are good things and bad. Although there is inequality and an absence of real job opportunities, the people are amazing, the food is great, and the beaches are beautiful. In the coastal areas of São Paulo and Rio, the sights are breathtaking, and if you travel north to areas like Recife, Natal, and especially Fernando de Noronha, you would have unforgettable memories of crystal clear water, soft sand beaches, and beautiful girls. *You like beautiful girls?*"

"Rather," Mat replied, smiling.

Adriana locked her gaze on him. "I mean *real, exotic beauties* of mixed ancestry including Portuguese, Spanish, maybe some other European stock, and even some black thrown in dating back to the slave trade when plantation owners routinely jumped the fence for a little privilege."

"I get it," Mat said. "Exotic, sexy, Latino beauties," *just like you,* he was thinking.

Adriana continued, "Picture an almost endless expanse of white sand beaches, lined with palm trees waving in the trades under a brilliant, sunny sky, with stunning, chocolate skinned, long haired Latino girls in thong bikinis everywhere – none over thirty. Typically, they've got round, firm booties, tiny, sculpted waists, and the kind of breasts that men would go to war for, spilling out over the top and sides of their string bikinis barely covering their nipples, smiling and laughing like hyper-sexed bunnies, partying at the Playboy Mansion. *That's* Brazil."

Holy fuck! Mat thought. He was a little taken aback by such frank talk coming from a woman, but then clearly, this was no ordinary woman.

"Now you've got my attention," he said as the testosterone level in his blood momentarily spiked. He straightened up in his chair. "Tell me more."

She laughed at how easy it was to awaken his libido. *Typical guy!*

"I'll tell you all about it another time. But first, let's get back to business. How long have you known Jack Kincaid?"

Mat shook off the vivid imagery going through his head. "Around ten years. I met him just before I left the bank. A man I used to work for, Hyman Wexler, introduced us. He said that Mr. Kincaid was a man of many resources who may be able to bring me some special opportunities." Mental pictures of breasts in string bikinis, firm booties, chocolate skin, and tropical sun still vexed his concentration.

"And I take it, he has done so on other occasions," Adriana said.

"Oh, yes. We've done business together a few times. How about you?"

Adriana explained, "I met him when he needed legal work done for his business. He was importing goods from South America — a locale I have some knowledge of. Turns out he was bringing in drums of coffee that had been rejected by quality control in Colombia. It was deemed unfit for sale there, but Jack got onto it and purchased it at ten cents on the dollar. Then he had it shipped here under the radar of Canada Customs. It was given a stamp of approval by someone at the Canadian FDA who owed Jack a favor, repackaged and sold in supermarkets all over Western Canada as *premium* Colombian coffee. He did it all under a numbered company set up in Colombia, which he then dissolved immediately after the sale. He made hundreds of thousands of dollars if you can believe it, and he topped up my fee with a substantial bonus. He asked me to join him as an advisor on future transactions of a similar nature."

She smiled and Mat took particular notice when she ran her index finger around the rim of her wine glass, making it hum like a violin string. "I guess he liked the way I worked."

"Among other things," Mat replied, Christine's image reminiscing on his mind.

Adriana didn't miss the innuendo. "We're strictly business associates, Mr. Crawford. I assure you there is nothing of a personal nature to our relationship." She looked intently at Mat then added, "I wonder why you don't wear a wedding ring?"

"How do you know I'm married?" he asked.

"Perhaps because you're trying so hard *not* to be attracted to me."

There it was. Mat's crush on Adriana was out in the open. He was taken a little off guard by her insight. It almost seemed like she could read his mind, tap into his thoughts and emotions. Mat felt something odd. She was inside his head, and it made him a little uncomfortable. His eyes locked on hers and she smiled reassuringly. This lady's mystery continued to grow.

"It's that obvious," he said, awkwardly.

"I'm flattered, silly. Don't be embarrassed," Adriana reassured him. There was a pause in the flow of conversation. "Let me pay for lunch. You can get it next time, deal?" she offered.

Mat agreed and got the understated message that another informal *date* of this nature was set for the near future. He was, frankly, a little embarrassed that Adriana had intuitively picked up on his feelings toward her but at the same time he was glad that it was plainly exposed. Her acceptance of it and subtle reciprocation of the feeling was energizing. The two left the restaurant and went their separate ways, each a little giddy with excitement.

Inside however, another part of Mat wrenched his gut. He thought about Christine and he was in torment. He had meant to go home at lunch today to talk with her and patch things up from their tiff last night. Instead, against her wishes, he met with criminals, agreed to take on a money laundering job that placed him squarely in concert with organized crime at its worst, and had a flirtatious lunch with an engaging and mysterious, new woman. He set his mind on putting this fling behind him before it got out of control. He would go home to Christine and Hannah at once.

When he arrived, nobody was there. He called out to both Christine and Hannah but there was no answer. There was an ominous stillness in the house. The clock over the pantry was ticking, underlining the silence, otherwise. He looked both ways on the street to see if they might be out for a walk or something. There was no one at the park near their house. He had parked on the driveway and entered through the front door. Looking now in the garage, Christine's car was missing. Mat went upstairs to the master bedroom and as he entered the walk-in closet it struck him. She was gone. She had left him. All her clothes were missing from the hangers and shelves. Her toiletries were gone from the bathroom. Hannah's room too was missing all signs of its occupant.

Mat sat on the edge of their king sized bed and looked at a framed photo on the wall of them posing together in happier times — their wedding picture.

"Oh, Christine..."

CHAPTER 12

IN THE DAYS that followed Christine's departure Mat was miserable and wracked with guilt over hurting her with his admission to participating in criminal activities. He had taken to sleeping on the couch because it didn't feel right sleeping in the matrimonial bed without her. When he tried, he always woke up on his own side, as if she were still there.

Alone in the house at night, he went to the bottle more than he normally would or should, and it drew him inside his thoughts and tormented him with all that he did to cause this and what he would have to do to see it through now that there was no turning back. He was an emotional wreck and he realized how much he loved and missed the two people that were the driving force of his life. Christine and Hannah meant everything, and if they were gone, he saw little purpose to carrying on. For a fleeting moment, the possibility of suicide even crossed his mind.

He realized, however, that his thoughts and mood were more along the lines of mania than depression. His mind was racing, not mired in defeat.

"No," he thought. "I'm not that desperate. I'll work my way out of this and make things right. I can do this thing and make us rich beyond our dreams and then I'll win back my wife and daughter and we'll be a family again."

It was late one night, perhaps around 2:00 or 3:00 a.m. and he was stirred from his restless, booze induced sleep on the sofa. He looked up through blurry eyes and there she was, Christine, in the same satin robe and night dress that she wore on the last night they argued. She was sitting on the coffee table beside the sofa looking down at him. Her blonde hair tumbled around her pretty face and down the front of her shoulders. She was as beautiful as ever. God, how he loved her. He reached out…

"Chris, what are you doing here?" She was speaking but his brain was foggy, and her words were inaudible as though coming from another room or through a muffled filter of some sort, like there was cotton in his ears. But through her manner, that married couples synchronize with each other, her message was clear enough. She was speaking to him about love, and marriage, and family, and commitment, and responsibility, and doing the right thing, and he strained to listen to her, trying to make out her words, but as he concentrated and focused harder, he was awakened from his state of semi-sleep and the bubble burst. He rubbed his eyes, and she was gone. He was alone.

He sat up in his day clothes, having fallen asleep without even changing into night-ware and realized that he had been dreaming, again. His eyes welled up and he felt an unmanly sadness and remorse. It was 2:43 a.m. now and he was awake. If he could do something to turn this nightmare around immediately he would, but he was entangled now with the underworld of drugs, and money, and hoods, and corruption, and if he backed out and ran now, it would mean almost certain disaster to him and Foley and Kincaid, and possibly Christine and Hannah and others. He had to carry through with his end of this deal, or there could be drastic consequences. He was alone, miserable, and desperate. He stumbled off to bed to try and get a few hours sleep before facing the music again tomorrow.

Had he known that he would hear from Christine in the morning it might have made him sleep better, or not at all.

She had called him from a blocked number and said, "Mat, it's me. First, don't worry about us. We're fine and Hannah wants to say hello. I'll put her on in a minute. I don't know what to say to you, baby. I'm *so* sorry it has to be this way."

"Where are you, Chris? I miss you too. You don't have to do this. Come home, so we can talk."

Christine replied, "No, not now. I need some time to think and get my life in order. Anyways, we've talked about it before and it always comes back to you carrying on with this appalling thing while Hannah and I are just supposed to stand by until something terrible comes of it. I don't think I can live under the same roof as a criminal money launderer. God knows what else you might be into, and for now, I don't even want to think about it."

"What are you going to do?" Mat asked her.

"I'm going to wait out the rest of the summer, then when school is back in I'll return to my job and probably file papers for separation. I need some time to settle my mind on how to handle all this. I'm not going to sit back and let you do this Mat, because knowing it and not reporting it makes me an accomplice and I could be charged as well. For the record, you never told me anything about this thing, all right? From here on, you do your thing, and I'll do mine. That's the way it is."

"No problem. You don't know anything, but I'm not going to get caught and neither are you. I love you Chris. Can we please get together and work this out?"

"No, I need to figure this out on my own. Anyways, it's not just that. There's something else... well, never mind for now. We'll talk about it another time. I'll get Hannah from the other room and you can talk to her. Tell her the same thing I have. Mommy just needs some time away from daddy to sort some things out. We all still love each other and no matter what else, you'll always be her daddy."

"Chris, *it will* all get sorted out. I'm getting out of this like I told you before, but it will take some time. You'll see."

"Daddy?" Hannah came on the line. "Where are you? I miss you, Daddy."

Mat tried to sound brave for the little girl. "I miss you too, sweetie. Are you and mommy safe and sound together?"

"Oh, yes. Mommy even took me for an ice cream today. I had a blizzard, cookie dough."

"Daddy loves you, Hannah... *I love you*," he clarified, putting it into first person. "Don't ever forget that, okay? You do as mommy says and be an extra good girl for her. Remember, I'm always thinking of you."

Mat talked with his daughter for a few minutes longer, then brave *goodbyes* were said and the call was ended. He accepted that Christine needed some time to sort through her feelings and he had little choice but to abide her wishes. He was perplexed by her passing comment that there was *something else*, but for the moment, he paid it little mind.

Unfortunately, he didn't have the luxury of wallowing in grief and self-reflection, because the cocaine money would be starting to flow. Mat knew he had to pull himself together and get organized with putting his plan into action.

He remembered in high school how the coach had told him after an injury that he had to *play through the pain*, so with a burdened heart and troubled mind he went about his task like the professional he was. If things were ever going to be better in his life again, he had a bridge to cross and that bridge was the contract he agreed to with Kincaid and the Kings Crew. He had to get the job done — quickly, efficiently, and without incident. He took a deep breath, shook himself off, and committed to the task at hand.

Three weeks after Christine had vanished Mat and Foley were called to the offices of Evergreen Import Export International. Jack Kincaid had known that Mat had a business partner in his security company but until recently he didn't know that Karl Folkestad was also in on the money laundering. With a project this big, Mat decided that it served little purpose to pretend otherwise and he advised Kincaid of Foley's role in the matter. Kincaid had requested the meeting to start the transfer of money received from the street sale of the stolen shipment of drugs.

Mat and Foley entered the office to find the pretty receptionist sitting dutifully at her desk. "Gentlemen, welcome," she said. "Mr. Kincaid is expecting you. Mr. Crawford, I haven't had the opportunity of meeting your associate. I'm Crystal Waters." She extended her hand to Foley and smiled.

"Karl Folkestad," Foley replied forthrightly to her cleavage. "Most folks just call me Foley. That's a mighty catchy name you've got there, Miss. "

Mat looked at Foley, then did a double take and smiled, noticing that old Foley's radar was registering the same thing Mat's did the first time he met her. He thought to himself, *You dirty old dog. Wouldn't you like to get your hands under that angora sweater?*

The two men proceeded to Jack's office and were shown in. Crystal smiled politely and left the room. Having been thoroughly entertained by eaves dropping on their last meeting, she then discreetly turned on the speaker at low volume to her intercom connected to Jack's desk phone. She pulled her chair up close to her desk and tuned in attentively. This eavesdropping was starting to be real interesting... *fun, even!*

The purpose of this meeting was indeed to turn over an installment of cash. Jack closed his door and took a suitcase from a large steel safe behind a false wall in his office. He put it on his desk with a heavy thud and snapped open the locking hinges. Inside were hundreds of high denomination bills in neat piles held together with elastic bands. They were stacked to the top of the suitcase.

"How much?" Mat asked.

"I've got four more pieces of luggage just like this one. Five million two hundred and fifty two thousand, one hundred and forty six," replied Jack. "I'll need you to sign for it."

"Why? So they can sue me if any of it goes missing?" Mat scoffed.

"Just to prove to them that you saw it, counted it, and took possession of it. And if it goes missing, they'll do a lot worse than sue you."

"Well, let's start counting then," Mat said, dreading the task ahead of him. Two hours and forty minutes later the count was complete and the amount was correct, to the dollar. It was now going on 5:00 p.m. and Mat and Foley were ready to leave.

Mat said to Kincaid, "Jack, I need to get this money out of the country to a bank in Central America where it won't be questioned. It's going to take about three weeks to move it around and bring it back as laundered currency. Just so you know the timing involved here, in case our friends start gettin' jumpy about where their money is."

"Run with it, my friend. Work your magic and earn your money. Just don't, for Christ's sake, get caught," Jack replied.

"I'll take that under advisement," Mat responded. Looking at Foley he said, "Hey, can you get the wheels?" Foley left the room.

A few minutes later the car pulled into the alley where the suitcases would be discreetly transferred from the back door of the building to the vehicle. Once both men were inside and rolling down the road a feeling of relief came over them that the first transfer had gone without incident.

"That was a little risky," Foley said, in uncharacteristic dryness. "We should plan the pick ups of these cash bundles so that we are certain nothing can go wrong. What if the Red Sun Boys were onto Kincaid and just waiting for someone to walk outta there with a suitcase or duffle bag full of money. We could have gotten aired out with an AK 47 or had our guts opened up with a stiletto. I've seen how quick in can happen when I was a kid in the army."

Mat agreed. "Ya, next time we'll cover our asses better. Handling cash is such a liability. It's the riskiest part of this business."

"True, but there are perks too," Foley replied.

Mat looked at him inquisitively. "Like what?"

Foley took a slip of paper from his shirt pocket and opened it. He handed it to Mat. The paper had a woman's handwriting on it which read, *Crystal Waters* with a local phone number. Foley smiled a broad grin and said, "Still got it, son!"

"You old horn dog! When did you score that little tidbit? I'm not surprised. The way you were looking at her sweater when we went in, I thought you were going to have an orgasm."

"Well, she is a cute, little hen, you'll have to agree. When I left to get the car I stopped by her desk and acquainted her with the old Folkestad charm for a moment. She was flirting with me, so I asked her if she'd like to go to a movie or something, some time."

"Right on! I can imagine what you had in mind by 'or something'. She's got a pair of blowers on her that would rival Pamela Anderson," Mat pointed out, tastefully.

"Really? I didn't notice. Out of principle, I make it a policy not to sexually objectify the fairer sex," Foley replied.

"Well, I was just about to add what a vibrant, charming personality I thought she had, also."

Foley came back, "Ya, but a woman with a nice personality and a great pair of hooters grabs my attention faster than a woman with a nice personality every time! It always comes down to *tits*, son. It's an age-old question — *Why do men like women's breasts?*"

Mat piped up, "Because when we see them, it usually means we're in for something good. We're like Pavlov's dogs... Au-hoooo!" Mat howled like a wolf, and the two pals laughed raucously together at their locker room humor. Then Mat said, "*Ah, Jesus, save me.* For now, we've got work to do, so your love life, and certainly mine, will have to go on the back burner."

"Ya, I suppose you're right. How you gonna start washin' this cash? You got a plan yet?" Foley asked.

"I've always got a plan, old chum. This money is goin' into the Canadian banking system and then it'll be transferred to an offshore account in Central America. I'll be flyin' down there in a few days to personally see that all the details are to my liking. From there we'll put it through the process of *now you see it, now you don't.*"

"Foley looked impressed and replied, "And what part do I play in the whole plan? Do you want me to come along? Keep you company?"

Mat pondered the question. "No. I'd rather you stay here and watch over the business as usual. We don't want to both be out of the country together in case any suspicion arises that we're up to something in a known offshore banking refuge. Besides, I need you to watch closely in case trouble arises between the local gangs and that Hong Kong group. We're still sittin' on a powder keg and someone needs to protect our interests. In other words, keep an eye on Kincaid and don't let any grief come to him before the next cash transfer. One other thing, try and figure out where my wife and daughter are holed up. I'd like to know they're safe."

"Will do, Buck. I think I can handle that assignment," Foley said with confidence.

With five million, cash, in tow, Mat and Foley rolled casually down the Lougheed Highway being careful not to speed or do anything that might attract attention from some overly-diligent traffic cop. In a few days it would be transferred to Panama and the laundering process would be underway. Mat was glad that the wheels were finally turning because all the preamble of meetings, discussions, proposals, and discord with his wife were taking a toll on his nerves. Mat was a man of action and putting his plan into play made him feel and function better on a physical and mental level.

The following morning Mat went to his front door and collected the morning newspaper. As he scanned the first few pages over a coffee, his eyes fixated on one headline on page three with a brief news report following. It read:

Ship's Captain Found Murdered

Captain Montgomery Furlong of local freight and cargo forwarding company, Westgate Shipping Lines, was found shot to death early Thursday morning. Complaints had been made to local police about a ruckus overheard in his North Vancouver home by neighbors. Witnesses say two cars stopped at his address just after midnight. Several men smashed a window at the rear of the house and entered the home where the melee ensued.

Sources say robbery appears not to have been the motive as nothing of value was taken and the incident lasted no more than five or ten minutes. His wife and two sons aged fourteen and eleven were home at the time and were shaken but unharmed during the confrontation. Grief counselors are working with them.

Captain Furlong had enjoyed an exemplary career with Westgate Shipping Lines for some fifteen years and had made frequent voyages across the Pacific to Japan, China, Thailand, and the Philippines.

"He was well respected by crew members and management alike, and will be sorely missed," reports a company representative.

Police spokesperson, homicide detective Jerome Lundgren, said police are concerned about the escalating level of hostility and horrific bloodshed throughout the mainland.

"This appears to be a classic example of a senseless, violent act with no apparent motive other than a malicious home invasion and the murder of an innocent citizen," said Lundgren.

Mr. Furlong had been shot multiple times and had virtually no chance of survival, prompting speculation that it may have been a targeted execution for reasons unknown at this point. He died at the scene. Perpetrators remain at large and investigations continue.

"Ah Jesus, God, no!" Mathew cursed out loud to himself. "It's started. I've got news for you, my old friend detective Lundgren. Captain Furlong wasn't quite the innocent citizen you *think* he was. He took a bribe from organized criminals and now he's paid for it with his life."

Worse, if they found out about Furlong's complicity in the matter of their stolen drugs, they would be learning other aspects of the caper as well. Mat knew that the trail could eventually lead them to him as the principal launderer of the money that by rights should be theirs. He feared a fate like this might await him as well. Mat immediately picked up the phone. This call had to be made right now.

CHAPTER 13

"KINCAID, HAVE YOU read the morning paper yet?" Mat said immediately after Jack answered his phone.

"No, what's up?"

"Your Captain Furlong's been murdered. It's on page three. You better talk to those accountants that we met with from the Kings Crew and find out if they know anything about it. We might have to all go into hiding if they're planning on wiping out everyone connected to this heist," Mat said. "And since *you* set this whole thing up to begin with, you're the next logical candidate for a hit. What are you going to do?"

Jack paused to consider his options. "I have another office I can work out of 'til the project is complete, and I *will* talk to Dom and Carlos. We always knew they weren't going to take this lying down and I've been assured that the Crew have a contingency plan for dealing with a backlash if, and when, it arose. It wasn't entirely unexpected. Let's not shit our pants just yet."

Mat knew that Jack was correct on that point. The Kings Crew were capable of taking care of their interests in these matters. They were, after all, the pre-eminent crime family operating in BC. This was their turf, and for the time being, Jack and Mathew were playing on their team, so they would fall under their veil of protection. It was unlikely, at least at this point, that Mat or Kincaid would be targeted for execution because the parties most directly culpable in the theft of these drugs were the Kings Crew themselves, and violence was most likely to erupt between them and the Red Sun Boys.

The biggest concern for him was that he avoid any possibility of being falsely implicated as one of the thieves. If he was ever confronted by Asian gang members he would have a hard time explaining that he was only a disinterested third party in a hired role providing a service for a fee. On reflection, he then realized that, if he thought he could proceed with impunity on that basis, he was only fooling himself. The Red Sun Boys would kill *anyone* remotely connected to the theft or sale of their drugs.

Jack spoke into his cell phone. "From this point on I'll be working from my other office. It's in an old house near Arbutus and west 48th. I won it in a card game a few years back. Few people know about it so it should be quite secure. While I'm gone, Crystal can hold down day to day matters at my business. I'll stay in touch with her by phone. I'll move out of my home and use my brother's condo downtown 'til this all blows over. It's vacant and he has it up for rent, but that'll have to wait for now."

Jack's brother was in fact, his half-brother, on his father's side and four years younger. According to family history, Jack's father had only lasted a few months with his mother, before he threw her out, literally, over a furious fight about something shameful, but ever after unspoken of, and went his separate way. Her clothes and personal effects had been strewn across the front lawn and she had been evicted from the matrimonial home like garbage. She had been cast off by her husband with revulsion and rage, then he sold the house and moved out himself, closing forever the chapter on her, and the spurious marriage. Eight months after he left, Jack was born. A couple of years later he married someone new, and that marriage produced his half brother. As an adult, the fraternal half brother got into debt with bookies to the extent that his life was in severe danger. Jack bailed him out with ill-gotten money of his own, so the favor of using his condo was a given.

Mat brought Jack up to speed on his plans too. "In a couple of days I'm going to Panama City to make some arrangements to move the money to an offshore account. Foley will stay behind and I've asked him to keep an eye on things, including you and your business, so he'll be watching from the wings. You won't even know he's there. Take my word for it, the bugger's good at providing security and surveillance."

"I hope so, because there's another development I haven't mentioned just yet," Jack responded.

"What's that?"

"Wo Shing Chu has sent an ultimatum to the Red Sun Boys — 'Pay up the remaining five million immediately or face the music.' They've threatened to send over an army of mongrels that will let loose Armageddon on the streets of Vancouver if their debt isn't settled *RFN*," Jack explained.

"RFN?" Mat questioned.

"Right now," Jack explained.

"Cute… How do you know that?" Mat replied. "Gang wars in Vancouver. Now *there's* something new."

"Carlos Garcia told me. These guys work with a bunch of bikers and hoods, but that's their world and they've got their ears to the ground when it comes to gathering information."

"More likely a gun to someone's head," Mat replied.

Jack sighed a repressed laugh. "True enough. Well, we knew this was goin' to get interesting at some point and it looks like this is it. We've both got some preparations to make so I suggest we hop to it. Anything else?" he asked Mat.

"Nope, let's rock 'n roll. Keep your cell with you at all times. I'll call you if anything develops," Mat said.

✲ ✲ ✲

Two days later, Mat was aboard a plane bound for Panama City in the Republic of Panama with an appointment to meet a lawyer named Marcos Del Rio. There's but one sure and safe way of placing a large amount of money into a financial institution without attaching your name to it and that was by setting up an offshore trust through the law firm of Diaz, Cordoba & Del Rio in Panama. Mat had done his homework diligently and discovered that handling this much cash was a special challenge because of logistical considerations. $5 million was a lot of money to deal with by sheer weight and volume alone, never mind getting it into an account somehow without raising alarm.

He had decided to get it placed into the financial system through the establishment of a special *trust agreement* with a local law firm where it could then be manipulated through the layering process before being returned to Canada in a useable form of currency. The whole process was complicated and Mat would have to maintain tight controls.

✫ ✫ ✫

Back in Vancouver, Foley was running the security business and keeping an eye on matters to do with Jack Kincaid, as Mathew has asked. Mat was scheduled to be out of country for several days, if not more, and it allowed Foley to also look into where Christine might have gone. He staked out her elderly parents home for half a day thinking that would be a logical refuge for her to turn to. No luck. He wondered about other links to her. Where did she do her banking? Forget it. Everyone banks online these days. Where did she buy groceries? Nope. If she was staying on the other side of town she would just shop somewhere local. He checked with information to see if she might have registered a new telephone number, without success.

Then it came to him. Hannah had an interest in synchronized swimming and she was enrolled in lessons at 7:00 p.m. at the West Vancouver Aquatic Centre. Foley waited in the parking lot that evening from 6:30 p.m. on, and sure enough, Christine pulled into the lot and escorted little Hannah inside the building. An hour later, the two returned to their car and as they drove out onto the main street, Foley followed, at a safe distance. Christine must have rented a suite because she stopped at a small, three story apartment complex and went inside the main doors. Foley pulled up and watched closely. He took out his cell phone and photographed the front of the building, showing the address… *Click.*

Then something happened that took Foley by complete surprise. A man met Christine and her daughter in the foyer. Foley readied his cell phone, finger on the *capture* button. Hannah ran down the hall ahead of them. They kissed briefly, on the lips, and exchanged a few words. *Click, click.* Then they put their arms around each other's waists and they walked together into the building. *Click, click. What was that? Who was that?*

Foley wasn't naïve but he didn't want to believe his eyes either. *Christine has a lover,* he said to himself in disbelief. Mat would have to know, but he would have to be told in person. No way, was Foley going to drop a bomb like that on him over the phone.

☆ ☆ ☆

It was the end of a long week, and Danielle had been answering customer calls, sending out invoices, recording various data in company records, paying bills, making bank deposits, filing, and doing just about everything else that made Foley and Mat's business of Bull Dog Security operate, and business was good. It dawned on her that the two principals seemed to be distracted or off on other matters a lot lately, and that she was running the show more or less by herself.

Still, they treated and paid her well and never took her for granted, so she was committed to doing her best. She quietly thought to herself, *I'm happy coming to work here. I'm well taken care of financially. I like the people I work with. Life is good.*

The chime sounded, signaling that the front door had opened. An attractive, professional looking woman entered, smiling pleasantly, and approached the reception area.

Danielle welcomed the visitor. "Hello, can I be of help?"

"Oh, I sure hope so. It's been one of those weeks. Never thought it would end." The lady fanned herself with her hand.

"I hear ya, girlfriend. Fridays don't come soon enough," Danielle agreed.

The lady gestured to a legal sized envelope she was holding. "One last job to take care of here and I'm officially off duty 'til Monday. Hey, I love your hair. It frames your face perfectly. Where do you get it done?"

"Oh, thanks! Anthony's Hair Care on Burrard. They're good but not cheap," Danielle replied. "Ask for a guy named Ronny if you drop in. He's gay as a blade, but who cares? He's the best, and he'll talk your ear off."

"I'll just do that. I've had this old do for too long now. I feel like I need a makeover. Ever get the itch to try something new? A new hair cut, or color, a new car, a new beau?" she winked. "New shoes are always fun. Maybe a new job – that's not so hard? I don't know."

"Well funny, I was just thinking about my job, and I sort of decided that, ya, I do work too hard, but I still like it here because my boss treats me well, and gives me loads of responsibility, and seems to respect my opinions, and certainly pays me very well... You know, I'm one of the lucky ones who can honestly say, *I love my job, actually!*" Danielle confided in her new friend.

"That's wonderful, but I'll bet even *your job* could get better, somehow. Oh, I'm sorry. Didn't mean to take up your time with small talk. Speaking about your boss, I just wanted to drop these off to Mr. Crawford," the lady said, holding out a large brown envelope stuffed with papers. "It's *urgent* that he have them this weekend."

"What is that?" Danielle asked, concern registering on her face.

"A prospectus and legal papers for a business venture he'll likely be entering into next week. He wanted to review all the details over the weekend. I'm afraid I can't really say much more than that," she explained.

Danielle had an *Uh-Oh* look on her face. "Well, I'm afraid that's not going to be possible."

"Why not?"

"He's gone for the day and he's on a flight to Panama first thing in the morning. I know what. If it's urgent, I could drop them off at his house tonight before I go home," Danielle offered.

"Oh, my gosh, I wouldn't dream of asking you to do something like that. If you're anything like me, there's a cold glass of Chardonnay calling your name from a quaint little bar, or your own living room right about now. Do you know where he's staying down there? I could send it by rush courier and he'll get it in a day or two, max," the attractive lady asked persuasively.

"Well, okay, he's at The Villa Tropicana Suites. It's in the financial district of Panama city. I made his reservations but I'm sorry I don't have the address handy," Danielle explained.

"No problem. I can look it up on the net. When did you say he's going there?"

"Tomorrow morning. Flight leaves at 10:15."

"WestJet?"

"No, Air Canada."

"Great! Listen, I won't keep you any longer." Pivoting towards the door, she added, "Thanks, you've been a great help. Maybe I can return the favor some time. In fact, *I promise.*"

"Wait, can I tell Mat who stopped by? I didn't get your name," Danielle called out.

"Just tell him I hope he enjoyed his surprise package in Panama," she replied, as the front door chimed again, then closed behind her.

CHAPTER 14

AT 8:00 O'CLOCK Monday morning Crystal Waters unlocked the front doors at Evergreen Import Export International as usual and entered the office. She turned on the lights and powered up the computers, fax machine and photo copier, checked the answering service for messages and prepared a pot of coffee on the counter at the far wall of the kitchen with her back to the door. She pulled opened the sliding window over the sink several inches for fresh air. As she turned around to return to her desk she was startled by the presence of three Asian men blocking the door. Two more thugs stood vigil at the front door to the main office.

"Can I help you?" she said, trying to appear calm.

One man was about thirty-five years old, with a pronounced scar stretching from his chin to his upper cheek. His glossy black hair was combed straight forward into bangs of a sort, and his clothes were designer label and obviously expensive. The other two looked to be younger, mid-twenties possibly, and were dressed in black leather jackets and blue jeans. None of them smiled. In fact, they all looked quite pissed. She knew she was in trouble.

The man with the scar stepped forward and spoke with a Cantonese accent. "Listen me. I ask da question, and you ansah da question. If I don' like or believe yo' ansah, dis be yo' last day alive. My two friend here like white trash like yo' and dey have dey way wit' you, den you be eliminated from gene pool. You follow? We clear?" He offered up a reptilian grin.

"Get out of here!" she yelled in horror, and Scarface back-handed her with a brutal slap to the face.

"Wrong ansah!" He said. "We don' seem be gettin' off very good start. Bring her ova' here, boys," he gestured to a kitchen chair by the wall. The other two men each grabbed her arms and forcibly sat her on the chair, where her arms and legs were duct taped to the wooden rails. Scarface removed a switchblade from his pocket and with a quick flip of his wrist the blade locked into place with a metallic snap.

"Now, we try again, yes?" he said. "Listen, little girl, you way out yo' league here. Understan' dat you but dispensable pawn in much large picture. You provide me wit information or I slit yo' throat ear to ear and you bleed out quick, easy. Den my friend and me go have breakfast. Steak and egg sound pretty good to-day. What you tink?"

The one side of her face was welted and turning blue already with a bruise coming up.

"Please... *don't.* I don't know anything," she pleaded with him.

"About what?"

She remained silent, looking terrified.

This time he shouted. *"You know nothing about what?"* He paused for a few moments and returned to a normal speaking tone.

"You take guess, why we here?" and he placed the tip of the blade under her chin, lifting her face to meet his, only inches away. His breath was foul with last night's booze, cigarette smoke, and stale coffee.

"Yo' *want* die?" Her chin was bleeding slightly at the point of his switchblade.

"I'm just the secretary. You're asking the wrong person," she muttered.

"I be judge dat," he reassured her, menacingly. "Okay, I be more specific, we see. Maybe you wake up tomorrow, or maybe be zipped up in body bag. Someone steal our cocaine, and we out lot of money. Tell me what you know from start to finish. You *really don'* know nothin', I afraid you no use to us and you, unfortunately, *expendable.*" The men at the door laughed and looked at each other like scavengers.

Crystal was in horror, crying. "Look, all I know is that the Kings Crew took your drugs."

"Tell me something I *don'* know," said Scarface.

She continued, "They bribed some ship's captain."

"And we already deal him," replied her interrogator.

Outside the building Foley had been surveilling the area as Mat had asked him to, from just before business hours, until now. He had seen the five Asian men enter the office and through binoculars he could now see that two of them were guarding the front door. That meant that three of them were in the back someplace doing something with, or to the girl that he was sweet on. As much as he wanted to help her, he couldn't risk a confrontation of five on one, and his specific orders were to guard Jack Kincaid, not Crystal Waters. He was torn between taking action and holding back.

"Okay, which one you go first?" Scarface said to his cohorts, as a torture tactic. "She no cooperate, so I guess she only good one thing." One man started undoing the belt on his pants.

"Wait!" Crystal begged. "There's more. So far about $5 million has come in. It's going to *Central America...* or maybe *South America.* I forget." Her voice quivered.

The three men looked at each other. One man at the kitchen door said, "She know more dan what she say."

Scarface rejoined, "*Shut up!* I do da talkin'." He looked back down at Crystal. "And where dis five million dollahs now?"

Crystal answered, trembling and terrified. "Honest, I don't know where it is." She prayed he wouldn't force any more information out of her or find out that she really did know that the money was now under the care and control of Mat and Foley. The last thing on earth she wanted to do was *rat them out,* and she regretted that she even mentioned the five million.

Now, after forcing her to cough up this much, Scarface supposed that she probably was just a bimbo secretary who had picked up bits and pieces of overheard conversations and was of no further use. He was all out of patience. They were sent here to pick up the trail to either their drugs or the money and the real information would come from Jack Kincaid, whom they had learned was the author and architect of this escapade, shortly before executing Captain Mo Furlong.

"Don' kill her. She still be useful, maybe. *Keep her quiet,*" he said to the two goons in leather. "We see what her boss say when he arrive, den we finish dem off, both." He horked back and spat out a gob of yellow mucous on the floor then left the room for the front office.

By now Foley was getting very concerned. The five men had been in the office for over twenty minutes and he was convinced that something very bad was going down. He had decided to get a closer look at matters from street level. As he approached the front of the building, he walked along looking this way and that as if out for a casual morning walk. Inside the two sentries watched him cautiously through the glass doors. Other passers-by were beginning to mill about as well as the business day got under way.

Now the two men remaining in the kitchen had freed Crystal from the duct tape on the chair. They were laughing excitedly, making sport of shoving her back and forth between them as she tried in vain to break free. Crystal was screaming, "Stop, *stop it...* Leave me alone!" and it was a scene that was growing ugly and noisy. Chairs were being overturned, cups and dishes from the counter were smashing to the floor and the game was escalating into something that was perversely arousing to the two depraved bullies.

"Ya! *Bitch slap* her good, soften her up!" one hood encouraged the other, as they viciously assaulted their victim.

One man grabbed Crystal by the arms and locked them from behind inside his arms while the other one ripped her blouse open at the front, pearl buttons scattering like marbles across the tiled floor. He removed a pocket knife and lifted the satin link with it that held her bra together in the middle. *One little tug*, seconds later, and it would slice through, revealing the erotic treasures beneath. He hesitated, to savor her terror, and to relish the anticipation.

Out front, Scarface was sitting at Kincaid's desk, rifling through files and papers for any clues about where their drug shipment might be stashed. He heard the racket going on in the kitchen and was annoyed, but didn't have sufficient interest or compassion to do anything about it.

The attack upon Crystal continued to escalate and at its peak one punk said to the other, "I bet she secretly enjoy dis. You tink so?" They both laughed savagely.

A moment later Scarface heard a horrific scream in the kitchen from Crystal like she'd be burned with a branding iron. Enough was enough. He marched back into the room and stepped between the two hoods and Crystal. Her face was bleeding, her blouse had been torn open, and her skirt was hiked up around her waist. She was stretched out prone across the table, one brute holding her by the arms in front. The other was standing behind her with his pants around his ankles. She had been used and degraded by these beasts and was sobbing and terrorized.

Scarface pulled his switchblade again and snapped it open, this time holding it threateningly towards the two hoodlums.

"I tell you jackals keep dis Jezebel *quiet*, not have *stag party* in here wit' her. Next time you defy me, I slit yo' bellies! I no repeat myself again... *Quiet!*"

He stared at them with cold black eyes, deadly serious. Like wild canines fighting over a wounded doe, they complied dejectedly, while the one pulled up his jeans from around his ankles. Each took a seat at the table, snarling and cursing. Scarface pocketed the knife and walked out, slamming the door behind him.

The two goons looked at each other, then at Crystal. *This time* they stood and approached her again, taking a cotton dish towel from the counter to wrap around her mouth. Crystal was in for a sexual assault, gagged with a dish towel from these monsters — a text book rape, no escaping it. Like a horror movie, the horrible act played out, one grisly, disgusting scene after another, until she was a heap of degraded, used flesh lying on the floor — beaten, humiliated, and defiled beyond any sane man's imagination.

Foley was a few feet from the front door now and while it was barely audible, he did hear Crystal's cry through the partially opened kitchen window around the side of the building. He knew this meant trouble and he wasn't going to abide whatever violence was being perpetrated on Crystal. It was a call to action. Foley kept on walking and opened the front door to Kincaid's office. The two men inside stepped forward and blocked his way like bouncers at a night club. They stood defiantly side by each in front of him.

"Hello, Fellas. Say, do you want to hear a funny story?" As he made that comment he put his hands on top of each sentry's outer shoulder. They looked at him oddly, as though in disbelief of his buffoonery. In the micro-moment of their hesitation, Foley acted with lethal swiftness. He shifted his hands upward and shattered their heads together like two watermelons exploding in a spray of blood, spit, and snot. It made a sickening *crack*, as though a baseball bat had landed simultaneously on each of their skulls. Both men went down like they had just been executed by a firing squad.

Now Scarface was on his feet and coming at Foley from across the room with his switchblade drawn. It was evident that he was a skilled knife fighter, as he took a crouched stance and waved his other hand in a distracting manner, looking for an opportunity to stab or slash his large opponent. Foley took a defensive posture as well, and glanced around for something to use for defense. He regretted not having brought any weaponry with him, but he never thought for a moment that he would run into anything like this. On Crystal's desk, there was a large mug filled with pens, a ruler, yellow highlighters and the like. Among its contents was a letter opener, dull on its edges, but pointed, nonetheless. Foley grabbed it, spilling the other contents of the mug across the desk.

Scarface lunged and Foley evaded the switchblade by inches. Then he slashed at Foley, missed again, and Foley smacked him across the face with an open palm. Next he ran at Foley swinging the blade wildly up and down, back and forth. Foley raised his arm to block a thrust and the knife went right between the radius and ulna of his forearm. In doing so, however, Scarface was now in close contact with the big man and he gripped the knife impaled in Foley's arm tightly. Foley dropped the letter opener, grasped the wrist of the man's knife hand and twisted it upwards and around back in a hammer lock. Now with his injured arm wrapped around the man's neck, Foley had seized him in an inescapable death lock. Scarface struggled but was no match for Foley's brute strength and combat skill. Foley squeezed the man's neck in the vice grip of his bicep and forearm and in only moments, the creep went limp. His face was bluish from asphyxiation and with vacant eyes wide open, his tongue hung out — revolting and undignified, like a dead beast. Foley let go and the body dropped to the floor with a thump.

By this time, the two men who had been brutalizing Crystal had heard the commotion, pulled their drawers back up and emerged from the back room. As they entered the main office area, they took one look at the two fallen sentries at the front door. One was sitting up in a state of semi-consciousness, blood streaming from a gaping wound in his forehead. He looked like he'd been hit by a car. The other lay motionless, bleeding profusely from both ears, with his eyes rolled back into his head. Then there was their boss, rumpled, blue-faced on the floor at the far side of the room showing no signs of life whatsoever, with Foley standing over him like a victorious gladiator.

Foley looked at them with ferocity in his eyes, the knife protruding from his lower arm. He expected to have to fight them as well, and he felt like he was just nicely warmed up for the task. He reached down and extracted the blade with a grimace. Blood dripped down his finger tips. He raised the knife and readied himself for battle again, stepping forward.

"Wanna dance, girls? Come and get it," he dared the two.

The two miserable curs looked at this pissed off, wounded giant holding a bloodied knife, freshly pulled from his own arm, then at each other, and ran straight out the front door, jostling the injured, but still alive, sentry to his feet in the process. Like frightened vermin – *sewer rats* that they were, they bolted down the street without looking back.

Foley raised his injured arm and rolled the sleeve up to survey the damage. It was bleeding, but the wound must not have involved any arteries because, if so, it would have been spurting blood much more freely. He went into the kitchen to check on Crystal.

Entering the room from the hallway his heart dropped when he saw her. She was laying face down in the middle of the floor, nude, but for her skirt rumpled like a twisted scarf around her waist, her ass humiliatingly exposed. She had obviously been horribly defiled. Her clothes were scattered. She was bleeding from the loins and he thought she was dead, but then she stirred, just slightly. He approached her and gently turned her over. As he held her head in his hands, her eyes opened through puffy slits. Her face had been punched or kicked repeatedly and it was bloody, swollen, and ugly. One of her breasts had a hideous bite mark on it. She was a bloody, beaten mess.

"You're going to be all right, little darlin'," Foley tried to reassure her, though in truth, he was utterly disconsolate by her condition. He grabbed a leather coat left behind by one of the hoods and covered her with it.

"Foley, *they* did this to me. I tried to stop it," she attempted to account for herself.

"*Sshhhh*, don't try and explain it. Now, listen to me. Do you think you can stand up?" Foley asked.

"I think so... But my clothes..." Crystal responded.

"Of course. I'll help you. We've gotta get outta here." He knew that the three punks that escaped might be back, and with an army of riled up soldiers this time. He gathered up all the garments that he could and helped Crystal to her feet. She covered herself laboriously in clothes torn to ribbons and stepped into her shoes. Foley looked down and tried not to watch. Then he wrapped his injured arm with a tourniquet made from a cotton dish cloth."

"Time to buck up and clear outta here," he said.

He looked at her beaten face and torn clothing and felt a pang of pity and compassion over the sadism and indignity she had suffered. Physical violence with men who were your enemies was one thing, but anyone who could perform such a brutal act of depraved hostility on a defenseless woman deserved damnation.

"Wait here a moment. I'll be right back," he said to Crystal, almost as a military directive. Foley walked with resolve to the front office. He picked up the lifeless corpses of Scarface and Mr. fractured skull, each by the scruff of his neck, and dragged them together to the back door of the building. He checked outside for possible witnesses, and saw no one. One by one, he took each body out and hoisted it into the dumpster in the alley.

He threw several flattened cardboard boxes on top of them that were stacked behind the building. In a couple of hours they'd be dumped at a Vancouver landfill, along with the rest of the garbage.

Foley returned to the office. He put his arm around her shoulder, led her to the front of the office and out the door, locking it behind him. It was 8:45 a.m. and business was closed for the day. Then he took Crystal home to care for her and give her the safety and security she would require during her period of physical, mental, and emotional recovery.

"God forgive what I do to any man that might try to hurt you like this again," he whispered. "I gotcha, sweetheart. Don't you worry. Ol' Foley's here and you're gonna be alright," he had said to her back at his condo. Crystal nestled her head against Foley's shoulder, breathing heavily. She cried, softly, "I didn't deserve this."

"No you didn't. You deserve better, and I'm gonna make sure you get it."

He held her tightly with both arms, and they leaned back together into his leather sofa. They closed their eyes, and drifted numbly into relaxation.

CHAPTER 15

MATHEW'S SATURDAY FLIGHT to Panama City was uneventful and he managed to put his head back for a couple hours of sleep. The stress he had endured lately with Christine and Hannah disappearing, and all the plans he had to make for managing the money coming in had put a great weariness upon him. He watched the overhead monitors, flipped through the In-Flight magazine, and read the National Post.

He glanced through the obituaries and wondered what each of the deceased would do if they had their lives to live over again. One day, his picture would be in there with a write up that tried, and failed, to summarize his life's aspirations and achievements. He realized that time is precious and washes away like sand under your feet on the beach. There are no second chances at living life and he had to get it right — now, the first and only opportunity he was ever going to have. And getting it right meant acquiring a lot of money, then investing it wisely, living the rest of his days in luxury with financial security, and leaving a nest egg for Hannah.

Moments later, the flight attendant was advising passengers over the intercom to raise their seat backs and trays in preparation for landing at the Tocumen International Airport in Panama City. His mission was underway.

On the cab ride to The Villa Tropicana Suites, Panama, Mat reflected on all the events that had shaped his life. At the outset, he and Christine had set out as innocent, young lovers on an adventure of building a home and life together. Their future lay before them like an open road stretching over the horizon. But life has a way of changing things, little by little. He had been lured into the money laundering game years ago when his mother had left him the fifty thousand. He supposed he could have walked away from it after that first foray into the business but his old friend and mentor, Hyman Wexler had quietly encouraged him into other financial opportunities outside the strict parameters of the law. Once Jack Kincaid, whom he also met through Wexler, was sending him business, he became more or less a professional money launderer. It soon became very profitable and, like most things you practice, he got better at it over time and clients came to him. Like the addage goes, *Most things in life are easier to get into, than out of.*

He was never ashamed of what he did, but it wasn't exactly something you go home and share with your wife either, though he always knew he would do just that at some point. Try as he might, he couldn't suppress the soundtrack in his head about all the events and issues that made up the fabric of his life.

His legitimate employer, the bank, unfairly pulled the rug out from under him when they fired him, or *displaced* him, in the terminology of the day, and he had bitterly decided from that point on never to be sucker punched again in business or in life. Ironically, the weakest link in the persona of his criminality was also the greatest driving force behind his determination and his commitment to success, Christine. And now she was gone, possibly forever. He was conflicted and disheartened to his core.

Worse, she hadn't outrightly said so, but he realized that she was disappointed in him and it hurt his pride. He did what he did in large part to provide a bright future for her and Hannah, and she had rejected it as unnecessary, unwanted, and morally unacceptable. Viscerally, he felt betrayed and slighted that she could just self-righteously take the high ground without due consideration for why he did the things he did, and he was perplexed by how she could simply discard the marriage and run off with their daughter without even telling him where they went. She didn't even leave a letter.

The more he thought about it the more he felt a creeping emotional disconnect from her. He wondered, *Do I love the real Christine, or was I in love with who I thought she was? The woman I believed her to be would never do this. For that matter, was she in love with the real me? Who am I, really, for that matter?"*

So he was left disillusioned and alienated from his wife, or soon perhaps, *ex-wife*. There are few things in life that are as deflating as finding out, too late, that you have invested yourself emotionally, and every other way, in the wrong person. When people don't love equally, it's a recipe for heartbreak, and nothing hurts more than a broken heart.

Yet, on another level, he understood her estrangement completely. By voluntarily engaging in this covert money laundering crime, Mat had made his own choices. He had no right, however, to draw Christine and Hannah into it against their knowledge or will. He thought about a *Dr. Philism* that had made an impact on him once: *When you choose the action, you choose the consequence.* Thinking objectively, it made *perfect* sense. Or it made *no* sense, depending on which position he took.

One thing was clear. He had made a deal with the Devil, and like always, now it had a real potential for going bad. Mat sensed Lucifer laughing at him from the sidelines.

How come nothing's ever simple? he wondered privately. *You are a prisoner of your own device,* he thought to himself.

In the end, even if he conceded to her wishes, he couldn't just bring it to a dead stop like she seemed to think he could. He had always hoped she would be at his side, no matter what, but now she had rejected him and deserted their marriage. He had to play out this final hand and then strategize how to proceed, free of the seedy underworld of organized crime, drugs, gangs, murder, theft, police and dirty money. He was trapped.

This is getting way out of control, he thought to himself. For a long time he had understood criminal activities, unlawful proceeds, illegal profiteering, and money laundering. Now he understood loneliness, fear, and despair. In his memory he kept seeing a gun barrel pointed squarely at him across the table and Dominic Hall's steely eyes fixed upon him. *One little pull and we're onto candidate number two.* He felt like a snared rabbit, and struggled with his fate.

The hotel was a palatial structure a few blocks from the beach. It was in the heart of Panama City's financial and banking districts. Patrons were a mix of smartly dressed, obviously affluent business people and well off visitors and tourists. They were spending money lavishly, in U.S. dollars, on everything from expensive restaurant meals, to designer label clothing, to fancy items from the gift shops. Shoppers entered the lobby headed for their rooms with arm loads of plastic bags and boxes containing items purchased from local merchants. The air was floral scented, humid and warm, and people everywhere had a cheerful and prosperous manner about them.

Mat had done considerable reading and research on this country of well over three million people and was duly impressed with what he learned. Much of what he'd read resonated in his head.

The city and country are a virtual paradise, with tropical climate, wonderful outlying rainforests, a dollarized economy, low crime rates and stable democratic government. Metro Panama City has a population of around a million people and extends for a full six miles along the Pacific coast. It's one of the most diverse and cosmopolitan Central American cities and has been among the top five retirement locations in the world for the last several years.

Many of the Fortune 500 companies are based here and the business climate is growing at a healthy rate, fuelled largely by being in the free trade zone. Panama's principle trading partners are the USA, EU,

Central America, The Caribbean and Japan, so the economy is lively and expanding.

Real estate is a sound investment in Panama, and opportunities to move here and take up full residency are relatively easy. There is no tax on real estate, capital gains, interest income, or foreign source income. The cost of living is quite reasonable, and international banking is one of the principle services offered in the country.

Mat knew that he would fit right in here and was excited by his arrival to this exotic and beautiful place.

The attendant at the front desk gave Mat the encoded card for his room. A friendly bellman assisted with his luggage and showed him to the suite. He greased him generously in case he needed him again at some later point. Upon entering the room, Mat felt almost like he was on vacation.

It was a large, well furnished suite with Greek style wall draperies, a luxuriously quilted queen sized bed, richly carpeted floors, big screen TV, spacious spa-like bathroom that glistened with shiny brass appointments and mirrors, and supplied with thirsty, white towels and complimentary robes; and in the main sitting area there were solid, wooden, coffee tables, a wet bar, and a writing desk. Mat's suite, and the entire hotel, for that matter, had a grandeur and elegance that was undeniable.

Too bad, he lamented, *I don't have anyone to share this with.*

He walked over to the window to take in a panoramic view towards the city's Metropolitan Natural Park and it was breath taking. In a reality check moment, Mat recalled of his real purpose for being there. He was set to meet with Marcos Del Rio to arrange the establishment of a trust agreement with his firm to accomplish the goal of anonymous banking.

There was a knock on the door. *Must be hotel staff again,* Mat guessed. He crossed the room and opened the door.

"You! What are you doing here?" he said with delight and surprise.

"Well, I hope you're happy to see me. I know you don't *need* me, but you did say I could, uh, *'tag along for the ride.'* Isn't that how you put it?" It was Adriana Santos, sassy as ever.

"Yes, something like that anyway. But how did you find me?" Mat wondered aloud.

"Jack had told me you were coming today. I stopped by your office and spoke with Danielle yesterday. She made your reservations, remember?"

"Uh huh, and she just told a complete stranger where to find me in a foreign country?"

Adriana explained, "Not exactly. We made some girl talk for a while, and I found out that she feels you work her too hard, for the amount you pay her."

"Really? She never mentioned anything about that to me," Mat replied with concern, as he looked away in thought.

"Yes, you're not very approachable, apparently. If you want my opinion, she certainly seems like a *keeper* to me. Maybe you should think about giving her a raise... and more time off." Mat's head snapped around and he stared hard at her for a moment.

"Anyways, then I told her I needed to forward some legal documents that were of urgent importance to you. She trusted me and gave me the name of the hotel. There were only two flights from Vancouver to Panama City today and I took the other one. I just waited in the lobby for you to arrive. The young bellman that assisted you discreetly told me what room you were in, after a wink and a tip. I assured him you would be pleased to see me. You are, *aren't you?*"

"Uh," Mat was distracted in thought. "Oh, of course I am!" Mat nodded. "Well, I'm sorry. I don't mean to interrogate you in the hallway. Please, come in and join me for a libation of a sociable nature, won't you?" Mat's tone turned playful and engaging.

"I'd love to," Adriana replied, "But I won't stay long. You haven't even unpacked yet and I don't want to intrude."

"Mat countered, "Nonsense. You're a sight for sore eyes. I was just thinking that it would be marvelous to share this experience with someone spe..." He stopped himself.

"*Special?*" She finished the sentence and looked at him with her penetrating, dark brown eyes, smiling coyly as she spoke.

"I keep doing that, don't I? *Open mouth, insert foot,*" and they both laughed together as they exchanged a friendly hug. They walked to the leather sofa with a heavy coffee table in front. Mat poured them each a Canadian whiskey over rocks with a splash of water.

"Here, drink this nectar. You'll find it has a calming effect. To the success of our mission, *partner,*" Mat toasted.

They both sipped their icy drinks from crystal glasses, sweating already with condensation. She made a face indicating she wasn't accustomed to drinking hard liquor. Mathew smiled.

"So, tell me. Since we're partners, *what is* our mission here? Would you like to share the details of your plan?" Adriana inquired.

"Sure. I'm meeting with a lawyer who'll make an arrangement for us to do our banking here in Central America with almost complete secrecy. We'll only need to keep the account open a few months and when we're finished, we'll close everything down, eliminate all records and '*get outta Dodge*' before anyone's the wiser."

Adriana persisted, "Details, details..."

"Well, understand first that the proverbial numbered account, in Switzerland or anywhere else, is non-existent today. The FATF stipulates that bankers, above all, should *know your customer,* so bank accounts have to be linked to someone with verifiable identification. Countries who don't comply with this basic tenet can face dire economic consequences because the international banking community could blacklist them and choke off trade with other countries." Mat was in lecture mode again. Adriana was a willing and perceptive student. She studied his mouth, and eyes, and hair, and mannerisms as he talked.

He continued, "However, many countries have strict rules governing the disclosure of information about their customers to protect their privacy and this makes it difficult for outsiders to learn anything about money that is being held offshore in places like Panama. Some countries also have tax treaties with other nations that call for information sharing about bank accounts. Panama and Guatemala don't have any of these treaties, so your information and privacy is quite secure here."

"I'm starting to understand your notoriety in this field," Adriana remarked, as she drew another sip from her drink.

"Now, the closest thing you can get to completely nameless banking is by setting up a *trust agreement* with a law firm who then forms a Guatemala Corporation called an *Empressa*. Then they open up an account for the company with a reputable Guatemalan bank, one worth many billions in assets to ensure the security of your money. The only signatory on the account is the law firm. Your identification is legally verified by a passport and driver's license with the law firm, but it's protected under attorney client privilege which is like *iron clad* privacy in Guatemala.

"To put an even greater firewall around your financial matters, we can have a Guatemalan judicial seal placed on the trust agreement and bank account records, meaning that the records cannot be opened unless the judge who placed it, or a higher Guatemalan court, authorized it, and you're more likely to see a snow storm here in July than have that happen."

"Yes, thank you for explaining what a judicial seal is. I'm an attorney," Adriana reminded Mat.

Mat said, "Listen up, councilor. I'm not finished yet. Through the trust agreement, you maintain power of attorney over the corporation and access to online banking pass codes so you can see the account history, balance and send international wire transfers. You also have an ATM card and secured Visa card, neither of which have your personal name on it.

"There are also safeguards built into this arrangement against all the '*what if's*' that might crop up, too. Part of the trust agreement contains a *distress clause* covering the unexpected, such as a messy divorce, a lawsuit, arrests, blackmail, extortion, whatever. This allows them to remove your control and power of attorney over the account in the event of some catastrophic personal event. Since you don't have any control over the funds, in favor of the law firm, it also provides you with an alibi in the event that some legal action is taken against you back home. You provide and define through the agreement what signals the beginning and end of the distress period, and how the funds are to be handled or invested during that period.

"And how do you fund this corporation?" Mat queried himself. "Through wire transfers directly to the trust account in Guatemala. Everything is done through this account and everything is under the sacred protection of attorney client privilege."

Adriana pointed out an important detail. "But you have to get the cash into an account someplace else before you can wire transfer it to the trust account."

"Ah, she has a lawyer's eye for details, doesn't she?" Mat teased, referring to her in third person. "I may have mentioned previously that a highly placed accomplice can discreetly open the door to the vault. I can deposit the money in a Canadian bank at night, but I've got to transfer it almost immediately, so the records can be jimmied before opening time in the morning."

Adriana looked more puzzled than informed. "What *are* you talking about? How are you going to accomplish that?

"Well, you don't launder large sums of cash without enlisting some specialized help along the way. Here's how we get the whole ball rolling," Mat said. He was beginning to feel a pleasant buzz from his Canadian Club and felt talkative. He stood and poured them each another glass of the golden liquor. Adriana shifted herself closer to him and crossed her leg in his direction on the sofa. She fixed her eyes on his face, almost hypnotically and looked at his lips while he was talking.

"I used to work for a man who believed that basically all banks and governments were intrinsically corrupt and greedy. He felt that making money by creating and bending the rules was not just a privilege of banks, big business and government, but for every day people too, when opportunities arise. It was a *risk reward* calculation for him and not a moral dilemma when he discovered an open window to prosper. The more I understood his position the more I agreed with him."

Adriana interjected, "What are you trying to say, Mathew?"

"I'm saying that I have a contact that will arrange the deposits and wire transfers of vast amounts of cash without disclosing it to the authorities. He'll work the system from inside a bank and we'll all make truck loads of money in the process." Mat smiled. "Before any of it is accounted for, the money will be transferred out of Canada and securely deposited in the Guatemalan trust account. Then we'll move it around the globe through a network of transactions and finally obscure it back into the Canadian economy as legitimate capital. It's not as difficult as you might think."

Adriana asked outright, "Who is this man?"

"Hyman Wexler. My old friend from my banking days. He's now the general manager of a Schedule B bank in Vancouver."

"And you're in quick sand right up to your eye balls in all this," Adriana responded. "You're doing business with the Kings Crew, the worst crime syndicate on the west coast, who are on the outs with the Red Sun Boys, who, in turn, have an outstanding debt of $10 million with some mainland China mob."

"Wo Shing Chu," Mat interjected. "And by the way, the war is about to get under way between those two. The China mob wants the balance of the money owed for the drug sale or they're gonna start something on the scale of the Iraq war."

"Right. And if all hell breaks out between that bunch and you doing this, there's a good chance that you'll get caught in the crossfire. Even if you survive that, if the law ever catches up with you on any of this, you're probably going to be locked up until you're kids are senior citizens. And by then, you'll have no assets or material wealth from legitimate sources, and your wife will be so long gone she won't even remember the name of the guy she married *after* you."

Mat was taken aback. "*Okay then,* I guess you've pretty much summed up the risk elements of this enterprise. I remind you that by being here and contributing to the project, you're also an accomplice and could face similar consequences yourself."

"I know. Don't think for one second that I haven't considered that," Adriana said. "It's odd how we sometimes make decisions that are foolhardy and dangerous. It's like gambling. You know the odds are against you, but you put down your bet and roll the dice anyways. How do you explain that?"

"Because life is an adventure that you embrace, or it's a boring movie that you sleep through," Mat replied. "We all make our choices. People fall into two camps: *Stick your neck out and embrace the adventure,* or *play it safe and die a slow death.*"

The two looked at each other thoughtfully without speaking further. Over the TV music channel, Michael Buble was crooning *Haven't Met You Yet,* as if it had been written and performed just for them. Adriana was sitting close to Mathew on the sofa and they were postured toward one another. The drinks had loosened them up and the intimacy of the moment was drawing them together.

Adriana's dark, thick hair tussled seductively to her shoulders and around her face. The swell of her breasts heaved invitingly into her chenille blouse as her breathing deepened. Her lips were moist, and she was close enough for Mat to sense the faint smell of liquor on her breath. Something in her demeanor whispered, *take me...* Mat moved his face closer to hers and he looked deeply into her eyes. In response, she tilted her head back, subtly availing her lips to his. He leaned forward and kissed her, softly at first, then passionately, almost violently. She responded eagerly and put her hands around his shoulders and neck. Their tongues danced upon each other's lips in sensual play and they moved their bodies and heads rapturously. If there was one thing they would each agree on now, it was that this was *bloody wonderful!*

Adriana broke the embrace. "I'm sorry," she said. "I shouldn't have allowed that. I'm feeling a little tipsy."

Mat looked puzzled. "What happened to *'Don't be embarrassed, silly, I'm flattered'* from our little lunch thing in the restaurant? Are you in a relationship?'

"No. I mean, not really."

"What does '*not really*' mean? Yes you are, or no you're not?" Mat pressed her.

Adriana looked a little uncomfortable. "Well, there *is* someone I see from time to time, but it's nothing serious."

"You see him? What do you do, play cards, exchange recipes, go for coffee?"

"No, don't be *daft*. He takes me for dinner, or we go to the movies, that sort of thing. It's just a date," Adriana explained.

Mat's eyes were locked onto hers trying to interpret what she was telling him. She was dating someone but not to establish any kind of relationship. He didn't quite understand. What was the point of it all?

"Adriana, have you ever been in a serious, committed relationship?"

"Not since I exchanged rings with Lenny Himmelfarb in high school," she replied, wryly.

Mat inquired, "You're an attractive, perfectly eligible, mid-thirties woman in the prime of your life and career. How is that possible?"

Adriana took a delicate sip of her drink and said in a frank tone, "Well, yes, I am in the prime of my career, and that seems to rule out the likelihood of a traditional man-woman relationship. Most men are scared away by successful, professional women, and when I spend upwards of fifty or sixty hours a week at my career, it doesn't leave much time or energy for playing the mating game. And I make more money than most men, and that turns them off."

"And so, you have these casual dates with someone you're not really interested in to pass the time," Mat concluded.

"You could put it that way. And since you seem to want to hear all the sordid details, I have creature needs that have to be met occasionally, and so does he, so we go out and pretend that we're dating, and then we go home and consummate the evening with something physical but meaningless, and I try and fool myself that it's something more and that we just need time to let the relationship grow, but it never does, and it never will. It's kind of pathetic actually, but there it is. Happy?"

Mat was a little shocked by Adriana's frankness. "No I'm not happy, I'm embarrassed, actually. Sorry. I didn't mean to corner you into discussing personal matters. You should have told me to mind my own business."

Adriana cooled off after a moment and responded, "Truthfully, it's the most honest conversation I've had with a man in a long time. I don't really have a lot of people I can share personal things with. I don't even have many girlfriends, and it does get lonely at times. It's puzzling. How can you live in a great city, amidst millions of people, and not have *anyone* you regard as a real friend?"

"I don't know," Mat replied. "I have Foley."

"Is he real?" she asked.

Mat paused momentarily. "*Oh, ya.* He'd *die* for me, I believe, even if I begged him not to."

Adriana gave him a hard look. "Let's hope it doesn't come to that. You're lucky to have such a friend."

"Yes, I suppose so, and I'm counting on fate that my luck holds out." Mat wondered how such a captivating woman could not have at least one close friend also. "There's really *no one* you can share your private thoughts and feelings with?"

"Not really. You're the only person I've admitted all this to and it feels kind of liberating. You're a good man at heart, and I think you try to understand."

"Doesn't your date, friend, try to understand you?" Mat asked.

"God no! He gropes around at me and does his thing, then he gets dressed and leaves. Can you believe the last time he actually *thanked* me? He treated me to a meal at a nice restaurant and then I took him home and asked him if he'd like to come in for a night cap which, in the parlance of dating, is code for something... *physical,* and at the time I hoped, meaningful." Adriana expressed herself with reserve and Mat was boring holes into her with his eyes, trying to grasp her story.

"He indulged himself in my bedroom like some *grunting animal,* then said 'Thank you,' and left. He didn't even use my shower. I thought he was going to shake my hand or leave a hundred dollars on my bureau for my services. I laid there blankly after and felt used, dirty, and ashamed and vowed I'd never do it again. Do you know what it feels like to be given the subtle message that your only value to a man is as an outlet for his carnal pleasure? Men are just horny pigs... Sorry."

Mat did understand. Successful women in business often sacrifice respect as real women with human needs, and traditional values, for career advancement. Most men want independent, undemanding women whom they can have their fun with, but not have any responsibility to afterward.

And women have needs that they are compelled towards, biologically and emotionally. We're all human, and men and women can be awfully callous when it comes to another person's feelings and self esteem in the name of sexual fulfillment. People connect at a primal level through sex, and when one person feels they have made that connection only to find that the other was just meeting a physical need, it can be heart breaking. It's sad how people drift in and out of each other's lives looking for meaning through empty sexual encounters.

He paused reflectively on her comments then slowly, he said, "Adriana, I am not exploiting you in any way and I didn't ask or expect you to come to Panama. There's no need to pull away from me. I'll *never* hurt you, trust me on that. I'm attracted to you and I surrendered to the urge to act upon it a moment ago. I think you enjoyed it too. Extend your hand, and I'll kiss it tenderly, or withhold yourself and tell me I'm wrong." Mat took her hand into both of his.

Adriana was visibly moved by Mathew's romanticism. "No, you're not wrong. But moral values die hard, and I have a problem with doing something like this with..." Her voice trailed off.

Mat finished the sentence, "a married man."

Adriana replied with lawyerly summation, "It's not my *MO* to close in and seduce some woman's husband on the pretense of doing a business deal together, even if it is illegal and in league with the criminal dredges of society. I still know what's proper, and what's not."

Mat wanted to tell her she was dead wrong. "It's not that way, actually. I am married, but... *we're not together.* She left me and I don't even know where she is. She will likely be filing papers for separation before next month. I thought she was my soul mate and life partner no matter what, and instead, she turned tail and ran at the first sign of trouble. It's easy to run. It takes guts to stay together and ride out the wrinkles life throws at you. Some soul mate."

Adriana swallowed, looking downward, then asked, "You still love her though, and want her back, don't you?"

Mat hesitated, but had to answer truthfully, "Ya, a part of me will always want that, if it was ever real. And I miss my little girl. I'm just a bit twisted about it all right now. It's hard to keep on wanting someone when they don't want you."

She watched and listened with compassion. "I won't tell you I understand. I've never had someone I cared that much about and I've never had someone who cared about me. We all want what we don't have. I wonder which one of us is worse off."

Adriana paused and jingled the ice cubes in her empty glass. "But I'm getting really woozy. This stuff is like drinking chilled gasoline. Let's call it a night and meet for breakfast. When do you talk with that lawyer about the trust agreement?"

"Monday... day after tomorrow," Mat replied, then he looked at her and said sincerely, "Hey, thanks for coming to Panama. I am glad you're here, really. Please don't take any of my comments too seriously. I'd like to blame the booze for being sentimental. Listen, you are *a very special* woman and friend, and I'd like to be the same for you."

Adriana paused and looked at him quizzically. "A woman?" she replied.

"Get outta here," Mat said, trying to sound dismissive. They stood and walked across the room together. "I'll call you around nine for breakfast." At the door she gave Mat a loving smile, pressed a lingering kiss to his cheek, and then left the suite, glancing back momentarily. He let the door swing shut on its spring-loaded hinges, then with his back against the wall, he stared into space, thinking.

CHAPTER 16

MAT DIDN'T WANT to appear too eager to start the day with Adriana, so he waited as long as he could until after the scheduled 9:00 o'clock Sunday morning to make the call. At 9:03 sharp, he eagerly picked up the phone and dialed her room. She had been showered, perfumed and fully dressed since before 8:00 o'clock, with makeup and hair done perfectly. She even took the time to shave her legs and under-arms in the shower that morning, even though it could easily have waited another couple days or so.

"Good morning, Adriana Santos," she answered in a reserved tone, as if it might be any of a number of callers.

"Good morning yourself. I hope you're as perky as you sound," Mat replied. "Hey, we've got some time to kill today, so I've made some arrangements to have some fun. I'll tell you about it over breakfast. Can you meet me downstairs in five?"

"I'm just getting ready. Slept in," she lied. You go ahead and I'll be there as quick as I can. It's a brunch buffet, so start without me if you have to." Twenty minutes later Adriana checked herself one last time in the full length mirror in her luxurious bathroom... *perfect!* Then she left her suite to join Mat in the dining room.

Mat, along with nearly every other male in the room, took notice of her instantly as she entered the restaurant. He pushed back his chair to stand as she approached the table. "Morning," he greeted her. "You look wonderful. Sleep well?"

"Passed out completely, more like it," Adriana replied. "The buffet looks delicious. Have you tried anything yet?"

"No, I was waiting for you. They're serving Champagne and Bloody Marys for starters. Try some?"

"Love to. It'd be a shame not to be decadent in a place like this. Alcohol for breakfast. You're corrupting me, completely," Adriana remarked as Mat waived over the waiter.

"Just wait," he replied with a devilish grin, which she returned.

After sipping their aperitifs, the two approached the buffet items and each made a few selections, being careful not to overindulge. As expected the dishes included tropical fruits like red bananas, pineapple, kiwana fruit, exotic berries, seedless red and green grapes, kiwis, passion fruit — which Mat offered to Adriana with a wink and a smile, cactus pears, guava, pomegranate, mangos, and sliced melons that neither had ever seen before, never mind eaten.

The main course dishes included spiced pork roast, curried chicken, lobster tails, giant scallops and prawns fried in garlic and lemon butter, steamed sea bass and tuna, impossibly pink smoked salmon with Philadelphia creamed cheese, capers and sweet onions, Cajun blackened chicken, and roast beef munificently sliced off a Baron of Beef by a jolly, fat server in a white uniform complete with a towering chef's hat.

There were potatoes — scalloped, roasted, mashed, and baked-creamed corn, fiddlehead greens in a buttery, salty glaze, salads of every description — three bean, Greek, Caesar, seared Ahi tuna, garden greens, cold pasta, fresh Cole slaw, sesame ginger spinach, gelatin and molded creations that seemed a shame to dig into and ruin the sculpture. As well, there were traditional breakfast items for the less adventurous, like eggs sizzling on a skillet right before their eyes, however they chose, with hollandaise and béarnaise sauce for the taking. Pancakes, corn bread, bacon, ham, fried hash browns, toast, English muffins, and croissants. They could have spent the whole day just enjoying the culinary experience, chatting and laughing together. They were like giddy teenagers on a first date.

At the end of the meal, a handsome, young waiter came around their table and offered them each a mouth-watering baked apple oozing with melted brown sugar, cinnamon, and whipped cream, sitting in a dish of thick, caramel drizzle. They decided to share one together and asked for two clean forks, which the cordial, young attendant graciously provided with over-the-top hospitality.

Mat had commented, "They're treating us like we're *honey moaners*. I mean *mooners*, I mean *honey mooners!*" and Adriana laughed right out loud.

Finally, after they both had failed miserably at not eating too much, Mat said, "Listen, my meeting with the law firm isn't until tomorrow, so we have today to enjoy the sights. I made some calls and it would be fun to go on a sail boat ride. I've booked one for just after lunch today. Please tell me you don't get sea sick."

Adriana smiled and simply said, "I hope not, after this meal. I've never actually been on a sail boat, but I don't get motion sickness in cars or aircraft."

Mat chuckled in amusement and said, "Well then, how different can it be — cars, planes, boats? Let's walk off this food and then get ready for some fun on the high seas."

Looking forward to their sea cruise, the two left the dining extravaganza and headed out to stroll through the bustling streets of Panama City to walk and talk and take in all the new experiences that this tropical Central American metropolis had to offer. In all their fun and merriment they nearly forgot the gravity of their mission in Panama and how crucial it was that everything go according to plan, and in a timely and controlled manner. Perhaps, for one day anyway, that was a good thing.

✼ ✼ ✼

Back in Vancouver, Jack Kincaid had been advised by Foley of the calamity that had occurred at his office Friday morning. Crystal would not be back to work any time soon. Nor would Jack be seen anywhere near his usual office or residence with those Red Sun hoods looking for him. Before executing Captain Furlong, they had extracted enough information out of him to put Kincaid as the mastermind behind their missing drug shipment. Jack was now in hiding and had even purchased a toupee and artificial goatee to disguise his appearance if he had to go out for any reason.

Foley himself realized that he'd been made by the three *sewer rats* that escaped, but they had no way to put together exactly who he was or how he was involved. He saw no good reason to lay low, as long as he stayed clear of Kincaid's office, but he did take to carrying his Beretta 93R 9mm semi-automatic pistol, as well as his throwing knife and a small, but highly effective, black-jack. No more getting caught off guard for Mister Karl Folkestad from now until this job was complete. He knew Mat would be back in a few days, and he would bide his time until he could discuss the situation with his partner and friend. As for his wounded arm, he had doused it in alcohol then wrapped it tightly in a gauze bandage. His hand was stiff as hell, but he expected the injury to mend on its own and luckily, it wasn't his dominant hand anyway

Foley took some much needed time to attend to Crystal's injuries while Mat was away. She had been badly beaten up by those vile thugs, and worse, she had been raped brutally by each of them. Her face would require weeks to heal properly, although it was fortunate that her injuries were largely superficial. With both eyes blackened and swollen, she would not be able to leave the house without drawing gawks from anyone who saw her. Miraculously, her nose and jaw were intact, although two of her teeth had been broken, but that could be corrected in time by any good dentist. Otherwise, there were no broken bones anywhere else in her body.

She was torn up where the men had forced themselves into her sexually, however that would heal in due course as well. Foley had immediately swabbed her bite mark with alcohol and applied a gauze bandage to reduce the chances of infection such as tetanus. The physical injuries would repair themselves, but emotionally and psychologically she might never be the same again, Foley realized. She carried a rage and humiliation that overshadowed good sense and closure and she might never let it go to resume life normally again. He tried not to let on the true extent of his concern.

The day after the attack Crystal had said, "Those *bastards*! I want to go to the police and file a report. I'll charge them with rape, and break and enter, and uttering threats, and unlawful confinement, and common assault, and brandishing a weapon, and attempted murder!"

Foley repressed a smile and tried to be sympathetic to her bitterness, but he knew that none of that was possible. "Crystal, first, you don't even know who they were, so how would you expect the cops to find them. How are you going to describe them, a bunch of Asian punks up to no good? Now that really narrows the field in a city like Vancouver, doesn't it? Second, if you go to the cops, they'll pry the whole story out of you, bit by bit. Are you going to tell them we're involved with the Kings Crew processing millions of dollars worth of drug money, and that your boss is the front man for the entire sordid deal including bribery, drug dealing, money laundering and murder?"

Crystal shot back furiously, "Well, they can't just get away with this. Look what they did to me. Look at my face. He bit my breast. They were going to cut my throat! What if they gave me HIV? *Those pigs!* What if it happened to you? You'd be looking for pay back, no questions asked. They should be beaten down with clubs then castrated. I wanna kill them. *Dead...* is what they deserve. We should hunt them down like dogs, and kill them!" She was incensed beyond all reason.

"I know, I'm not saying you're not entitled to the way you feel. Don't forget, two of them *are* dead, and if we ever catch up to the ones that did this to you, I'll put a slug in each of them too, you've got *my word*. But we have to keep a level head and stay focused on our assignment. Listen, I'm not too experienced at counseling women on how to cope with something like this, or anything else, but what you've been through is horrible beyond all measure and no one but you can decide whether you're going to survive it and *just be Crystal* again, or carry around a hurt for the rest of your life that never heals and never, ever grants you freedom from your past.

"Ma'am, I'm pretty good at readin' people, and I think you've seen your share of hard times and hurt, but... here's the thing," Foley continued, "Life is a river, and its eddies and currents mark our course more or less at random into rocks and obstacles, over white waters, and through rough weather. But we all go one direction only — downstream, and if we wanna survive we have to keep on paddling, no matter what. We've got a long journey ahead of us yet, Crystal. Don't let this thing capsize you before we pull ashore. You follow me?"

She looked on and listened to Foley and recognized that this man was sensible and wise in his own way. He empathized and understood her anguish, he spoke to her sincerely, and he was just *special. He even called me Ma'am,* she reflected, smiling.

He continued, "Whatever you fix on, I'll be here with you and I'll try to understand, because you're a special lady and you deserve a friend, a *real* friend. I can tell you this much. I've been around dust ups like this before and this probably ain't over yet. Don't be flabbergasted if we run across those boys again. Like the saying goes, *'Be careful what you wish for'.* Revenge is not a pretty thing. Let's just take one day at a time for now, and get you healed up and well again."

Crystal knew Foley had seen her indignantly naked, bruised and bleeding and still he had compassion and respect for her, and moreover, he valiantly defended her in deadly circumstances. That was something that wasn't ever before seen in her world and her heart told her to listen to this paradoxically kind and brutish man. She felt that at last, she had an ally in life that she could rely on. Reluctantly, and with welled up eyes, she yielded through halting sobs of misery and surrender. Foley embraced her, reassuring her with a crushing bear hug and a loving pat on the back, and she hugged him back like she'd never hugged any man before in her life.

And so Crystal had agreed to take up residence with this Foley, partly so he could nurture her back to health, but mostly just because the two of them had taken to each other. Sometimes you know instantly when you've found *the one*, and it appeared that these two were now unofficially, but never-the-less, a couple. Foley had always prided himself on his independence and freedom, but now he felt needed and loved by a real woman and he took a notion that that might be a good thing in this chapter of his life. He wasn't getting any younger, he rationalized. Crystal too felt loved, understood and secure with this man, and she just felt right being at his side. But, romance aside, they still needed to get on with the job and all its hazards.

CHAPTER 17

AS MAT AND Adriana approached the Shelter Bay Marina by cab, they took note of the palm lined, white sand beaches along the way. There were surfers, parasailors, and recreational boats skirting the shores by the dozens. Out-door recreation, sunbathing and water sports were everywhere.

Adriana remarked to Mat as they took in the sights, "Is *having fun* all they do here?"

The ocean was bright aqua blue beyond imagination, and it blended into the horizon of the tropical sky, accented with white puffs of slowly drifting clouds. At their destination Mat paid the cab driver by Platinum American Express card, and he and Adriana stood together looking at a large sailboat marked *Matri-Ark of the Sea* on its hull. They couldn't help feeling just a little touristy.

"Well, this is it. We're supposed to ask for Captain Paulo Toromenta," Mat said.

"At your service, sir," a gruff voice rumbled cheerily from right behind them.

Mat and Adriana turned around and were greeted by a large, bearded man bearing a wide, friendly grin and dressed in Khaki pants with a white tee-shirt and blue runners. He was, perhaps, in his mid-fifties with thick, wavy grey hair that hadn't been barbered in months and he had a healthy, cheerful vitality about him that was instantly magnetic. He set down two pails of ice he'd been carrying and extended his hand to Mathew.

"Mathew Crawford," Mat introduced himself. "Captain Toromenta, I presume?" he said and shook the man's hand. He noticed immediately that the Captain's hand was obviously accustomed to hard work as it engulfed his like a large adult's would that of a child.

"Yes sir," the captain replied. Welcome to Panama. We're going on a little sailing excursion today, *si*?" He spoke with a Spanish accent, but his English was good.

"Absolutely. We've been looking forward to it," Mat said. "Is this your sail boat?" pointing to the large, docked vessel.

"Yacht," the captain responded, smiling at Adriana. "It's called a Yacht, son — fifty four feet of poetry in motion on the open seas. And may I welcome you also, young lady? How would you like to be addressed?"

"Why, thank you. Just Adriana would be quite fine with me, Mister Toromenta."

Mat noticed she had a giddy grin on her face like a kid about to go for her first ride on a Ferris Wheel. Then he realized self-consciously that he was smiling broadly as well.

"Alright, *just Adriana.* Why don't you both come this way?" And he picked up the pails of ice, handing off one to Mat, then led his new friends down the gangway to his boat — *Yacht.* They hadn't even left harbor yet and already they were having terrific fun.

"Aye Aye, Skipper," Mat replied, immediately dropping into the character and lingo of a sailor. "Let's set sail on the open sea!" Adriana rolled her eyes and laughed as she followed along behind the two men.

On board, there were several other passengers also awaiting the day's adventure on the high seas. Another couple — retired,

Mat guessed, likely in their mid sixties, were smiling, holding hands, and waiting patiently. Two other ladies, both around thirty, were talking animatedly, but in a hushed tone about something that must have been terribly controversial, judging by their behavior. *Looks like they're auditioning for Sex in the City,* Mat thought to himself. Then there was a young man — a father, around thirty five, maybe a little more, with two young sons that looked to be about six and eight. It looked like he was treating the boys to a special voyage, far outside the realm of their usual world.

Onboard, after Captain Toromenta went over some basic safety principals for Mat, Adriana, and all the passengers and issued them each with a comfortable life jacket, the docking cables were untied and, before long, the mainsail and two foresails caught the wind and carried the large vessel out to open water of the Pacific Ocean. Both Mat and Adriana were surprised by the speed and agility that the ocean craft exhibited under the control of Captain Toromenta and his two crewmen. The salty sea spray felt cool on their faces and Mat watched the warm wind blow Adriana's hair luxuriously as if she were in a shampoo commercial demonstrating beautiful, healthy, clean hair. She lifted her chin into the breeze and smiled happily, and Mat could tell she was truly enjoying this experience.

It was entertaining watching and listening to the Captain bark orders to the crewmen. "Bring her about! She's *heeling* too far. Trim the *mainsail.* Loosen off the *downhaul.* You there, Bobby, *starboard helm,* then hold that *tiller* while we're headin' out to sea. *Belay* those lines once the sails *luff,*" and the like. It was a language unto itself.

His men treated him with obedience and respect and willingly followed his orders without hesitation or question. Nautical terms were mostly Greek to Mat, but he admired the captain's expertise and mastery of his craft and crew. The day's expedition had an authentic sense of adventure about it.

"Here, better use some of this before the sun gets to you," the Captain said, as he tossed a tube of Coppertone SPF 50 to

Adriana and Mat. Each of them lathered on a liberal amount, rubbing each other's noses, cheeks, and shoulders to ensure even application, but moreover to seize an opportunity to engage in some tactile, affectionate touching of one another.

Once they were out to sea, with the shore barely visible, Captain Toromenta trimmed the sails and the vessel straightened up to an even keel in the water. She was sailing along now, perfectly balanced at a comfortable speed, and it was easy and safe to walk around the deck. Mat and Adriana strolled from one end of the vessel to the other and euphorically enjoyed the sights, and sounds, and smells of being on the wide-open water, far out on the brilliant Pacific Ocean.

"See that land mass over there?" the captain commented, pointing his finger west. "That's the Pearl Island Archipelago. That's where they shoot the television series 'Survivor'. Its operations are based on Contadora Island, or *Isla Contadora*, in Spanish." Everyone peered off into the distance at the tropical paradise rising majestically out of the sea. It was beautiful and fascinating.

"We'll have some chow from the galley brought up in few minutes. Everyone feeling up to a little something to eat and drink? How about it? Adriana, Mat?" the Captain asked briskly.

"Yes, that would be wonderful," she answered for both of them. Then she looked out at the water racing by and shouted, "Look! What's that out there? It must be *sharks*." Everyone raced to the starboard side of the craft and stared out onto the water with rapt anticipation.

Captain Toromenta squinted into the area where she had pointed, then let go a loud belly laugh that infectiously got the rest of them going as well.

"What's so funny? Don't you see them?" Adriana persisted.

The captain replied, "Those sharks are actually dolphins. A whole pod of 'em by the looks of it. Sometimes they'll follow us, racing around the fore and aft of the vessel actually having fun, teasing and chattering at us like playful children."

Adriana looked at them again with marvel in her eyes that something so graceful and free could be living out here in the open ocean. There were birds flying overhead performing a discordant avian symphony of squawks, quacks, whistles, and screams; the waves were slapping against the hull of the vessel; the dolphins were showing off like speeding little torpedoes, darting in and out of the water; the sails were bulging magnificently in the humid sea breeze under the dazzling, tropical sun; and Captain Toromenta and his crew mates seemed like born seafarers who could not be happier or more in their natural element. It was breathtaking and when she turned and looked at Mat, she saw astonishment in his face as well. He returned her gaze from the other side of the deck and in harmony they smiled warmly at one another and silently communicated their mutual affection.

Moments later a steward emerged aboveboard from the galley, with a trolley of fresh sandwiches, exotic European cheeses, deli meats, Kalamata and Manzanilla olives, lox and pickled herring with capers and sweet Vidalia onions, crusty French bread with olive oil and balsamic vinegar, cooked prawns on ice, raw oysters on the half-shell garnished with sliced lemon, condiments, and rock salt, a fancy assortment of Italian breadsticks and crackers, jalapeno jelly, tropical fruits, and strawberries that were surely huge enough to make it into the Guinness Book of World Records.

There were bottles of carbonated ice water, red and white wine chilled in decanters, and several kinds of beer — Tuborg, Heineken, Kilkenny Crème, Stout, Ale and Guinness, as well as good old standbys, Budweiser, Coors, and Millers, that had been chilling in a cooler of ice since the vessel left harbor nearly two hours ago.

The crew and their guests sat around a solid wood table in the shade of a large canopy on the deck and leisurely enjoyed the meal and each other's company, while sailing along tranquilly under the balmy skies of sunny Central America. On a ghetto blaster sitting at one corner of the bar Jimmy Buffet was singing *Margaritaville,* lamenting something about a lost shaker of salt, a brand new tattoo and wasting away his life in the tropics over a lost love, and the mood was festive and relaxed among all the passengers.

Mat sat across from the dad and his two young sons, and noticed the man talking supportively with both boys, explaining various aspects of the vessel and the sea. The lads were bundled tightly in life jackets and listened like eager Boy Scouts. It was evident that there was a strong bond between the three of them as they talked and laughed together. Both boys sat up straight along side their dad and watched the crewmen with keen interest and admiration. One of them looked over and noticed Mat watching, and he raised his hand and waived cheerfully as if to say, *Hi Mister. We're on a high adventure at sea with our dad!* The boy's dad looked over too, and Mat brought his right hand to his brow and gestured a friendly salute towards him.

I love my little Hannah to pieces, but it would have been nice to have a son too, Mat thought to himself.

Adriana perused the cheerful sailors, several other happy guests, the harmony of the sea, sky, wind and marine life, and her captivating new friend — *boyfriend?* As they talked, sipped, ate, and experienced a wonderful afternoon, she felt like she had a naughty secret inside her and she wanted to share it with Mathew.

In understatement, she said, "This is *really nice.* Thank you, Mat, for arranging this."

"Naw," Mat replied, smiling. *"This...* is really nice," taking her hand in his, squeezing it gently and looking into her eyes. The captain and crew mates watched them with amusement and exchanged nods and winks.

"Captain, how long have you been sailing?" Mat asked the big man, initiating conversation.

"My whole life, pretty much. I used to go with my father, who was a fisherman, and we'd be out at sea from dawn until dusk talking and catching fish to bring back and sell on the docks the next morning. We were never wealthy, but I grew up with a full belly and the love and companionship of my father and family. I never really wanted to do anything else," Captain Toromenta explained between chomps on his sandwich.

The comment about the bond between the captain and his father were not lost on Mat and privately, it saddened him that his boyhood relationship with his dad was so very different. "What kind of fish would you catch?" Mat inquired.

"Oh, whatever swims the seas was fair game. Black marlin, bill-fish, sailfish, yellow fin tuna, wahoo, dorado, roosterfish, sea bass, red snapper, grouper, barracudas, amberjacks... to name a few.

"There's more? Sounds like you just named them *all*," Adriana quipped, then laughed heartily at her own joke.

The Captain chuckled. "We used to fish Hannibal Bank, Coiba Island, and Isle Montuosa. Did you know the word Panama means *abundance of fish and butterflies?* The earliest inhabitants of the isthmus joining North and South America named it some fifteen hundred years BC. When a man has all this, why would he need anything else? Sometimes we overlook wealth, beauty, and happiness when it's sitting right under our noses. And tell me Mathew, what line of work are you in?"

Mat paused, calculating his answer. "Well now, I own a security company with a partner and we provide businesses and home owners with protection, mostly against break-ins, burglary, theft, and fires."

"Ah, *so, so much crime* in the world. Sad, that people need to take such measures to protect themselves from the dishonesty of others. Too many people look for shortcuts to find fulfillment and meaning in their lives, when plain hard work and honest living are their own rewards. And what brings you to Panama, just a little vacation?" the captain inquired.

Mat exchanged a quick look with Adriana. "Call it a *working* vacation, I'd say. We're here to transfer some money. Panama is an international banking centre and a great place to shelter your investments."

"Well, money is one subject I don't have much knowledge of," replied the captain. "My boat is paid for, my wife and three kids are all clothed and fed with a good roof over their heads. We really don't want for much, and I sleep well most every night. I have simple needs, and I am a *truly happy* man, I guess you could say. I believe it is a great treasure in this world for one to have a contented heart and a peaceful soul," Captain Toromenta reflected, looking out to sea. He reached into a satchel at his side and took out a pipe and small bag of tobacco.

The captain's tone had turned philosophical. "If I may ask, Mathew, would you say that, as a man, *you are happy* with most things in your life? Are you a *contented* man?" he continued, holding a match to his pipe and drawing heavily on it, until its contents glowed red, producing plumes of blue grey smoke.

Mat considered the question and glanced at Adriana. "Not quite yet, sir, but I'm workin' on it. Just a few wrinkles to iron out and I'd like to believe I'll be very content in the near future." The humid sea breeze picked up and the crew men scurried to adjust the sails and rigging.

Adriana looped her arm through his elbow on the bench seat they were sharing and pulled herself tightly to his side. *"I'd like to believe that too,"* she whispered softly into his ear.

He turned and as they looked into each other's eyes, a realization came over Mat that his life finally held the potential for true happiness; free of the anger and bitterness about getting fired unfairly at the bank years ago; free of the need to react and rebel against society's laws, rules, and constraints; free of the resentment he carried over his unhappy relationship with his father and the anguish over his mother's actions; free of the hurt and disillusionment brought to bear upon him by Christine's disapproval and rejection of him, and her flight from the marriage. It was like a dark veil had been lifted from his eyes, exposing a luminous world of beauty, opportunity, and fulfillment.

Here was a wonderful, intelligent woman at his side, his equal, availing herself to him without reservation or conditions. They were in a paradise of sorts, worlds apart from the moral corruption, violence, and depravity of Vancouver's criminal underworld, and Mat saw fresh new beginnings and possibility all around him. He had only to complete this last assignment and he felt sure his life's course could be altered forever. It was all so simple, and yet so difficult.

"You always this nice to be around?" Mat asked her, rhetorically.

"No, actually, hardly ever. Something's come over me, it seems," Adriana responded. "Would you like to spend some time *really* getting to know me?"

Mat paused, more for effect than because there was any doubt. "I think I would… Yes, I would indeed."

The afternoon's sea cruise was a joyous and defining event in the lives of Adriana and Mat. Each had reservations about starting something that they couldn't, or shouldn't finish, but to deny it would have been even more painful and a bigger lie. Relationships are sometimes — usually actually, complicated, and don't always happen when or where you want or expect them, or at a convenient time, and they don't always follow a sensible path. Sometimes they just dance onstage, unannounced and unanticipated, and you just have to embrace their arrival with gratitude and humility. Although it makes you feel like a new world has opened up before you, like a parent with a new baby, it also reminds you of how small and lucky you are that this is happening, here and now.

Whatever else lay ahead for these two, one thing was certain; they were connected now and there was no turning back. Whatever course it would lead them on, they were committed to follow, together.

With the sailing tour finished Mat and Adriana were tired but had thoroughly enjoyed the day. They returned, hand in hand, to Mat's room in the hotel and more or less fell onto the sofa together. Mat reached over Adriana's shoulder and put his arm around her and she obliged by snuggling closely to his side. They ordered in a light snack and some ice wine as they talked, and cuddled, and prepared for the meeting with Marcos Del Rio the next day. It was good, real good, being together.

At 8:00 o'clock the next morning, the door to Mathew's room swung open and Adriana emerged into the hotel corridor, followed by Mat, each looking rested and pleased. Both were smiling contentedly. They were well groomed and dressed professionally for the meeting downtown.

Riding down the elevator to catch their cab, Mat looked at Adriana seriously and said, "Adriana, about last night, and this morning..." He raised his eye brows.

She locked her eyes with his and replied, "Yes?"

"*Thank you.*"

The words hung in the air. Although he tried, he couldn't repress a small grin. She hesitated momentarily, then replied, "*You jerk!*" They both laughed at the private joke as the lift doors parted from the middle in the lobby, then they headed for the street.

At the outset, Jack Kincaid had said, "You'll be glad I introduced the two of you before this is done. That's a prediction I'll make."

His prediction had proven true.

CHAPTER 18

OUTSIDE THE OFFICES of Hall Garcia and Barlow a panel van slowly rolled by with a man in wayfarers in the passenger seat surveying the two story building and all its surroundings. "Slow down," he said to Jimmy Yang, the driver, who was sporting a colorful tattoo of a coiled snake with fangs exposed on his cheek.

"Nelson," Jimmy replied, "Don' be so obvious. Anyone watching us would know we casing the place." In the cargo hold of the van sat six more thugs, armed with semi-automatic weapons, pipe bombs loaded with screws, ball bearings and glass from broken pop bottles, knives of varying descriptions, and an assortment of close contact weaponry.

"Pull up over there," Nelson Hi Wo ordered. "Beside that newspaper box. Everybody ready back there?" he called out to the gang behind him.

The Red Sun Boys had learned of the heist of their drug shipment by the Kings Crew from Captain Furlong. It was corroborated by the secretary at Evergreen Import Export. They tracked information provided by Furlong to the accounting office just steps away from the parked van. Time *was not* on their side. At *YVR*, Vancouver International Airport, a contingent of six alleged Hong Kong businessmen had just landed and was clearing customs. They were preparing to pay a surprise visit to some business associates in Chinatown, Vancouver. Wo Shing Chu had arrived and time was up for the Red Sun Boys.

"What are we waiting for? Let's do 'em," one of the soldiers in the back asked maliciously. They were here to recover their drugs and, if necessary, in doing so wreak havoc on the accounting office. Now bristling with wicked anticipation, they were about as patient as trained pit bulls awaiting the starting whistle in a dogfight ring.

"Lock it down, back there! Await my orders," Nelson commanded. "First we put them all in one room for interrogation. We need to get our product back and any money that might be on hand. We're not here to just slash and burn, so don't get trigger happy or we'll just end up in a showdown with the cops. We do this quietly at first and, if we have to, we'll leave a calling card of death and ruin. Anyone straying from my orders will wind up with a third eye socket in the middle of your forehead."

Nelson Hi Wo, at forty-two, was a seasoned member of the Red Sun Gang and had been well known to the Vancouver police as a career criminal since his early adolescence. He had evaded capture and arrest numerous times and was rumored to be a brutal, remorseless killer with the blood of a desert scorpion flowing through his veins. The police had profiled him to be resourceful, capable in Cantonese, and completely fluent in English, self-educated beyond the norm for criminals, and a predatorily intelligent psychopath. His only family appeared to be the gang he belonged to and, outside of criminal pursuits, his life seemed to have little purpose other than, paradoxically, his fascination with the Lord and a preoccupation with Christianity. Homicide detectives referred to him as the *bible thumping serial killer.* He was on the most-wanted list of the authorities, but had the transparency of a ghost.

His job here was to spearhead the task of recovering the drugs, or the money, or both, and he earned this assignment through the merit of previous successes at similar jobs. Nelson and Jimmy were senior management within the ranks of the Red Sun gang and it fell on them to resolve this problem, and fast. Knowing that Wo Shing Chu had issued an ultimatum from mainland China that payment was due, they were on fire, and they had to move fast.

Even if they found where their cocaine had been stockpiled they wouldn't be able to liquidate it fast enough to raise the five million, but at least they could recover costs, over time, when they sold it themselves. If they couldn't find a way to recover the drugs, they would be faced with paying the five million out of reserves – a huge blow to their organization, or waging a war with the more senior and better organized Wo Shing Chu. Without question, that alternative was second choice.

It was 11:40 a.m. and the door to the building opened. Two ladies walked out and headed for the parking lot. "Most of them will be going for lunch soon," Jimmy said. "If we want to do this thing, we'd better move fast or it will have to wait until this afternoon."

Nelson agreed. "Okay. Bones, Spike, and Digger, you go around back and wait by the door. Anyone tries to leave, you stop 'em. We'll let you in after we've secured the place. Rocky, Ice, and Fats... you guys come with us. Remember everyone, stick to the plan." The Red Sun Boys opted for nick-names in addressing each other for the most part — to signify club membership, and because their real Chinese names were so foreign to North Americans.

At that, the boys exited the van and broke into two groups, one heading for the front door, the other moving around the back. Nelson pulled down the front of his sweat shirt to conceal the hand gun tucked into the front of his pants. The five men scaled the stairs leading to the front door. Nelson and Jimmy entered first, followed by the other three. Spike carried a duffle bag containing the pipe bombs and other assault hardware. A matronly lady in her mid fifties sat at a reception desk. Her name tag said *Betty Dow* and she immediately looked at the group disapprovingly.

"What can I do for you?" she said curtly, as they approached her desk.

"You can *shut up* and don't touch a fuckin' thing on that console, bitch," Nelson said as he pulled the weapon from under his shirt, pointing it at her face. The lady looked like she'd just experienced the anti-Christ incarnate, horror registering on her face. "Stand up, now. Get over there and say your prayers," he said, pointing to the chairs in the waiting area.

Nelson continued, "Ice, nobody leaves the building, and if this old cow makes a sound, kill 'er." Ice leveled his semi-automatic on her, and smiled.

"Where's the boardroom, *Betty Dow?*" he asked mockingly, looking at her name badge.

With halting breath, she said, "Down that hall. First left."

"Second thought, come with me," he ordered her. "Watch the door," he said to Ice.

Betty led them to the boardroom where they shoved her into a seat at the large rectangular table. "How do we get to the back door?" he said to Betty, pointing the gun at her.

"Go farther down the hall we just came from. There's a door leading to a stairwell. It's in there. You'll see it," she said with forced compliance.

Nelson addressed Jimmy. "Go let them in, and do it quietly." Jimmy left the room and returned moments later with the other three thugs.

Nelson summarized their plan. "Ice has the front door. Bones, you guard the back door. The rest of us, gather up everyone in the building and bring 'em in here. Do this floor first, then the second." Each of the gang dispersed and started going office door to door. One by one the accounting staff were brought into the boardroom. Nelson entered a large corner office, nicely furnished with windows on three out of four walls. Carlos Garcia was at his desk and immediately looked up at the intruder.

"What's this?" he demanded.

"Outta' your chair, motherfucker," replied Nelson holding his gun menacingly sideways on the man.

Carlos remained sitting, defiantly. With his left hand he pressed a panic button on the inner panel of his desk, beside his chair. It took no more than a second and went unnoticed by his captor. In a matter of minutes the Kings Crew would be arriving.

"Who are you, and what do you want?" he demanded.

"I *want* to put a bullet right through your head, asshole. Give me a reason to, please. Now get outta' that chair and do as you're told." Carlos stood up and followed instructions. Like the others, he was led down the hall to the boardroom.

Further down the corridor, Fats entered the office marked *Dominic Hall* on the door. The office was empty, or so he thought. The distinctive red light and digital beep activated by Carlos's signal had alerted him to a security problem. He immediately grabbed the snub-nosed revolver from his desk drawer and stood behind the folding door to a supply closet in his office. As anticipated, an unwelcome Asian guest had entered his office and he watched him silently through the crack of the folding doors until he left. "Red Sun Boys," he whispered to himself.

Systematically, office workers and bystanders chatting in the halls and around the water cooler were confronted by gang members and marched at gun point towards the gathering room. Their protests and demands for explanation went ignored by the hoods. Both the front and back doors were guarded by armed sentries so there would be no frantic attempts at escape.

Now, most everyone in the building, with the exception of Dominic, had been herded into the boardroom. Some eighteen people were assembled at the table and none, save Carlos Garcia, knew their firm had any connection to the biker gang or drug money. Most thought it must be a stick up. All of them had had a gun waived in their face and all were scared. The six gang members stood all around the room holding their guns on the crowd. Two others remained at the front and back doors. All cell phones were confiscated by the gang members. The power cable to the business land line was cut. The employees of this firm were now captive and subject to the whims of a brutal and merciless gang bent on recovering their drugs at any cost.

Nelson started the interrogation. "Okay, I'm going to be asking some questions here. Know what happens if I don't get the right answers?"

There was a long pause among the hostages. A cocky young man in a blue pin striped Armani suit was leaning back in his chair trying to be cool in the face of danger. Finally, he spoke up.

"What's going to happen?" he said.

Nelson immediately raised his gun and fired it once directly into his belly. The man let out a grunt, grabbed at his gut with both hands, and fell out of his chair. A collective gasp went around the room. Some ladies let out a scream, and everyone was stunned.

"That, for starters," Nelson said. "Now, I caution you, *do not lie to me.* I will know if you're lying and it will not go well for you. Sorry Buddy... *you alright?*"

Down the hall Dominic heard the shot. He had moved from the closet and opened his door a crack to survey the hallway for information about the intrusion. There was no movement in the hall from what he could see. He waited, unsure of how to react to it all.

"*Make no mistake.* We mean business here and we are leaving with answers," Nelson assured them. The wounded man writhed on the floor and moaned. His hands were already awash with blood.

"*Of course* he's not alright. He needs help!" A lady near him said. "Call an ambulance, *please.*"

"Give me the information I need and *perhaps* he'll live," replied Nelson.

A woman at the far end of the table started screaming incomprehensibly and lost complete control of herself. Rocky was standing close to her and locked eyes with Nelson. Nelson nodded, and Rocky pistol whipped her once across the face and she tumbled out of the chair onto the boardroom floor. On her hands and knees, she coughed and choked up fragments of white teeth, ropy saliva, and blood onto the carpet.

"It's all in the wrist," Rocky smirked.

"What do you want, for God sakes?" demanded a fifty something, overweight accountant with bifocals and a bad comb-over, as he stood up from his chair.

"Ah, now *that's what I'm talkin' about*," Nelson patronized. "What do we want? We want our cocaine back. Now!" he shouted, "or all of your lives will change forever, if you live at all."

"Don't be ridiculous!" bellowed the man with mock authority. "Jesus Christ! We don't know anything about any damn cocaine."

Without hesitation Nelson lifted his gun and shot the man through his thigh, shattering the upper leg bone and perforating the femoral artery. He hit the floor like a slaughtered bull and lay nearly motionless, rendered unconscious almost instantly from the pain, shock, and horrifically rapid loss of blood. Without immediate help, the man would surely fall victim to death by exsanguination, in a matter of minutes. Women and men alike were crying in terror. These guys were ruthless, blood thirsty monsters and the atmosphere in the room was one of shock, horror and fear.

In a pompous tone Nelson said, "See, now that was a fib, wasn't it? Didn't I say *not to lie* to me? You will show me *respect*!"

Outside, a contingent of perhaps a half dozen bikers pulled up on choppers a block away from the offices of Hall Garcia and

Barlow. Another four men in an F-250 SuperCab pick up rolled into the back lane of the building. They were all well armed and crudely trained for assault.

Nelson walked over to another man of about forty who was nervously turning the wedding band on his finger. He noticed this and from behind, Nelson yanked his chair away from the table and pointed his gun at the man's groin. The guy looked mortified and started hyper-ventilating. "Tell us, friend, have you ever been unfaithful to your wife? You know, the tenth commandment? *Don't lie to me.*"

His eyes widened with panic and he started gasping for breath, his diaphragm spasming involuntarily, like a child crying. There was an agonizing pause as he tried to compose himself. *"Please..."* was all he could manage, cupping his hands over his crotch, *like that* would protect him if the gun fired.

Nelson straightened his arm, preparing to shoot.

"Yes! God, yes, once, only once I swear," he blurted out and Nelson laughed, sadistically. Then he discharged the weapon into the chair between the victim's legs, missing him by inches. The man startled violently, then turned his head and threw up on the floor.

"Who's the senior man here?" Nelson asked the room. "Who's in charge of you pathetic bunch of suits?"

People huddled, frightened of the dreadful consequences of a wrong answer. No one spoke, and no one dared move with goons pointing guns at them from all around the room.

Nelson grabbed an attractive young girl in her twenties by the back of her hair and lifted her out of the chair. She cried out and tears streamed down her face. He stood behind her and tucked the gun into his pants. Then he pulled a smooth, surgically sharp knife from behind his back, held it to her throat and said, "Has anyone ever seen a live decapitation?"

"Noooo! *Please* don't hurt me," she plead. An awful anticipation hung in the air. The gruesome scene about to unfold in this nightmare was beyond imagination.

Still, no one answered, but one timid looking male office worker made eye contact with Nelson, then cast his gaze on Carlos Garcia, one of the firm's partners. Nelson took the hint. He released the girl and walked over to Garcia.

"Give me your wallet," he ordered, returning the knife to its sheath in the small of his back. Carlos immediately complied. Nelson first took all the cash and put it in his pocket, then he removed the driver's license. *"Carlos Garcia,"* he said. "As in *Hall Garcia and Barlow?*" Carlos remained stone faced, looking directly ahead, not answering.

Nelson ordered him, "Stand up, now, *thief.*" Carlos stood. He pointed his automatic and put a penetrating stare upon him. Then he softened into a philosophical posture, like a warped leader of some misguided cult. Charles Manson wouldn't have been scarier.

"Do you believe in God?" he asked like an evangelist.

"Will you have salvation through the acceptance of Jesus Christ into your heart?" He paused while everyone held their breath in dismay.

"Relax, your journey is complete and revelation will soon be yours. *I bring death,* and I shall deliver you from perdition into the kingdom of God, your savior. We will now hear your testimony. *Where is our cocaine?*"

The atmosphere in the room had turned surreal. People were open-mouthed in disbelief at this madness. He slowly lowered the muzzle of the gun, inches away from Carlos's thigh, and fixated his eyes upon him, like a snake on a rodent.

Carlos was sweating. Droplets ran down the side of his face and his upper lip trembled uncontrollably. He looked down at his injured colleague lying comatose in a widening circle of blood, only inches away.

"I'll count backwards from five," Nelson said. "If you hear the number one, *you're looking at your fate.* You better start talking, or I'll sacrifice you and every one of these sheep, if I have to. God has chosen me."

The reception lady finally snapped and shouted, "You know nothing about God, you sadistic little coward! How dare you invoke His name in this travesty? You're worse than a bunch of Nazi, skin-heads, you heathen bunch of devils... Damn you to hell!"

Nelson's face hardened, then he turned and instantly shot her through the middle of her forehead. She convulsed out of her chair, dropped to the floor and twitched once, before relaxing into a lifeless body. Her eyes were still wide open and saliva streamed grotesquely from her mouth. The on-lookers reacted with unified disbelief and revulsion. Women held their hands to their mouths. Men showed unimaginable fear and contempt on their faces.

"Anyone else?" Nelson addressed the room.

Carlos had been witnessing the slaughter of innocent employees, one by one, and he stood now on trembling legs, a puddle of warm urine pooling at his feet.

In a slow, calculated delivery, Nelson said, *"Where is our cocaine?"*

Bones was at the back door waiting patiently, as ordered. No one was to exit the building and he watched down the hall with his UZI machine pistol at the ready. What he wasn't watching for was someone *coming in* the back door. Silently, the Kings Crew biker slid the key into the deadbolt and turned it over. He and his three comrades entered the back hall of the stairwell. They were separated now by only a few feet from Bones, on the other side of the door to the office hallway. Very carefully they turned the door handle and looked through a narrow opening, seeing an armed man standing guard. With precision one man raised a Ruger 9mm fitted with an HTG silencer and fired once. Bones life ended instantly. With military stealth the four men worked their way through the building. They could hear crying and talking in the boardroom.

Nelson started his countdown: *Five... four...*

The bikers could see now through a glass wall that someone was holding a gun on their man, Carlos. They could see other bodies on the floor as well.

"Three... two...

"Wait! *I'll tell you everything.* Don't shoot me," Carlos begged.

"Make it fast," Nelson said. "Time's up," and he placed the muzzle of the gun in his victim's ear.

"The cocaine is being stored in grain bags marked *Wheat* on pallets in a warehouse."

"What warehouse? Where?" Nelson pressed him.

"It's called Driftwood Warehouse, in Burnaby. Unit fifteen." His voice was reduced to a trembling whisper and he looked ashen with dread.

"We'll go there together and see if you're right. God help you if you're lying," Nelson said.

Waiting no longer, the biker-hoods took decisive and deadly action. Two of them raised their weapons and fired together through the glass. The wall collapsed in a shower of disintegrating glass and Nelson dropped to his knees then fell face forward, his skull blown apart with two exit wounds the size of golf balls.

At the front door, Ice heard the exploding glass and came running down the hall. Seeing the four Kings Crew, he raised his weapon and trained it on them. Just as he fired two of the bikers returned gun shots and struck Ice in the chest. Now Ice was dead and one of the Crew had been hit also. Inside the board room it was chaos.

The remaining Red Sun Boys returned fire indiscriminately, hitting innocent employees in the crossfire, including a fatal volley from a machine pistol into Carlos Garcia's back. It was a chaotic barrage of bullets in both directions, sending the Crew-bikers in the Hall running for cover. There was screaming and some of the men struggled with Spike and Digger trying to disarm them. Others cowered under the table in fetal position, covering their heads with their hands. From the hall, the Kings Crew continued firing, and terrified hostages scrambled desperately for safety.

The front door of the building burst open and the six bikers stormed the scene, each flaunting an automatic weapon, not sure where to go or who to shoot at. Some started shooting blind, unsure of who was friend and who was foe.

In the turmoil, Jimmy grabbed the duffle bag and pulled out two pipe bombs, a foot long each, packed with C-4 plastic explosives, fire accelerant, and improvised deadly shrapnel. He twisted the cap, arming the fuse and lobbed one into the hall towards the front door. It rattled down the linoleum hallway to the reception area. Seconds later, a horrendous explosion ripped through the front office, killing or maiming three out of the six bikers who had just entered. The concussion of the blast blew out all the front windows of the structure in a dust cloud of shattered glass and twisted metal. A fire erupted where it detonated, sending a fog of choking, black smoke throughout the building. Chairs, tables, coat racks, and other furniture in the waiting area had been scattered and overturned as if a bar fight had broken out.

On the floor at the reception desk lay a broken, gold framed photo of Betty Dow smiling happily with her family, unaware of the life challenges she would face in the future, like having her brains blown out by a madman.

Rocky and Fats escaped the commotion and ran for the back door. Dominic was watching through his partially opened door, and just as they approached his office in the hall, he opened the door and shot his Colt .38 Special twice, in rapid succession. The rounds found their mark and both men dropped to the ground, gravely wounded and likely dead in moments. Then Dominic made good his escape and ran for the front door.

Now Spike's gun went off accidently as the two men struggled with him. He managed to break free and immediately shot one of them, point blank. The other one dove for cover behind some scattered chairs. Digger was not so lucky as one of his attackers swung a heavy glass water jug and clocked him squarely on the head with a debilitating blow. He fell to the floor, out cold and bleeding, possibly fatally struck.

Jimmy twisted the cap of another pipe bomb and tossed it into the hallway with a metallic *clack, clack, clack.*

"Take cover!" someone yelled, and the remaining bikers and hostages scattered in all directions. Another detonation sent a firestorm of fragmented metal, glass, nails, and ball bearings through the walls and ceiling, killing hapless victims who weren't fast enough to get out of the way. The building was a maelstrom of bedlam, wreckage, spattered blood, and death. Electrical wires had been exposed and were sparking wildly, fires were burning with searing intensity from a ruptured gas line, and people were screaming hysterically, *"Oh my God! Oh my God!"* The overhead water sprinklers had turned on, and steam was hissing madly from a bullet grazed heat radiator. This was a scene of hell on earth.

Jimmy and Spike were all that remained of the original group now and Jimmy motioned his cohort to follow him. Bodies, rubble, and carnage lay everywhere. Running past a fallen biker still showing signs of fight, Spike plugged him once midline and he slumped back, hands gripped, claw-like at his chest. Deep red blood bubbled from his lips, pursed in agony, malice, and regret. He surrendered a final breath, gurgling deeply from his blood-filled lungs, and then just stared blankly through lifeless eyes, dead.

Together Jimmy and Spike scurried down the hall to the back door and slipped out, running full tilt once their feet hit the pavement. The sirens of police and emergency vehicles were wailing off in the distance.

They had escaped, amazingly, and if their Intel was correct, they knew where their drugs were being held.

CHAPTER 19

THE CAB PULLED up in front of the Ocean Plaza Building in Panama City, where the offices of Diaz, Cordoba & Del Rio were located. Mat and Adriana approached the building eagerly anticipating their meeting with Marcos Del Rio. Entering the law firm's offices, they were greeted by a pretty Latino girl behind a reception desk. She was clad in a flowery dress suitably styled to the sunny, warm climate of the region. She smiled genially and said, "¡Bien venidos! ¿Cómo puedo ayudarles hoy?"

Mat struggled to reply, "Lo siento… No habla español."

"Ah," the attractive receptionist said. "Welcome, my friends. How can I help you?" She spoke with a thick accent, but her English was much better than Mat's Spanish.

Mat replied, "Thank you. Mat Crawford to see Mr. Del Rio. I have an appointment."

"Certainly," and she pressed some keys on her PBX console. "Yes, I have a Mr. Crawford to see you," she spoke into her wireless headset. Alright, sir."

"He'll be right out," she advised Mat and Adriana.

In a few minutes a mid-forties man, smartly dressed in a tailored light tan suit with salt and pepper hair appeared from a corridor. He wore a crisply ironed shirt, silk tie, and soft brown,

Gucci loafers. He looked to be in the prime of his career, first-class, successful, affluent. Mat deduced from his appearance alone that business was good.

"Mr. Crawford. I'm Marcos Del Rio. Welcome to Panama City," he said with a Spanish inflection and a pleasant tone, extending his hand.

Mat reciprocated and replied, "Thanks, we've only been here a few days and we love your city already. This is my associate, Adriana Santos."

"Very pleased to meet you, my lady," Marcos replied. "¡Bienvenida."

Del Rio nodded to the receptionist. *"Gracias, Tesoro."*

"Right this way. We have much to discuss, my friends," Marcos said, gesturing to the hallway. He led his two new clients to his office and officially assumed his place behind a large desk constructed of a rich exotic wood, with a matching credenza behind. Glass floor-to-ceiling windows formed two of his office walls, and there was a buttery leather sofa and an overstuffed chair with a marble coffee table in another corner of the room.

An original oil painting of the Panama City skyline as viewed from the harbor hung from an adjoining wall. Behind his desk hung his Bachelor's, Master's, and Law Degrees, nicely framed in black and gold, along with a picture of him shaking hands with Manuel Noriega, while each smiled towards the camera for a staged photo op. His credentials, experience, and expertise were self-evident. Once they were all seated, his office door opened and Tesoro entered, carrying a tray with coffee, tea, cream and sugar.

"My guests, please have a refreshment," Mr. Del Rio said, extending his hand towards the decanters. Adriana reached across and poured Mat and her a cup of hot tea.

Mat started the conversation. "Mr. Del Rio, you understand that we are interested in setting up a *Guatemalan Trust Account* to shelter a large amount of money. Are you certain that this type of arrangement meets the criteria we discussed by phone?"

"Yes, of course. We have many clients from the US and Canada, as well as other parts of the world, who use this type of investment vehicle to ensure the confidentiality and privacy of their wealth and savings," Marcos assured them. He leaned forward and filled a cup with coffee.

"Adriana said, "I think I understand how it all works, but can you run the salient features of this trust agreement by me again?"

Marcos obliged the request willingly. "Of course, I'd be happy to. First, our firm is situated in Panama, but due to the uniquely stringent laws in Guatemala protecting bank record privacy, and attorney client confidentiality, we conduct this transaction in Guatemala.

"Quite simply, we become the *trustee*, for you, the *beneficiary*, however we act under your advice, control, and direction. As we discussed, we form a Guatemalan corporation — an *Empressa*, then set up a trust account to manage it's affairs. The trust account will be opened under our firm's name, not yours. Attorney client privilege will guard the privacy of your affairs and is a sacredly held relationship throughout Central America, particularly so in Guatemala. In legal and practical terms, nobody could force us to reveal your name or involvement with the account in any way."

"And you've done this before? And it's withstood scrutiny from outsiders?" Adriana asked.

Marcos smiled confidently as he answered, "Miss Santos, this is a *specialty of practice* for our firm, and one reason, among others, that Panama is an international banking centre. Nobody wants to expose their wealth unnecessarily to gratuitous taxation or examination by outside parties."

"Taxation is the least of our concerns," Adriana commented. "It's more the *examination by outside parties thing* we're hedging against."

Marcos Del Rio was very sincere and very convincing. "We understand your skepticism, but we know what we're doing. The privacy of your financial affairs is our first priority, and we can do it within the law."

The three discussed the details of the agreement at length, Adriana focusing on the fine points of legality, and Mathew on the assurances of impenetrability by outsiders. In the end, it was as secure an arrangement as could be hoped for and Mat said, "Well, I'm satisfied that we can proceed. We'll start transferring funds to the account as soon as I return to Canada. Marcos? Adriana? Do we all agree? Do we have a deal?"

"Sí señor, es excelente. Vamos a empezar!" Marcos enthused. *Yes sir. This is excellent. Let's get started!* "We can proceed at your direction. I have all the documentation ready and with some signatures and seals we can formalize the agreement today."

The requisite passport and driver's license verification of Mathew's identity was completed, all contracts were duly signed and executed, and Mat and Adriana left the meeting sharing a sense of accomplishment that a plan was under way. A good plan, that would work, without any surprises, they hoped.

Back in Canada, the first call Mat would be making would be to Mr. Hyman Wexler. Mat had a deposit and wire transfer he'd like to make ASAP. $5.2 million and change, to be exact.

✠ ✠ ✠

Wo Shing Chu had sold the cocaine to the Red Sun Boys on terms and conditions not unlike those of any trader of commodities on world markets. They were criminals, but they were also businessmen and expected their buyers to adhere to the terms of the agreement. Five million up front, and five million on delivery, no questions, no deviations from the agreement. A deposit, then the rest C.O.D. upon arrival in Vancouver. Standard procedures of trade and commerce among buyers and sellers, anywhere.

In truth, the Red Sun Boys had passed themselves off as bigger operators than they were and they had underestimated the clout that Wo Shing Chu had on a global scale. The criminal syndicate from China had operations around the world and could accurately be referred to as the Chinese mafia. They were well organized, richly funded, integrated with legal business and government through bribery, pay offs and extortion, and had the ability to do just about anything, anywhere, anytime they wanted.

The Red Sun Boys were a bunch of penny ante criminals who managed to raise the first five million through robberies, cargo theft, drug sales, and buttlegging or cigarette smuggling, but the balance of payment, another five million, wasn't something that they had readily on hand. Their roughly calculated plan was to sell the cocaine fast, stall for time, and make payment through the proceeds. Contrasting the business-like procedures followed by Wo Shing Chu, the Red Sun Boys were a gang of Asian thugs and hoods operating in the underworld of the West Coast, and came by their alias of *Sewer Rats* honestly, in a manner of speaking

Understandably, when word filtered back that the drugs had gone missing and the Red Sun Boys were hedging on paying the balance owing, Wo Shing Chu recognized that this was a past due receivable and it was time to put the matter to collection. Being thirty days delinquent with them was the same as defaulting on payment to a loan shark with the mob. It was suicidal.

There was the matter of the money, yes, but additionally, there was the issue of *precedent*. If word circled the globe that a small time gang of hoodlums in Canada had pulled one over on the infamous Wo Shing Chu, it would be an invitation for larger, better organized crime syndicates to target them as well. The world proliferates with groups like the Russian, Italian, and Indian Mafias, the Japanese Yakuza, Mexican and Columbian drug cartels, and even terrorist organizations like Al-Qaeda and Hamas, all of whom have a need for large scale funding through untraceable, and therefore illegal, sources. Wo Shing Chu is one supplier of capital to such groups and cannot afford negative press in the criminal world. And so, the Red Sun Boys were in line for a *fireside chat* about the importance of honoring contracts and paying their bills promptly, or else. In short, they had failed payment by purchasing a Ferrari on a Hyundai budget, and now the bailiff was at their door.

The Red Sun gang conducted most of their activities on the streets, however they did maintain a business office, under a loose definition of the term, at the Hotel East on Gore Avenue, Chinatown. It amounted to a rundown room with a sink and a toilette at the back of the building that would never rent out to any regular guest seeking accommodation, so, for a nominal fee, the gang paid to have a private place to meet and plan their high jinks. Wo Shing Chu had this address, as well as the last known addresses of several of the kingpins of the gang.

Leaving the Vancouver airport for Chinatown, Ming Kang and Huang Ku, the leaders of the group from Hong Kong, had decided that violence and bloodshed were remedies of last resort and they would first try and collect the five million peacefully.

Jimmy Yang sat in the office, still stunned by the melee he had just survived. He was contemplating whether today's mission was a failure, due to the loss of Nelson Hi Wo and several other gang members, or a success due to the disclosure by Carlos Garcia of where the drugs were being stored. It didn't go down the way anyone would have predicted, and nobody wanted as much bloodshed as it produced, but it was done now and couldn't be changed. Even Jimmy, a hardened criminal himself, felt remorse over the extent of cruelty and cold blooded killing that took place. He wondered whether their organization was better off with, or without Nelson Hi Wo. In any event, he hoped that the cocaine would be where Carlos claimed it was.

Everybody knew that a stash of cocaine of that magnitude would have to be kept somewhere safe, secluded, and disguised in some way. Nobody would be interested in bags of grain in a warehouse and considering the duress that Carlos was under at the time, it was doubtful that he would have had the guts or imagination to make up a lie. They would have to go and get the drugs themselves before they could be certain. Carlos Garcia was dead now, so he couldn't tip off anyone to rush out and move the stash, but nevertheless, Jimmy would mount up a team of gang members and go to retrieve the treasure posthaste.

A knock at the door caused Jimmy to snap out of his musings. At first he was wary slightly, but he then considered that the knock was soft and unthreatening so he crossed the room and carefully opened the door, with the chain still attached for security. In the hall stood Ming Kang and Huang Ku. Jimmy knew who they were, although he wasn't expecting them. He had no real choice in the matter but to welcome them in with false hospitality. Ming and Huang entered the office, followed by four husky, armed body guards. They looked like Sumo wrestlers in suits.

The Red Sun Boys had no respect or concern for Caucasians or the general public, no matter what their race or creed, and felt no compulsion to treat them with fairness, dignity, or honor. They were merely pawns to be manipulated in the pursuit of wealth and power by the Red Sun gang. Among Asians, however, there was an unwritten hierarchy, and Wo Shing Chu were clearly a cast well above these boys. Jimmy was obliged to treat these emissaries with utmost esteem if he expected any chance of living what you might call a normal life again, or for that matter, living — period.

The conversation took place entirely in Cantonese.

"Mr. Yang, hello. I hope you and your family are well," Ming said.

"Hello. Yes, we are all fine. We weren't aware you were coming to Canada. Welcome. Please come in and have a seat. Would you like anything? A drink?" Jimmy showed the two men in and they all sat around a small table with wooden chairs with false cordiality.

Now Huang spoke. "I'm afraid this isn't a social visit, Mr. Yang. You have defaulted on payment for the product we sold you. This violates the terms of our agreement. You dishonor us."

Jimmy tried to explain. "There's been a complication. We never received the shipment. It was stolen en route and we have been trying ever since to recover it. We didn't expect to have this problem."

Huang and Ming looked briefly at each other, then Ming spoke. "*We* don't have a problem. *You* have a problem, and our agreement made no provisions for such matters. You will pay us now, or you will suffer the consequences. It's our custom. It's business."

Jimmy spoke as if he were addressing a superior. "Understood. We ask that you be generous and tolerant after you hear the whole story."

"Speak."

With humility and respect, Jimmy gave the details. "We have learned that the shipment was diverted by the freighter's captain, after he was bribed by another gang, the Kings Crew. He paid for his treachery with his life. Then, just today we learned where the drugs are being held. I was just planning to gather a team to go and retrieve them, when you arrived. As it stands, we have a little liquidity problem. We have to sell the product before we can pay for it. If you can graciously grant us an extension, we can retrieve what's rightfully ours and sell it, then pay for it, as originally agreed."

Ming was visibly angry and replied, "Originally agreed?" He paused like he was repressing an outburst of rage.

"There was never any mention that you had to *sell the cocaine* before you could make payment," he said emphatically. "You were to pay us the balance of five million when the freighter reached port. Now you say the drugs are stolen and you don't have the money? That's not our problem and not how we do business. You'll be lucky if your entire family isn't executed for such deception." He stared down Jimmy like a cruel head master in a boy's reform school.

"I humbly ask your forgiveness," Jimmy replied. "Please allow us some latitude. *We will make payment.* We just need some time. Or, if you prefer, we will return the product to you when we find it."

"First, it's not *when* you find it, it's *if* you find it. And we don't want the drugs returned to us. We're not Walmart. We want *our money.* If we return to China without it, we will look like fools."

"We meant you no disrespect. This just got out of control and we've been trying to solve the problem. We're making progress. Please, indulge us some time."

Ming and Huang sat quietly as an uncomfortable air hung in the room like a foul smell in a public bathroom. Jimmy hoped that the silence meant that he would be spared. Finally, Ming said, "If we grant you some time, you must give us *something for something… A favor for a favor.*"

If there was to be an extension of time granted for payment, it would have to be on a basis of *quid pro quo,* a common bargaining tactic among the Chinese, allowing the aggrieved party to botched a business transaction an opportunity to save face.

"Sir, what favor can we provide?" Jimmy asked.

"The terms of payment have been contravened. If you want an extension, we will grant you thirty days. In return, you will pay a balance of *$7.5 million.*" Ming waited, arms folded across his chest, with cold patience.

"$2.5 million for thirty days?" Jimmy asked incredulously.

"Take it, or leave it," Ming said. Huang looked on disapprovingly.

Jimmy had no real choice. His guests could have enough China men here in a matter of days to rebuild the Canadian

Pacific Railway. If he declined such an offer, Wo Shing Chu had influence around the world and could have an army assembled before Monday that could wipe out the Red Sun gang, all their families, all their friends, and most police officers that might get in the way, easily. Reluctantly, he agreed, with a false smile.

"Very well. We will not disappoint you. Thank you for your generosity and kindness," Jimmy said.

Ming and Huang stood and Jimmy did as well. The three men faced each other and bowed from the waist. The meeting was concluded and new terms had been agreed upon. There would be no second chances again. As the two men and their four guards left his office, Jimmy immediately picked up the phone and started calling for backup. They were going to find the cocaine at once.

CHAPTER 20

IT WAS 6:45, Tuesday evening, local time in Vancouver when Max Wexler's phone rang. Glancing at the call display before answering Wexler noticed that all it said was *Out of Country*.

"Hello?"

"Mr. Wexler. Mat Crawford. How are you, my friend?"

"Mat, I'm fine. It's wonderful to hear from you. Has everything gone according to plan?"

Mat and Wexler had met and talked over the particulars of this deal well prior to Mat's trip to Panama. Mat had not forgotten Max's offer years ago to participate if Mat ever happened across an opportunity to make some big money on the sly. The two of them had shaken hands on an agreement for Wexler to deposit the money at his bank for immediate and covert transfer to the Panamanian law firm of Diaz, Cordoba & Del Rio.

It was a win-win arrangement. Mat got the cash through the *placement* stage of the money laundering process and ready to be transferred into the accounts of the *Empressa*. Mr. Wexler manipulated the deposit and wire transfer records at the bank late at night, erasing any evidence of the transactions, and eliminating the requirement of reporting *large sum deposits* to FINTRAC.

Both Mathew and Max would earn their respective fees in the process, making them each quite wealthy. The first installment of some five point two five million was ready to be put through the laundering procedures. They would eventually incorporate it back into the mainstream capital of the Canadian economy, and into the eager hands of the Kings Crew.

Mat responded to Wexler's question. "Well, the 'plan' is an evolving thing, I'm finding. But yes, everything is proceeding along nicely. I can have the package delivered to you whenever you give the *go ahead*. Are you ready to do magic on your end?"

"I can be by the day after tomorrow. How much are we talking about?"

"A little over five point two mil."

"Very good. Have it delivered to the back door in the alley at 2:00 in the morning and it'll all be done well before opening time in the morning."

"Sounds like a plan," Mathew replied. "Max, listen... *Be careful.* I know I'm wasting my breath and I have complete confidence in your abilities, but I don't have to remind you of the dangers involved here."

"No, you don't. And don't worry about me. I wouldn't be doing this if I thought the risk wasn't worth the reward. You watch your own back, Son, and let me do my part of the job. We're good?"

"Yes sir. We're good, always."

The next phone call Mathew would be making was to Foley to make arrangements for the cash to be delivered to the location designated by Mr. Wexler. Foley's cell phone vibrated on his hip as he was driving home from a grueling workout at the gym. He was a big man naturally, but it was no accident that he was extraordinarily fit. He managed his diet scrupulously, trained on weights, ran laps on the track, practiced karate at a local club, and took exceptional care of his health. With his physique, knowledge, and credentials, he could easily qualify as a personal trainer, among the best.

Like Wexler, Foley's display read, *Out of Country*.

"Hello, Foley speakin'."

"Hey, Foley. It's Mat."

"Mat who?"

"*Christ…* Mat Dillon from Gunsmoke, who do ya think, ya hammerhead!"

Foley chuckled. "Oh, Bucky, I was gettin' worried about you. You managing to stay outta trouble down there?"

"Ya, I'm a magnet for trouble back home but down here, all I've been doing is working – around the clock," Mat lied. "I'm just on my way back to the hotel, so I can only talk a minute or two. Listen, we're ready to start moving the money. Can you get it over to Wexler's bank at about two in the morning, Thursday? Take it to the back door in the alley, and I don't have to add, *be careful!*"

"Ya, I will. You know me. I take it you're planning on staying down there for a while yet. You talked to that law firm and everything's on the up 'n up?" Foley queried.

"You bet. It looks fool proof, as long as we get the money placed into Wexler's bank and transferred here pronto, and without anything unexpected," Mat assured his partner. "One other thing. You better contact Jack Kincaid and let him know that it's under way. We haven't talked in a few days and he may be getting antsy. Tell him to reassure his cohorts that the laundering process is in progress and they'll have their money in due course."

"Done. You want me to contact that lawyer gal of his and tell her as well? Jack seems to wanna keep her nose in this whole business too," Foley asked.

Mat paused before answering. While he wasn't planning on mentioning that Adriana Santos was down there with him, he didn't want to lie to his friend either.

"Well, actually, that won't be necessary," Mat waffled.

"Why not?"

"She's... here, sort of."

There was a long silence on the other end of the line, then Foley started to laugh a *knowing laugh.*

"I thought so. You and she had this whole thing planned as a little tête-à-tête, didn't you? I thought there were some sparks between you two. Don't try and fool old Foley, you cunning little schemer. I'm like a bloodhound on an escaped prisoner in Louisiana. You should know that by now."

"No, you got it wrong! She just showed up. I didn't ask her to come."

"But you didn't send her home either."

"How could I do that? Anyways, she's smart and talented, and we're getting a lot done here, together," Mat defended himself, poorly.

"I can imagine what you're *getting done,* together son," Foley carried on. "I'm curious. Did you... ah, accomplish anything of merit with her yet... *sort of?*"

Even put in Foley's unique lexicon, Mat knew exactly what he was driving at.

"Foley, for Christ's Sake!" Mat complained. "I don't have to explain myself to you! She's here, we're putting the deal together with the law firm, and okay, maybe there's some chemistry between us. You'd do well to get a woman of your own so you didn't have to watch over me like some perverted voyeur."

Foley wanted to boast, just a little, about his adventure and escapades with Crystal Waters. *No time like the present,* he decided.

"Geeze, touchy! Sorry if I hit a sore spot there, buddy. Listen, my cell phone is running low. I'm down to one chiclet so I can't talk long, but here's some news for you too. Some goons broke into Jack Kincaid's office — roughed up the secretary pretty bad tryin' to get information out of her. She's gonna be alright, in time, but I've got her bunked down and resting at my place."

Mat interrupted, "Who were they? What were they looking for?"

"They were an Asian group of young thugs, though they didn't have the courtesy of introducing themselves properly. They had some cock 'n bull story about someone stealing a stash of cocaine from them. Crystal was the only one there at the time and they slapped her around pretty good... and did some *other* stuff."

"What kinda stuff?"

"The kinda stuff that brings payback, if anyone objects to punks brutalizing and raping a good woman."

"*Here we go.* Who did ya kill this time, Foley?"

"Some little Oriental Fauntleroy in expensive clothes who came at me like Jackie Chan in a *roid rage.* Meaner than a cornered badger. Stabbed me right through the forearm with a switchblade, though it didn't do much damage. I had no choice but to send him to his maker, and two others who got in my face when I simply knocked on the door. I banged their noggins together and one of 'em died on the spot. The other one escaped with just a bad headache I think, lucky for him."

"Perfect. Can you get through a day without getting into a bloodbath with someone? What about the bodies?

"Gone."

"And Crystal? Did she tell them anything?"

"She doesn't know anything."

"Don't count on it. She's Kincaid's assistant. He may have let her in on some of the details, one way or another. Think about Danielle. She knows more about our business than we do."

219

"Well, certainly more than you do, but that's another discussion. Anyways, Crystal told me she didn't tell them *squat* about anything. And I believe her," Foley added. "Oh, and by the way? She won't be movin' outta here, anytime soon. We kinda hit it off together, so you're in good company if you're thinkin' you're some kinda James Bond ladies' man."

"Well, I'm glad something good came out of it. So you and her *hit it off?* What does that mean, Casanova? Come clean, did ya get a little?"

"A little what?" Foley sounded defensive.

Mat was laughing now. "You know… did ya, *do the nasty*, or have ya even felt 'er up yet?"

"A gentleman never kisses and tells, young fellow. And I'm a little disappointed you'd even ask such a blunt and vulgar question, frankly," Foley replied, indignantly.

Mat burst out laughing and guffawed at the hypocrisy. "What? You asked me, but I can't ask you? And I'll take that as a *No.* You've probably fooled her into thinking you're a *really nice guy.*"

Foley defended himself. "Well, this is different. She ain't just some cheap tart and she was hurt, bad. Brutalized beyond sanity, and I helped her. You'd have done the same. She's a special lady, Buck, and I care about 'er. You would too, in my boots."

"In your *shorts*, more like it. Ah, that's beautiful. *She completes you!* He offered his honor, and she honored his offer, and all night long, he was on 'er and off 'er!" Mat mused aloud.

"Very funny. Now you're *a poet*. Bad one, at that."

"Hey look, we can catch up on each other's love lives later. I'm in the hotel parking lot now, so I better go," Mat said.

"Wait, there's more. And this part ain't good," Foley pressed on. There was some kind of invasion down at the accounting firm where those two Kings Crew guys worked. One of 'em is dead and the other has gone missing. It was all over the papers and covered on the TV news. There'll be less damage on judgment day, I swear. Looked like a scene outta *Terminator Two*. A bloody massacre. Bikers and china men shot dead and blown to hell everywhere. Explosions and fires and burst water pipes, smoke, hysterical screaming, blood, bodies — the works. A lot of innocent office workers got caught up in it too. The whole building may be a write off. No one's sure what exactly happened, but a survivor reported that there was talk of missing cocaine, and that they coerced a confession outta one of the hostages before they strafed him dead with machine gun fire."

"What? This is turning into a disaster. The cops will be having a convention at the Hyatt over this," Mat shot back.

"Ya, well, I think I might have told you this was a bad idea from the get go, but what do I know?"

"Wait, you said they coerced a confession out of him? A confession about what?"

"About where the drugs were being hidden, what da ya think? Cops wouldn't give any more details than that to the media."

"Damn! If those scheming little rats steal back the cocaine there won't be any more money to launder. This was supposed to be the big one, the *last* one."

Mat paused momentarily for thought, then added, "Foley, call Kincaid and tell him to pull in whatever money is on the street, *now*. This caper may get stopped in its tracks before its barely gotten started.

"No problem. I'll call him soon as we're done here."

Mat made one more inquiry. *"Hey Fole,* one last thing. Did you manage to find out anything about Christine and Hannah?"

Mat paused, waiting for a reply. *"Fole? Foley? Hey buddy, you there?"*

Foley heard the question, but pretended his cell phone was dead and the connection was lost. He pressed the *end* key. "That one will have to wait 'til later, Buddy."

CHAPTER 21

A DAY EARLIER, Jimmy Yang had assembled a group of gang members to proceed to the Driftwood Warehouse, in Burnaby. According to Carlos Garcia, the coke that would buy the gang out of a shitload of trouble was stored there on pallets. The stolen Hummer H2 that they drove accommodated four of them easily with an assortment of weaponry on their laps and in the cargo hold, just in case. Following behind was a Dodge RAM 2500 pick up, with suitable payload capacity to transport the product – bags and bags of cocaine.

As they pulled up to the warehouse facility, Turk and Foggy jumped out early with a semi-automatic each and skirted both sides of the building in case there was a trap. Jimmy and Shade waited with the engine running and slowly backed away from the building, keeping their field of vision clear in all directions. Moments later the two scouts appeared around each side of the building and signaled a thumbs up to their comrades. Jimmy pulled ahead and parked the Hummer close to a loading dock. In the pick up, Moe and Ripper waited on the far side of the parking lot near an exit point.

With the aide of an acetylene torch and a crowbar the entrance door was easily dismantled, after the overhead phone lines had been cut to disable the security system. These boys were career criminals and had graduated basic training school, including *Break and Enter 101,* a long time ago.

Flashlights in hand, the search for a pallet of grain bags was quickly underway. The men stood inside the doorway looking around nervously.

Jimmy gave the orders in Cantonese. "Alright, each of us will cover one quarter of this building. It's two stories high, so we do the ground floor first, then we move upstairs. Turk, you do the back left wall to the centre point and cover everything forward to the middle. Fog, you do the same, only start on the back right wall. I'll do the front left wall to the middle, and Shade you start at the front right wall. Be thorough boys. If the stuff is here, we gotta find it!" The four men fanned out in all directions.

It was getting close to midnight and four blocks away, Constable Casey Murdoch was patrolling his usual beat in a police cruiser. Nothing noteworthy had occurred on his rounds in over three months and while he wasn't exactly complacent, he may not have been described as *sharp as a tack* either. He sipped a 'coffee to go' from Tim's, forgoing the usual Boston cream doughnut to counteract his expanding waistline from sitting in a police car six hours a day. He would do a quick run through the Driftwood Industrial Park just to make sure everything looked normal. Over his police radio he listened to the usual drone of a female dispatcher's impassionate voice describing a litany of car accidents, domestic disputes, a liquor store hold up, and an altercation near the Steam Clock in Gastown, with nearby cruisers responding as required. Business as usual, no shortage of customers.

Murdoch had put in twenty three years and was looking forward to retirement soon, so he wasn't about to go searching for trouble at this point of his career. *I'll do my job, but that's it. Nothing to prove and a whole lot to lose by sticking my neck out unnecessarily,* he privately said to himself. He steered the cruiser down Beta Avenue proceeding at a lazy speed, trolling for any irregularities or bad guys.

Back in the warehouse, the boys had been searching for close to ten minutes when Turk hollered, "Hallelujah, the lord taketh away, and the lord giveth back! I hit pay dirt, girls."

224

Jimmy Yang, working maybe twenty feet away from him, responded, "Shut up! You sound like that crazy religious bastard, Nelson Hi Wo. He nearly got us all killed today!"

"Well come look at what's under this tarp. These are grain bags, alright, but I slit one with my knife and look what's here. It's coke!"

The four hoods quickly assembled in front of the two pallets with grain bags marked *Wheat,* just as Carlos Garcia had said.

"So he wasn't lying," one of the gang members remarked about Garcia.

"Of course he wasn't. He was so scared he was pissin' his pants, and you would be too if that lunatic Hi Wo was holding a gun on you," Jimmy replied. "We better not stall. Get all these bags out to the truck *Chicken Louie,* and let's clear outta here. Move!"

Constable Murdoch turned the corner just in time to see the Dodge Ram pickup pull across the parking lot and back up to the loading dock. *Odd. No lights around the building, no signage on the truck, and why do a warehouse run at midnight?* He thought to himself. *Better call it in.*

"Dispatch, unit 421."

"Go ahead 421."

"Checking a possible *B 'n E* at Driftwood Warehouse on Beta Avenue. Suspicious activity around a loading dock. Probably nothing."

"Roger that. Do you want backup, just to be safe?"

"Not yet. If it gets ugly I'll transmit again," Murdoch answered, breaking the cops' protocol of *take no chances,* and the policeman slowly pulled the cruiser towards the loading dock.

By now, Moe and Ripper in the pick up noticed the police car approaching and made a hand signal recognized by the gang members that meant *police.*

Jimmy cursed in native tongue, "Shit! Now the fuckin' heat is at the door. Turk, hide behind those cargo boxes," pointing to some containers near the door of the building. "If it goes bad, fire at my signal. Remember, he'll be wearing body armor, so go for the legs." Turk took his position, readying his MAC-10 machine pistol. "The rest of you, keep working like there's no problem, and I'll try and talk our way outta this."

According to plan, the men worked in an orderly fashion, carrying grain bags from the two pallets to the back of the pick up. Constable Murdoch pulled up to the scene. He stepped out of the vehicle, engine still running, and walked toward the loading dock. He attempted to pull up his pants, but they stalled at the overhang of his paunch.

"Evening Fellas. Can I ask what you're doing here tonight?"

Jimmy spoke up in English. "Hello, offica'. We just pick up grain bein' trucked Alberta first thing tomorrow morning."

"You in charge here?" The officer inquired.

"Not really, but dey tink I am, so I keep givin' da order," and he smiled. The others laughed at the attempted humor.

"Maybe I'll have you break out some ID for me, sir," Murdoch continued.

First, Jimmy Yang didn't even have ID, aside from a lengthy rap sheet downtown and the deportation papers he had been issued a long time ago. He wasn't even licensed to drive in Canada, and if this cop ever actually made him, he'd be locked up faster than Paul Bernardo.

"Sorry, no can do dat. No tink we have any trouble with law tonight. My wallet at home." The others kept loading the pick up. One pallet was almost empty.

Jimmy's demeanor turned serious. "D'ere no problem here, sir. We just finish job so we get home for good night rest? It late now."

"What's your name, son, and where do you live?"

"I live Alberta – Calgary. Just visit friend here."

"This your truck?" the officer continued.

"Ya," Jimmy replied, knowing almost instantly that that was the wrong answer. The truck had stolen British Columbia license plates, *and he'd just said he lived in Alberta?*

Officer Murdoch took out a small coil spring notebook and wrote down the BC license plate numbers of the pick up and Hummer. This wasn't going well.

"I'll have you all step down from that platform please and wait right here," pointing to the brick wall of the building. One by one the boys complied with his command. He reached down and withdrew his SIG P226 service pistol, as he reached for the *push to talk* button on his shoulder mounted radio.

In a snap decision, Jimmy whipped out the handgun he had tucked in the waistband of his pants, at the small of his back, and met the officer's challenge. The others followed suit. Constable Murdoch was now facing five handguns pointed with intent at his head and legs as the boys quickly started to spread out, covering him from all angles.

"Don' touch radio, asshole!" Jimmy shouted. "Drop yo' fuckin' piece, now!"

At all the commotion, Turk stepped from behind his hiding place and leveled his weapon on the officer, whose training and experience told him was a rapid fire machine pistol. He was out numbered and out gunned. Slowly he bent over and set his gun to the ground.

"Fellas, you don't want to do this — killing a police officer." Murdoch didn't have the words or stomach to continue, but he was in no frame of mind to be a hero. In two years he'd be vested of his career service duty and retired with full benefits and pension, if this didn't prove to be his last day alive. How scared he really was right now would only be verified on laundry day.

"Do as you tol' and maybe, just maybe, you come out dis alive. Now, over here, fat guy," Jimmy ordered pointing to the inside of the building. "What you? Model for *before picture*, L.A. Weight Loss advertisement?" Jimmy's cohorts laughed.

There were metal floor to ceiling racks designed to hold stacks of pallets and storage bins. The portly officer obeyed without resistance.

"Now *you break out* handcuffs and attach yo'self to dese rack, big shot," Jimmy demanded. "Tell *me* break out some I.D., asshole. You only know who I am, who we are. You don' control us, we *tolerate* you, long as you stay out our way!" The officer attached one cuff to his own wrist and the other to the metal rack. Jimmy searched him, took the handcuff keys, and pulled the radio off his shoulder, then he bound the man's mouth with mover's carton tape, several times around his head. Task complete, he cuffed the back of his head with a disciplinary *dumb ass* slap and commented, "Sit tight, flatfoot. You no goin' nowhere."

"Be tankful I no put few strand of dis around yo' nose too. Be kinda hard breath, yes?"

Officer Murdoch's forehead was glistening with perspiration and he shuddered with the thought of suffocation. With the acrylic tape, Jimmy tightly bound his arms and legs and entire body again, and again, around the racks making it impossible for the officer to move a muscle. Jimmy had immobilized him like a bug all wound up in a spider's web. He was gagged, handcuffed, and hog tied and wouldn't be going anywhere until someone else found him.

The boys resumed the job at hand. In Cantonese, Jimmy ordered, "Moe, get in that cruiser and pull it around the far side of the building, outta sight. Turn off the engine. The rest of you, finish loading this pick up and we roll this candy back where it belongs!"

In the police car, Moe heard the radio, but didn't know who the dispatcher was trying to talk to.

She said, "Unit 421, please report the status of your possible B and E. 421, do you copy? 421, what's your twenty, please?"

Although Moe didn't get it, central dispatch already knew something had gone wrong at the Driftwood Warehouse with Constable Casey Murdoch, and backup was on the way.

The Dodge pick up now held all of the phony grain bags in its cargo box, and Moe and Ripper started pulling away from the warehouse. Jimmy Yang and his three companions jumped into the Hummer. Jimmy turned the key and ignited a controlled explosion of V8 power under the hood until the engine growled into a steady idle. He banged the tranny into drive and hit the gas, creating a G-force that momentarily pinned all of them into their seats. As they left the parking lot, at the far end of the street another police cruiser was approaching with two occupants. The blue and red LED lightbars immediately activated on the cruiser's roof and front grill.

"Ah, kiss my ass. Not *again!*" Jimmy cussed.

The Dodge had been leading the way, but Moe hit the brakes and Jimmy sped past him towards the police car. Jimmy hammered it and aimed the Hummer straight at the approaching car. In less than a city block the vehicle reached a speed of nearly a hundred kilometers per hour, and the faces of the two cops registered sheer terror at the prospect of a head on collision with this SUV on steroids.

Reflexively, the cop driving yanked the wheel to the right at the last possible second, and as the Hummer sped by it clipped the cruiser's tail section, sending a rear quarter panel careening into the air. The Dodge and Hummer were in full flight now, and each nearly took the corner on two wheels.

After a brief pause, the officer driving slammed his own foot down, and the cruiser fish tailed into a screeching pursuit amidst clouds of burning rubber and blue smoke. The passenger cop had the radio mic in his hand feverishly advising dispatch of the situation.

Jimmy knew that they didn't have much time before half the cops in Vancouver would be upon them. Handing his cell phone to Turk he yelled, "Quick, call Moe!"

In the pick up following behind, Moe's cell phone rang and the display indicated who was calling. "Ya, talk…" he answered.

"Tell Ripper to throw everything you've got at those bastards. We've gotta take 'em out, now!" Turk shouted in Cantonese.

"Gotcha."

Moments later, with the police cruiser on the chase and closing, Ripper reached out the window with a sawed off shot gun and fired three rounds of buckshot at the officers' windshield. Exploding glass and disabled roof lights were the result, but the car didn't slow down. These cops were young, full of fight, and pissed that some petty criminals would *dis* their authority so blatantly. All three vehicles were now mingling with other traffic and Jimmy started swerving and weaving in and out of an oncoming stream of cars. Moe followed his lead and did the same. With millions of dollars worth of drugs in the back of the pick up, getting captured was simply not an option to the fleeing Red Sun Boys. After a felony of this magnitude, they'd have nothing better to look forward to than three hots and a cot for the rest of their days.

This time, Ripper grabbed the crowbar used earlier in the evening to break into the warehouse, and banged out the rear pane of glass in the pickup. He pointed and shot right through the open back window of the cab with a Tec-9 pistol, illegally converted to a fully automatic capability. In a matter of seconds, the fifty round magazine was empty. The cop car following swerved erratically left and right with screaming tires and the windshield plastered with bullet holes and shatter lines. Miraculously, the officers didn't appear to be hit as their heads popped up from below the dashboard once the firing stopped.

"Take out the tires," Moe yelled. Ripper reloaded with a fresh clip.

"I can't get a good shot from this angle. I need a shot from the side."

"Okay, hang on. I'm turning on the boulevard. Wait for your opportunity, then let 'em have it!" The boys were chattering back and forth in Cantonese.

Moe jumped the curb onto a grass median, pulled the wheel to a hard left, and jammed on the brakes. In a matter of seconds, the truck spun around on the slippery grass until it was now facing the approaching cruiser. Moe stomped on the gas and sped towards the cops, mud and grass pluming violently behind the vehicle. Ripper aimed the pistol at the side of the car and opened fire, peppering its lower region to target the wheels. Both the front and rear tires of the vehicle deflated instantly. In response, the officer riding passenger returned fire of his own and blasted the side of the pick up with two volleys of shotgun pellets.

"Ahhhh!" Ripper cried out, grabbing at the side of his face. "I'm hit!" Moe buried the pedal and sped away, leaving the disabled police car behind.

"Where?"

"My shoulder... my face. Turn around, I'm gonna kill that prick!"

"Not a chance. We gotta scram or we're gonna have a lot of company in about one minute," Moe responded, wisely.

Jimmy and the boys were well ahead now and out of sight of the skirmish between the pick up and the cop car.

This time Moe called Jimmy's cell. "Go ahead, *Moe-man*," Jimmy answered.

"Problem solved, buddy!" Moe responded.

"You took 'em out?"

"Ya, easy as hell, except Ripper bought some lead in his face and arm. He'll live," Moe informed his boss with false bravado.

"Okay, slow it down and get outta the area. Take the back roads and make your way to the club house," Jimmy said, meaning the grungy little office at the Hotel East on Gore Avenue.

Following the flow of traffic, the pick up blended in with thousands of other vehicles, eventually making their way west on the Trans Canada Highway, then turning left onto East Hastings, and left again at Gore Avenue. Included among this sea of vehicles was a handful of police cruisers approaching the area with lights and sirens in full activation — too late by minutes, however. The hoods had made good their escape with a payload of millions in contraband drugs destined for mainland BC.

The Red Sun Boys had stolen the coke that had been stolen from them — not without violence, property damage, bloodshed, murder, police involvement, and danger to the general public. All typical events in a day of normal business among the criminal underworld on the streets of Vancouver, British Columbia. Jimmy steered the Hummer into the nearest parking lot he could find and removed all the weaponry in its hold, stashing them behind a nearby dumpster for pick up later. This vehicle would attract too much attention and they would just have to steal something less conspicuous. A minor challenge for the likes of the Red Sun gang.

All in all, Jimmy and the rest of his *Sewer Rats* were pleased. They had just recovered their stolen drugs with a street value, originally, of close to $50 million. And they would be able to pay off their debt to the mainland China mafia. And they would be able to stay alive and breathing by avoiding Wo Shing Chu's retribution. Not a bad day's work. And then there was the satisfaction of having tripped up the Kings Crew on their own caper. Now it was pay back time.

"Get ready for hell," Jimmy Yang said to the Kings Crew, looking into his bathroom mirror.

CHAPTER 22

DOMINIC HALL HAD narrowly escaped the confrontation at the office between the rival gangs with his life and he was shaken to his core. After he escaped the meltdown at his accounting firm, he went to his lawyer's office, for refuge and advice as to what the hell to do now and stormed into his office, forgoing the formalities of checking in with reception.

"Dominic, always a pleasure. You look a little haggard," the lawyer said.

"You got a TV here?" Dom replied. "Turn on the news."

He had missed the conversation in the boardroom between the Asian gang and their hostages, so he only had limited information as to what actually went down at the melee. Until that is, he watched *Live, Breaking News* on his lawyer's wall mounted, Samsung, plasma HDTV. They each pulled up a chair, faced the TV, and watched the newscast with rapt attention.

A microphone clutched in her right hand, the pretty young reporter gave on-the-scene coverage of the incident.

"Today a vicious gun battle erupted at these offices of local accounting firm, Hall Garcia and Barlow, resulting in numerous injuries and killings, as well as extensive property damage. Witnesses say that shortly after noon there were several gunshots in the building. A group of armed assailants believed to be members of the infamous biker gang, the Kings Crew, were seen entering the front of the building. A blast from an unknown source destroyed the front entryway to the structure and gunshots were exchanged extensively shortly thereafter. Fires erupted inside and smoke was seen billowing out several windows of the business."

There was a west coast drizzle of rain and a cool Pacific breeze blew the attractive blonde's bangs across her forehead as she delivered her report with a look of due concern on her face. Dominic's lawyer, Jesse Novak rose from the chair and walked over to his desk. He pressed his intercom button and a secretary's voice responded, "Yes, sir?"

"Nancy, will you please bring in the Hall Garcia and Barlow file?" he asked, then returned to his chair by the TV. Dominic was glued to the screen with his mouth open.

The TV reporter continued, "Police advise that although investigations are underway, it is too early to speculate on the cause of the battle. Witnesses interviewed immediately after the incident say that an Asian gang may have been seeking to recover drugs that had been stolen from them and that one of the firm's partners, Carlos Garcia, may have held information pertaining to the matter. He was, sadly, one of the many casualties in the skirmish, so obtaining comments from him will be difficult, according to a police spokesperson. Foul play is suspected," she said with unintended absurdity.

"As the facts emerge, we will keep our viewers informed about this very unfortunate incidence of fatalities, injuries, and property damage, likely the result of drug related violence. Mackenzie Oliver, CTV News, Vancouver. Over to you, Bob."

In the background, live TV coverage displayed a burning building, stretchers with the wounded being carried here and there, and police and emergency vehicles parked askew everywhere. Curious rubberneckers were being held at bay from the scene by yellow police tape and blue uniformed officers standing vigil around the perimeter.

The secretary entered the room with the file Novak had requested and was stopped dead in her tracks as she approached the two men.

"Fuck! Fuck!" Dominic shouted, articulating his thoughts to the best of his ability. He stood up and paced the room, nervously.

"Those cock suckin', murderin', little slant-eyed, Asian, fuckin' bastards!"

"Nicely put," Novak commented. "Nancy, have you met Mr. Hall?"

"I haven't had the pleasure," she replied, her eyes like saucers.

Novak was a criminal defense lawyer, on the take, who represented the bikers when the law occasionally caught up with them. He knew crown prosecutors, judges, high ranking police officers, and prison guards, among others, and what buttons to push to have charges given minimal sentences or stayed altogether. He was arrogant, smooth as silk and as corrupt as any person working in the legal system could be. Never was he seen in anything other than Harry Rosen or Armani suits with silk ties, Bally shoes, and white shirts with monogrammed French cuffs fastened with mother of pearl cuff links. He was sort of a legal equivalent of *Dog, the bounty hunter,* only he worked *on behalf* of criminals and was an advocate for their rights, defense and release. Without question, *Dog,* a convicted and reformed felon, was the better man.

With a smile and a few choice words, Novak could make his position known, without actually spelling it out, and usually, whomever he was plying for a favor got his message, and the implied reward for cooperating. Occasionally, they also understood the threat to themselves, other family members, or exposure from past indiscretions, like accepting bribery or complicity in other criminal acts. *A real gem,* this guy.

He wasn't in the law profession because of his love and dedication to the Canadian legal system. He was in it for the money, and desperate criminals usually pay very well for effective representation, by cheque, when everything was legit, and by cash and other favors, otherwise. He was aware of this cocaine heist from the outset — part of it, in fact, as a clandestine silent partner and retained for his special talents in case something might arise that required a devious legal mind.

After escaping the skirmish, Dominic had immediately gone downtown to his colleague's office on Robson to lay low and confer with Novak on how to deal with the problem.

"Christ, now what?" Dominic cussed. "Put two and two together. If they're reporting over the fuckin' evening news that Carlos *may* have known something about a shipment of stolen drugs, what are the odds that those Asian freaks pried *it all* out of him? We've gotta send someone over to the warehouse to check on our stash. It'll have to be moved immediately."

Novak was contemplative. "Don't jump to conclusions too fast. The reporter said he was one of the casualties. It's possible that he wouldn't cave in, so they killed him."

"It's possible, but we don't know and we can't stand by and just hope that our inventory is safe. There's millions of dollars at stake. The Red Sun Gang are just getting started. We're going to have to wipe that scurvy carrying pack of slimy rodents off the face of the earth. And now we've got the fuckin' law all over this, too. They're gonna be looking for me since I'm one of the firm's partners, you can bet your balls.

"Goddamn it! We couldn't just stick to prostitutes, marijuana, gambling, and what we *know*. We had to poke our noses into the business of mega, hard drug sales, and get in the middle of a family fuckin' feud between those dirty little Asian bastards here and the fuckin' mafia in China." Dominic was glistening with sweat and his mind was over stimulated and panicking. Right now, a strong dose of something like Prozac might have been a good idea.

"I agree, you have to take action to protect your interests. You'd be wise to send someone over to the warehouse to transfer the product to some other secure location. Keep yourself at arm's length from all communications and get it done immediately," Novak counseled.

"You'll also need to calm down and get your story straight as to what you know about this invasion into your business, and whether there is any truth to the allegation that Carlos Garcia, or your firm, was in on any kind of drug deals.

"The short answer is, *You know nothing.* Don't try to cook up some convoluted yarn that implies you may be covering something up, or know more than your saying. The cops will see right through it and they'll interrogate you for hours and hours until they trip you up on something, and if they find a little hole in your story, they'll pry away at it until it's a gaping, bloody wound, and then they'll crucify you.

"Keep in mind that drug dealing, by definition, involves money laundering. They're two sides of a coin. The proceeds of drug sales need to be put into some useable form of currency, and that's illegal with a *capital I.* And dealers sell to vulnerable people, minors, or others who have probably engaged in criminal activities to raise the money to buy the drugs, in the first place. It's a self feeding, black hole of criminality. Consider how it would look for a professional accountant, *even possibly* being party to any stage of that process and his likely involvement in the money laundering process. The cops will be all over you like sharks on chum in a feeding frenzy in the Georgia Strait."

Dominic's face looked like he'd already been charged, tried, convicted, and sentenced to life in the electric chair — old *Sizzlin' Sally.* He sat back down, looking dejected.

"Remember, aside from you and Carlos, none of your employees know anything about any drug heist, so the cops won't get anything from them. Carlos is dead so he won't be talking, and that only leaves you. Your answers to their questions should be, *'I don't know, I don't recall, I have no idea, I don't know that person,*

I'm not sure, I have no recollection,' and don't be evasive but don't motor-mouth either. Keep your answers short, and don't volunteer information about anything that you're not directly asked.

"They might play *good cop, bad cop* with you. Don't trust the good one and don't let the bad one provoke you into an argument. Or they may just sit you down in an interrogation room and not ask you *any* questions to see what you cough up on your own... Don't say a bloody word!"

Dom finally buckled under the pressure. *"Don't, don't, don't...* What *should I do,* is the pressing question, for Christ sakes!" standing up again with both arms in the air.

"Okay, sit down, and we'll talk about what you *are* going to do," Jesse replied as he sauntered over to the granite and smoked glass bar in his office and poured them each a glass of premium scotch over ice. He removed his suit jacket, undid the top button of his starched white shirt, and loosened his tie.

"A good scotch helps settle the nerves and focus the mind. *Glenlivet, eighteen years old —* better than sex, with my wife, anyways. Drink up and let's strategize. *Salute.*"

Dominic and Jesse spent the next good hour discussing the types of questions he might face, and the direction the interrogation might take. Dom would cooperate unless the questioning started implying that he was culpable in some way. Until he was read the Miranda rights he would simply be being detained for questioning and not under arrest. If the proceedings turned into a formal arrest, he would call Jesse Novak immediately without saying another word.

"Gosh, I feel so much better now," he said, as he walked to the bar and poured himself another double scotch over ice, then another, stirring them both with his finger and gulping them down like water.

"Call me a cab," he said to Novak. "Drinking and driving is illegal in BC."

✧ ✧ ✧

The next day, after Mat had spoken with Wexler and Foley, the plan for putting the first five million into the laundering process was underway. As instructed, Foley called Jack Kincaid.

"Hey, Jack, I hear you're sportin' a new look these days. How's that toupee and goatee workin' for ya? Any better luck with the ladies?"

Jack replied, "I don't need luck. When I want some poontang, I simply peel off a couple hundred and buy the services of a good whore. Last thing I need is some woman raggin' on me 'cause she thinks I owe her the time of day in exchange for a little pussy. The disguise is to keep my identity incognito in case anyone's looking for me. What can I do for you?"

Even to Foley, Jack Kincaid's vulgarity and crude logic was an insult to decency, and he chuckled, shaking his head. *Talkin' to this man is like shaving with a dull razor.* "Just talked to Mat. He says to tell you that the washin' machine is running full tilt, and for you to let your buddies know everything's on schedule. Also, for your guys to pull in all the money they can from the street, straight away. Word has it that the Red Sun gang may know where it is and recover it, right quick. That happens, we're outta business. We gotta move fast, *capiche?*"

"Ya, I watch the evening news too," Kincaid replied. "I'll talk to Dominic and see what we can do. I have a hunch they're already all over it. Shouldn't take me more than a day or two to get back to you."

"Alright, Bud. Call me when you have it all bundled up and ready for counting and processing and I'll lay low 'til I hear anything else. Be careful, Jack. This is like gettin' in between a mongoose and a cobra. Know what I mean?"

The call ended there, and Foley went about the business of running Bull Dog Security and tending to his new girlfriend-patient, Crystal Waters. As near as possible, he tried to continue living life as normally as usual, however, *hooked up* with a good woman, for the first time ever.

At about the same time, Dominic had issued the command through an intermediary, keeping *at arm's length from all communications,* as Jesse Novak had advised him, to check on the stash of coke, and move it to another secure location. He would soon learn, however, that the coke *couldn't* be moved, because it was *gone* from the Driftwood Warehouse. Incredibly, the Red Sun Gang had raided the accounting firm, secured the information they needed, and recovered their imported treasure of drugs from China.

As bold and brash as the Kings Crew were in bribing Captain Furlong and redirecting his ship to an alternate port terminal at the last moment, they had underestimated their rivals and had now lost control of the payload. If Dominic Hall was having a bad day so far, it would only get worse.

He went to his residence and sure enough, a message played back on his telephone voice mail.

"Mr. Hall, Inspector Jerome Lundgren with the Vancouver P.D. calling. No doubt, you're aware of the incident that took place at your business yesterday. A full investigation is in progress and we have some questions we'd like you to answer. Would you return my call as soon as possible, please?" and a local phone number was left for him.

Alright damn it, let's do this thing, Dom said to himself. He gingerly picked up the phone and placed the call to the detective. Although still apprehensive, he felt better prepared by his coaching session with the slippery lawyer, Novak. All he'd have to do is dodge a few questions convincingly about some alleged drug heist, that he knew nothing about, and the police would redirect their efforts towards the warring rival gangs – the Red Sun Boys and the Kings Crew.

The line rang once, then twice. "Lundgren," the detective answered.

"Yes, this is Dominic Hall returning your call. You're investigating the break in at my business. I got your message."

"We sure are. Thanks for getting back to me. We'll need to get together to see if we can piece together what happened, and why. Can you come down to precinct, right away, Mr. Hall?"

"Yes, of course. I'll be there within the hour," Dom offered cooperatively.

"Even better, I'll have a car pick you up. We can drop you off when we're finished. Where are you right now?"

"I'm at my residence. 602 Hastings Street West, suite 604. Have them buzz me from the lobby, please, and I'll be right down."

The two men finished the call and a squad car was on its way.

Here we go. I hate cops even worse when I have to be polite to the pricks, Dom said to himself.

Twenty minutes later Dom's intercom sounded from the main floor foyer and he said out loud, "Looks like my ride's here." He grabbed his coat and pressed the PTT, *push-to-talk* button, "I'll be right down."

Waiting in the lobby were two blue uniforms looking appropriately official.

Outta uniform, you pair of clowns would just be two more shoppers carrying the bags, probably wearing sandals with socks, and being led around the mall on a leash by some woman with bleached-blonde hair and an arse like a Clydesdale, he thought.

"Mr. Hall?" One of them spoke up. "Right this way, sir," and out the front door they proceeded to the black and white parked curbside.

Dom sat in the back seat while the two boys – neither of them was more than thirty, he was certain — sat up front. *Punks,* he thought, *What do you know?*

On the ride downtown Dominic mentally rehearsed the answers he had been coached on by Jesse Novak. If he sailed through this interrogation, which is exactly what it was, he would likely walk away and never be questioned on it again. On the other hand, a couple of mistakes could land him in hot water and expose things that the police had no business knowing, at least in his opinion. In a short time, he would be in the precinct and face to face with homicide detectives.

"Mr. Hall. Inspector Lundgren. Good to meet you," the detective opened up the conversation.

"Likewise, glad to be of help."

"Can I get you something to drink — coffee, pop, water?"

"Thanks. A coke would go down nicely, if you have one."

Lundgren asked an administrative girl just outside his door to help out.

"Mr. Hall, this is a colleague of mine, Inspector Julia Drummond," he went on. "She'll be assisting me today. We need to find out all we can about this apparent invasion of your business."

Drummond stood and shook Dominic's hand, which was damp already with nervous perspiration. She was a butchy looking woman, without any trace of feminine appeal, who Dominic immediately assumed played on the other field. Dom thought to himself, *There's something just wrong about women wearing a necktie, black service boots and a man's hat, in any job. It's like men wearing leg warmers in an exercise class. People who dress off code, for their gender, are immediately suspect, and rightfully so. Who'd disagree?*

"Okay, well, let's get started. How can I help you with our *apparent* invasion?"

"You're one of the firm's partners, I gather," Lundgren said.

"Yes, that's correct."

"And what kind of work does your firm do?"

"Accounting. General accounting services, from tax work to book keeping to business consulting. We do corporate work as well as services for individuals and families." *Shut up... Don't motor mouth!*

Lundgren was studying the man with steely eyes. "I see."

"And do you know who these assailants were, that entered your firm, Mr. Hall?" he continued.

"No, never seen them before," Hall answered succinctly.

"I understand that you and your employees were forcibly detained in the board room, and that there was an allegation that you may have had information about a drug theft," the inspector said.

"Yes, they were. I mean, *no, not me.* I hid out in my office stationary closet when I heard the commotion. They never found me, and I wasn't privy to any conversations in the board room." Dominic was struggling not to look or sound nervous. He sipped his coke casually.

"Do you know anything about an alleged stolen shipment of drugs, or have any reason to suspect that anyone else in your firm may have knowledge or information in this regard?" Lundgren asked.

"No sir, unless one of the people murdered knew something. And if they did, they won't be of much help to you now," Dom said, introducing some dry wit. Novak's coaching sounded off in his head *Only answer the question. Don't say more than what's called for.*

"Someone like who? Mr. Garcia, perhaps?"

Now Dominic was starting to understand Novak's expertise in such matters. These cops seize on every little detail you mention to try and pull you into a full confession. He tried to clarify himself.

"Really, I have no idea what anyone else in the building, or on the planet for that matter, might know about the whole thing. We were conducting business normally like any other day, and all of a sudden there's a bunch of Chinese guys running around the building waiving guns in people's faces. Next thing I know, a gang of hoods, in leather and beards burst in the front door and a full scale war breaks out. When the coast was clear, I made a break for it and ran out the front door. That's all I know about anything, period."

"Do you think you could identify any of the participants in a line up, in this incident?" Lundgren asked.

"Not really. Like I said, I was hiding and couldn't see much," Dom replied.

"But you could see *when the coast was clear* to run out," the detective said, feeding his own words back to him.

"Ya, I opened my office door a crack when things were dying down. But by then most everyone was either dead on the floor or had left the building. It was a fire storm in there, by then. I had to get out."

"Well, if it was practically over, why did you flee the building?"

"Because I was scared shitless! I wasn't planning on sticking around to see who else might come around the corner with a fuckin' piece aimed at my head!" Dominic burst out. "Pardon my French," he said nodding to the butch-lady cop, thinking remotely, about what she might be doing to her *partner*, off hours.

The two detectives looked at each other. Neither spoke. Drummond was scribbling madly in a hand held note book.

Inspector Lundgren continued gathering the facts, as well as Mr. Hall was able to recollect, for another twenty or thirty minutes. By the end, Dominic had given a good accounting of himself, he believed, and didn't get tripped up by any surprise questions. He was never read the Miranda rights, so nothing he said must have aroused much suspicion.

Wrapping up, Detective Lundgren said, "Thank you for your cooperation here today, Mr. Hall. I am sorry for your loss in this incident. Rest assured we will pursue the perpetrators of this crime with due diligence. I do ask that you notify us of your whereabouts until further notice."

"Why? Am I some kind of suspect?" Dominic replied.

"Just trying to keep tabs on all possible pieces to the puzzle. We wouldn't want to find out that you'd moved to Argentina over the weekend." Lundgren smiled. "I'll have a car run you back home." And that, was that, for now.

CHAPTER 23

JACK KINCAID HAD been holed up for a few days in his brother's condo in downtown Vancouver, and he was starting to feel a bit of cabin fever. The fridge was getting down to bare bones, the liquor supply was running low, and he decided to venture out for supplies and some exercise. Since he was downtown, he had the safety of blending in with hordes of office workers, shoppers, and other pedestrians. He felt relatively safe, especially in disguise, and he'd left the building several times before without incident.

With precision, he donned the toupee and goatee and checked himself one last time in the hall mirror. Everything looked good. Even his own mother wouldn't recognize him, and if she did she'd probably look the other way. He'd been nothing more than a nuisance to her while they were together. She'd been a drug addicted prostitute and had a string of low life men in and out of their social aid apartment daily for all Jack's life, until he finally ran away at fifteen.

Meandering now back to his childhood, Jack recalled that his own father had even rejected him, claiming he wasn't at all certain that Jack was even his child, like it was Jack's fault. He remembered the sickening, violent fights between his parents; how as a little boy he felt responsible in some way; how he'd listen to the grunting and moaning coming from the other room daily, when his drug obsessed mother turned to hooking for a living; how she abandoned him in the end, and only agreed reluctantly to feed and clothe him in rags, to keep him alive and off the streets.

Some people start out with a leg up from someone – a parent especially, to arrive at better things in life. Not Jack. He'd been a loner and a cast out from the start. No wonder he had worked his way into the underworld of organized crime and racketeering.

He checked that he had his shopping list and opened the door to the hallway, looking left and right before venturing from the safety of his brother's condo. The coast was clear, so off he went.

No sense in being paranoid. I've taken every reasonable precaution to conceal myself, he thought quietly as he pressed the down arrow of the elevator call button. He waited patiently as the lights flashed one by one from floors one to eleven. Soon he would be on the street, out in the open, and vulnerable to any pay backs that gang members might want to execute upon him.

He warned himself, *They killed Captain Furlong. They killed Carlos Garcia, and many others at the accounting firm. They nearly killed Crystal. They know I'm involved with the heist somehow. I've got to get my supplies then get back under cover 'til this thing blows over.*

Jack exited the elevator doors and walked across the marble floored foyer of the condominium complex. Others were gathering their mail from the metal mailbox compartments mounted in the wall. A couple was chatting quietly about something on the leather sofa in a waiting area off to one side. A realtor was spreading brochures advertising the property at a table set up to display the units still available for sale. The sun shone brightly through the glass wall of the entryway. Outside, a plethora of passersby were bustling every which way on the streets, mostly oblivious to each other and each on their own mission of importance. A typical busy scene in downtown Vancouver.

Jack left the building and headed towards the curb to hail a cab. As he stood and waited he looked both ways to see if one might be anywhere close by. There... a yellow cab was approaching from his side of the road, a half block away. Jack raised his arm to signal the driver, and at that moment, a piercing jolt of debilitating pain shot through his right chest like he'd been struck by lightning. There was no sound, no assailant, only knee buckling, devastating pain.

In falling to the ground, Jack's toupee twisted all out of position on his head, giving him an almost comical appearance in parody of himself pathetically attempting disguise. Now, lying supine on the concrete sidewalk, his hand reflexively went to the source of his anguish, and all he felt was the feathered end of a small arrow, oozing at the wound with warm arterial blood.

In actuality, it was a sixteen inch carbon crossbow bolt fired by one of the Red Sun Boys who had been incentivized with a thousand dollar bonus for killing Kincaid, *with verification.* The feathered vanes protruded slightly out the front of Jack's chest and the razor sharp, four-sided broadhead extended out his back by inches, its shaft lodged in his rib cage. His right lung and its pulmonary arteries had been destroyed by the projectile, spinning like a drill as it penetrated his body.

The crossbow was a perfect inner city weapon of assassination. It was compact, silent, accurate, and lethal. The shooter had waited patiently with a cohort in a car parked across the street from the condominium building until he caught sight of Kincaid, disguised or not. He'd raised the weapon, fixed the sight on his victim out the car window, waited for a kill shot, and squeezed the trigger at the perfect moment of opportunity. Jack's lanky frame, well over six feet, left little doubt as to who this fool in the phony toupee really was. One moment he was standing with his arm in the air hailing a cab. A second later, he was on the ground, mortally wounded.

The Red Sun Boys knew that Jack was not staying at his usual residence and were smart enough to figure out that his brother owned a vacant condo downtown. With little effort, they located their man and delivered restitution for his part in the theft of their drugs.

"Mommy, what's wrong with that man?" a little boy asked. People were quickly gathering around the fallen Jack Kincaid with curiosity, dismay, and alarm.

"He's... been shot with something, some kind of arrow, it looks like," she replied sympathetically to her son. "Come away, Calvin, don't look!"

"Oh my word! Someone call an ambulance," another lady called out. By now a crowd of at least a dozen people had descended upon Jack. Sadly, his fate was now set, and he gasped for air through a pierced lung and other internal injuries. Moments to go, and he would be dead. He looked up, and a circle of onlookers peered down at him, shock on their faces.

In all the fuss and mingle of emergency efforts and people converging on the scene, two Asian youths, perhaps in their early twenties, approached the dying man from across the street and looked down upon him.

"Wow, he must really piss someone off, deserve dis kind payback," one of them remarked, well within earshot of the victim.

"Ya, but in end, they all get what they deserve when they stick their noses where it don't belong," the other replied. They looked at each other and smiled sadistically, then knelt down beside Jack.

"Don' worry," one whispered close to his face. "There be others. Red Sun Boys *say hello*. We send message. Mess around in our affair, and dis what you look forward to. You not first, and you not be last. Rest easy, it all over soon." He flipped open a cell phone and took a few pictures of his victim, to *verify* the kill. *Click, Click, Click...*

Jack looked up through watery eyes, his chest feeling like he'd been run through with a bayonet and weakly coughed out a red, coagulated wad of blood, which leached out the corner of his mouth, to the morbid delight of many of his onlookers.

"Punks," he murmured weakly. "You'll rot in hell."

"Then we see you later, I guess," one of them replied.

Jack wondered in his dying moments if Mat, and Foley, and Adriana would eventually fall victim to a similar fate, if they hadn't already. The pain of the wound was subsiding now, and he eased into a state of submission — mentally, physically, and spiritually. As so often happens, men find faith in times of mortal desperation and his mind spoke to him.

Oh Lordy, Lordy, why did it come to this? I wasn't born lucky, but I was determined to make my way in the world, somehow. I know I strayed from Your guidance and did some bad things in my life. Things that were illegal, immoral, corrupt, and flat out wrong. I wish I could take it all back. Oh, Lord, for another chance. I squandered my life in crime and kept company with riff raff, and now this, the payback for sin. And I hurt so many others... None that deserved to be harmed, or killed. Most, only flawed, regular people, guilty of the mortal error of falling away from innocence, like me. What man hasn't yielded to temptation in his life? I'm so sorry I caused all this. I gambled. It was greed, I admit, and I brought down a disaster. I'm so, so sorry. Mistakes... I made so many in my life. I wanna start all over. I just wanna go home. God, mercy.

He took a few more shallow breaths, and the memories of his life churned and whirled one last time in a vortex, like a view through a kaleidoscope, then Jack's body released all its tension and he lay still, almost relaxed. He felt no pain now. Oddly, he did feel *loved*, at long last, although no one in his life *had ever* loved him. Neither mother, father, brother, woman, nor friend. The Elephant Man would have garnered more affection than Jack did throughout his life. Now, he felt that he was being *welcomed home*. Knowing his time was running out fast, he spoke his final comforting words, internally:

The lord is my shepherd; I shall not want.

He maketh me to lie down in green pastures: He leadeth me beside the still waters.

He restoreth my soul: He leadeth me in the paths of righteousness for his name's sake.

*Yea though I walk through the valley of the shadow of
death, I will fear no evil: for thou art with me...*

He breathed in, and out, in halting gasps through his one
good lung. Time was running out, fast.

Hovering now above the scene below, he looked upon the
mishap and his own body lying gravely wounded on the pavement
and he felt a beckoning to a higher place. In his own mind, he
fell into a deep, calm sleep and embraced the irresistible pull of
finality, falling with arms outstretched, gently and willingly, into
a beautiful, radiant starburst of white light before him. It was
done. At last, Jack Kincaid had found peace *and love* in eternity.

To those watching, he simply succumbed to his injury before
help could arrive. And so closed the book on Mr. Jack Kincaid,
from humble beginnings as an unwanted and unloved child, to
an import-export, criminal entrepreneur, to murder victim in
uptown Vancouver.

"Quite a show. Gang warfare yet again on the streets of
Vancouver. The paramedics should be here any minute, then the
news people, then the cops," a smartass young bike courier remarked, donned in the unofficial uniform of Oakley sunglasses,
fingerless gloves and Puma runners, as he slung his tote bag over
his shoulder and pedaled off to his next urgent delivery, recklessly dodging oncoming cars by inches.

✵ ✵ ✵

As instructed, at 2:00 o'clock Thursday morning, Foley
pulled into the back alley of the Cambridge Mercantile Group
on Burrard Street. The panel van he was driving was packed
with hockey sized duffle bags full of cash, some $5 million worth.
Slowly and quietly Foley rolled up to the rear of the building,
and as planned, Wexler opened the back door to the bank.

"Mr. Wexler, you're a sight for sore eyes. Gotta tell you, this
makes me nervous as hell," Foley confessed.

"Come along now. Let's not delay this. Turn off your engine and get these bags inside quickly. I'll handle the rest," Max Wexler instructed.

Foley wasted no time in complying with his instructions and in a matter of a few minutes, the bags were off loaded and Foley was back behind the wheel driving along Burrard Street and obeying all the traffic laws to the letter.

"I love it when a plan comes together," he said out loud, quoting one of his boyhood TV heroes, Hannibal Smith, played by George Peppard on *The A Team. They just don't make TV programs like they used to,* he mused to himself. *Reality shows out the ying yang... Good Lord!*

Wexler, meanwhile was busy counting and sorting the money. By opening time in the morning, he would have $5.25 million intermingled with regular cash deposits, bank drafts, cheques, and other monetary notes and wire transfer documents, ready for pick up by Loomis Armed Courier. Of course, all records of the irregularity attached to the five million would be erased by Wexler and the money would blend into the system without suspicion. From there, Mat would transfer the money to the account of the Empressa, controlled by the Panamanian law firm of Diaz, Cordoba & Del Rio. This was the magic of modern, high stakes money laundering in action, and Mat Crawford was taking centre stage as the David Copperfield of his craft.

In the realm of Vancouver's criminal underworld, the Kings Crew had discovered that their stash of stolen drugs had been repossessed by their underestimated competitors, the Red Sun Gang. Also, word quickly got out that the mastermind of the whole caper, Jack Kincaid, had paid the *ultimate* price for his role in this treachery. There would likely be more bloodshed before the whole matter was finished. The Red Sun Boys had demonstrated resourcefulness and nerves of steel in their actions thus far, and they were incited to complete their payback with certainty. They were out to *send a message.*

Still, life and business goes on, and the Kings Crew were not about to stand idly by and let a setback like this put them out of business. They were still the dominant crime syndicate in the lower mainland and they had many other business interests that financed their booze, and drugs, and broads, and Harleys, and they refused to roll over and play dead over a minor change in plans. Money is money and it has the whole world as its source. And the more illicit the source, the more money is available. *Just watch.*

CHAPTER 24

BACK IN PANAMA, Mat and Adriana had arranged the Empressa with the lawyers, taken in all the sights, and learned all they needed to know about Central America — its laws, customs, culture, and economy. It was a good place to visit, live, and work, and more importantly, invest. They had exhausted virtually all of their reasons for staying there without formally declaring it a vacation, so it was time to board a plane and head back to Canada to complete their assignment.

As the powerful Rolls-Royce turbo fans roared, the Boeing 757 surged upward to cruising altitude, destined for Miami, Florida, the stop-over, before transferring to another aircraft bound for Vancouver.

After a brief delay in Miami, Mat and Adriana were finally aboard an A321 Airbus in executive class destined for home. A matronly, middle aged flight attendant came around glowering at the business class passengers, like a vigilant elementary school mistress, for any infractions of the regulations. Immediately, Mat didn't like her.

She offered complimentary beverages.

"Some OJ and Champagne, here?" she asked with false cordiality.

"Love some. Fill 'er up, good lookin', but hold the Tang," Mat answered back cheerfully. "Don't be shy, now."

The attendant was taken aback at Mat's familiarity and looked at him oddly as she tipped the bottle of Asti Spumante, perhaps the cheapest version of the beverage available anywhere.

"Atta girl," Mat said. "Nuttin' but the best." He winked at her.

"Just OJ for me, please," Adriana remarked.

Sipping on his beverage indulgently, Mat said to Adriana, "For an impromptu, unplanned visit to Panama, it's been quite an exciting few days, you'll have to admit."

"You didn't plan this trip?" she queried.

"Not me, I was talking about you. You did this on the spur of the moment, I take it. Kind of a spontaneous act, or an impulsive decision. Not something you planned in advance, right?"

"Well, there are long range plans and short range plans, and this was a short range one, true enough. But I had a general game plan in my head for some time, probably since you gave your little speech about the money laundering process back at the accounting firm. I took an interest in you and decided to explore it. By the way, when that one man, Dominic Hall, pulled his gun on you, your upper lip was sweating, Mister Tough Guy."

"You don't have to remind me. Those guys are all tangled up in one illegal scheme or another, and they're popping each other off one by one in the process, or their enemies are, and if you associate with them long enough, it's a pretty good bet you'll find yourself *toes up* on a coroner's slab too. I'm getting tired of it all, to be honest. When this is over, I'd like to make other plans for my life in a safer line of work... you too, I'd hope."

"You mean us — together?" Adriana replied, somewhat stiffly, looking straight ahead.

Mat paused, then commented on *the elephant in the parlor.* "I don't honestly know what's going to happen with my wife. She said she was likely filing for separation. I'll find out soon enough," he said.

"And if she doesn't file? Then she's in and I'm out? Am I your fall back girl if your wife leaves you? And if not, then *we'll always have Panama?* What a compliment. I feel like I'm in Casablanca." Adriana's tone had turned decidedly defensive.

"No, Adriana, you were definitely not a fling of some sort. I'm sorry, I didn't mean for it to sound like that. Look, it's complicated, is all I'm saying. I've been with her for a lot of years, since we were kids really, and we have a daughter, and truthfully, I love her, but it's never been like us. We have something special together. You mean a lot to me. I feel something different with you."

"Like what?"

"You know, I just... *connect* with you. We're on the same page all the time. We work in the same business, if you can call it that. We're compatible. We laugh a lot together. Haven't you noticed? Don't you get it?"

"I get it. I'm not sure *you* get it," Adriana replied.

"Get what? Why are we arguing? We'll find a way to make this all work out."

"Mat, say it. You haven't so far — *at all.* You know, I'm a lawyer and a criminal maybe, thanks to your little project, but I'm still a woman, and I need to hear the words. Do I have to draw you a picture? We connect? We're on the same page? I mean a lot to you? *Please.*"

"Okay, okay," Mat relented. "I think I get what you're driving at, and I have no problem spelling out my true, sappy feelings. But if you laugh, I'll never confide in you again." He looked down at his complimentary champagne, served by nurse

Ratched of the flight crew. Thoughtfully, he paused, choosing his words carefully. "Ready?"

"Do I *look* ready?" Actually she looked uptight, and pissed, Mat noted.

"Adriana... I really, really, I mean I truly, and honestly, and genuinely... *dig you, baby*. Stick with me and we'll go to the moon together! How's that?" Mat looked at her with phony romance on his face, trying pitifully, to be funny.

Adriana looked at the man more like he was from Mars, never mind the moon. She'd gone fishing for those three little words that have a world of meaning and he responded with humor, although his feelings for her really weren't in any doubt — *unless she was misreading him and she was just his little play thing*. Compatibly, they seemed to fit together like adjoining pieces to a jigsaw puzzle. The words would have to wait. He wasn't ready, she realized, and she didn't want to pressure him.

Adriana and Mat locked eyes for a moment then they both erupted with laughter. "You dig me? Sometimes you're an idiot, you realize," she remarked, exasperated.

Though he didn't actually say it, Adriana was reasonably certain that their relationship was on a solid footing. But she was a woman, nonetheless, and hearing the words from her new man would have meant a lot. *Why are men so afraid to commit?* she wondered to herself.

This was a man on a mission with big plans, unbelievable nerve, and a healthy lust for her, she thought with self-conscious delight. She wanted to be part of his plans and would apply her feminine wiles relentlessly to ensure he was thoroughly smitten, starting right now.

Leaning back and resting her head in her first class over-sized seat, Adriana smiled, sipping her OJ, *sans* alcohol. She closed her eyes.

"I think I'm pregnant."

Mat's eyes widened and the scene did a *freeze-frame* with his champagne glass locked midway between the table tray and his open mouth... *What?*

"Wadda'ya mean?" Mat said after he finally collected himself and stopped exhaling effervescent champagne into a napkin through his nose.

"I mean, *with child*, as in when a woman conceives and is carrying new life in her womb," Adriana explained. "And I said, *I think*, I'm pregnant."

"Well, you're capable of delivering quite the bombshell, aren't you?"

"Yes, and there'll be more, I expect," she replied.

"Oh, I'm sure. But why do you *think* you might be pregnant? We've only been here a little over a week."

"Yes, and I'm late by a *little over* a few days *or more*, or do I have to explain what that means to you as well. What? You think we have to do it a hundred times before conception is possible?"

A hundred times last week sounds about right, by my score card, his little voice said. "I assumed you were on... like, protection," Mat fumbled.

"Well, you assumed *like*, wrong. I told you, I've been off men for the past while. I wanted to give my system a rest from drugs. Then along came you, and your wicked little needs, and now this," Adriana replied. "Surprised?"

Mat got it, and was thinking out loud now. "Ah... The questions about the *future* of our relationship."

"What about it?"

"You're concerned that *if* you're pregnant and you decide *to have* the baby..."

"Which I will," Adriana interrupted.

"Okay, that you may have to face the prospect of being a single mom, and raising a child on your own," Mat surmised.

Adriana laughed quietly in a *don't be ridiculous* way. "I make a good living and I can hire all the support I need to help me raise a child, if it comes to that. This is the twenty first century, Mister. Women can work at a career *and* be good mothers without compromising either, if they're resourceful and committed."

"That's certainly true of you, but I don't know if I'd generalize that to the whole population. Sometimes single parenthood is not optional for people – women or men, but it's never a good substitute for a normal, stable, two parent family," Mat replied. "Anyways, let's not get ahead of ourselves. You can get tested and find out for sure when we get back home. Either way, I'll stand by you, if you'll have me," he assured her.

"I know you will. I was just pulling your chain, Rover. But *I am* tired. Think I'll try to sleep a bit," and she put her head back for some rest. Moments later, her deep, rhythmic breathing told Mat she was in dreamland. A flight attendant came by with a champagne bottle and topped up Mat's drink.

Mat tried to read, but couldn't really get interested in anything. Tried to watch the In-flight movie, but it was some silly thing about *Mr. Magorium's Wonder Emporium*. Tried to sleep, but couldn't relax. Tried to listen to music, but couldn't get the headset to fit right on his ears. Tried to eat, but salty pretzels and honey roasted peanuts didn't turn his crank. So he just sat still and looked out the window at the canopy of clouds, now well below the altitude of the airliner, flying at thirty seven thousand feet.

He wondered about what Christine and Hannah had been occupied with while he was in Panama on a clandestine adventure with the extraordinary, exotic Adriana Santos. He replayed the conversation with Foley in his head about Crystal Waters being assaulted, and how his partner seemed to have evolved into a new, better man over her. Mat speculated quietly about the gang invasion at the accounting firm of Hall, Garcia and

Barlow, with all its devastation and bloodshed. He wondered if, and how, they might be able to process any more money through the Panamanian law firm, if the Red Sun Boys had succeeded in recovering their contraband. He questioned whether the privacy and security of his financial affairs was as iron clad through the Guatemalan Empressa as Marcos Del Rio had assured him. Adriana bought his story, and he trusted her judgment.

He was curious about what other developments might have taken place in his absence from Vancouver over the last week. He puzzled over the strange and crooked path that his life had taken down this long and bizarre road of money laundering in the first place. He worried over the safety, one by one, of Christine, Hannah, Foley, Adriana, Crystal, Danielle, himself, and others, as a result of his involvement in the world of criminals, drugs, and deception.

As he looked below, his mind a moving collage of thoughts, images, issues, rewinds and playbacks, worries, plans, and *what ifs*, it occurred to him how small and remote the problems of the world seemed when viewed from high above the earth. Looking below, it reminded him of the assignment he had once helped Hannah with as part of her science homework. Mat and his young daughter were powerfully and emotionally impacted when they viewed Carl Sagan's presentation on YouTube, *Pale Blue Dot*, about the uniqueness and value of the earth in contrast to the vast expanse of the universe. It was an eye opener from a gifted astronomer, scholar, and remarkable human being, that made him appreciate the earth and mankind from a new perspective.

His mind was at gridlock and mildly lulled by the champagne. Mat's eyes became heavy and he closed them for a moment or two to regain his composure. He drifted off and in moments the blackness of past due sleep had overtaken him. He was gone.

"Mat, wake up... wake up, hon." Adriana was running the back of her hand up and down his cheek. "We'll be landing in a few minutes. We have to get ready. C'mon, sleepyhead, sit up."

"Wha...? Oh, my neck's sore," Mat mumbled out groggily. "How long was I out?"

"Not sure. A couple of hours, anyway. You're *great company* on a long plane trip," she teased. "You must have contracted narcolepsy or something in Panama. What's wrong? A few days with a good woman wear you out?"

Mat and Adriana both put their seatbacks in the fully upright position, as ordered, and got rid of sundry items like magazines, headsets, pillows and blankets that they had gathered during the flight. In a few minutes YVR was just ahead, and the huge airliner touched down with a gentle thump, reverse thrusters in full roar. The passengers clapped like they were audience to a gifted artistic performance, instead of high paying customers who had entrusted their lives to the pilots, flight service crew, and equipment. Anyone would think they were lucky survivors on US Airways flight 1549, piloted by Captain Sully Sullenberger, after ditching the plane in the Hudson River.

Inside the terminal, Mat and Adriana were herded like cattle to be checked in with a nice customs officer who looked them over like they were *criminals,* before grudgingly stamping their declaration forms. He looked at them like, '*Get the fuck outta here, before I change my mind.'* Then they waited patiently for over a half hour, hoping their luggage made it back looking like it hadn't been dragged behind a *just married* car, if it arrived at all.

"I don't know why I like travelling," Mat said wryly as the luggage carousel final started turning. Travelers, looking weary and disheveled, immediately crowded forward, each claiming their own little piece of real estate in front of the moving belt, *as if that* would help them retrieve their belongings faster. *Me first! Me first!* Mat thought of the other travelers to himself. *What ever happened to common courtesy? Step back until you see your bag, bunch of vultures!*

As exciting and successful as their trip together was, Mat and Adriana each took separate cabs to their own homes. There were clothes to be washed, letters to be opened, phone calls to be returned and other housekeeping duties that needed attention. There was a sense of *back to the real world,* and they each tried to shake off the euphoria of their working vacation together.

They parted company at the arrivals area where cabs queued up like next generation rickshaws in Calcutta vying for fares, and spoke to each other simultaneously.

"I'll call you," Mat said.

"You'll call me?" Adriana said over top of him.

They laughed together, pecked each other on the lips, and went their own ways.

In the cab, Mathew opened his cell phone and immediately called Foley. The line rang twice.

"Hi, Foley here."

"Hey, it's me again. I'm just leaving the airport for home. I'm totally bagged, so make it fast, will ya? Anything I should know about?" Mat inquired.

"Christ almighty, where do I start?" Foley replied.

"How about with whether the drugs have been found by the China men. And whether we're still in business."

"I wish I could tell ya. All I know is what's been on the news. It's been a real shit show here for the last week or so. I tried to call Kincaid yesterday but, well, we'll talk about that later," Foley stalled.

"What?" Mat pressed on. "What about him?"

"Oh, nothin' that won't wait 'til tomorrow, trust me. I'll fill ya in on everything when you're fresh."

"Okay then, I just wanted to let you know I'm home. I'm going to my place for a major snooze, then I'll call you tomorrow and we'll figure out how to proceed. Okey-dokey?"

"Okey-doke," Foley replied, trying to sound optimistic.

"Foley, thanks for holding down the fort while I was gone, and everything else you do here. It may seem like grunt work, but what you do is critical, you know that, right?"

"No problem, bud. We're a team and I know my place, and yours. Everything's cool. Go home, get some *zeds*. We'll kick ass tomorrow."

Foley could tell Mat was tired — *too tired* to deal with the news of Jack Kincaid's *death,* and too tired to process the prospect of his wife's involvement with another man. *Rest well, young friend. Tomorrow your world is gonna change,* Foley thought to himself.

"Good plan. Missed ya, buddy. And don't worry, I'm home now, *you'll be fine.* Talk in the mornin'," Mat completed the call and snapped shut his cell.

CHAPTER 25

EARLY NEXT DAY, Mat woke up feeling surprisingly energized. He was on fire to do something ambitious and he wanted to get this project finished. After a shower and a shave, he stepped into some fresh clothes and went downstairs for a bite of eggs and toast for breakfast.

I know what. After a week and a half of eating and drinking to excess, I should hit the gym and go on a fitness kick for a few weeks. Gotta get buff while I still can, after all. Mat reasoned with himself. *I'll call Foley. He spends as much time at the gym as at the office.*

It was going on 9:00 a.m. by this point, so Mat picked his phone and dialed the office, knowing Foley would be at work by now. After a couple of rings, the line was connected and a pleasant female voice Mat recognized instantly as Danielle answered professionally.

"Good Morning, Bull Dog Security, Danielle speaking. How can I help you?"

"Hi there, girl Friday – and *every other* day. Did you miss me while I was gone?"

"Well, listen to you! Nice to have you back, Mathew." Danielle replied cheerfully. "How was your trip? Get everything done you wanted to?"

"And then some," Mat responded, smiling. "How's business been? Any major problems?"

"None that I couldn't handle. A lady came in just before you left with that package of documents you were expecting. She was going to courier them to you in Panama. D'ya get them alright?"

"Documents? A lady? What was her name?" Mat inquired.

"I never did get it. She was really nice but seemed to be in a big hurry. She asked me where to send them so I told her what hotel you were staying at. I hope that was alright. She said to tell you, 'I hope you enjoyed your surprise package in Panama,' or something like that."

Mat paused, connecting the dots as to what must have gone down, then he started laughing quietly, amazed again at the mystery and allure of this woman, Adriana Santos. She was a schemer, a planner, a thinker — like him.

"Yes, I got the package alright. And I *did indeed* enjoy the surprise," he said, grinning widely.

Changing the subject, Mat went on, "Hey, has Foley come in yet. I'd like to talk to him."

"Ya, sure. He's right here. I'll put him on," Danielle said.

"Good. Oh, wait, Danielle?"

"Yes?"

"Is there *anything else*, we need to talk about?" Mat tried to ask discreetly.

"No, I don't think so. Like what?" She seemed puzzled.

"Everything okay with you, as far as the job is concerned?"

"My job? Ya... I guess so. Why do you ask?"

"First chance I get, we're going to have a sit down and review everything – what you do, all your contributions and rewards, your whole job description, and how well you're doing at it, okay?"

"You mean a performance review?" she asked, apprehensively.

"Not really. We're a small company, and I don't like the formality of those things. They just put everybody on edge and usually cause more friction and resentment than anything. Let's just call it a good, honest discussion. Don't worry, there's good things, *better things*, in store for you here. I just wanted to let you know. You're one in a million and I don't want you getting quietly frustrated without letting me in on it. Okay?"

"Okay, Mr. Crawford. I'll get Foley now for you. Hold on a sec," and she transferred the call to Foley's line. She gazed out the window by her desk, perplexed as to what that was all about.

"Hey, Fole, you doing anything important right now?" Mat opened up.

"No, just talking to customers, dealing with Revenue Canada, paying bills, ordering stuff from suppliers, and fixin' a broke down photocopier that should have been replaced two years ago. Just the usual."

"Got your gym bag in the car?" Mat went on.

"Always."

"Drop what you're doin' and let's go for a workout. I'm in the mood to start a fitness program. Meet me at the gym 'bout ten? We can talk about everything while we're there," Mat persuaded.

"Alright, sure. Not my usual time of day for this, but I can change it up, I guess."

Mat walked into Gold's Gym a few minutes before 10:00 o'clock and Foley was already there, easily finishing his second set on bench. Two plates on each side at forty five pounds each plus the bar, put his opening resistance at two hundred twenty-five pounds. Not bad, nearly his own weight.

"Hey, Buck. All rested up and ready to sweat?" Foley spoke up as Mat crossed the floor.

"Yup. I'm going to take a few weeks here and try and get some semblance of fitness back. All I've done is eat and drink for months, the last week especially," Mat replied, regretfully.

"'*kay*... So your first couple o' weeks will just be breaking in old muscles that haven't been used much lately. Guess that leaves out your love muscle," Foley put in a playful dig.

Mat laughed and replied, "You're one to talk! I gather you've up'd your batting average lately, although anything better than a dead stop is an improvement, I suppose."

"Honestly, she's been too injured for any kind of carryin' on in the bedroom, but when she's better, and ready, I'm pretty sure she'll give me the nod," Foley countered.

"Can't wait to hear you brag about it, now what about a training schedule."

"Okay, Arnold, so you wanna pack on some muscle, do ya? Here's the plan. Week one, you'll do high reps, low weight, and finish with twenty minutes cardio. You'll target all the major muscle groups, including legs, and go on a four days on and two days off rotation. You'll also focus on your core strength and work your abs and lower back. On your days off you'll still do cardio, but at lower intensity.

"Your diet will consist of sixty percent carbs, mainly fibrous veggies and a limited amount of fruit, and forty percent lean protein — fish, chicken, high quality beef and the like, and you'll supplement with whey protein powder twice a day and multivitamins. You'll cut out all processed foods, fats, dairy, and white starchy carbs like bread, pasta and rice until your body composition is lean and mean, and you'll eliminate the use of salt, sugar, and alcohol at the table."

"Jesus," Mat interjected. "I said I wanted to get in shape, not train for Mr. Olympia!"

Foley replied, "Oh, come on now, it'll be fun if you get your head around it right. Think of it as a military boot camp, like you're preparing to join the army. You just need a drill sergeant to help you reach your goals. I'll guide ya down the road to discipline and excellence!"

"Alright then, *Sarg*, but what if I go to all the trouble, and it doesn't work? Will I just be wasting my time? What if this wasn't a good idea."

"*Negative. At ease, soldier.* What if my aunt had balls? Then she'd be my uncle. It'll work, by God. I'm a personal trainer who gets results! What do I look like, Richard Simmons?"

"No, I do."

"Not when I'm done with ya. Weeks two and three we'll start upping the weight your lifting until a couple months down the road, your at your maximum resistance. Pushin' hard and heavy activates the testosterone production in your knackers, and that's where you'll really start packin' on the beef. You'll find that your mental alertness and overall energy will gradually improve too. It's not just a physical thing, this weight training. Am I goin' too fast for ya? You payin' attention?"

"Maybe I'll just call Jenny," Mat replied.

"Sorry, there's a big difference between losing a ton of body fat through some temporary diet manipulation, and developing a strong, densely muscled, well balanced, hard body for the long term. One's a treatment for obesity. The other's a lifestyle change and a commitment to health and fitness. Don't worry kid, when you've reached your goals, more or less, you can start cheatin' just a little, and sneak in the odd beer or desert.

Remember, climbin' the mountain is the hard part and you have to show intestinal fortitude, then it gradually gets easier."

"Sounds like it'd be easier to win the *Tour de France*, but okay, let's get started." Mat conceded.

"What are you whining about? Lance Armstrong did it seven times – after he beat cancer, and we don't hear him *belly achin'* about how difficult it was. Which reminds me, Arnold Schwarzenegger, another *pretty good* athlete, won Mr. Olympia seven times too. But then what did he ever amount to after that?" Foley remarked.

Mat looked on and replied whimsically, "A movie star? Governor of California — a state with roughly the same population as all of Canada? Married into the Kennedys? Ya, he should have done better."

"My point, exactly. Now get on that tread mill and warm up. A great journey begins with but a single step. From a small acorn grows the mighty oak."

"*Oh, Jesus,*" Mat said, stepping on the machine.

"One other thing," Foley added as Mat was starting to jog on the moving belt. "While you're in training, there can't be any foolin' around with females, whatsoever. You'll have to completely suppress the libido. Makes you weak, and fat, and interferes with your focus."

"Mat's head snapped around and he looked at Foley speechless, like *enough was enough.*

Foley grinned and relented. "Okay, maybe just the odd time, if it's *quick*, and the word *love* never gets mentioned, and no cigarette afterward," and they both laughed out loud.

Mat picked up the pace on the treadmill and started breathing harder. Foley coached him, "Remember now, to inhale and exhale, deeply. You want to oxygenate your blood. Breathing is very important during exercise."

"Also, at *all other* times," Mat pointed out, insightfully.

As Mat worked up a rhythm on the tread mill, he asked, "So what happened while I was in Panama? You get the goods delivered to Wexler alright?"

"Sure did. Went down slicker 'n snakes in a snot barrel. You'll have a hay day clickin' away on your laptop, movin the money around the globe," Foley replied.

"Keep your voice down. There's lots of people in here," Mat cautioned. "What about Kincaid? What were you trying to tell me about him last night?"

Foley hesitated and looked uncomfortable before answering. "Mat, I'm sorry to report, Jack won't be returning calls anymore."

"What? What are you saying?"

"He was coming out of his brother's condo downtown where he was layin' low couple days ago, and someone shot him with a crossbow, right through the chest. Poor bugger died on the spot."

"How'd you find out about all this?"

"I tried callin' him to see how much more money was comin' in before you got home and couldn't find him anywhere's. Finally I tracked down his brother and he gave me the news. He was pretty shook up."

"Ah, don't tell me... *Jesus, Jack, how did they find you?*"

"That part, I can't tell you," Foley replied.

Mat weighed up the situation. "Okay, so let's think... *think*. Who's going to be our contact point for cash transfers from now on? I guess the million bonus for executing the whole process without incident is history now. Who do we deliver the money to once it's been laundered?"

Foley rubbed his knuckles across the stubble on his jaw. "Dunno, but this whole damn project is comin' down like a house of cards, if you ask me. If I weren't a better man I'd be tempted to say *I told ya so,* right from the start."

"I don't disagree, but there's no turning back, I'm afraid. We have to work this thing to a point where they'll willingly release us. We signed on to launder the drug money from the cocaine they heisted from the Red Sun Boys. Until that's complete, I don't really see any way out."

"We're headin' downhill toward a steep cliff in a bus with no brakes if you want my opinion. Better to jump out now, than consider our options when we're in mid air," Foley reasoned.

Mat was sweating now from working the tread mill but still smiled at the analogy. "As usual, you have a way with words that uniquely illuminates the situation, my friend."

"Just tellin' it like it is," Foley replied.

"So, Kincaid is out of the picture. What's the good news?" Mat pressed on.

"There ain't any. In fact, it gets worse," Foley said.

"Worse?"

"Ya, it's about Christine."

"What about 'er?"

"She, uh, appears to have found herself a… *boyfriend,*" Foley said, looking down to avoid eye contact.

Mat stopped jogging the tread mill. "What? What are you talking about?"

"Well, I found out where she's been staying, and I followed her home one night."

Foley shared with Mat all the difficult details he knew and saw, and if a picture is worth a thousand words, he reluctantly opened up his cell and showed him the captured images too, to Mat's astonishment. Then he put the phone away and stopped talking, and both men just stared blankly, digesting the uncomfortable facts.

"I guess I shouldn't be surprised. Did I think she was going to live in a nunnery without me? And I'm one to be judgmental, after the week I just spent in Panama." Mat looked sick.

Foley consoled his friend. "Don't be too hard on yourself, Buck. The book of any man's life is full of surprises. Not all of 'em are good. C'mon, we gotta keep workin'. There's always excuses to cave. Quitters cave. We ain't quitters. You march on, no matter what life throws at you. Did I mention that before? Your pecs need some work, by the way. Here's another thing, we've been followed since we arrived here. See those guys over there with all the tattoos and piercings? They've been watchin' us like we're movie stars the whole time we've been here. They don't know it, but I'm watchin' them too."

Mat looked and sure enough, three guys were working together on gym equipment that they obviously weren't familiar with. They were watching the two men with interest, alright, and Mat shifted his gaze so as not to make it obvious that they'd been made. *That Foley's good*, Mat thought to himself. *Got a sixth sense, that bugger, I swear.*

"Who do ya think they are? And why would they be doggin' us?" Mat wondered aloud.

"Dunno. But maybe we should put the question to 'em personally. Let's go have a little chat and see how they account for themselves," Foley replied as he paced across the floor to the Smith machine where they were attempting squats with the worst form imaginable. *They probably won't be able to climb stairs tomorrow*, he wise cracked to himself. He approached the three men and stood before them without speaking.

"You wanna work in?" one of them asked.

"No, thanks. I wanna know if there's something my friend and I can do for you guys. Maybe you'd like an autograph or something?" Foley was pumped from heavy lifting and he was an imposing and threatening sight.

By now Mat had crossed the gym floor as well and stood a few feet away from Foley at his side. The three body building imposters looked nervously at each other and one of them spoke up.

"Hey Mister, we're not lookin' for any trouble here, okay?"

"No? Well I get kinda jumpy when I see three guys watchin' me like they're up to no good. Suppose you let us in on the secret. Why are you tailing us?" Foley asked directly. He didn't look like he was in any mood for *smart ass* answers.

"Just doin' our job. We're *not* up to no good. We work for the Kings Crew," he said quietly. We're *associates*. Trying to prove we've got what it takes. Our boss wanted us to tag along behind you, that's all. Wants to know where you hang out, what you do with yourselves all day, where he can find you if he needs to."

Mat entered the conversation. "We're going back to our office at Bull Dog Security, after this. He can reach either of us there almost anytime. If we're not there, he can leave a message and my secretary will track us down. And your boss doesn't need to spy on us. We made a deal and we're holding up our end of it. Questions?"

The one doing the talking just shook his head. The last thing these three wanted to do was get into an extended conversation, or anything else.

Foley added, "Okay, and take that foam pad off the bar. Real lifters don't use 'em. They're for the ladies." The bikers looked at each other laughed embarrassedly. Foley and Mat went back to their workout.

After more than an hour of pumping iron and conversation, the boys showered and changed back into street clothes and headed back to the office. When they arrived, Danielle had slipped out for lunch, but she left them a message on a sheet of foolscap.

Hi Foley and Mat,

I'm just out for a quickie — lunch, that is! Should be back by about 1:00.

Someone named Dominic Hall called but didn't leave a message. Said he'd call you back later.

Foley, you're supposed to call Crystal. Needs you to pick up a few things for her on the way home.

BRB,

D.

P.S. Mat, missed you. Welcome home!

CHAPTER 26

"DOMINIC HALL... *YOU remember him,*" Foley said with exaggerated cheerfulness. Mat's palms got clammy, remembering his last encounter with the revolver-pointing, accountant-biker. The deal was that Jack Kincaid was supposed to be their only point of contact in this arrangement, but obviously, that was no longer possible.

"He must know that Kincaid bought it," Mat replied. "Or he wouldn't be contacting us directly."

"What do you think he wants?"

Mat put a *duh* look on his face. "Oh, probably wants to know if we'd like to join him for tea and biscuits this afternoon."

Foley laughed like a good sport. "Don't patronize me. You can't be this good lookin' and smart too."

"Sorry. Honestly? I think he wants to get the drug money to us directly from here on, since Jack's outta the picture. What else could it be?" Mat said. "Guess we'll have to wait 'til he calls back."

Mat looked at a pile of letters on his desk and said, "Looks like I need to wade through this snail mail. Mind watching the phone 'til Danielle gets back?"

"Well, I'll answer it if it rings. Don't think I need to watch it too."

"I see what you mean. *You are* good lookin'," Mat replied.

Mat started fumbling with letters and envelopes on his desk and Foley sat down in his office. Since it was quiet for the moment, he picked up his handset and dialed home to talk to Crystal.

"Hello?" She answered.

"Hey, buttercup, it's me. Danielle left a message that you called," Foley said. "What's up?"

"Oh, hi Karl. Listen, I need a few things and I don't really want to go out until the bruising is gone from my face. Do you think you could help out with some shopping?"

"Absolutely, anything you want, sweet thing. What can I do for ya?"

Foley listened quietly for a minute or two and developed a troubled look on his face. He wrote on a slip of paper, a shopping list for Crystal.

"Uh huh, okay, Ya, I can do that, I guess. I suppose other guys do it." Another moment or two went by. "How do ya spell that? Never heard of the stuff. What does it do. *Really?* What if I can't find it?" he continued. "Well, no, it's not that. I suppose I could ask for help. It's not the kind of thing most men normally do, but, I'm okay with it, for you." Foley waited and listened patiently. "Ya, I understand, *I get it.* You'll be all healed up and back on your game in no time," Foley reassured her. "Leave it with me. I'll be home by happy hour. Put the wine in the fridge. I'll see ya soon, Rocky." He finished the call and hung up, looking concerned.

Mat walked out of his office and strolled down the hall by Foley's door.

"Bills, bills, bills. This business is a money pit," Mat griped. "What's eatin' you? You just get notified you're being audited?"

looking in at Foley, sitting pinch faced and crouched behind his desk.

"No, I'm fine. No problems here." Foley replied a little abruptly.

Mat let it go and carried on with business matters.

At around mid afternoon everyone was working busily at Bull Dog Security when line one lit up and Danielle responded by answering it promptly. After a brief interchange she transferred the call to Mat.

"Mat Crawford, can I help you?"

"Hello, Crawford, Dom Hall here."

"Ah. I've been expecting your call. Are you alright? I heard about the invasion at your business. Sorry to hear about Carlos."

"I'm alright, thanks for asking. You wouldn't believe what those animals did to our place. Ransacked the building. Killed a bunch of innocent employees, and ya, we lost Carlos too."

"So, where do we stand now? Where's the stash of drugs? Did they find it and steal it back? Are we all still in business?" Mat asked in rapid succession.

"I love the way you tip toe around a subject, Crawford. You'll find out, as we find out. You probably know as well that Jack Kincaid was murdered too by those fuckers," Dominic went on.

"Yes."

"I got your message just before he was killed. We pulled in as much money from the street as possible. A little over three million," Dom explained. "We'll have to meet someplace to transfer it."

"Okay. You'll need to buy enough large duffle bags to transport it, then we can meet someplace secure by tomorrow afternoon. How about that vacant building we all met in the first time? The one on 146th in Surrey," Mat proposed.

"Sure, don't see why not. I'll send some scouts ahead of us to make certain everything's cool. How's four tomorrow sound?" Dominic said.

"Sounds like a plan, *for now*. But listen, word has it, the punks forced Carlos at gunpoint to say where the rest of the stash was being held. Did they manage to steal it back?" Mat asked again, bluntly.

"Well, let's just say they put a minor dent in our operation, but we're not outta business, by a long shot. There'll be enough cash flow to keep you busy for a while yet," Dominic said with confidence. "First things first, let's get this next package in the system and back to us as *legit* currency. Your fees will be close to a million by my calculations. Pretty good incentive?"

"Pretty good. Let's talk at 3:00 p.m. tomorrow to make sure everything's 'a go'. I've got the number your at now on my received calls list. Shall I use this number?"

"Ya, it's my cell. I'll be waiting. Tomorrow then at 3:00." And the line went dead.

Mat had that feeling in his gut that something wasn't right, or maybe it was just all the murders and mayhem that had gone down lately. After a moment, he dismissed it and went about his business. He decided he needed some comfort and wanted to talk to Adriana, so she was his next call.

"Hola, señor Crawford," she answered seductively. "Still diggin' me?"

"You bet. Haven't seen you in nearly twenty four hours. I'm having withdrawal symptoms I think. I take it you have call display," he said.

"I have women's intuition, even better," she replied. "I knew you'd be thinking about me and just *have* to call by now."

"Pretty confident, are we? You *knew* I'd call?" He was smiling, and picturing her pretty face and feminine manner.

"Yes, I always know what you're thinking, near or far. Don't ever forget that, Mister," she said in a sultry, vamp-like voice. It was a little scary, actually. She was controlling this conversation, he realized.

Mat replied, "What are you, psychic?"

"No. I'd prefer to call it connected. It's like I'm plugged into your thoughts and emotions at all times. I can feel you, *like warm sunshine* on my face."

Mat was amused (and smitten). "Warm sunshine? Glad I have that effect on you."

"Yes, and maybe sometime we'll talk about some other effects you have on me physically, at a primal level." She made a purring sound, like a cat. *"Prrtttt, prrtttt, prrtttt…"*

"Oh, you are good," he schmoozed.

"You should know. Not many secrets between us anymore."

"No, but we share some secrets together, don't we?" he reminded her. "Tell me something."

"Anything," she replied cooperatively.

There was a pause. "What are you *wearing?*" he asked with a quivering voice, like a pervert.

Adriana tried, but failed to stifle a laugh. "Well, I have on a garter belt, and black fishnet stockings, with six inch stilettos, a teensy bra with tassels, crotchless panties, and… Do you realize I'm at work!" she interrupted the fantasy.

"Ya, thank god you stopped," he replied. "A few more seconds and I might've had an accident. Goose bumps all over."

"You're such a *guy!*"

"Translation — Pig!" Mat confessed.

"Right. Hey, actually I'm really glad you called." Adriana took a more serious tone. "Do you think you could stop by my place after work, *and not*, to finish our little role play. It won't take long."

"Of course. Need me to fix a faucet, or something?"

"No, actually, there's someone I'd like you to meet. I think you'll find him interesting. I certainly do," she said convincingly.

"Who is he?" Mat asked.

"It's a surprise. C'mon, I played along with your little game," she said. "Now I really do have to get back to work. Come by around seven. I'll make dinner. Deal?"

"Okay, I'll be there, gorgeous," Mat said. "Oh, Adriana, *wait*. One other thing…"

"Ya?"

"I take it you haven't heard about Jack, yet."

"Jack? No. What about him?"

"I'm sorry to pass on bad news. He's been killed, I'm afraid. Murdered."

"Oh, God… no! When? How?" she asked, almost panic stricken.

"Couple of days ago. Someone shot him with an arrow. Likely the Red Sun Gang. How they tracked him down, I don't know," Mat explained. "But this changes things, I don't have to tell you. It's getting more dangerous by the day and we're going to have to finish up this assignment and make our exit, fast."

The two discussed details of the matter as fully as Mat knew them and agreed to process all outstanding funds through the accounts of the Empressa. The original timeline for completing the project was three to four months. Considering the pace that things were falling off the rails, Mat suspected that that estimate might be shortened considerably. He and Adriana agreed to march forward with their end of the agreement and launder the funds as quickly as they came in.

By quittin' time everyone at Bull Dog had had enough of the place for one day, thank you. Mat had to return a week's worth of calls and open the same amount of mail. Foley had done his usual chores around the office and had visited some customers, and had his weight workout mid-day rather than after work. Danielle had been on pins and needles all day about what it was Mat wanted to have an *open, honest discussion* about. But then he didn't say another word about it to her all day.

After saying goodbye extra nicely to Danielle, Mat went home to freshen up before going to meet the *mystery man* at Adriana's. Foley tucked his shopping list for Crystal into his shirt pocket, and proceeded to the nearest mall.

No biggy, I've handled harder assignments than this, he thought to himself, stoking his courage for the job ahead. He took the closest parking spot he could find to the mall doors to make a hasty retreat once his mission was accomplished. Images of the IKEA lady shouting *'Start the car! Start the car!'* while running frantically to her vehicle danced through his head.

Entering the mall, he located the Pharmasave on the floor directory. There it was, Section F, store number 24. He walked purposefully down the mall corridor until the subject store was in front of him. He walked in looking left, then right. He noticed his palms were sweaty. Picking up one of those little carry baskets, he reconnoitered until he found his way to the battle zone... Feminine Products, *Isle C.*

He turned and walked down the isle as cautiously as if he was entering a mine field. Words like Maxi, Ultra, Kotex, Tampons, KY, Vagisil, Canesten, and Summer's Eve screamed out to him from the labels of little boxes of female fixations that no man in his right mind would get caught even looking at, much less buying. This might be harder than he was expecting. Truthfully, he would gladly take on Scarface and the goons all over again, than go through this.

"Can I help you with anything?" a female voice said from behind him as he was examining the label on a box of Carefree Feminine Light Pads.

Foley nearly jumped out of his skin, turned and shot a look at her like he'd been caught peeking in the keyhole of a women's washroom. Standing before him was an official looking lady, perhaps forty, garbed in the blue store uniform with her name badge 'Vicky'. If any more blood had rushed to his face he might have been in danger of suffering a cranial aneurism.

"Uh, *fine thanks*, I mean, uh, no, no!" he blurted out. *Piss off, and mind your own goddamned business,* is what he wanted to say.

"Excuse me?" she replied.

"Oh, well I... need some, stuff," he mumbled, almost incoherently.

"You?"

"Well, it's not *for me*. My girlfr... er, *my wife*, wrote me out a list," he lied.

"Maybe I can help," she said, taking unwelcome control of the matter.

Now other customers — women, were gathering 'round, curious about this intruder in *sector C*. One lady with a push cart containing a small girl in the child carrier moved by and gave Foley the *evil eye* as she passed. Men at both ends of the isle walked by and glanced at him suspiciously, clearly in a *no go zone*. He reached into his shirt pocket and fumbled with the piece of paper, now damp with perspiration.

"Let's have a look at that," the Gestapo sales lady ordered. *Your papers!*

Foley's hands were trembling slightly and in a fluster, he dropped it to the ground. He stooped down to retrieve it and clumsily bumped it under the shelf unit with his boot.

"Sir, *please*, let me get that," she said and bent over revealing the *T-bar* of her thong panties out the back of her skirt. The other shopper-ladies glared rays of fire into Foley like a flock of Madame Godzillas from all directions, as he looked involuntarily at her backside.

She reached under the bottom shelf and retrieved the folded piece of paper. Opening it up, her face registered surprise and she said almost accusingly, "Well, this is a *man's* hand writing. You said your *wife* wrote it."

Oh God, this was getting worse by the minute. Foley had not only been sent on a mission to hell, but now he was caught in *a lie* to boot, by Miss Busybody here.

"Well, ya, we did it on the phone, actually. I just wrote it down," he said awkwardly.

"Did it?" she repeated.

"Dictated... She dictated it, and I wrote it down, is what *we did*," he mumbled, his composure now utterly dismayed.

She put a questioning look upon him, not saying anything, which was ten times worse than discussing the matter, so he could make her understand his plight. *This is entrapment*, he thought.

Just as he was about to break down and storm out of the store empty handed, his eyes locked on someone turning down the isle that, rather than meet her here and now, he would have gladly donated a kidney, without anesthesia.

"Hi Foley! What are you doing here?" Danielle chirped, with two girlfriends in tow. "This is Cindy, and Pearl," she introduced her two pretty companions. They each extended their hands to greet Foley, their new friend, unaware of the depraved task he was undertaking.

285

Foley's face looked like he had just personally witnessed the eruption of Mount Saint Helens.

"Oh. Hi, Danielle. Just picking up some groceries and... *things*," he replied, lamely. Danielle's two friends circled and flanked him on each side preventing escape as they engaged him in torturous conversation.

By now the sales lady had efficiently collected all the items on Foley's list: feminine pads with wrap around wings, extra absorbent overnight poontons, or whatever they're called, Nair, little Vagisil wipey things, cotton balls, FDS, Lady Speed Stick, Midol, Salon Selectives hairspray, some kind of KY lubricant, Lady Schick razors, and an assortment of other *exclusively girl* items.

"Sir? Sir?" She barged into the conversation between him and the young ladies. "Here are the items on your shopping list." She dropped them into his basket. "Can I get anything else for you?"

How about my semi-automatic? Foley thought, silently.

Danielle and her friends looked wide-eyed at the incriminating evidence in Foley's hand basket which he was now holding like an unstable pale of nitro glycerin.

"I can explain," he said, pathetically.

"Hey, look, we're in a hurry too. You finish your shopping and have a nice evening, okay? See you tomorrow, Foley," Danielle said looking at him oddly, and the three girls rushed off, whispering to one another.

By the time Foley got back to his car, he felt like he'd just made a life altering escape from some televised new reality show highlighting the perils and humiliation of coupledom, with many more to follow — worse, he was certain. He vowed never to set foot in a drug store again, unless it was to buy men's shaving cream, Zam-Buk, or aspirin.

Although not normally prone to stunt driving, this time Foley floored it and laid a patch as he sped out of the parking lot. On the radio, Lady Gaga was belting out something about *'Caught in a bad romance,'* and Foley turned the volume up full blast as he made good his exit, singing along to the weird lyrics and tapping his fingers on the steering wheel to the mesmerizing beat.

CHAPTER 27

MAT FINISHED UP with some trusty old Aqua Velva after a quick shower and put on some fresh clothes before heading over to Adriana's place. It was only six so he still had an hour before he was expected. No rush. Try as he might, he couldn't imagine who Adriana might have lined up for him to meet. Someone she works with? A neighbor? Someone who might be a good business contact? *I think you'll find him interesting. I certainly do*, kept ringing through his head.

In keeping with the novelty of their relationship, Mat wanted to please her with an unexpected gift, so he stopped at the market on his way over and selected a lovely bouquet to present to her. She'd receive it with an appreciative hug and lingering kiss, one leg raised at the knee behind her back, as he pictured it in his imagination.

By the time he pulled up to her house, it was still only 6:50 p.m. but she did say, *around 7:00*, as he recalled. He slowly parallel parked the car and killed the distinctive growl of the BMW M3 engine. Taking hold of the fragile flowers carefully, he walked up the winding path to her front door and rang the bell beside the solid oak front door. Waiting, he observed that she lived well. This was a nice, expensive house, and he reminded himself that she did all this by herself — a single, career woman.

The door opened, and to Mat's surprise, it was a Filipino woman, maybe in her mid thirties.

"Hello, You must be *Mat-you*," she said in a welcoming tone, however in a distinctive accent.

"Yes, I'm here to see Adriana," he said.

"Of course. I'm Mina," extending her hand. "Please to meet you, sir. Won't you come dis way?"

She led Mat down the hallway of a long hardwood foyer into a large kitchen, amply lit by overhead skylights, where Adriana was working on what looked like a salad of some sort in a large glass bowl. She had on an apron, and her hair was pinned up behind her head in a messy, but pretty bun, uncharacteristic of any way he'd seen her in before.

"Hi Mat! I hope you're hungry. I've prepared one of my favorite meals. Caesar salad, Brazilian style, with Cajun blackened chicken and fettuccini. You've met Mina?"

"Yes, she introduced herself at the door." He held out the flowers to Adriana. "Here, something for your table."

"Wow, thanks! How thoughtful!" She set down the knife she was working with and embraced Mat with a quick hug. "Mina, can you finish this up, please?" she asked, as she snapped off the apron and led Mat to the family room.

"Can I get you something? A glass of wine?"

"Love one. Chardonnay?"

"House specialty," she replied, and proceeded to the bar, pouring them each a glass of chilled, velvety Lindeman's Bin 65.

He took note that this was the first time he was actually on her turf. They weren't in a hotel in some central American country now. They were in her comfortable surroundings, her safe haven, her home. Her sunglasses and car keys had been set on an Oprah magazine on the coffee table. He sat back in a plush, velour couch and sipped the ice cold, oak-scented wine from a long stemmed glass. It was creamy and smooth and just *good*.

"This is nice," Mat noted, tilting the glass up to the light.

"*Sunshine in a bottle*, they call it," Adriana replied. "Australian."

"You live well. I didn't know you had help," he said, referring to Mina.

"Oh yes. Couldn't do it without her. We've been together nearly ten years. Her full name is Yomina, but it's commonly shortened to just Mina in the Philippines."

"I guess you meant it when you said there weren't many secrets between us anymore," Mat quipped.

Adriana looked at him over the top of her wine glass as she sipped it sparingly.

"No, there aren't many more. Mat, before we go any further, I want you to know all about me, I mean us."

"Us? You and me?"

"Not exactly. I said I wanted you to meet someone today. Sit tight a moment and I'll be right back, okay?" She set down her glass, stood and left the room down a hall that seemed to lead to private quarters, bedrooms, or a reading room perhaps.

"Sure," he replied, baffled as to what to expect next.

In a few moments she returned, accompanied by a young boy, maybe ten, with her arm draped gently around his shoulder. He was a handsome lad with a shock of unruly dark hair shooting out from a ball cap jammed down tightly, backwards on his head. He had on blue jeans, a Vancouver Canucks hockey jersey, and white runners. He looked at Mat suspiciously with large, dark brown eyes.

"Mat, I'd like you to meet my son. This is Manuel. Manuel, say hello to Mat. He's my *friend*," she said.

Mathew and Manuel looked at each other, speechless. Adriana tried to read the expression on Mat's face, wondering whether this would be the end of everything, or the start of something wonderful. She regretted not having mentioned this detail earlier but in the hubbub of their whirlwind romance and all the events they experienced together, she just didn't.

After a pregnant pause, Mat stood and reached out to the boy with his hand, "Glad to meet you, Manuel." *Nice try*, but Mat still looked shell-shocked.

Manuel reciprocated, and reluctantly shook Mat's hand with a weak effort. "Hi, same."

With near inhuman restraint, Adriana didn't come to either's rescue. They would have to get over this introduction and come to terms with each other on their own. She tried to look busy, fluffing the throw pillows on the sofa.

"You must be about twelve, are you?" Mat encouraged conversation.

"No, ten."

"Wow, you're a big guy for ten. Play any sports?"

"I play soccer and take lessons in tennis and karate."

"Any good?"

"Got my green belt already. Sensei says I'm a *tiger*. You dating my mom?"

"Ya, *sort of* — no. It's like this, your mom and I are *seeing* each other. I mean we might…" Mat stopped himself, and addressed the boy more one on one, like buddies. "See, you can *date* someone, or you can really, really *dig someone*, like their *special*. Like they're *the one*, you understand?" Now he looked seriously at Manuel, eyebrows raised.

Manuel just looked at him, expressionless. Ten or fifteen seconds passed. "You wanna see my room?" he offered.

"Love to. You got any bugs, or spiders?"

"I got a garter snake. C'mon." Off the two boys went down the hall to share the treasures of Manuel's private quarters. Mat looked over his shoulder and locked eyes with Adriana. '*You blind sided me!*' his expression screamed.

Adriana might have been chained to the couch to prevent her from running down the hall to participate in the boys' one-on-one with each other, but instead she went back to the kitchen to attempt finishing making dinner with Mina like everything was the same between her and Mat.

Fifteen, twenty minutes later, everything was ready and Adriana called down the hall, "Boys, dinner's ready." No answer. "Boys, hello?" louder this time.

"Ya, we're coming," Mat called out in a muffled voice from a far away room. Together, Mat and Manuel emerged from the recesses of the boy's private place, where girls weren't allowed, and re-entered the kitchen. The ladies had set a lovely table and Mat's bouquet was placed in a crystal vase at the centre of it all, making the setting look inviting and fresh. Adriana scrutinized the faces of each of her men for clues as to how they got along, and it was obvious they had struck up a friendship.

"Mom, Mat knows how to catch a bird with a box and a string. And there's a place we're gonna go where you can drive go-carts and climb a rock wall," Manuel said excitedly.

Adriana looked at Mat and before she could say anything, he shot back, "Don't worry, it's safe."

"And Mat says we can rent a boat and go out in the harbor off Vancouver Island and catch wild salmon, then bring 'em back and gut 'em and cook 'em right here in our kitchen! He's gonna show me how to filet a fish, so the skin comes right off 'em with a knife. 'Fish guts from asshole to tea kettle', "Manuel said, making a slicing gesture with an imaginary razor sharp blade with his hands.

"Lovely," she remarked, casting an accusing look at Mat for the language.

"And he wants to come to my karate tournament next month, and I said he could. Can he Mom, *please?* Oh, and watch this. Mat can wiggle his ears. Show 'er Mat!"

Adriana interjected before she heard any more of these wild promises made to her son.

"In just fifteen minutes, you two seem to have covered a lot of ground down there in your dungeon. I'd hate to see what happens if you're together all day."

Mat smiled with a sparkle in his face that Adriana hadn't seen before. "Hey, Manuel, let's wash up. Dinner smells like heaven. I'm starving. How 'bout you?" Away the boys went to the washroom together, chattering about guy things the whole way.

The dinner went down like an unplanned party and Mat, Adriana, Manuel, and Mina each shared stories of their experiences and lives. Often the pitch of conversation was so animated that all four people were talking at once and there was laughter and happiness around the table that was spontaneous and genuine.

Mat even showed Manuel and the girls the static-electricity-finger trick, where you rub one index finger atop the other while balancing a quarter on its edge on the table to build up an electric charge. Then you run your top finger quickly down the other and, unperceivable to the others, clip the edge of the coin with the tip of your thumb making the coin spin like a top — due to the electric charge it acquired from rubbing your fingers together, *not.* Mat's audience was spellbound and amazed at how this was possible and, of course, no one else could replicate the feat.

"I don't know how you're doing that," Adriana said, "but I'm sure there's some trick of deception going on."

Mat replied in the tone of the head master in *Harry Potter*, "Oh yes. Sometimes the trick lies in the smallest of details, Hermione."

"*You* would know," Adriana made the astute observation.

Mat said, "Let me give you an example. Are you good at physics?"

"It wasn't my specialty, but I suppose I get by," she replied.

"Okay, picture this. There's an electric train roaring down the tracks travelling at fifty miles per hour. But there's a tail wind blowing at sixty miles per hour. Which way does the smoke go?"

Adriana puzzled over the question for a moment, performing mental calculations.

"Well, it would go forward, since the wind is going ten miles an hour faster than the train."

"*BZZZZD!* No — you flunk."

"Why not?" Adriana demanded.

"It wouldn't go anywhere. Electric trains don't make any smoke," Mat pointed out. The table erupted with outlandish laughter.

"Okay, I'll give you another chance. Try this one... If Billy-Joe rode into Amarillo, Texas on Friday, and stayed in a hotel 'til Monday for six days, how is that possible?"

The table was silent as everyone labored for an answer.

"Alright, I give up. It's *not* possible, mathematically," Adriana finally said.

Mat grinned. "It's easy. The horse's name was Friday!"

Adriana put her head back in her hands and said, *"Oh... My... God. And I graduated top of my class!"*

Then she responded with a challenge of her own. "Okay, wise guy, try this one. A boat is moored in the harbor at low tide and it has a ladder hanging off the back with five rungs, the fifth one just at the water line. The rungs are each spaced exactly one foot apart. Then the tide comes in at a rate of six inches every half hour. After two hours, how many rungs will be above the water line?"

Manuel's hand shot up almost instantly. He was certain he nailed this one.

"Manuel?" Adriana said.

"Three," he announced confidently.

Adriana looked at Mat, then cross examined, "Mister Crawford, do you agree?"

Mat paused, smiling. "No."

"Why not?"

He was clearly suppressing a smile. "Boats float. It would rise with the tide and there'd still be five rungs out of the water."

Clearly frustrated, Adriana dissed him, "Oh you're such *spoil sport.* You could have given me this one!" She threw a dinner roll at him across the table, but he ducked it like *Dubya* dodging an Iraqi shoe at the podium.

"Never try to outfox a fox. You're *O for two,* baby," Mat scoffed, gloating and laughing over his little victory.

"Food fight!" Manuel yelled, rising from his chair beside Mat and reaching for the bowl of dinner rolls.

"No, no, no, no..." Mat said holding Manuel's arm. "Your mom's right. A gentleman would have conceded the point. It

isn't nice to bully a lesser opponent. Men shouldn't outsmart girls."

Adriana looked thoroughly insulted — in a feminist sort of way. "Men? Girls? Outsmart? Be careful, buster, or you'll be dealing with a lot more incoming than just a wild bun!" They all laughed like rival family members taking verbal jabs at one another.

By the end of it all, Mat said, "Well, this certainly was an exquisite dinner. You didn't tell me you could cook."

"I was just the under study, I'm afraid. Thank Mina," Adriana replied modestly. Mina waived her hand like it was no big deal.

"You didn't tell me a lot of things, actually," Mat remarked.

"Manuel, why don't you go get your things ready for tomorrow. It's the start of sports camp, remember? You'll need to organize your back pack," Adriana instructed her son. "Why don't we retire to the family room and try and settle down a bit. Mina, can you put on some coffee, please."

Manuel pushed away from the table and said, "Okay, mom. See ya later Mat!"

"See ya later, buddy," he responded warmly.

Mina took charge of the clean up and started busily picking up dishes and putting pans and utensils in the sink.

Adriana led Mat into a room off to the side where they sat down together on a couch in front of a bay window with a picturesque view of Vancouver. Neither spoke as they admired the sparkling lights of a great city at night shimmering before them like luminescent stars in a velvet black, summer sky. Mina had lit the fireplace earlier, and it was snapping away, sending up sparks and smoke, filling the room with a pleasant burnt larch aroma. The two of them sat, cuddling, chatting, and sipping icy, white wine for a half hour, or so.

Finally, Mat said, "I thought you said you'd never had a serious, committed relationship."

"That's true. I haven't."

"But, Manuel?"

"I was young. It was just a date, we were partying and things got… Well, you know. Later I found out I was pregnant. It was a mistake. *Have you* ever made a mistake?" Before Mat could answer, she went on, "Men have dates and sex and go their merry ways. Women do it and sometimes there are consequences. I was carrying life, and I couldn't bear to put an end to it. Suddenly, he was part of me. I wasn't proud of it, but I wanted him desperately, and I decided to take responsibility for it. I *wanted* my baby, and I had him, and here we are."

"You should have told me."

"I was scared."

"Scared? Of what?"

She paused, weighing her words carefully. Her eyes glassed over. "Scared of losing the first real thing I've ever had. Scared of killing an opportunity for love and companionship before it got a start. Scared of having nothing in my world but business and career and my son. Scared of remaining single and lonely, but for Manuel and Mina, for the rest of my life. Scared of growing old and missing out. Scared of…"

"*I get it,*" Mat interrupted. "Don't worry. We're in this together. I'm not going anywhere, and I hope you're not either. I'm here for you, Adriana. On the flight home, I said I'd stand by you, no matter what, remember? Which reminds me …"

This time Adriana interrupted. "Don't worry, I'm *not* pregnant. It was a false alarm." She wiped her eyes with her hand and sniffled back, suppressing a giggle.

"Did you get a home test kit?"

"Didn't have to. Nature gave me the message this morning, loud and clear. I must have just been off my schedule from travelling and all the excitement. Had you going there for a while though, didn't I?" and they both laughed together, not certain whether to be relieved or disappointed at the news. Mat put his arm around her and kissed her temple.

"Anyway, lover boy, you still have a wife and daughter out there, I hesitate to remind you," Adriana pointed out.

"Ya," he replied, adding nothing further.

Sitting side by side, they watched the distant lights of downtown Vancouver's streets, traffic, and buildings pulsating before them almost like a living organism, and contemplated their situation. How would drugs, and crime, and gangs, and money laundering, and deception fit in with this new world of happiness and opportunity opening up before them? How would Mat resolve his marital problems, whether Christine wanted to come back, or whether she had left for good? Adriana wondered where she really stood, under either scenario. Mat had a pleasant buzz on from the wine by now, and just stared contentedly at the lights of the city.

As if on cue, they each lifted their glasses and took a liberal sip of the tasty, soothing wine.

CHAPTER 28

THE NEXT DAY, Mat prepared for his meeting with Dominic Hall in Surrey. Aside from the revolver incident during their first meeting, Mat had a queasy feeling about the man. The more he thought about him during their first encounter, the more he decided that he was just a biker in a phony suit, without many redeeming qualities. Dom was a good actor — he'd give him that. He could act like a gentleman, but underneath he was just a foul mouthed, scheming hood, plain and simple. He wouldn't trust the man or take his word at face value under any circumstances. Still, he had no option but to meet with him, get the next transfer of cash and proceed with the money laundering. *Get it over with.*

Driving to the office that morning his damned internal voice was chattering away, like usual. *Who am I to take the high road. You're dealing with some biker posing as an accountant that you knew from the start was a drug runner and criminal, and you don't trust him? There's a surprise. But you're a fine, upstanding money launderer… That's different, and you've got principles and values that distinguish you among regular criminals. That'll work in your favor in court… Eligibility for parole in fifteen, rather than twenty.*

And let's talk about Christine. She disappoints you because she walked out of a marriage where her husband and confidant kept secrets from her about his criminal activities. You not only put yourself in jeopardy but her and Hannah as well, and she put her foot down and said, 'I'm opting out on this plan, pal.' You did lie to her after all, didn't you? Because your ego is so big, then you find it hard to believe that she would engage in an extramarital affair after she left you? And just what do you think you were doing in Panama, Mister Double Standard?

"Okay, shut up already!" Mat said out loud. "The time's over for second guessing it. Nobody's perfect!" *Least of all you,* his little voice persisted. "Shut up, I said."

Mat pulled in and parked, then walked into the front door of his office.

"'Morning, Danielle. Everything copacetic?"

"Copa-who?" she replied. "Isn't he some director in Hollywood?"

He chuckled. "Never mind. Foley come in yet? And it's Coppola, as in Francis Ford," he added.

"Ya, he's in his office, and you have a visitor as well."

"I do? Who?"

"Your wife. She's waiting in your office."

Mat stopped dead in his tracks. Wherever a conversation with his wife might go now, it wouldn't likely be anyplace good. Mat took a deep breath and with false courage walked down the hall to his office door. He entered the room and there she was — *Christine,* his lovely wife, mother of his child.

She wore a white summer dress with a pink floral pattern and a wide brimmed hat with blonde, wavy locks falling around her shoulders, and she looked wonderful, beautiful. For a moment, his heart fluttered with delight at her presence. No matter what, he would always love her — his *first* love, beyond measure.

"Hello, Mat."

"Hi. You didn't tell me you were coming."

"No. I just decided this morning that it's time we talked. I can come back if it's not a good time," she said.

"No, that won't be necessary. I don't think my wife needs an appointment to see me. Now's fine." Mat called down the hall for Danielle to hold his calls. He closed the office door.

The two looked at each other awkwardly. "Well, where do we start?" he said.

"Mat, I'm so sorry that it's come to this. I want you to know that more than anything I don't want anything bad to happen to you. *Please...* take care of yourself and don't put yourself in a position where you might end up in jail, or hurt, or worse."

"No, I wouldn't want that to happen," he agreed, compliantly.

"See, I'm not like you," she went on. "I can't live a normal life and pretend everything is fine and dandy when you're engaged in something dangerous and illegal and *stupid,* frankly. I'm not the adventurous type, I guess. I wanted a colonial style house with a white picket fence and two kids and a dog. And a husband that sold insurance or managed a bank branch, like before."

"I tried that format, remember?"

"Yes, I remember, and you got fired. So what? It happens all the time, and people don't all turn to crime when it does. You've got to get over it. It's eating you up like a smoldering fire and one day it could, no — it *will* kill you!"

"I am over it. Couple of months and I'll just be the co-owner of a small security company, earning a regular living, paying taxes, curling on Saturdays, and attending church on Sundays."

"Somehow, I doubt that. But I want you to know a few things."

"Like what?"

"First, you've probably guessed by now. I'm *not* coming back." She paused and they looked at each other painfully. "And it's not just because of your involvement in money laundering."

"What do you mean?"

"There's someone else, actually. We've known each other for a long, long time at work, and we started out as friends, but over time it grew, and now…"

Mat cut her off. "Okay, I get the drift. You're seeing someone else who you met at work, the elementary school. What, another teacher?"

"Well, a guidance counselor," she specified.

"Oh, that's just perfect. And does this counselor specialize in promoting marital estrangement for his own personal gratification? Did one thing lead to another and before long the two of you were rapturously entwined in his bed?" Mat was starting to lose his temper.

"No, it wasn't like that. We've been friends for years, and I'm not going into a long explanation about it. Look, I've known that something's been wrong between us for a long time now. You brood. You go inside. You're preoccupied with something private. You don't talk, except when you're with Foley. It's like your mind is somewhere else all the time. We don't really act like lovers any more."

"Pretty hard, when we're not sleeping under the same roof. I'm involved in something big here, Christine. I have to march ahead with it and I don't have the luxury of analyzing and grooming our relationship right now."

Christine wouldn't be side tracked.

"We've just sort of grown away from each other, Mat. It happens. People meet and fall in love, and sometimes even get married and have children, but then their lives take them in different directions and before long, their love story has ended. And other times, people stay married in misery, when they should have let it go a long time ago. This thing about *for better or for worse, 'til death do you part,* is a lot of phooey. When a marriage comes apart, the vows don't trump the need and desire for change. People get married and take those vows *two, three, six times* in a lifetime. It's just a ceremony to cement a new love relationship, and when it's dead, it's dead, understand? I know you do!"

She looked lovingly at Mat and try as he might, he knew her words were true.

Mat looked down but didn't argue the point. Despite his new found relationship with Adriana Santos, someone he connected with at a much more gut level at this time and place in his life, he *still* wanted Christine. Irrational and impossible — *yes,* but she was his *wife,* and a part of him didn't want to let her go, ever. But it doesn't work that way, does it? *You can't have both,* his little buddy spoke in lament.

Mat replied softly, "I don't know what to say." He wiped his eye with the back of his knuckle. He loved her, but this thing was stuck in the mud.

Christine picked up easily on his mood and spoke again, "No, baby, don't look at me that way. Our time together was good. We'll always remember the magic we had together. We were *in love,* and we have Hannah to show for it. Don't ever let that fade away, Mat. Life goes on. Things change. Nobody can stop that."

"Couldn't... if I wanted to," he said. "What about Hannah?"

"Hannah will always be your little gem, that's obvious. Whatever problems we have, you're still her daddy and she loves you. I don't want to play games between us with her as the prize. There'll be no custody disputes started on my end of things. We can work out a schedule for her to be with us both, if you're agreeable."

"Of course I'm agreeable," he said. He marveled at how she remained fair and reasonable, even when cutting the ties to their relationship. Many, would not. No wonder he still loved her.

After all, Mat relented to what seemed inevitable. You build a life with someone, then through no one's fault, really, you find yourself asking, *Who are you? Who am I? What happened to us?* Mat and Christine talked together for thirty minutes or so and came to an arrangement to end things amicably. *My attorney will be in touch with your attorney,* seemed a surreal way to close this episode of their lives.

In the end they still loved each other, but Christine's comments about growing apart were well taken. Sometimes, in the book of failed marriage it's better to preserve the love you had in the early chapters with good memories, and not let the relationship deteriorate into something ugly that ruins the whole story. This marriage had had a good run, but it was over.

Christine and Mat stood, looked at each other one last time as soul mates, and hugged like intimate friends parting at a fork in the road. "I'll walk you to the door," Mat said. "Don't expect you'll be back here any time soon."

"No, I guess not."

"Christine,"

"Ya?"

"Are you in love, *real* love, you and this guidance counselor?"

She looked downward, thinking and adjusted the brim on her big hat, then said, "Who knows what real love is? This isn't the movies, it's life. By the time you get it all figured out, it's too late, probably. We all just do our silly best a day at a time, until it's over. He's good to me, and Hannah, and he earns his money legally — *sorry.*"

"No cause to be sorry. You're more right than wrong, I'm afraid."

Mat saw Christine to the front door and as her car pulled away from the building, the remorse of his actions and involvement in crime settled with a grave weight on his chest. Now he'd succeeded in estranging his lovely wife, and achieving part-time status as father to his young daughter.

The image of lovely Adriana drifted across his mind, and he pondered, on the scale of things, whether it was really all worth it. *Trade offs. 'Exit wife, enter girlfriend.'* Go figure, he thought quietly as his mind drifted momentarily. *How many other guys have gotten messed up in their personal lives about women.*

Paul McCartney's first wife, Linda, passed on, then he married Heather Mills, after a whirl-wind romance and promptly got divorced six short years later, at a cost to Paul of $50 million.

Is Tom Cruise really any better off with Katie Holmes than Nicole Kidman? He's sixteen years older than her. How much can they have in common? When he made Top Gun, Katie was two years old, in diapers, learning to walk. What do you think they talk about at night. No wonder he was jumping on Oprah's couch like a fool declaring his love for a little girl young enough to be his daughter. He's into Scientology. There's a surprise! What about Brad Pitt? How long do you think he'll hold out with the gorgeous, but eccentric, Angelina, before he runs back to Jennifer, a much sounder choice in life partners? Mr. & Mrs. Smith is one movie role you should have walked away from, buddy.

Snapping back to reality, Mat realize he was trapped. He had to continue carrying out a money laundering operation that might well land him in jail or Mountain View Cemetery along side Jack Kincaid, his erstwhile partner, Captain Furlong, and numerous others caught up in this heist, soaked in the blood of almost everyone involved. *Sorry? Christine, I'm the one who's sorry. Sorry as hell, and caught in a dirty money trap.*

By 3:00 o'clock, Mat and Foley were sitting and talking together in Mat's office. As planned, Mat called Dominic Hall on his cell.

"Dom Hall," he answered.

"Hi, Dom. Mat calling. We still on at 4:00, in Surrey?"

"You bet. There's five duffle bags. Everything's set on my end."

"Sound's good. We'll be there at 4:00 p.m., sharp."

Both cell phones snapped shut and Mat started cleaning up his desk for the day. He and Foley talked about the cash transfer and decided to go in separate vehicles, just to be safe. Again, Mat clipped on his radio transmitter and Foley took the receiver.

As they were finishing up, Mat heard the front door chime and he heard Danielle say, "Well, Hello again, mystery lady!"

"Hi. Great to see ya! Still workin' for Mister Slave Driver?"

It was Adriana's voice. Mat wasn't expecting her and he wouldn't be able to visit long because of his meeting with Dom Hall.

"Ya, I'll be here 'til they fire me, or bury me, I guess." Danielle said. "You here to see him?"

"Please. Let him know it's Adriana."

Mat walked out of his office and greeted her personally. "Well, we have a surprise visitor. What, just in the neighborhood and decided to drop in?"

She reached out to embrace him, but he discreetly pulled back in front of Danielle. She didn't know anything about the complications of his social life yet.

"C'mon into my office. Let's talk," he said. *This room's getting more action today than the marriage counseling clinic down the street,* he thought to himself. Mat closed his door. Foley was still sitting in a chair in front of Mat's desk.

"You want to talk privately together?" he said. "I can clear out."

"No, I just didn't want Danielle to see something that she might misinterpret," Mat said.

"Boy, could I tell you a story on that subject," Foley replied.

Adriana was cheerful and spoke right up now to Mathew.

"Hey, business hours are nearly over, and I wanted you to help me pick out a new bike for Manuel. It's his birthday next week. Then I'll treat you to dinner at Earl's, or Montana's, or Joey Tomatoes, or where ever you want. How 'bout it?"

Mat paused. There's nothing he'd like better than to help out with a new bike for his new, young pal. But duty called and this was one meeting that could not be put off.

"I'd love to, really, but I have to meet with that biker-accountant, Dominic Hall. Foley's coming too. Since Jack Kincaid is out of the picture now we have to deal directly with the accountant. We're picking up a truckload of cash that'll go straight to the Empressa."

"Oh, I didn't think another transfer would be ready so fast," she said. "Alright then, I'm coming too!"

"No you're not. Don't be crazy!" Mat shot back.

"Why not? It's not like I'm new to this deal. I was in the meeting that got this whole thing off the ground, remember? Dominic already knows me, after all, and he knows my role was to act as your assistant and advisor. That's how Jack positioned it," Adriana argued.

"She does have a point," Foley added, earning a harsh stare from Mat. "It might show that you're holding to your part of the bargain and using all the resources that were made available to launder their funds quickly. They want their money back in a form that's usable, that much I know."

"See, Mat? Foley agrees with me," Adriana said. "You're right, he's smarter than he looks." Foley turned and shot a dirty look at Mat.

Mat argued, "Something unexpected or dangerous could happen. This is major crime we're involved with here. It doesn't draw the best people out of the woodwork," Foley looked them both up and down.

"Sort of goes with the territory in this business. I think that's what you told me a while back when this whole thing came up. She's a big girl — *figuratively speakin', Ma'am,"* Foley back peddled to Adriana.

Adriana jumped on it. "*Figure?* What about my figure, Mister Folkestad? Just what do you mean, *big girl?* I'm a size four!" she fibbed.

"No, Jesus! What is it with women? I just meant you're all growed up and capable of making your own decisions. Listen up, Mat, I say we take her, but it's up to you two, and I ain't sayin' another word, damn it."

Mat hesitated and clearly wasn't comfortable with it, but he relented.

"Okay, let's get ready then, or we'll all be late. Adriana, you ride with me. Foley will hang back in his own vehicle in case there's any trouble," and off the trio went.

Outside, Foley hopped in his own vehicle, while Mat and Adriana buckled into the cockpit of his sporty BMW. After ignition, Mat's engine rumbled with an understated, German engineered, signature growl. He pushed the stick into first and looked across the lot at his partner. Mat and Foley nodded to one another through their windows and the two autos pulled forward. The next cash pick up was under way.

At 4:00 p.m. Mathew and Adriana entered the building in Surrey where they'd all met the first time to launch the plan. They went back to the fourth floor and entered the suite, like before. In his Dodge Durango, Foley waited outside, a half block away, with his receiver turned on to overhear everything Mat talked about during the meeting.

"Hello again, my friends," Dominic called out from the far side of the room. "I see you two have managed to build a working relationship together, after all." He was sitting behind an old desk, with a can of coke, pullin' on a Cuban cigar. "I guess two heads are better than one." He exhaled a thick plume of blue-grey smoke up into the air.

"Especially when one head looks like hers," Mat replied, complimenting Adriana.

"And the other one *thinks* like his," she added.

"Come in and sit down, please. How has it gone so far, processing our money?" Dom asked.

Mat replied confidently, "Good, the first five million has been moved to an offshore account. We'll be able to transfer it back to Canada in a few days, in smaller sums as you need it. It won't attract any attention from the authorities. Simple wire transfers, they go on by the thousands, every day."

"Excellent! Jack was right about your skills in this field. I believe this will be the start of a long and profitable association," Dominic predicted.

Not on your life, mister. Once we're done laundering your drug money, you won't see us for dust, Mat thought.

"You said you had five duffle bags for us today?" Mat went on.

"Ya, downstairs in a van. Four of my most trusted colleagues are watching over it. You can just take the van and stash the cash until you can get it into the financial system. The *placement stage,* I think you called it," Dom replied.

"Very good," Mat tried to sound impressed at Dom's accurate recall. "How much this time?"

"$3,250,000."

"Alright then, shall we?" Mat said and Dom flipped him the keys to the van's ignition across the desk.

"I'll walk you down so my boys know you're part of the *good guys*."

"I can't say I've heard of the Kings Crew referred to in that context before," Mat commented, as they proceeded to the elevator together.

In the alley where the van was parked, two men sat inside and two more were positioned outside, one on each side, a few feet away. They were dressed in the informal uniforms of blue jeans, jack boots, and leather jackets, without any identifying insignias on them. They did not want to attract anyone's attention, as Kings Crew, on this occasion. No doubt they were all armed and experienced.

Dominic addressed them, "Boys, we'll take it from here."

The one who seemed to be the leader nodded, and the four of them disappeared, around the corner of the alley, onto the street. Moments later the distinctive *wap, wap, wap,* thunder of Harley Davidson choppers sounded as they sped off in formation.

Mat spoke to Adriana, "You take my car back to the office and I'll drive this van." He handed her the keys to his BMW M3. "Try to keep 'er between the ditches. Remember, rubber side, down."

"*As if,*" she scoffed, smiling.

Dominic said to Mat, "Call me when you've unloaded this stuff. I'll rest better knowing it's safe."

"You and me both. Keep your cell with you," Mat replied.

"It'll be in my hand, don't worry."

Adriana emerged from the alley back to the street where Mat's car was parked, and fumbled with the keys in the door lock, being unfamiliar with the vehicle. Suddenly, there was a piercing screech of tires and two cars roared towards her from half a block away. One, a Ford Expedition, pulled in directly behind the BMW and the other rolled up along side, pinning her vehicle in. Two men, Asian punks, jumped out and grabbed her, one on each arm, and forced her into the back seat of a Mercedes sedan.

She screamed and called out, "Mat... Help! Help!" The door of the vehicle slammed shut and both cars accelerated away. The entire incident took no more than ten or fifteen seconds.

Mat was still in the alley and ran to the source of the commotion, only to see the two cars speeding off. By now, Foley was alert to the situation and drove his Durango past Mat and Dominic in hot pursuit of the kidnappers. The red tail lights of all three vehicles quickly disappeared into traffic.

Mat was dumbfounded. "Jesus! What was that?"

"I'd say your lady friend just got snatched," Dom replied. "The snatch got snatched," he remarked in a crude play on words.

Both men stood there looking, helpless to do anything. Mat couldn't even give chase. Adriana had his car keys.

Down the road, Foley was behind the Mercedes and was torn between bringing payback to these culprits if he could catch them and returning to Mat and the enormous sum of cash in his possession.

"I saw what you bastards did to Crystal... Be damned if I'll let it happen again," he said as he stayed right on their tail. The cars turned several corners and finally ended up on a quiet street in an industrial area with little traffic or pedestrian activity. The Mercedes slowed and turned left, while the Expedition turned right. Foley stayed with the Mercedes as it slowed down considerably.

Should I ram it and try to put 'em off the road? he wondered. *Don't want to risk hurting Adriana in an accident."*

Now there were bright lights in Foley's rear view mirror and he was being tailed by another vehicle. As he looked closer, he could see it was the Expedition. It must have circled the block and caught up with him from behind. Suddenly, the Mercedes slammed on the brakes, and reactively, Foley did as well so not to rear end them. The vehicle behind rolled to a stop right behind him and in an instant two men jumped out of each vehicle in front and behind armed with machine pistols of some sort and pointed them at Foley through all four sides of his truck He was trapped.

"Get out... Now!" one of them yelled.

For a moment Foley considered pulling his own gun and taking a stand, but he realized, just as quickly, that it would be suicide.

"Get out!" the goon repeated. "Hand on head, asshole!"

Foley opened his door and complied. He was turned to face the dodge, and frisked at gunpoint. They found Foley's weapons — his Beretta 9mm, his throwing knife, and his black-jack.

"Cute," one of the assailants said. "You tink yo' take down Red Sun gang dese trinkets?"

Foley didn't have time to answer. Something cracked the back of his head with blinding force. He felt like his skull had been split in two, then saw a bright flash of blue light, then blankness. He fell to the ground unconscious.

"Hmmff!" One of them mocked. "Dis work pretty good," holding Foley's black-jack in his hand. Foley was loaded into the trunk of the Mercedes, hands tied behind his back, and the vehicles pulled away again.

✫ ✫ ✫

Back at the old office building in Surrey, Mat was desperately trying to decide what to do. He couldn't exactly call the police for assistance, and he had no idea where to start looking for them even if he *could* get his car started. They were long gone by now.

Dom said, "Look, why don't you get in this van and get the cash to wherever you keep it. I assume you have a safe place to store it. The show's over here for now, and we'll just have to wait for them to make their next move." For now, he was thinking more clearly than Mat, who was in the throes of blaming himself for ever allowing Adriana to come along on this escapade.

"Ya, okay," he responded weakly. With no real other alternative, Mat climbed into the van, with $3.25 million in the back and drove back to his office. On the way back his mind was racing. *What if they hurt Adriana, or kill her. Jesus Christ! Foley will catch them. He always does. What about Manuel? I'll have to call Mina and tell her Adriana won't be home tonight, or maybe ever. Her office will have to be told something, or they'll alert the police that she's missing. I'll have to call Wexler so I'm not holding this cash any longer than I have to. Can anything else go wrong with this cursed, damn drug deal?*

When Mat got back to the office, it was after hours and Danielle had shut everything down for the day. Mat pulled around back and pressed the remote to open the service bay where his technicians operated. He drove the van in, locked it and closed the door. It wasn't the most secure place in the world to keep over $3 million, but it would have to do.

He went to his office, opened his credenza door and removed a bottle of Canadian whiskey he kept for just such an occasion. Mat then poured a stiff shot into a glass, and downed it in one swallow. Sitting back in his leather chair, he closed his eyes and felt the burn in the back of his throat from the hard liquor. He set down the glass, and with his elbows on the desk, put his face in his hands.

"Oh God... don't hurt her!"

CHAPTER 29

AFTER A SLEEPLESS night, Mat got up early and had a scalding, hot shower. He tried in vain to get control over his anxiety. He called Foley's home and Crystal answered, telling him that Foley was missing and hadn't contacted her. She said she had tried his cell number several times, but it was turned off and always went to voicemail. She, too, was worried sick. Without discussing the events of the night before, Mat ended the call.

Foley, where are you, my friend? You always pull through these things. I know you'll call me as soon as there's anything to report.

Mat went downstairs and put on a pot of strong coffee. He had to regain some measure of mental alertness to face this thing with a clear head. While it was brewing, he called the office and left a message for Danielle on voice mail.

"Danielle, it's Mat. Listen, something's come up and I won't be in for a while today, and likely, neither will Foley. There's a van in the service bay. I put it there last night. Please ask the guys to just leave it for now. It's all locked up and I'll move it later. Make sure the automatic door is closed and locked at all times. There's some *valuables* in the van and I don't want to run the risk of a theft. Call me on my cell if you need me. Thanks."

Trying to get on with business, Mat then called Max Wexler and made arrangements, again, to do a cash drop at the bank, after hours. It went without incident last time, but considering recent events, Mat felt certain that his luck was running out. During his second cup of coffee, Mat's cell phone rang and the call display said *Foley.*

'Bout time. I hope you've got good news, old chum. "Hello, Foley?"

The line was silent, then someone said, "No, I afraid Mister Foley, you call him, indisposed at da moment." There was an Oriental accent.

Mat barked, "Who is this?" He realized that they must have gotten Foley's cell phone somehow and looked up Mat's number from his contact list in the phone's memory.

"Shut up. I talk, you listen," the caller said. "You wan' see Miss Santos alive again, it cost you three million dollah. You understan'? *Now* you talk. "

"I understand. Don't you hurt her, you hear me? Let me speak to her. How do I know she's alright?" Mat fired off.

"Very well. Listen carefully," the caller instructed. There was a pause and some shuffling sounds on the phone.

"Mat, it's me, Adriana," she said in a distressed voice. Please Mat, don't..." and the phone was grabbed away from her.

"She alive, now, like I say," the voice assured Mat. "You have seventy two hour raise money. We contact you again, let you know where deliver. I don' tell you what happen you bring cops in on it. Now you get busy, smart guy."

"Wait. What about Foley?" Mat demanded.

"I afraid his fate already seal."

"What's that supposed to mean," Mat asked angrily.

"It mean *he already dead,* just like Miss Santos be in three day, you disappoint me," the cold voice explained.

"Impossible," Mat said. "An army of you parasites couldn't kill that man."

"Oh, I see. You want *verification?* Dat what we call in our organization. How about his head? Dat convince you? Say da word, I have it send over."

Mat was silent, in horror, pissed beyond imagination.

"Three day. We be in touch," and the line went dead.

✵ ✵ ✵

Jimmy Yang was never as sadistically violent as his late colleague Nelson Hi Wo, but he could be sufficiently threatening to bluff most others that he could be lethal, if necessary. It had come to him through the crude intelligence of the gang's network of informants, that Dominic Hall of *Hall Garcia, and Barlow,* had survived the attack on their firm, and he immediately put out an order to track him down.

He had been found and followed to the vacant office building in Surrey where he met with Mathew and Adriana the day before. Had they known that a cash transfer of $3 million was going down in the alley, they would simply have robbed the loot and forgone the complications of a kidnapping and ransom.

Now Yang was in debt an extra $2.5 million to Wo Shing Chu, and even though they recovered most of their shipment of drugs, he didn't have enough cocaine to cover that shortfall. He needed to find a way to raise big money, fast. He hoped that the life of Adriana Santos meant that much to someone in the Kings Crew camp.

They grabbed her without really knowing who she was, or what part she played in the whole thing. She'd been seen with Dominic Hall, Mat Crawford, and the four bikers, and she was very pretty, so it was a good bet that she was someone's little trophy bitch, and he intended to use her to leverage a big pay off.

✵ ✵ ✵

Oh Jesus, no! Not Foley too. This can't be happening, Mat thought to himself. The prospect of losing his life long friend, especially to a drug deal that Foley had been against from the outset, put a cloud of guilt and shame over Mat that was all but unbearable. His actions had already cost him his marriage. Now he might have gotten Foley murdered, and they might also kill Adriana. *God almighty. I wish I had a time machine,* Mat thought.

He decided to call Dominic Hall and solicit his help in trying to work through this. The Kings Crew were street fighters who operated on the *gang level* of the Red Sun Boys and they might be able to come up with a plan to rescue Adriana... and Foley, if he was still alive. Mat snapped open his cell and found Dom's number among his *Recent Calls* list.

"Hi, Mat, Dom here," he answered.

"Hi yourself. Listen, they've contacted me with my partner's cell phone. They're holding our lady for three million green, and they claim they've killed my partner. Can you meet with me, right away?"

"*Holy Shhh...* Alright, but I can't give you much time. We're getting our business put back together in a temporary office, until we can find a new building. I got staff issues, police sniffing around, mad clients that aren't being serviced right, and an arrogant little prick of an insurance adjustor that thinks they shouldn't have to pay for any of our damages. *They'll pay,* by Christ, or I'll arrange for someone to carve him a new asshole," he said distractedly.

"We've both got problems and they're all connected to this coke deal. Hear me out and maybe we can help each other," Mat said.

Dom gave Mat the address they were running the firm from short term, and Mat was on his way ten seconds after he closed his cell.

Twenty minutes later, Mat walked in the front door of *Hall and Barlow*. Since Carlos Garcia was now carved up like a Christmas turkey after his autopsy, and filled with formaldehyde, methanol, and ethanol, otherwise known as embalming fluid, Dom didn't see much point in keeping his name on the new articles of incorporation being drawn up. The Barlow part was the result of the firm's original founder, Charles Dudley Barlow, who had long since retired and taken up fly fishing and drinking scotch full time in Northern BC. That left Dominic Hall who was, in effect, running the firm by himself now.

"Mat, come on in. What's up, my man?" Dom said upon seeing him.

"Ah Jesus, I don't know where to start. First, they called me and said we had to raise three million within three days or they'll kill Adriana."

"How do you know they haven't already?"

"I talked to her, only briefly. They only let her say a few words to prove she's alive."

Dom pondered the situation. "Any idea where she's being held?"

"Not a clue. And they said if they catch wind of any police they'll kill her right away," Mat continued.

"Well, you don't want those meddling bastards poking their noses into it, that's for sure," Dom said with distain. "Bottom line, she can probably take care of herself. She's a bright girl. In any event, I wouldn't pay three million to have my own mother released. Good lookin' girls are a dime a dozen in this town, if you haven't noticed."

Mat looked at the man like he couldn't believe his ears. "She's not just a good lookin' girl, and I'm not going to stand by and let her get murdered. We've *got* to raise the money, that's all there is to it!"

Dom looked on without emotion. "What sense of the word *we* do you mean? She's not my problem. If you're so enamored with her *you* find the ransom money and pay it, so they can deliver her to you, good and fucked by a whole gang of stiff, little pricks, by then, probably."

"What are you saying?" Mat pressed on, clearly annoyed at the vulgarity.

"You think they won't pass her around like a plate of nachos among a bunch of hungry snow boarders while they have her? She's nothing more than a good piece of ass and a highway to money, and will likely be dead by the time you get to her anyway. Even if she *is* alive, her ass will be so sore she won't be able to stand up straight for a month."

Now Mat was sorry he was ever foolish enough to think that this reptile would have an ounce of compassion for Adriana, or anyone else. He didn't have time to argue with him or debate the worth of Adriana's life. And he had to track down Foley, whether dead or alive, and deal with whatever he might find.

"Alright, I've heard enough," Mat said summarily. "I'm going to try and help her, and our little money laundering project will just have to wait. And by the way? I'm trying real hard not to say something like… *Fuck you, you heartless, selfish bastard!* But I won't stoop to that."

As Mat stormed out of the office, Dom thought for a moment then ran after him.

"Hold up there, partner. Okay, okay, I can see you're serious about the broad. Okay, she's good lookin' and smart, and probably gives good head, judging by your reaction. C'mon, shake it off. Here's a suggestion. We got a lawyer who's as slippery as a fish. He always has good ideas when we run into trouble."

"What are you suggesting? I *sue them*, if they kill her? Or maybe we should draw up a contract stipulating the terms of her release, and we'll all sign it at the bottom?"

Dom laughed, "No, not at all. Just talk to the man, is all I'm saying. I'll call him and tell him you're coming. Let him know all the facts. He's part of the family, and we trust him. Tell you what, as a gesture of good will, I'll pick up his fee for advising you on the matter." Dom took out a piece of paper and wrote down the name and address of Jesse Novak.

"That's very magnanimous of you," Mat remarked.

Mat stuffed the paper into his shirt pocket and marched to his car. It was maybe a thirty minute drive across town to the lawyer's address at this time of day. By the time he arrived, Novak had been briefed by Dominic by telephone and had a good understanding of the situation. Mat rode up the elevator of the ornately designed office building and exited at the tenth floor. He entered the law firm through its heavy, wooden door and was greeted by Nancy, the secretary.

"Hello, you must be Mister Crawford," she welcomed him.

"Yes," Mat replied, knowing that true to his word, Dom had called ahead. "Is Jesse Novak available?"

"Darn sure is. He's expecting you," she said, showing Mat down the hall to her boss's office.

Mat walked in. Jesse stood and walked around his desk. He shook Mat's hand affably.

"Pleased to meet you, Mathew. May I call you that?" Jesse opened the conversation.

"Yes, of course, *Jesse*. I'm here at Dominic's suggestion, but I don't know that this problem will fall into your line of expertise, honestly," Mat explained.

"You might be surprised. Those guys wind up in all kinds of hot water, legally speaking, and in other ways," Jesse said.

There's a piece of news. Try robbery, bribery, fraud, murder, drug dealing, extortion, and money laundering, to name a few.

Jesse went on, "Okay, why don't I sum up all I know about the matter based on my brief telephone conversation with Dom before you got here, and then you tell me if I missed anything. Please, sit down. Would you like a coffee, something stronger?"

"No, thanks. Well, ya, sure, coffee, just black." Jesse buzzed Nancy at reception and asked her politely to bring in some coffee, which she did in two steaming mugs, moments later.

Jesse went on to feed back virtually the entire discussion between Mat and Dom less than an hour ago, and he gave a startlingly accurate account of the kidnapping incident the night before. It was like he'd been there, himself! *He must have a mind like a steel trap,* Mat surmised.

"So, now you have to come up with $3 million or, *they say,* they'll kill her in three days."

"Two and a half, now," Mat pointed out.

"Do you believe them?" Jesse asked.

"I have to. This is not something I'm prepared to gamble on."

"No, I can see that. Then the next question is of course, can you raise that kind of money — in two and a half days?" Jesse continued.

"Maybe. It would take some scrambling," Mat knew he could, in fact, collect that much money, if he pulled in his funds in various overseas accounts which he had deposited over the years. He had money in the Philippines, Bermuda, Switzerland, Argentina, Thailand, Fiji, Bali, Greece, and elsewhere, but he couldn't do it in only three days.

Jesse pressed on, "And, not to be indelicate, but assuming they stick to their word, and return her unharmed once you pay up, you understand that you get nothing back for your investment, *except her.* You sure she's worth it?"

"Yes, the hostage for the ransom. I think we're still on the same page, so far," Mat said wryly.

Jesse persisted as devil's advocate. "Mat, if you were them, and the Mark, that is *you,* in this instance, actually came to them with three million, would you just give back the hostage?"

"That's the deal. Those were the terms of their demands."

Jesse continued, "Or would you be tempted to say, 'Thanks for the money, but *oh, gosh,* we've changed our minds. We want *another* million… or two.' Why should they give back the goose that lays the golden eggs? The fun's just getting started. Get my point?"

Mat was getting frustrated. "So what do you suggest?" he asked.

Jesse folded his hands together and rested his chin atop his knuckles, elbows on the desk. He thought intensely for a moment.

"First, my best advice is, don't pay a cent. It's too risky any way you look at it. You'll have to deliver the money somehow, and they might just kill you, and her, right on the spot."

Emphatically, he pointed out, "You *never* take unnecessary chances, or put yourself in jeopardy, over money. It's gotta be a sure thing — no risk of failure. You get that basic premise of crime, right?

"Second, odds are strongly in your favor that they're bluffing, and in three days, your girlfriend is likely to pull up in a city cab, maybe just a little roughed up. She'll want to fix up her hair and make up, then probably go shopping. I doubt they'd actually kill her.

"Murder attracts a lot of attention from the cops. They don't want that. If I'm wrong, and they do kill her, it was out of your hands from the start, so don't beat yourself up about it. You may have lost your girlfriend, but at least you're not out three million bucks, too. You can always get a new girlfriend, but once the money's gone?" He shook his head, unable to finish. "Fifty percent of the population is female, and you'll find another. They're really just a commodity — pork bellies, coal, soybeans, women..."

"I can see why Dominic gets along with you," Mat sighed.

The wily lawyer continued. "Second scenario. Okay, so you're *gaw, gaw* over this skirt and can't bear to live without her, and you're committed to paying the dough for her release. *If* you pay, and again, it's *a big if,* you need to ensure that you don't turn over the money until you're sure she's safe and sound. Do not, under any circumstances, send over a suitcase of cash on anyone's good word that she'll be released, and you won't be bled for more ransom.

"It's a Mexican standoff. You're gonna say, 'Give me the girl, and I'll give you the money.' They'll take the position, 'Give us the money, and we'll give you the girl.' You have to ensure the security of your asset, before you make payment."

"*My asset?* Mat asked, incredulously, "And how do I do that?"

"Not sure, but I'd do some hard thinking on a fool proof plan before I called my banker." Novak advised. "You don't turn over three mil, without absolute *certainty* of your outcome. You *get that,* right?"

Mat and Jesse finished up, and Mat left his office trying to feel a little better that he had received some advice from a *qualified professional* on one of the few areas of criminal activity that so far, he hadn't been exposed to — kidnapping and extortion.

As he walked down the hall past the reception desk Nancy called out cheerily, "Bye, bye now. Have a nice day!"

She can't be serious! Mat's inner voice commented.

CHAPTER 30

MAT DECIDED TO go to his office and at least check in once for the day. He certainly wasn't going in to work, as his mind was far too distracted to accomplish anything. He pulled into the parking lot and walked in the front door. As usual, Danielle was sitting at reception working with files and clicking away on her keyboard.

"Mornin' Mat. I got your message. Is anything wrong?"

"Hi, Danielle. Please don't ask me any questions today, especially that one," Mat replied. "Anything going on here out of the ordinary?"

"No, business as usual. I'm on it, don't worry. Is Foley coming in too? You said he might not in your message."

Mat answered with difficulty, "No, Foley won't be in, I'm fairly certain. Some things are a bit up in the air right now. We'll know more in a few days."

"Okay, just asking. Crystal Waters has called for him three times already this morning. I didn't know what to tell her, other than he's not here yet," Danielle said with concern.

"I'll talk to her," Mat said. "Guess she has a right to some kind of explanation."

Mat proceeded to his office and called Crystal for the second time this morning at Foley's place. He explained about the incident the night before and that Foley had lit out after the kidnappers. He asked her not to panic because until Foley surfaced, one way or another, it would serve no useful purpose to assume the worst. He *did not* tell her that this morning's caller claimed Foley was already dead.

"Crystal, Foley is a trained soldier and security expert. He can look after himself, I assure you. He could just be laying low out there for any number of reasons, so sit tight and I'll call you if there's any more news," Mat had explained.

Or he could be at the bottom of Horseshoe Bay with a bullet through his brain, if he still has his head, that is, Mat's thought.

Crystal had little choice but to reluctantly go along with Mat's advice.

"Alright, but if you hear from him at all, please ask him to call me right away. This is turning into a horror movie. First I get beat up and raped by those animals, then my boss gets murdered, now Foley has gone missing... I *can't take* any more of this Mat. I never expected to be dragged into some kind of gang war. You and Foley are into something here that won't have a happy ending. This has gone way beyond weird. It's got to stop, or you'll get us all killed."

Mat consoled Crystal as best he could under the circumstances. He tried to be optimistic, but in truth, he was as worried about Foley, and Adriana, as she was. He finished up with her and set the phone down.

Staring ahead blankly he thought to himself, *I need to raise $3 million. I can't put Adriana at risk of being killed. I have the money, but it will take a couple of weeks, minimum, to get it here. Would they extend the deadline? I doubt it. It's already day two.*

Oftentimes, Mat did some of his best thinking while driving his car. Something about the solitude, the passing scenery, the steady procession of the road, and the motorcade of traffic that was never the same twice. He decided to go for a drive and just let his thoughts flow. Once behind the wheel, however, he found that he was driving in the general direction of his house, and he wanted to just go home and reflect on the whole situation. He pulled into his garage, entered into the kitchen, tossed his keys on the table, and realized he was exhausted. His eyes were heavy as lead, and he was beyond fighting it, done.

Mat suddenly felt an overwhelming need for sleep, as if he'd taken three valium earlier and they were just now kicking in. The lack of rest from the night before, the stress of the early morning phone call from the kidnappers, the worry about Foley's welfare, his meetings with Dominic Hall and Jesse Novak, and the pressure now of having to raise $3 million, put Mat's stress level on overload, and he knew he had to power down for a while. He went to the bedroom and fell onto the bed, pulling the covers over him, clothes and all. What he thought would be an afternoon nap, turned into an all-nighter, and he didn't stir again until nearly 6:00 the next morning when dawn's sunlight nudged him into consciousness.

When he awoke, the first thought that came to him was of the Econoline van parked in his service bay at the business. There were $3 million in that vehicle at his disposal, and no one would be the wiser if he *borrowed* it until he could pull in his own funds from all the various offshore accounts. Genius idea, or sheer stupidity? He wasn't sure, but wasn't going to let Adriana die with her ransom money sitting right under his nose. It occurred to him that he could wire transfer his own money, in various locales around the world, directly to the account of the Empressa, and just use the cash right here to save the life of Adriana Santos.

He jumped out of bed, flew through the shower, and grabbed a cereal bar from the pantry before turning over the ignition of his BMW with his spare set of keys. Mat had things to do and felt inspired to take action. Finally, he was on fire.

Once at work, Mat took out his cell phone, opened it up to check that it was fully charged, and set it on his desk. He didn't want to miss any calls today – it was *day three*. Using his land line, he dialed Max Wexler's number.

"Hello, Max Wexler."

"Max, it's Mathew calling. Do you have a moment?"

"Of course, Mat. What is it?"

"There has to be a change in plan. I can't bring over the cash tonight, Sorry, but my..." (he wasn't sure what to call her), "*colleague*, has been captured by some thugs. They're demanding a big ransom for her and I have to tap into this money to pay it. I have no choice, Max."

"Mathew is that wise? You could end up losing the money *and* your colleague, and it sounds to me like she's more than just that to you. Am I wrong?"

"*Ya, no*, long story. But for now, I have to go along with the demands of the kidnappers, or they say they'll kill her. Can't let that happen."

"Kidnapping is a heinous and violent crime committed by scoundrels and cowards. Rarely does it have a happy outcome," Max warned.

"I know, sir. I've been given that same advice by others. But I can't take any chances here. I have to pay it. I'm all out of options," he explained.

After a short interchange Wexler accepted Mat's reasoning, and wished him luck. The planned drop of cash at his bank would have to be delayed. As Mat set down the receiver, Danielle walked into his office.

"There's a gentleman here to see you. He's a detective — Inspector Lundgren, from Vancouver PD. What should I do?"

Oh great, him again... Now what?

"Show him in, I guess." Mat prepared for bad news.

The inspector entered Mat's office and Mat gestured with an open hand for him to take a seat. Lundgren sat down and looked directly at Mat, without saying a word. Finally Mat said, "Well? What brings you by, Inspector?"

Without answering, Lundgren took out an envelope from his inner jacket pocket and opened it up. On Mat's desk he fanned out several snap shots of Mat and Dominic talking together from their meeting two days ago in Surrey. They had been taken with a zoom, telephoto lens from a roof top or upper story window.

"Mind explaining what this was all about?" he answered.

Mat's mind raced for an answer. How could he explain his association with someone who the cops *might* know full well is member of the Kings Crew, and an active criminal in other matters?

"Well, that man is an accountant. He's been doing some work for me," Mat said calmly.

"In the alley behind a run down building in Surrey, he's doing accounting work for you?" Lundgren asked sarcastically. "I wasn't born yesterday, Crawford."

"No, we talked together inside the building. I was just borrowing his van. It came up that we need another service vehicle in our business and he happened to be selling that one. I borrowed it to try it for a couple of days."

Mat wondered if the question might be raised about the kidnapping, but from the vantage point of camera, all you could see was the alley, not the front street where they grabbed Adriana and sped off. He recalled that the whole incident didn't last thirty seconds.

"Inspector, if I may, why were you having me followed and photographed? What's your interest in me, in this matter, anyways?" Mat tried to sound puzzled.

Lundgren replied, "Are you aware of what took place at this individual's place of business recently?"

"Yes, shocking, that. Some kind of gang invasion. Are the police making any headway on getting to the bottom of it?"

"It's under investigation. Allegations are circulating that some kind of drug deal was behind the whole thing. Dominic Hall, and others, have been questioned on it."

Mat responded, "Is he a suspect of some kind?"

"Well, let's say he is a *person of interest*. See, I put a tail on him to find out what he might be up to. You can imagine my surprise when *your* face turned up in these photos. It seems you're developing quite a knack for showing up wherever there's trouble. First that suspicious death at The Sutton Place Hotel a few weeks ago... now this. When you've been doing this as long as I have Mr. Crawford, you learn to trust your nose, and right now, my nose tells me something stinks."

"Well, murder and drug deals are two things I don't take much interest in, I can assure you," Mat said.

Just then Mat's cell phone that he had set on his desk earlier started to ring. Mat looked down at it and the call display said *Foley*. It was the kidnappers again. Mat couldn't get into a conversation about hostages, and $3 million, and directions for the drop off right now. Not with a City detective sitting right in front of him.

"You gonna get that?" Lundgren asked.

"No. Its not important."

"How do you know? Who is it?"

"It's just my partner. You remember — Karl Folkestad."

"I don't mind. Go ahead, take the call. I'm in no hurry," Lundgren insisted.

Reluctantly, Mat picked up the phone and flipped it open.

"Hello?"

"Mr. Crawford. So far, yo' lady Santos still alive. You have da money?"

"Yes, I do. But listen, *Foley*, can you call me back in a few minutes? I'm just in a meeting right now." Mat was winging it, poorly.

"Dis not *Foley*, you fool."

"*I know, I know.* But I'm just with Inspector Lund..." Mat stopped dead in his tracks.

"What? Yo' bring police into dis?" the caller demanded.

"*No, no, no...* It's not that." Mat smiled towards the cop, deflecting suspicion of anything amiss. "Please just call me back later, and I'll help you solve your problem, okay?" The connection was cut and the line went dead.

Mat bluffed like he was still engaged in the call, "Alright then, I'll help you sort it out as soon as I'm finished here."

Then he acted like the call ended normally, "Sounds good, buddy. Bye now," and he folded the phone in half.

"Now, can I be of any other help to you, Inspector?"

"If I think you can, I want to know where I can find you. Please don't leave the city without notifying us of your whereabouts. Like Mr. Hall, you can consider yourself a person of interest in a police matter, and you'll be expected to govern yourself accordingly. Is that clear?" the detective instructed Mathew in an official tone.

"Clear," Mat replied, thinking *Up yours, Charlie!* "But if you'll excuse me, I'm running a business." Inspector Jerome Lundgren gathered up his photos, stood, and walked out of Mat's office to the front door.

Danielle watched him drive off then came back to Mat's office. "What was *that* all about?" she asked.

"Just a couple of unpaid parking tickets." His conscience twinged, for once, at having lied to her. She deserved better.

Mat didn't wait for the kidnappers to call him back. As soon as Danielle went back to her desk, he dialed Foley's cell number immediately.

"Hello." *Thank God,* someone answered.

"Ya, it's Mat Crawford calling. Sorry about that. Listen *I did not* bring the police into this thing. He dropped in unannounced on another matter. He doesn't know anything about the kidnapping, I swear."

There was a long pause. "You say you have da money?"

"Yes, cash. All of it."

"Okay. Listen my instruction, very carefully. One mistake cost yo' girlfriend life. Don' test me, got it?"

Mat put his phone on speaker, set it down, then picked a pen and pad of paper. Then he said something that even surprised him when he heard the words come out of his mouth.

CHAPTER 31

"SHE'S *NOT* MY girlfriend, or any one else's that I know of, but go ahead with your instructions." Mat didn't want to let the hood know just how attached he was to the lady. If he could convince his adversary that he wasn't emotionally involved, he would remove one card that he might try to play.

"Very well. You take da money Tsawwassen Ferry Terminal, 7:00 tonight. At entrance main parking lot you see dark grey Dodge RAM 2500 pick up with small Canadian flag attach to whip antenna — We patriotic new Canadian, yes? You follow, so fa'?"

"Yes, go on."

"The truck proceed in parking lot at slow speed, and you follow close, no matter where it go or how long take. Got dat?"

"Got it."

"When we satisfy no tail and no trick, it pull over and park and you transfer da money to truck. Den yo' lady be return you, as agree. Try anything cute, we find out how long yo' Miss Santos hold breath under water. We send you cell phone video, so you watch too. Understan'?"

"No way, my friend," Mat said with mock confidence.

"What?"

"You drive off with the money and we're supposed to just believe that you'll return the hostage? How do we know you won't kill 'er anyway. She *made you* after all, when you grabbed her. How do we know you won't hold her and demand more ransom? We want our lady back with us safely before we turn over the money," Mat said.

"You no position make demand — *We kill dis bitch!*" Mat's counterpart shouted out caustically. "Maybe do it right now."

"Do that and you won't see a dime, and you might become the focus of attention of the Vancouver homicide division, after they get an anonymous tip from some conscientious citizen. That would be stupid now, wouldn't it? We just want to have confidence that the deal goes down like we agreed. That asking too much?"

There was a delay while the hood thought. "What you want, den?" he finally asked.

"We want to ensure the security of our asset," Mat said, as if those were his own words. "Look, you wanted three million bucks and I have it, cash. I'll turn it over to you, from my hand to yours, as long as I know she's released from your custody and in a safe place. Here's my proposal. I'll bring the money to you in a public place in a non-descript panel van. You send one of your men to confirm that the money is there. When he tells you it's a go, you release the girl on a busy downtown street, and as soon as she phones me on my cell and tells me she's safe, the van and the money are yours. Plain and simple, everybody wins... Agreed?"

"You got some kind stones, lay out condition me, Crawford."

"Like I said, I've got the money, you've got the girl. Let's just do the swap, no tricks, we go our separate ways. You tell me where and when. I'll be there with the van and the money."

"Alright, make it front of Bridges Restaurant at Granville Island, 4:00 p.m. today. On Duranleau, near end street. I be in blue Navigator, someplace close by, and we watch for you in panel van. We see you, I send my man, confirm drop. We let girl go, wit' cell phone, but she be in our crosshair 'til I have money. Dis be on up 'n up, or we put bullet through her head. You too, later, don' worry," Jimmy warned.

"Deal. I'll be there, and *I will* be armed, so if your man tries anything other than looking at the money, things could get ugly, fast, and that will bring the cops down on all of us in one big hurry."

The deal was agreed upon by both parties, and the life of Adriana Santos hung in the balance. Mat looked at his watch and noted it was 12:45 p.m. Dominic Hall had given Mat $3.25 million in cash. He had just over three hours to skim off the extra $250,000, leaving exactly $3 million to cover the ransom. His first impulse was to take the van to his house and count the money in his garage, but he realized that if he might be under surveillance, so it was safer to keep the van concealed right where it was until show time.

"Danielle, I'll be in the back working on that van I brought in. No interruptions please, unless it's urgent," he called out to his manager.

Danielle replied, "We're a security company. *Everything's* urgent."

You don't know the half of it, sweetheart, Mat thought, looking back at her.

✻ ✻ ✻

Back in Chinatown at the Hotel East, Jimmy Yang set down Foley's cell phone after talking with Mat Crawford, and looked at his pretty hostage, tied securely to a wooden chair, blindfolded and gagged. Beside her, in the same condition was her companion, Karl Folkestad, *Mr. Foley*, his apparent nickname among his friends. With Jimmy were his cohorts, Moe, Turk, Foggy, Shade, and Ripper – sporting gauze bandages on the side of his face and neck, and in a corresponding, surly mood.

They sat, lined up like the cast of some Chinese equivalent of *Trailer Park Boys* — off beat, eccentric misfits, all of them. Almost comical under other circumstances.

Foley and Adriana had been warned to sit quietly and not make any sounds. They couldn't anyway, their mouths were gagged. But they could still hear, and Foley sat motionless and listening, taking in all he could. His military training taught him to learn as much as possible about his captors — *know your enemy*.

From Jimmy's end of the conversation with Mat, he learned that the ransom drop was to be made at Bridges Restaurant, a well known landmark to locals, at Granville Island at 4:00 o'clock today. He also knew that there would be two vehicles involved, a blue Navigator – pretty hard to miss, and some kind of panel van. He didn't hear how much the ransom was, but it was safe to assume it was a lot.

"Dis it," Jimmy announced. "Our ticket to redemption from Wo Shing Chu at hand."

"They've got the ransom?" one of them asked.

Jimmy rubbed his temples and replied, "Dat what da man say. We just have to execute da plan, no mistake."

"Speaking of execute, what about him?" Ripper inquired, nodding in Foley's direction.

"Ya, dis guy only gonna be trouble down road. He know us. He hear our name. He hear our conversation. He know about da coke. He already try run us down, once. And dey tink he already dead, anyway," Jimmy said, almost regretfully. "Ripper and Turk, take him down to dock. Do it quiet. Get rid of body. Use dis," he said, pulling open his desk drawer and tossing a black hood to cover the victim's head.

Foley sat still, listening. He knew they were planning to kill him, but sitting there, bound up like Houdini, there wasn't a thing he could do about it. So he waited. Waited to make his move, if an opportunity arose.

Ripper's face and neck were throbbing badly with his wounds from the cop's shot gun, and he was spoiling for an opportunity to take out revenge. From the table they were sitting at, he pulled on a thick pair of leather gloves, walked over to Foley, tied in the chair, and viciously drilled him hard with a closed fist, squarely in the face. Foley's head snapped back, and the chair rocked back on its rear legs then fell forward again. He slumped ahead, momentarily stunned by the blow.

"I tune him up first — prick!" Ripper demanded. "He ask for it!"

"Hold it!" Jimmy yelled in native tongue. "Don't get cute. There's nothing to gain by torturing him. Control yourself! Just follow my orders."

"Fucker... alright, boss." Turk stood and joined Ripper, dissuading him from any further assault. They tied the hood over Foley's head, undid the restraints holding him to the chair, and muscled him out of the room to a Ford Mustang GT with opaque tinted windows waiting outside.

"Don't try anything stupid, unless you want whack on head with yo' little, leather bag of hell, like last time," Ripper assured Foley, gripping the blackjack, and pushing him roughshod towards the exit.

Foley walked along compliantly with his hands tied behind his back. At the car, he was shoved into the passenger seat, with Ripper driving and Turk in the back.

"Now you sit like good boy or I blow yo' fuckin' brain all over dash," Turk said, placing the point of his index finger into the back of Foley's head, while winking at Ripper.

The sporty muscle car pulled ahead and growled out of the parking lot in the direction of Vancouver's shipping docks.

Back inside the posh setting of the Red Sun Boys' one-room, cockroach infested clubhouse, Moe beckoned his boss to the far side of the room and whispered, "Y'know, Jimmy, everything you say about big man – Mr. Foley, also true of dis one," gesturing with an open palm towards Adriana, tied to her chair. "She hear and see way too much not be a problem on street. She could go cops what she know, and they piece together enough info make our life hell."

Jimmy thought about it. "Yes, you right, but we need turn her over, get money."

"You mention something about keep her in crosshair. Why not we track her, wait 'til you got cash, den quietly bump her off, just be on safe side? I make sure painless. *Zip, wit' silencer,*" using his hand like a gun.

Jimmy was quiet. Killing a male operative that stuck his nose into the gang's affairs was one thing, but the cold blooded murder of a woman was another. Still, the security and success of the gang's business was paramount, and if she posed a threat to them, she would have to be expendable, in a *collateral damage* kind of way. He wanted to keep his options open and think about it.

"Alright, you follow her when deal go down. Don' shoot 'til you hear my command. You clear?" Jimmy ordered sternly.

Moe nodded his head and peered maliciously over at Miss Santos. He checked his cell phone to ensure it was charged.

✵ ✵ ✵

Back at Bull Dog Security, Mat finished up counting the money, ensuring exactly three million remained in the van and taking the rest to his office where it was locked into a cabinet. It was nearly half past three. Time to move. Mat went back to his office, unlocked the .45 Caliber Ruger pistol with a box of cartridges provided to him by Foley *for emergencies,* years ago, and placed the weapon in his gym bag. He walked out to the front to speak with Danielle.

"Danielle, I have to go now, for the day. If you don't see me here first thing in the morning, don't sweat it. I may be a little late. Just open up like usual and I'll call or be in *ASAP*, okay?"

"Okay, I guess," she replied.

"You guess?"

"Mat, something's up. What is it? I've worked with you guys a long time and I can read you. Both you and Foley are *way* too intense lately. Is anything wrong?"

Mat sighed and wished he could level with her. "I can't go into details, but ya, something's... *wrong,* and I have to make it right. Can you keep doing what you do, for now? I *need you,* Danielle. You're the rudder to this business. When it's over, we'll have a good long talk, I promise."

She looked flattered at the compliment and worried at the same time. "Okay," she agreed. "Go get 'em, *Double-Oh-Seven.* I'll hold down the business."

"More like Maxwell Smart," he replied as he headed back to the service bay to back out the three million dollar Econoline. "Wish me luck."

"*A prayer for your safe return* is probably more on the mark," she said, and blew her boss an open-handed, lucky kiss.

Twenty minutes later Mat proceeded across the Granville Bridge onto Granville Island. He swung onto Johnston Street and connected with Duranleau and there, ahead, was Bridges Restaurant where the transfer of cash would take place, once Adriana was freed. Mat slowly rolled ahead in the van and stopped in a loading zone, where it would be easy to speed away if something unexpected occurred. The late afternoon sun was hot and the streets were bustling with busy shoppers and sight seers. This place was a Mecca for tourists and locals out for a leisurely stroll or shopping excursion.

As promised, a half block away was a blue Lincoln Navigator, stolen, no doubt.

Mat flashed his lights once, then twice, and the passenger door of the luxury SUV opened. A slightly built, twenty something man in blue jeans, runners and a bulky hoody exited the vehicle and walked towards the van. Mat readied his auto-loading pistol releasing the safety. The punk held up both open palms as he approached, signaling that he was unarmed. Mat didn't believe that for a second, but waived him forward and reached back unlocking the sliding door on the side.

"I here check da money," he said in broken English.

"Back there. Make it fast," Mat agreed.

With deliberation, the envoy inspected all five duffle bags, confirming that there was a hell of a lot of money present. Ironically, the cash in the van was from the sale of drugs that had been stolen from the Red Sun Gang, so it was *their money*, so to speak. Mat held his gun at the ready where the young gangster could see it.

"Okay, I go now. We release yo' girl and she call you five minute. Keep yo' engine running, den you flash light again, leave yo' vehicle at once. Boss tell me any trick, we kill her, and you."

In his free hand Mat held his cell phone in his palm, clammy with nervous sweat. The passage of five minutes seemed like an eternity, and Mat wondered whether he might be executed like Jack Kincaid the instant he stepped out of the van. Finally his flip-phone rang. *Foley*, it said. In his haste, he dropped it, trying to open it with his slippery fingers. *Ah, Jesus, no!* It rang a second time, then a third. Finally, just before it went to voicemail, he fumbled on the floor and retrieved it.

"Hello…" he said anxiously.

"Mat, it's me. They let me go. I'm on the corner at Robson and Thurlow," Adriana said frantically.

"Are you alright? Did they hurt you?"

"Yes. I mean no. They didn't hurt me. I'm okay," she answered, clearly flustered. "Please, *come get me.*"

"Okay, tell me a store nearby that you can go into."

"There's a Classy Cameras across the street," she replied.

"Go there, now. Try and stay in a crowd of people. I'll be right there," Mat instructed her.

She closed the cell phone and proceeded across to the camera store. Not far behind her, one fine member of the city's Asian population followed her into the store, clad in a black leather bomber jacket with a Beretta 32, specially designed for *concealed carry*, tucked into the waistband of his pants.

"You're mine, Cinderella," he said under his breath. His forehead glistened in anticipation of the event.

Mat followed his instructions to the letter and left the van, running at a slow pace to the nearest storefront in the Public Market he could see, straight through to the back where it said *Employees Only* and right out the rear doors. He was trying to make it difficult, if not impossible for anyone to follow him, or in particular, shoot him.

"Hey!" someone yelled, as Mat dashed out the back door.

Then he ran down the back lane and in reverse, he entered the back door of a florist's shop and bolted out through the front door. He repeated this maneuver four times until he was back outside the Public Market, where a cab was parked nearby at a taxi stand.

"Hey, buddy, you for hire?" he barked at the cabby, a *new Canadian.*

"Sure, hop in my friend," the Indian immigrant driver said, happy to get a fare.

"Robson and Thurlow. Make it quick, and there's a nice tip in it for you," Mat coaxed.

"You got it, boss," the Sikh driver replied as he sped the yellow cab away — as fast as a rebuilt engine with 430,000 kilometers would carry it. In the rearview mirror, his dark eyes were framed by a pink turban covering a head of hair that had never been cut out of respect for God's creation, with a twisted black beard tucked up into it, as well.

He studied his nervous passenger curiously and felt an empathy for him, recalling the appalling troubles he had fled from in his own land many years ago, having lost his home, a career, three fingers, both parents, a sister, and a son to political unrest between the Sikhs, Hindus and Muslims. He knew what a troubled face looked like, and Mat had that face.

Now, in Canada, he drove cab, while in his homeland he had been an accredited architect, capable of designing office towers, traffic interchanges, airports, or a bridge crossing a great river, all lost forever, now. But he could drive, and make a living.

A few minutes later the cab pulled over at their destination, and Mat flipped out two twenties for a $24 fare.

"Thanks, buddy, don't spend it all in one place."

"I am wishing you *good luck*, my brother," he replied, genuinely.

Mat glanced back at him curiously, "*Thanks*, my friend," then jumped out of the cab and ran to the camera store where Adriana was waiting.

Mat entered the store like any regular shopper. He looked around eagerly, in hope of seeing his Adriana. *Close, so close now,* he thought to himself. The store had twenty, twenty-five people in it, some looking at telescopes, some chatting with clerks, some holding up and looking at the viewers of digital cameras. All, busy, affluent shoppers willing and able to spend upwards of a thousand dollars, minimum, for most high-tech products this store carried.

All except one scruffy, leather clad, Asian kid with greasy, black hair, dirty jeans, and a look that shouted, *'I'm a low life up to something bad.'* Mat's instincts were attuned to sense trouble as a result of the tumultuous events thrown into his life over the last several weeks, and this kid looked out of place. *I doubt your net worth is a hundred bucks. What are you doing in this place?* he thought.

Then, with relief, Mat spotted Adriana at the far side of the store, feigning interest in a display case of fancy picture frames. Trying not to reconstruct a scene of two long lost lovers calling out to one another while running in slow motion into each other's arms, Mat walked as normally as possible towards his girl. But wait, the other character in this scene, the creep in leather, was walking towards her, as well.

Mat moved forward with determination and purpose and it was clear that *Mr. leather-punk-troublemaker* was closing the gap on her faster than he was. Was Mat just being paranoid, and maybe this kid was just a shopper dressed in clothes that were making some kind of statement? Perhaps this was some variation on kids who wear baggy pants so their boxer shorts or the cleavage of their asses are hanging out the back, with the crotch drooping comically around their knees, looking like the whole garment is about to fall to their ankles at any moment.

No, this was the real deal and this kid — this *mid-twenties, gangster-hood,* was approaching Adriana from behind with one hand in his coat pocket. Mat quickened his pace, only a matter of seconds to act. He reached under his coat and grasped his hand gun, but, in a crowded store like this, out in the wide open public, he couldn't discharge a fire arm. He'd never shot anyone in his life. With a matter of ten feet between the hood and

Adriana, Mat scurried up behind and pistol-whipped the punk over his head with the butt of the gun.

The sound of blunt force against a human skull made a nauseating crack and earned the stunned attention of several bystanders. There, on the floor, lay a culprit obviously up to no good, with a handgun fitted with a silencer still in his hand. People stood, mouths agape, shocked at the scene.

"Security, call police!" someone yelled.

Adriana turned and looked at the supine body just behind her, warm blood starting to expand on the tiles under his head, then at Mat, and said, *"My God!"*

"You're safe, baby," Mat replied. "Let's move," and he took her hand and hurried out of the store.

"Wait! You'll need to make a statement," the store manager called out.

The two dashed out the front door and around the corner where Mat hailed another cab. The reluctant adventurers made it back to Mat's office, each traumatized but in one piece. By now it was after 6:00 o'clock and the place was quiet and deserted of all other employees.

Adriana said, "I can't believe how close I just came to getting killed." She was exasperated.

"I know. Why do ya think I'm trying to wind this thing up and get outta this game?"

"You saved my life."

"I paid for it with hard cash too. $3 million, no less"

"I'd be dead if not for you. That guy had a gun."

Mat looked at her like *enough already*. "Adriana, this game may be adventurous, but a long, secure life isn't something you can reasonably count on, the business we're in."

"Where did you *get $3 million?*" Adriana asked in a delayed reaction to his earlier comment.

"It was the drug money from the Kings Crew. If they ever find out I used their money for this, I'm a marked man. Now I have to replace it from my own accounts over seas. It'll pretty much clean me out. You still need to know whether I love you or not?"

"You're not cleaned out. You have me, and I have money – *plenty,* to get us through," Adriana said.

"I'm not worried about the money. Together we will always get by, but we really do have to wrap up this assignment. Our luck will run out one of these times. We're gamblers at a table and we've had a run of good luck. It's time to fold and walk away. The odds don't favor us any more."

"And what are you going to do next, buy a Dairy Queen?" she asked.

Mat chuckled. "No, I'm going to run this place with Foley – Bull Dog Security, and walk the line."

Adriana suddenly looked troubled. "Mat, they took Foley away. The orders were clear. He was going to be executed, just like me. We were gagged, blindfolded, and bound. There's no way he could have escaped."

Mat didn't answer. He looked ill. He stared out the window, pale and near defeat. As much as he believed her report of his partner's fate, he still held out hope that a miracle might happen. She didn't know Foley like he did.

"I'm sorry," Adriana said.

"*You* dodged the bullet. Maybe *he did* too," Mat reasoned.

"I was *rescued.* Face it, Mat... there's no one to rescue Foley." There was a long and thoughtful pause.

"No, I suppose not." Mat resigned himself to the facts, and slumped back into his chair, dejected and guilt ridden. Foley's luck had run out like he predicted it would for both of them. Mat had talked his friend into a criminal crap shoot with hoods and gangsters of the worst account, and now, like others, Foley had paid the ultimate price.

CHAPTER 32

MAT REACHED INTO his credenza and pulled out his old friend, Canadian Club. He splashed in a shot then rolled the glass between his hands.

"Join me?"

Adriana declined and just sat with her hands in her lap feeling helpless and dejected. For the first time in their relationship, they sat together for some fifteen, twenty minutes without conversation. So much had gone wrong. $3 million, vanished. Now he'd been identified by the Red Sun Boys, and Adriana too. And Foley, gone... But where? Chopped up in a dumpster? At the bottom of the ocean? Trussed up in some crate full of relief supplies headed on a cargo freighter for Haiti? Mat realized he wasn't quite the untouchable, professional criminal he thought he was, and he cursed his own inflated ego.

"I should have listened to Foley. He was against this assignment from the start, said it was too dangerous, too many players, we couldn't control this many variables."

"You can't blame yourself, Mat. Foley made his own choices, just like you," Adriana consoled. "We just need to cut our losses and get out alive ourselves. We should leave Vancouver, start over somewhere else, safe. They know us here now, and we'll never be safe and secure in our homes or businesses again. They're killers, Mat, monsters, and they'll stop at nothing for revenge, or manipulation, or profit. If we're gone, and they can't find us, they'll forget about us in time. It's our best chance." She spoke with remarkable clarity and insight.

"Ya, I suppose you're right," he replied weakly.

As Mat gazed out his office window, trying to come to grips with this nightmare, he saw a grey panel van turning into their parking lot. The setting sun shone brightly from the west and cast a glare on the windshield, making it impossible to see inside. Mat deduced it must be the Red Sun Boys who had tracked them back to his business somehow. This was payback. Another vehicle of hoods would be pulling up to the back door, no doubt. It was over. In another few minutes, he and Adriana would be shot dead, he was certain.

"What?" Adriana asked, seeing the change in Mat's demeanor.

"Look," Mat said. "There," pointing out his window.

"Who's that?" she asked.

"It's them. That's the van I delivered the ransom in today," he replied, picking up his gun. "We might be at the end of the line, Hon."

But something wasn't right. If this was a hit, it was too out in the open and too casual in its approach. Killers wouldn't just drive into the parking lot and pull into a stall, with the left signal light still flicking. The driver's side door opened. There was a pause. Nothing was happening — then, out stepped... Foley!

Mat's mouth dropped open and his eyes widened. "*Holy mother of God!* I don't believe my eyes. Told ya he'd make it somehow!" he shouted.

Mat dropped his gun on the desk and burst out the front door, sprinting across the lot to welcome his friend back to life. Adriana pursued like the second place finisher in the hundred meter dash at the summer Olympics.

If Foley had made it out alive it wasn't without a battle by the looks of him. He was banged up like a survivor pulled from the rubble of a bad earthquake, with blood streaming down one side of his head, and his nose likely broken. He was scraped and bruised with abrasions everywhere. One leg was obviously injured, and he was limping badly. His shirt collar was soaked crimson red on the right side, and he hadn't shaved in days.

"Jesus, Foley!" Mat cried out. "What happened to you? You look like shit."

"Why, what do ya mean? I feel fine. My hair okay?" he replied, wobbly on his feet.

"Should of known better than to ask," Mat said. "You're bleeding like a stuck pig. Come inside," Mat said taking his arm with Adriana on the other.

Together, the three amigos walked across the lot and back into Bull Dog Security. The gash on Foley's head was cleaned up and dressed and typical of head wounds, the profuse bleeding made it look worse than it was. He was lucid and showed no signs of brain injury. The nose would have to be re-set, just like Mat's was a few months ago.

"Okay, my friend, now tell us what happened," Mat demanded.

"Why are you still alive?" Adriana put in.

"Well, those guys herded me out to the front lot and put me in a car. We were driving down the road, and I knew we weren't goin' to have a café latte at Starbuck's, so I wondered what I should do."

"They had orders to execute you!" Adriana said emphatically. "And they tried to kill *me too* — in a camera shop, but Mat smacked this guy on the head with his gun and saved me, and all the other customers were shocked, and we ran out and caught a cab and escaped, and then we…"

"Ssshhhhh!" Mat scolded. "Let him tell the story."

Foley carried on, "One guy was driving and the other was behind me in the back seat. I waited about ten minutes until it sounded like we were outta downtown traffic. Those two fools were chattering away — half in Chinese and half in English, and I picked up enough to know we were getting close to the docks. Just as they were sharing a belly laugh over some joke they told, I swung my feet up from the floor and jack hammered the driver with all my might around six or eight times — head, chest, arms, whatever I could hit. The car swerved this way and that, and I put my foot down to the accelerator and pushed it to the floor. Then, with my shoulder, I leaned into the driver as hard as I could."

Adriana put in, "Foley, that was dangerous! Weren't you scared of the crash you were about to cause?"

"Scared? I was in danger of suffering a *myocardial infraction,* but that would have been preferable to a bullet through my skull with my hands bound behind my back."

"It's *farction,*" Mat commented.

"Huh?" Foley paused.

"That's myocardial *infarction* — a heart attack. Never mind, carry on." Mat said.

Foley continued, "Anyways, I put my head down and waited for a crash and sure enough, we ploughed right into the ditch. The car rolled I dunno how many times but we wound up wrapped around a light standard. I pulled my arms around my feet and wriggled outta my restraints. They'd had my eyes covered with a black bag, and I yanked that damn thing off too. After three days in the dark, the sudden daylight nearly blinded me. By the time I was free, one guy — the driver, was either dead or out cold, and the other one was layin' on the ground 'bout forty feet back."

"Saint Christopher, you're lucky you weren't killed," Mat said.

"Just call me Foley, don't need to be sainted, just yet. It was a calculated risk, and I didn't have a lot of options at that point. I figured the crash wouldn't be any worse than what those two fellas had in store for me. Anyways, I frisked the guy beside me and he was packin' a Beretta nine, so I borrowed it and kicked out the side window. Then I clumb out."

Adriana was astonished and asked, "Were there any witnesses? Did a crowd gather at the scene?"

"Oh ya, the *looky loos* were gathering like kids around the ice cream man, but I didn't wait about to sign autographs. I knew there was a deal goin' down at Bridges Restaurant, so I stopped a car and pulled out the driver. I turned around and headed straight to Granville Island," Foley reported.

"What! Now we've added auto theft and assault to our rap sheet?" Mat lamented.

"Well I didn't exactly have time to rent a car. It was getting close to 4:00 o'clock and I knew you were meeting with them to pay the ransom. Thought I might be able to get involved somehow," Foley explained.

"That's how you ended up with the van," Mat said. "What about the money?"

"Still there. It's in the back in them duffel bags."

"And how did you manage all that. They just hand you the keys and wave goodbye to three million bucks?" Mat asked incredulously.

"No, I arrived just in time to see you bolt outta that thing and high tail it into that shop. Looked like you were takin' evasive maneuvers, which was a good idea, I figured. You looked healthy enough, so I didn't follow."

"I didn't want to end up like Jack Kincaid," Mat interjected.

Foley continued, "Then two guys got outta the Navigator and headed straight for the van. Two other guys got out from the back seat and re-entered the vehicle in the front. I heard the one little guy call the other one, with the tattoo on his face, *Boss*, so I knew he must be the kingpin. I remembered too that he was the one doin' all the talkin' when they first captured me. I figure it was him who whacked me on the head with my black jack."

"They captured you? How?" Mat asked.

"Oh, they got me penned in between their vehicles then came to a quick stop. Next thing I know I'm lookin' at four machine pistols pointing at the car from every direction. Made me get out, disarmed me, and knocked me out cold. Woke up all tied down in a chair."

"Foley, my friend, why you're alive today is the eighth wonder of the world."

"Anyway, it didn't take much to lay out the little guy — one punch, and as soon as I did, the other two goons came running out of the Navigator, down the block. Old *tattoo face* went for his gun, but mine was already in my hand, and I held it on him and made him drop his piece. Then we both got into the van and I told him he better call off his dogs, or he'd finish today at the city morgue.

"By now we were gettin' some attention on the street so I knew I had to move fast. I made the two creeps get in the back at gun point, and I did too, then I had the *boss* drive us a few blocks away, where I kicked their butts out and drove off by myself. By the time they got another ride, I was long gone. Figured you two would be here, and here we all are. Kind of a boring story, actually," Foley finished up.

Everyone sat, quietly dumbfounded at Foley's tale. Then Adriana put her head back and laughed like Julia Roberts while Mat sat there speechless.

Finally, Mat shook loose and said, "You're going to have to get your nose looked at. What is it? Are broken noses a job hazard in this business?"

"Ya, one of those creeps blind-sided me when I was bound up in the chair — not very sportsmanlike, I'd say. I can run myself over to the clinic," Foley replied. "I'll just use one of our service vans, since my Durango is apparently stolen now."

"Oh, no, you don't. I'll drive you," Adriana insisted.

"Here, put this on," Mat said pulling a cellophane wrapped shirt emblazoned with the company logo from a shelf in the closet. If they ask what happened, tell them you fell from a ladder at work." Mat was becoming quite adept at fabricating stories to hide the truth lately. "Before you go you better call Crystal. She's worried sick and deserves to know you're safe. She's a good woman, Foley — You wanna treat her right."

Although he suppressed any outward sign of it, Foley's heart warmed that Mat recognized Crystal's worth and character. He wasn't prone to gushy feelings, but she touched a special chord in him that none other ever had and she meant the world to him. He proceeded to his office to follow Mat's advice without hesitation.

"What are you going to do?" Adriana asked Mat.

"I'll move Foley's van outta sight into our service bay and transfer the cash to somewhere safe. Tomorrow I'll set up a drop again with Max Wexler, and we'll place it into the system for transfer to Guatemala. Tonight, you, Manuel and Mina will stay with me," he said looking at Adriana. "And tomorrow morning we'll all meet here at eight and figure a way to finish this up without any more incidents."

At that, the trio had a plan and split up for the day. Incredibly, luck had smiled on them one more time. The question was, *would their luck hold out long enough to complete the mission?*

CHAPTER 33

LATER THAT NIGHT Mat and Adriana showered and changed into clean clothes. Adriana had Mina bring over her travel bag with toiletries and a couple sets of fresh clothes for her and Manuel. It was doubtful that there would be any further incident from the Red Sun Gang, at least for tonight. They made their play for collecting a ransom and failed, having lost the hostage and the money. Taking it further tonight might be walking straight into a Kings Crew trap. Nevertheless, Mat kept his gun in the same room with him at all times.

After Mina fixed them all a nice dinner of grilled salmon steaks from Mat's freezer with hollandaise sauce, steamed pearl rice and mixed vegetables, they all felt well fed and relaxed. An empty bottle of Mission Hill Chardonnay sat as testimony to the relief they felt at being home, safe and together again. Mina was cleaning up and Manuel was watching *CSI Miami* on TV in the family room. Horatio and Frank were in a shoot out with some drug dealing, low lives on the outs with the law.

Adriana scolded him, "Manuel, *you know* I don't like you watching those kind of shows. They're too violent!"

Mat looked at her and laughed, then said, "Sometimes truth is stranger than fiction. Let's go sit in the living room and relax for a bit." They strolled together out of the kitchen into the other room and flopped down, side by each, on Mat's sofa.

Adriana said, "That dinner was *soooo* good. Funny, how food tastes better when you've been practically starved for days."

"They didn't feed you much?" Mat added.

"Nope, chocolate bars and a few left-overs from the hotel kitchen. We were allowed to stand up two or three times a day, go to the bathroom, and eat maybe twice a day. They played cards for half the night, arguing and yelling like stock traders – half in English and half in Chinese, while we slept blindfolded on a mattress on the floor with our hands bound and tied to something heavy in the room. I don't know what – a piece of furniture, or a metal safe, or something."

"Foley too?" Mat asked.

"Yup. There, now I can say I've slept with both of you... *Ha!*" she cracked. The wine at dinner had her a bit tipsy and she seized the opportunity to tease Mat a little.

"Very funny," he replied. "Let's celebrate your safe return with a drink. Join me?" and he proceeded to the bar.

"Sure, don't make mine too strong," she said.

Mat came back with two Canadian whiskies, his considerably darker than hers. They clinked glasses.

"Le'chayim," he said and took a generous sip of the elixir.

She laughed, "What's that?"

"A Jewish toast, learned it from my old friend, Mr. Wexler. It means '*To life, or to your health.*'

"Charming. Did it ever occur to you that you drink too much? *You gotta ease up on that stuff, partner!*" she said, a little giddy with wine, herself.

"I probably do, but it's my only vice. I don't smoke or gamble or chase skirts, with the exception of yours. And I never lie, cheat, steal, or do anything dishonest, with the exception of that money laundering thing. But these are minor character flaws on a grand scale, wouldn't you say? I believe it was Mark Twain who said, *'Too much of anything is bad, but too much of good whiskey is barely enough.'* I always liked that man.

She rolled her eyes. "Give me a break — I thought your thing was money and finance. Now you're quoting Mark Twain?"

"Ya, well, I never like to be thought of as a *one trick pony.* So what? I have the occasional drink, being similar to Winston Churchill in that regard."

Adriana scoffed at the comparison, then added, "Ya, but... *See, it's like this.* When you have something to celebrate, it's *let's have a drink.* When you're troubled or worried about something, you brood with a glass in your hand. When you're bored or just relaxing, out comes the bottle. Everything that happens in life is an occasion to imbibe," Adriana observed.

Mat considered her comments for a moment. "I'll drink to that," he replied, taking another pull from his glass. "Stepping right into the role of nagging wife, are we? No wonder I drink."

"Oh, now it's *my fault,*" she said, and they both laughed.

"Okay," he continued. "I'll slow down on the stuff. I know you're right, but truthfully, *I like it.* What can I say? And it's almost like it has a... what's the word? A *habit forming* quality. Ever notice?"

"Well, what an insightful and original observation — liquor's addictive," Adriana replied with due condescension.

"And... *See, it's like this,*" Mat went on, mimicking her *intro* a moment ago. "It helps me cope with the *purposelessness* of the world. We're just a lonely little planet among billions of other celestial bodies floating around in the universe, populated by a sea of lost souls, and mankind is destined for extinction one way or another like all other species through time. Ultimately, our sun will go into super nova and burn up the entire solar system anyways, so what does *anything* really matter, never mind a little excessive drinking, here and now?" he asked her with a mock-serious, goofy face.

Adriana looked at him smiling and wondering how to address such a bizarre observation. "I'm not sure there's any such word as *purposelessness*, but in legal jargon, that kind of argument is called *reduction to the ridiculous*. Mind pouring me another one of these? And make it a little stronger this time." The two companions laughed heartily at their silly conversation as they each had another ill-advised glass of Canadian whiskey over ice.

☆ ☆ ☆

Under Foley's roof, a conversation of another sort was underway. Crystal had taken one look at Foley with a white strip of surgical tape across his newly-set-nose and a bandage on his forehead, and said, "See? I said you were going to get hurt sooner or later with all this drug business and money laundering. Look at you!"

"Oh, this'll heal in no time. I've been hurt worse sparing at the gym," Foley minimize his injuries. He had just showered and shaved after his three day ordeal, and was dressed comfortably in a thick, white terry cloth bathrobe. It was going on 9:00 p.m. by now and too late to bother dressing in street clothes.

She led her new man over to the kitchen table and sat him down. Then she dampened a rag with cold water to dab away some dried blood around his bandaged head. She pulled another chair up close, and Foley accepted the attention like an affectionate big dog. As she was administering care she looked into Foley's kind eyes and suddenly, each became aware of the intimate closeness they were sharing at this moment. Crystal became filled with emotion and felt a desire for her man that went beyond friendship and protection.

"What if I had lost you?" she said tearfully.

"You ain't gonna lose me, sweetheart. I'm sittin' right here, just a couple a days late for supper," he consoled her. Foley noticed she had a pleasant, perfumed scent, and her hair, and hands, and legs, and breasts beckoned his attention at an instinctive level. To Foley, she looked wonderful beyond any man's dreams.

"You're not Superman, Mister Folkestad," she went on. "You're just a man, and one that I plan on keeping around for a good, long time." She was looking into Foley's eyes very intently, and she began to feel the unmistakable stirring in her loins that signaled her readiness for him.

"And I know what a man wants, and I know how to give it to him, and make him *very, very happy.*" She held both of Foley's hands in hers, and slowly backed away from the table, leading Foley into his living room. The TV was on, and *Dr. House* was tormenting his interns with some impossibly cruel game to determine which of them would remain on staff as diagnosticians in training, and which would be cast off. Crystal reached for the remote and pressed the mute key, just after House called some poor bugger an *idiot* right to his face.

On the couch, Crystal immediately put her arms around Foley and kissed him passionately, taking him somewhat by surprise. He was no virgin, but he'd never been with a *hell-cat* like this who took charge so decisively and enthusiastically, like someone had spiked her wine with a potent aphrodisiac earlier, and he tried to keep up with her like a male teenager on his first romp.

She licked his lips, and sucked his ear lobes and kissed his neck, all the while slipping out of her sweater and bra, unfurling a pair of trophies that any man would look upon with raw, animal lust. *Oh, my God!* Now Foley's robe was open and draped around his shoulders with his bare chest pressed against her warm breasts, and the feeling of skin against skin was ecstatic.

Crystal kissed Foley's neck then ran her tongue down his chest leaving a trail of sticky chest hair, knit together with saliva. She knelt on the floor and pulled apart his robe completely, positioning herself between his legs. She looked down like a kid opening a Christmas present, then up at Foley's eyes, and smiled approvingly. Foley was a passive recipient, stunned with excitement to this point and felt a certain obligation to reciprocate her affections. He tried to reach down and caress her tenderly.

"No, this is for you," she said, rubbing his manhood across her heavy, naked breasts. Foley felt the warmth and softness of her flesh contrasted with the rough rigidness of her dark nipples brushing against his johnson, now engorged with blood, standing at attention like a new cadet, and pulsing with anticipation. Without apprehension, she leant her head forward and took him gently into her mouth, working it sensually, up and down, skillfully, with tongue, lips and hands, and not just for a few moments of foreplay but for a long, long time – as long, at least, as he could stand it. Too bad a film crew couldn't have gotten this. This would have been an award winner in the $12 billion a year U.S. porn industry.

After a short period, Foley said, "Crystal... I can't take much more," giving her the ten second fair warning, in gentlemanly tradition, in case she might not be aware of the consequences of her actions. He looked at her blonde hair bobbing around his hips and held back for dear life. His face looked like he was being tortured.

"It's okay," she paused. "Do what you have to, baby," and continued performing her special favor.

Foley closed his eyes and arched his head back in submission on the sofa. Soon his body would convulse with the ultimate pleasure. Then, he'd exhale spasmically — and *vocally*, like it might sound if a man was giving birth.

Seconds later, it was, "Ah! Ah! Ya... Oh Ya! Oh, don't stop now, baby!"

Foley breathed in and out forcefully through pursed lips, as if he was in labor, then finally declared, "Okay, here we go... *get ready*," then, "*Ahh! Ahhhh!* Oh, Jesus, God in heaven! Who's yo' daddy? Hang on, Darlin'! Ah, Lord have mercy! *Wooooh!*" A grand mal seizure wouldn't have been more electrifying.

All in all, this was a performance of man, *and woman,* made sounds, gymnastics, and convulsions that can't really be portrayed accurately in words, but it was quite a scene... quite a scene, indeed.

Moments later, Foley uttered, 'Darlin'? That was... *somethin',* by Christ! "

Miraculously, the neighbors weren't banging on the walls yelling, *'Hey, keep it down in there!'*

Foley was fully spent now, and he lay back almost in disbelief of what he'd just experienced. She moved off the floor and lay beside him on the couch, stroking his hair and holding him close. She was pleased with her performance and truly loved him at this moment.

"How was that, tough guy?" she whispered in his ear.

"Wonderful." For once Foley didn't have a clever comeback.

After a few minutes, Crystal stood and removed her skirt and panties, revealing her plump, nude body, lit only by the flickering glow of the muted TV screen. Modestly, she stood directly before him, slowly turned a full three-sixty, and smoothed down her pubic hair with one hand, trying to look appealing to her man. She smiled affectionately, and he gazed up at her through loving, attentive eyes from the sofa.

"Lord," Foley muttered looking at her. *It must be awful to be blind,* he thought to himself. To him, there was no more beautiful woman on planet earth.

She grabbed the throw blanket from the other chair and laid back down, covering them both up. Against Foley's warm body, she felt safe and snuggled closely. He wrapped his arms around her, closed his eyes, and held her securely against his chest.

"Let me know when you're ready again. You're not done yet, Huggy Bear," she said quietly. "My turn next."

CHAPTER 34

BY NEXT MORNING everyone was assembled back at Foley and Mat's business. Mat took care of arranging to drop off the cash to Max Wexler for a midnight deposit, Foley tended to routine matters around the business, and Adriana talked extensively with her office about transferring files for other lawyers to work on, while she was on a sabbatical of sorts. Even Crystal tagged along and sat along side Danielle, getting the hang of what her job entailed. Everything was moving forward in the two lines of business Mat and Foley were involved with, one legal and above board, and the other, not.

Mat's cell phone vibrated on his hip and he pulled it from its carry case – *Dominic Hall.*

"Crawford here, Good morning."

"Mornin', Dom calling. What's the news on your kidnapped girlfriend?" He jumped right on the problem.

"Fine, thanks. How are you? I like the way ease yourself into a subject." Mat replied.

Dom backed up a little. "Sorry. My Dale Carnegie training is a little rusty. But what about your predicament? Is she alright?"

"All taken care of, and it didn't cost me a dime, more through sheer, blind luck than anything else." Mat explained.

"Was she hurt at all?" Dom asked, *like he cared.*

"No, just a little shook up. Three days tied up in a chair with nothin' much to eat or drink, wondering what her fate might be... *Not* a real morale building experience. You get it?"

"Ya. Glad to hear it. She's a survivor, I'm confident. Listen, you got our money going through the dry cleaners? Just checking." Dom moved on to *his* business.

"You bet. Money laundering around the globe to beat the band. A few more days and you can start transferring funds into your own accounts," Mat replied.

"Excellent! This is turning into a first class partnership," Dom said.

Mat wanted to set the record straight. "I'd call it more of a *project* than a partnership. Nothing personal."

"Well that's something we'd like to talk about further. It's why I called actually. Hey, can you meet me at Jesse Novak's office later today, say, around 2:00 o'clock? I think you'll like what you hear," Dom persuaded Mat.

Although wary of his motives, Mat saw no compelling reason not to agree, so he went along with Dom's request, and the meeting was confirmed. Mat worked around the office on every day matters until it was time to leave, and he was quite curious about what this meeting might be about.

By 1:30 p.m., everyone was working busily in the office, and it occurred to Mat that he liked having everyone together at Bull Dog Security, almost like a family business — Foley, Adriana, Crystal, Danielle, Mat himself, and this business didn't pose a risk to your health or freedom. *I must be getting old,* he said to himself.

✳ ✳ ✳

It was in the back of Mat's mind all morning and past lunch, what, exactly, Dominic Hall wanted to talk about at Novak's office. True, he had the intention of finishing up with the present money laundering job and cutting ties with the Kings Crew and this whole sordid mess, but, at the same time, Dom's words '*I think you'll like what you hear*', kept repeating in his mind. *I'd like to wash my hands of all this, but I'm a whore for the money,* sounded off internally. He wasn't proud of it, but there it was. If all heroes have a fatal flaw, his was the inability, as Nancy Reagan said, to 'Just say no.'

As 2:00 o'clock approached, Mat excused himself from Bull Dog, hopped into his car, turned the ignition over and shifted into first. He popped the clutch and darted out of the parking lot and around the corner like an eager job candidate going on an interview.

Motoring to his appointment, his mind was in hyper-drive. *I'm not going to take any more work from this outfit. Keep an open mind. You're done with these guys, once and for all. Hear them out — it's a business decision. This was a bad idea from the start, like Foley said. You're in a risky business… you've known that all along. Suck it up and play the game. No one's caught you yet. Use your head, for once, and make tracks away from all this, you fool! Adriana wants you to quit, start something new, together with her. I'll attend the meeting, and hear what they have to say. Anything wrong with that?*

He parked the car in front of Jesse Novak's building and looked up at the tower, wondering how much dirty business, besides what Novak and Hall were up to, was really going on up there inside other offices. It's happening everywhere, after all. "Okay," he said out loud. "Let's do this thing." He slammed shut the BMW's door with a sturdy thud, walked across the sidewalk and marched into the front foyer towards the elevators.

As Mat walked into the law firm of Jesse Novak, Nancy was at her usual station behind her mahogany reception desk, typing while staring blankly at an LCD screen, with a headset on.

"Hello again, Mr. Crawford," she greeted him warmly, snapping out of her trance. "The gentlemen are waiting to see you. I'll buzz Mr. Novak."

Mat was almost ten minutes early. He wondered why they might be together already. No doubt strategizing about something. *Guess I'll find out soon enough.*

Jesse came out immediately and escorted Mat back to his office. Dom Hall was sitting at a granite meeting table with several chocolate colored leather arm chairs around it. He stood up and extended his hand to shake with Mat in a gesture that seemed a little too ingratiating.

"Thanks for coming, Mat," Dom said. The three men each took a chair.

"Yes, we appreciate your cooperation. We know you're a *busy man*," Jesse added, and he and Dominic laughed together at the private reference to Mat's money laundering enterprise. "Can I get you anything — coffee, tea, something stronger?"

"No, thanks, I'm good. So what can I do for you?" Mat got right to the point. His curiosity was roused.

Dom and Jesse exchanged a look like *Where do we start?* Dominic said, "Mat, I haven't shared this with you before now, but I want to be right up front with you."

Mat listened intently. "Please do."

"This whole drug heist that we pulled off hasn't exactly gone down like we expected. Christ, my business was raided, people were killed and wounded, the building is likely a write-off, there's cops nosing around, your girl was grabbed off the street, Captain Furlong and Jack Kincaid... well, you know what happened to them."

"Who would have ever thought that anything could go wrong?" Mat said, dryly.

"Ya, well, that's why we hired a professional to handle the money. You see, we can manage relatively small amounts of cash, a few thousand at a time, but when we start getting' into hundreds of thousands, or millions, it's just out of our league, and there's no room for error, or the cops will be all over us," Dominic explained. "From what we've seen and heard, you've got this money laundering down to a science and we think there's a bigger place for you in the organization."

Mat could see the direction this was headed, and he thought he better put the brakes on it right now.

"Fellas, I want to make it clear that I signed on to launder the proceeds of the coke shipment you commandeered from the Red Sun Gang. The street value of that heist is around $50 million, and so far we've moved around eight million bucks. I'm hoping we can pick up the pace and get the rest in the system and ready for transfer back to Canada. After that, I'm out, and I'm really not interested in taking any more assignments."

Dom looked at Jesse and there was a pregnant pause. Jesse stepped in.

"Let me handle this, Dom," he said. "Mat, here's the thing. We've moved all the money there is from that little caper. As Dom said, things didn't quite go according to plan, frankly."

"Mat interrupted. "What do you mean? There's still $42 million outstanding, by my math."

"Jesse said, "Well, there *would have* been. But the Asian gang got wind of where the drugs were being stored and went and hijacked it back again. It's out of our possession, I'm afraid."

"Goddamn it!" said Dominic. "We found out those slippery little pricks got to it, right under our noses!"

Mat was, if anything, relieved. Now he could drop this whole matter and get on with life.

"You can't sell drugs you don't have," he summarized.

"There ya go," Jesse responded.

"Then it's over. We're out of business."

"Well, not so fast," Jesse said. "Of course, we're disappointed that the upside wasn't nearly as high in this initiative as we had hoped, but as Dom alluded, it really wasn't our ideal involvement to begin with. The problem from the start was that it contained an inherently high degree of competition."

"The Red Sun, sons-a-bitches," Dom interjected with signature profanity.

Jesse went on, delivering his words carefully and slowly. "The enterprises that the Kings Crew are best suited to, like any business, are the ones that have little or no competition. Ones where you can demand a price, and your customer will pay it gladly, because you're the only supplier. And ones where you don't have to be looking over your shoulder the entire time wondering if somebody is going to do something that your life insurance carrier would disapprove of." He smiled at his own humor and adjusted the French cuffs of his shirt in the sleeves of his jacket.

"I think that's called a monopoly," Mat replied.

Jesse carried on, "Yes, exactly, and the Kings Crew didn't get where they are, as a world scale crime syndicate, by not diversifying their business interests. There's still lots of money coming in, and it'll need to be laundered, and we think you're our man."

"Gee, and I thought they were just a bunch of hoods on motorcycles engaged in enough petty crime to keep them in beer, mary jane, and a stable of chicks with double-D's in halter tops."

Dominic jumped in to the defense of his organization. "Now just a minute there, Bud. I could take exception to that. We don't all just chase after beer and marijuana…"

The three men looked at each other, paused, then laughed together at Dom's clarification of the issue.

"Bra-busting chippies are quite another matter, you understand," Jesse commented. "Double- Ds are always an interesting diversion."

Dom smiled, stood from his chair, and moved on, walking the room as he spoke. "Mr. Crawford, we're engaged in a whole wide variety of money makers, I can assure you. Things that you would never dream could be so profitable. See, when you're creative, there's hardly any limit to the things you can get involved with that will generate buckets of money. There's the Kings Crew motorcycle club, and then there's the Kings Crew business... That's us, my friend."

Mat observed, "Oh, I see. Then you're a regular Fortune 500 enterprise, with a business plan, diversified interests, and a vision for the future."

Dom smiled. "*Right you are*, and the only real difference between us and other corporations is that we don't pretend to be honest, law-abiding, tax paying, good corporate citizens. Most of them are as dishonest as we are. They spy on competitors, evade taxes — whenever and however possible, manipulate markets, deceive buyers, pay out bonuses in the hundreds of millions, or more, to senior executives for mediocre managerial performance, bribe government officials, and engage in stock market fraud to inflate their share values. Crime — white collar, and otherwise... It's mind boggling, when you delve into it. But you know all that, don't you? You're the financial expert."

"Expert? I don't know that I'd ever make that claim, but I do know from a long list of learning experiences what makes business tick, and how to get around some of the rules to turn a profit. I never said I condone the practices of big business, but you can't work the system by ignoring reality. You can bend some rules and get away with it. Stick your neck out too far and you're liable to lose your head, as *your last* learning experience."

"Mat, you're good at what you do because you understand all the parameters of your business, and just how far you can push the envelope. I like that. We understand our business too, and our basic philosophy is that we're gonna make money in a world of business that's already dirty. Don't tell us to play by the rules, because the rules are stacked to favor the house, and the house is corrupt."

"What do you mean, exactly?" Mat pressed his associate since he was feeling talkative.

"Well, the thing is, the whole business model that our society is built upon is like a huge Ponzi scheme. It assumes endless growth and an infinite supply of new consumers, new markets, new products, new money, new jobs, new taxpayers. It's a self feeding, pyramid-based system designed to keep corporations and governments wealthy on the backs of consumers and taxpayers. So we've decided not to participate, simple as that. We do, however, plan on staying in business and making money by our own means. They're the lions, Mat, and we're the Hyenas, and we're natural, mutually exclusive competitors, each making a living off scarce prey on the savannah of Vancouver's streets, and around the globe.

"Let no one forget, we're the Kings Crew... no less. We're into more shit than the man could catch up to in three life times, and if he starts gettin' too close, his lifetime might not last too much longer. Our motto is *When we do right, nobody remembers. When we do wrong, nobody forgets.*"

Mat listened on with interest and distain. The last thing he needed at this point was a dissertation on the scruples and tactics that the Kings Crew were capable of. He, himself, was a victim of their coercion and entrapment techniques.

"Would it surprise you, Mr. Crawford, to learn that we have infiltrated many of the highest offices of business, industry, and law enforcement in Vancouver, and all over North America for that matter? Bribery, extortion... don't matter to us. If we need you, we'll have you."

Mat looked skeptically at the man, wondering where he was going. Were they going to coerce him somehow into joining the Kings Crew as their exclusive money launderer?

Dom continued, "Not all Kings Crew are a bunch of bearded, easy-riders in sun glasses on Harleys, wearing colors and flaunting authority. Those are the foot soldiers that follow orders, and that's the side we show to the public. We work quietly too, behind all the hoop-la. Look at me. Look at Jesse. We're on the board of directors, my friend. *We're the money.*

"The image we display for the public is a group of fun loving bad boys who ride noisy bikes and take a lot of flack from the authorities, mostly without cause. We organize public service events like *Toys for Tots,* and stage blood drives to demonstrate our charitable side. So whose side of the story is the public going to believe — ours, or the heat? We don't have to convince anyone of anything. All we have to do is plant a little doubt. Are we any worse than politicians out shaking hands with common citizens, cutting ribbons, issuing cheques to charities, and kissing babies, before taking office and engaging in dishonesty and the manipulation of power? Where, exactly, is the line between right and wrong, honest and dishonest, law and crime, good guys and bad guys?

"Mat, we also have members in key roles in big business, who know how and when to look the other way… open or close doors. Circumvent the rules. Know what I mean? We have dirty cops. *Oh yes,* and even some judiciary. Everyone's a partner when the Kings Crew come a knockin', 'cause everyone, and I mean *everyone,* is on the take."

Mat interjected, "I won't call you a liar, but I think you may be over-estimating your influence, just a little."

"No, no, my friend. All it takes to recruit willing participants is to find someone who may be just a little disillusioned, who refuses to be constrained by all the laws and rules of conventional society. Someone fed up, disgusted. Someone who thinks they may not be getting their fair share. Someone who thinks they're entitled to a little more — if they can get away with it. Someone with a little greed at their core.

"Remember Gordon Gekko — Michael Douglas, in *Wall Street?* 'Greed is good. Greed is right. Greed works!' Someone who may feel cheated — maybe rightfully so, and wants some payback. Most everyone has their price, my friend, and if they're sure they won't get caught, most anyone can be bought. *It's all about money, Mat.* For the right price, most anyone will do anything, as we both well know. *Money talks.* It's that simple." Dominic paused and looked at Mat intensely, "Do you know anyone like that?"

Mat looked on but didn't answer. He wanted to offer a rebuttal, but was a little stumped as to where to start. The son-of-a-bitch made sense.

Dom pulled his chair around Mat's side of the table, sat down with his hands on his knees and said, "Mat, I'm gonna level with you about something. The drug money? It's all ours — Jesse's and mine. Carlos was in on it, but he's toast now. We master minded the bribery of Captain Furlong and the heist of the cocaine in the first place. We put it out on the street, and all the proceeds that have come in. *Ours, and ours alone.* $8 million. And the nice thing is *we stole it,* so there's no one we have to pay for it. Found money. One hundred percent profit.

"We're offering you a million bucks, cash, to join us at your usual fee schedule on future transactions. What do ya say?"

Mat *didn't* know what to say. He blurted out, "What about the rest of the Kings Crew? Where do they stand with all this money?"

"They're just workers, soldiers. We pay 'em good, buy 'em plenty of beer and broads. Keep 'em in shiny, noisy choppers, their chief source of identity in the world. Don't worry, they're happy, long as they don't find out we *freelanced* this drug deal.

Mat looked puzzled. "Freelanced?" he repeated.

Dom carried on, "Well ya. How would you react if someone in your organization was out doing business on the side, without turning in the proceeds to the company? It'd be a real shit-show, I can tell ya, but no worries, our secret is safe with Jesse and me.

And now, me! Mat thought.

"Tell you what," he continued, "You come with me tomorrow, let me show you some things. It'll blow your mind when you see the scope of our operations. If you don't want to take part in it, you can walk away, no obligations."

Mat felt compelled to argue a point. "That's what I understood last time, until you pulled a gun on me across the table. So much for *no obligations*."

"Oh, are you still sore about that? Christ, we were just two-steppin', feelin' each other out, is how I read it. If I was going to bump you off, I wouldn't do it myself. We have operatives who specialize in that sort of thing. C'mon, tag along with me for a couple hours tops, tomorrow, and I'll educate you on how we make a hell of a lot of under-the-radar-money. What have ya got to lose?" Dominic said laughing, like one good ol' boy to another.

Mat wasn't in the business of laundering proceeds of crime for big, tax-free returns by accident. To a fault, he was fascinated by the game and he was good at it. Although he realized the time had come to get out, like an addict, he wanted one more hit, and couldn't resist Dom's offer. He *wanted* to see what Dom was talking about.

Reluctantly, he gave in, his curiosity piqued, "Alright, but I want to bring my partner along too. We're in this together and I'll want his input."

Dominic looked slightly amused. "Then I take it the kidnappers didn't *off him*, after all."

Mat recalled their conversation before. "No, they tried, but he's got kind of a rare talent for dealing with bad guys. Trust me, he can be one nasty sum bitch, when the spirit moves him."

"I do trust you, or you wouldn't be here. But okay, bring along your pal. We'll make it a party."

On that note, the trio broke for the day and agreed to meet up again at Dominic Hall's office tomorrow at 9:00 a.m. to go on a guided tour of the Kings Crew's more rewarding operations. Mat wasn't comfortable with doing any more business with the group, but Dom's offer of having a look with no obligations lured him into agreeing. There was nothing to lose, he reasoned, by taking an opportunity to learn something new and gather some information.

What he was about to learn however, would easily fall into the colloquial category of *too much information.*

CHAPTER 35

"I DON'T LIKE it! All you're doin' is encouraging them to keep on pullin' you deeper and deeper into their affairs, and they're playin' you like a fiddle," was Foley's reaction to the story laid out by Mat.

Danielle entered Mat's office with two cups of steaming coffee and set them down before each partner. She smiled, but Mat wondered whether she might secretly resent such a favor as sexist and demeaning. In the back of his mind he confirmed his intent to have a heart-to-heart with her, like Adriana had suggested in the hotel room in Panama. "She certainly seems like a keeper. *A raise and more time off,*" were her exact recommendations, as Mat recalled silently.

"Well, I'm not crazy about it either. I understand your cold feet, but there's no harm in having a look. We can walk away at any time, just tie off the loose ends of the money being laundered in Panama, and call it a day. Where's the problem?" Mat countered.

"Christ almighty, you never learn. You stick your right hand in the fire, then turn around and put your other hand in right behind it, not happy 'til both are good and burned. And when that's all done, you'll lean forward and poke your head in."

"Fole… Relax. We're just goin' for a little drive to learn about the affairs of the people who are technically, still our employers. Take a pill, and back me up. We're only born to learn and grow, so let's not throw up the white flag just yet. C'mon, bud. Where's the Foley I grew up with? Are we caving under a little pressure, or are we still kickin' ass?"

Foley exhaled heavily and relented to the inevitable pressure of Mathew's curiosity about what lay ahead. He sensed that Mat was close to hangin' 'em up, but the boy still had issues that needed to be explored and Foley felt duty bound to follow along, as always before.

"Goddamn it, no, no, no!" Ten seconds, or so passed. "Okay, you win, like usual, there's no *quit* in you, is there boy? We'll do this thing, and then, it's over, for your sake and mine. After this, I'm out, understood? I didn't sign up for no suicide mission and that's what this is turning into. Clear?"

"Clear. I knew you'd see the light, Buddy, once it was explained in plain English. And here's the good part — I insisted that *you* come along, and they agreed. I think it's important that you get a first hand look at what they're doing so we can decide *together*, if we should have any further involvement in their business. Considering your apprehension, I'm wondering now whether that was a good idea on my part."

Foley sat up a little straighter in his chair. "No bloody way. That was the first smart thing you've done since we got sucked into this cyclone. I'll be glad to have a look at what other shenanigans these boys are up to. I warn ya though, if I don't like it, I'm gonna say so — in *plain English*."

"Well, there's a surprise — Foley's gonna speak his mind, for once. Anything else, and I'd probably grow a set of tits, which reminds me… Why don't you go home now and tell some lies to Crystal? Maybe you can finally coax her into the bedroom. I think she actually digs you and it's about time for some *heavy breathin'* after all, or you're going to fall into that black hole of being *just friends* forever. Here's a tip Foley, my old pal and mentor, guys and girls can never be *just friends,* There's always sexual chemistry to one extent or another, and if you don't strike while the iron is hot — well, the iron cools off, and so does she. Leave it much longer, and you'll have a better chance of getting lucky with your sister. Does she even know you're *hetero-*sexual? *You are, aren't you?"*

Foley didn't dignify that question with an answer.

Then Mat punched an upper cut in the air with one arm, illustrating the intent of his message. "Get 'er done — tonight. I'll see ya here at 8:00 tomorrow morning, with a big, guilty grin on your face, I hope. It's kinda sad when the student surpasses the teacher, but like the saying goes, *it is what it is."*

Foley looked at his naïve young buddy and smiled slightly, reminiscing, but didn't say another word.

Mat finished the last gulp of his coffee and banged the empty cup down authoritatively like a judge's gavel, signaling *case closed.* Both men rose and left the room, Foley heading out the front door with a nod and a wink towards Danielle, and Mat stopping at her desk looking at her intently. She looked up then did a double take, noticing the odd look on Mat's face.

"What's up? Why are you staring?" she asked. "Is there ketchup on my face?" she quipped.

"Danny, I said we were going to have a talk, about — things. Remember?" Mat replied.

"Ya, and you said something was wrong and you were going to make it right. Did you?"

"Yes, I did. For now, anyways. We're not out of the woods yet, but let's talk about you. Mind if I sit down?" Mat pulled a chair closer to her desk.

"Alright. What's on you mind, boss? Did I do anything wrong?" Danielle asked, turning serious.

"No, God, no. That's just it. You're a big part of the fabric that holds this place together, day to day, and I wonder if you know how much you're appreciated," Mat said to her as sincerely as possible. His internal voice was replaying Dominic Hall's words from the day before — *'Money talks, It's that simple.'*

Danielle was visibly flattered and she responded, "Why, thank you. It's always nice to be complimented but my job comes with rewards, and I feel you should know —" She paused searching for the right words to express how pleased she was to have her position and how she wouldn't dream of leaving the firm or even bother looking at another job. She couldn't be happier, or so she thought.

Mat was convinced otherwise, however, and between Adriana's friendly advice on how to hang on to this valuable and rare employee, and Dom Hall's candid speech about how greed is at the core of basic human motivation, and it's all about *money, money, money*, he took Danielle's partial statement differently than where she was trying to go with it. All he heard was something about *her job* and *rewards*, and he assumed that she was trying to diplomatically ask for a raise.

"Let me interrupt you right there," He jumped in. "I won't have you thinking that we don't value your contributions to this place, your consistent expertise in running this business and dealing with daily issues, and your fun, friendly personality around the office. There's a cost to an employer for that kind of service, and I'm prepared to pay it."

Danielle looked across her desk wide-eyed and surprised at her boss's sudden and new found appreciation of her work and character.

"Tell you what," Mat continued. "I'm going to give you an immediate salary increase of... *twenty* percent." He looked at her to gauge her response.

Danielle was open mouthed by now. She wasn't looking for *any* increase and she certainly didn't want to put her job in jeopardy by costing the company too much money. She was shocked, quite frankly, and she looked it. Mat, however, took her expression for disappointment, so he immediately upped the ante.

"No, make that *twenty-five* percent. You're worth every penny of it and it's overdue. And I'm also giving you an extra week of paid holidays from now on, and the company will be picking up one hundred percent of your health benefits. And your next review will be in six months — to see how we're all doing. Fair?"

Danielle wouldn't have been happier if she'd won the lottery, and she placed one hand over her open mouth. Her eyes welled up. Seeing this — and misreading it, Mat was getting desperate. He stood from his chair and raised both arms up in a gesture of frustration.

"Danny, What else can I do? What do you want?"

"No, no..." she stammered wiping her cheek with her hand. "You've done too much already. I'm happy, Mat, *really, really* happy. Please, no more. Thank you, thank you! I'll work even harder. You'll see," and she stood up and threw her arms around her boss and kissed his cheek in a display of affection that was uncharacteristically familiar. He was just a little uncomfortable, at first — she *was* an employee, after all, but then what man doesn't like being kissed by a pretty girl? Against all primal instincts, he restrained himself from kissing her back.

His ego suitably inflated now, and impressed with his own generosity, he patted her on the back and said in a more formal tone, "Alright now, back to work. I have to leave for the day, but I'll be in early tomorrow."

"Yes, sir," she replied, gathering control of herself and looking happier than the winner of *American Idol.*

Mat headed for the door and looked back over his shoulder on the way out. "Try not to burn the place down while I'm gone." The door closed behind him and she sat there, stunned, grinning.

Though unaware of the connection at this point, it was Adriana's final words to her when she first met Danielle that planted the seeds in Mat's head for this whole discussion and its fruitful outcome. Adriana's closing words were, "Thanks, you've been a great help. Maybe I can return the favor some time. In fact, *I promise.*" She had held true to her word and kept her promise — splendidly, in fact.

CHAPTER 36

THAT EVENING, MAT walked into his house and Adriana was already there with files spread all over the kitchen table. She was finishing off business from her law firm and closing whatever legal issues she could in what she expected to be a relatively short timeframe. She and Mat were in this mess right up to their necks with two of Vancouver's worst gangs, and the law, and her life had already been used as a pawn in trying to extort money out of the situation. It would never, ever, be over, and she knew it. She had decided to make preparations for an exit from the business, and likely from the city itself.

As Mat entered the house, he took one look at the scene before him. "So, it's come to this. Now you're working virtual from my kitchen table. How long have you been here? All day?"

She looked weary and stressed. "No, I dropped by my office this morning, returned a few calls and emails, picked up the files on my top ten clients and then came over here. Been here since around eleven, or so."

"Good idea. It's not safe for you to be exposed, out in the open, after what happened. Creeps might try something again," he replied.

"How about you? How's your day been?" she asked.

Mat's attention drifted back to the conversation with Dominic and Jesse, and to their agreement to go on a little excursion through the Kings Crew's business interests tomorrow.

"Well, I've had an interesting day, to say the least," he said. Adriana didn't have to ask what he meant. Her face said it all.

He went on. "I met with Dominic Hall and that lawyer, Jesse Novak. There'll be no more money laundering as far as the cocaine heist is concerned. The Red Sun Boys must have found out where it was being held when they raided the accounting firm. They stole it back somehow so the Kings Crew have lost control of their inventory. Can't sell drugs you don't have."

Adriana's face lit up. "Well, that's wonderful, isn't it? We're out, we're done!" She paused looking at him — no, *studying* him for a reaction. "There's more isn't there? I can tell. What is it, Mat?"

Carefully, he replied, or built an argument, more precisely. "Okay, keep an open mind here, Adriana. The Kings Crew are a widely diversified criminal organization. They have interests and involvement at practically all levels of business, law enforcement and government. They've infiltrated nearly all the institutions of society to one extent or another, and they'll stop at nothing to promote their interests and make money — dirty money, of course, and they want me to continue laundering it. They've asked me to go on a little tour around the city with them tomorrow to see some of the other things they're involved with that drives their cash flow. I expect there'll be casinos, marijuana grow ops, car theft rings — who knows?"

Adriana looked astonished. "You agreed? You're gonna let them pull you into their affairs even deeper? That's nuts! What were you thinking?"

Mat jumped to his defense, "I know, I know, but first, they've assured me that this is a one time, no obligations offer. If I elect not to participate, I can walk away. And second, I'd still be working for them anyways if the coke hadn't been recovered by the Asian gang."

"And what if they renege on that offer? What are you going to do? Sue them for *breach of contract?*" Adriana's legal mind went into action, even if with sarcasm.

Mat had a look of concern on his face but he went on, "Hon, it would be dangerous and foolish to just flatly refuse their offer. I already know too much about their affairs for us to just shake hands and part company. I'll have to remind them that I couldn't blow the whistle on them without incriminating myself, and why would I want to?

"We've been business partners and both made good money. Unless there are opportunities here to make some unbelievable green, I plan to cooperate with them then respectfully decline. I'll leave the impression that there's no bridges burned, that we may well do business again in the future. That's a lot safer than the *fuck you* approach and slamming the door on the way out, don't you think?"

"What I think is that is that if you want any kind of future with me you're going to have to stop freelancing like you're the lone ranger. You clearly subscribe to the belief that it's better to ask for forgiveness than beg for permission," Adriana said firmly.

Mat looked puzzled. "I'm not sure what you mean. Spell it out. "

She looked at him with a very serious demeanor. "Mat, I want a future with you, and I think you want one with me, but you can't make decisions like this without my input. We're partners, fifty-fifty, and we'll make the big decisions in life together, from here on. I'm not some mousy, little housewife that you can push around and do whatever you please. We're getting out of this money laundering thing of yours and never looking back, and you shouldn't pretend you're only window shopping with me if there's any chance, even remotely, that you're going to accept another assignment from these monsters... *or this isn't going to work.*"

At that moment, Mat realized that his mystery lady had a backbone of steel and she meant the words she was speaking. Was he in danger of losing the second good woman to come into his life over his involvement in the criminal underworld? He felt something akin to a controlled panic. *No way,* was he going to risk losing this woman.

"What do you want, exactly?" he said.

They looked long and hard at one another. Finally, she said, "I'm coming along."

"No, you're not!"

"Yes, I am. They know me, and that we work together, and they know you stuck your neck out to save me from the kidnappers. And to use your argument, if the coke hadn't been stolen back by the Asians, we'd still be on the first assignment — *together.* And if these operations are so lucrative, I want a say in whether you're going to participate. And like I said, the odds of that are a thousand to one. It's not negotiable."

Mat was adamant. "Look, you talked me into bringing you along the last time and you wound up as someone's hostage for three days. It's a miracle that we even got you out alive, and Foley too, and it nearly cost me three million, hard earned, dollars. No, absolutely not, and that's the end of it."

"I'm coming."

"No, *you're not,* discussion closed!" He put his foot down firmly, with authority and finality.

✷ ✷ ✷

The next morning shortly after eight, Mat and Adriana pulled into the parking lot at Bull Dog Security all set to go on the tour, together.

Mat reminded her, "Now remember, when we're looking today at the businesses these guys are involved in, don't make any judgmental comments or give any indications as to whether you're in favor of it or not. We have to *poker face* it all day long, got it? And you follow me and take my instructions. I'm the boss, as far as they're concerned. This *fifty-fifty* thing is just between us, okay?"

"I guess," she replied. "Let's look and learn."

They walked in the front door, said good morning to Danielle, who seemed unusually cheerful for so early in the morning, and back to Foley's office. Mat walked in first, and who was sitting across from Foley's desk? Crystal!

Mat piped up, "Hey Crystal, didn't know you were coming in today. What are ya doing, helping out Danielle again around the office?"

Crystal looked at Foley, who so far, hadn't said a word. He looked like he had something on his mind. Following Crystal's lead, every one shifted their attention to Foley. He took the floor and spoke up.

"See, it's like this, Buck. Crystal wants to come along on this little sight seeing tour that *we arranged* today. I tried to talk her out of it, but she wouldn't have any of it. I could go into a long explanation about it, but... *you wouldn't understand*. She's a headstrong woman and there's no talkin' sense to her when she sets her mind on somethin'. The bottom line is, she's coming along, or we're both out."

Mat's jaw dropped so hard it nearly hit the floor. "Oh, this is getting better by the minute! I wouldn't *understand?*" he said, looking at Adriana. "Let's make it a *double date* then, shall we? Why don't we see if we can't *all* get taken hostage, or killed, or arrested. Maybe we should bring along Danielle too. I'll call my *ex*, and see if she'd like to join us."

Foley piped in, "Don't be sore. You said it was just an observation tour, just a *reconnaissance mission*, as we called it back in my army days. And odds aren't strong that we'll take any more work from them anyways."

Now Adriana joined in. "The odds are a *hundred to one*, at best."

Mat noted quietly that that was an improvement by ten times from what she said last night, *a thousand to one*. Maybe this was moving in the right direction. He took over the conversation.

"Okay, okay, everyone. Looks like we're all in this together, but I want it understood that *I'm the money launderer*, the one who calls the shots, the one who does *the trick*, and all of you are my backup. Keep your comments to a minimum, don't ask questions, and don't piss anybody off, 'specially me. You're coming along today as observers, that's it — *against* my advice and wishes."

Mat's tone took a decidedly more serious note.

"One other thing. This may not just be a *recon* job. The unexpected is *always* just beyond sight. *Expect the unexpected* and look to me, and Foley, if anything off the wall goes down. We're playing with fire here, have no illusions. Questions?"

Everyone sat silent. Mat gathered up a leather bound writing pad, an extra clip of cartridges, and his pistol, which he tucked into the waistband of his pants at the small of his back. Foley did the same with his piece. They locked eyes for a moment and communicated their camaraderie like brothers. They nodded to one another and pivoted towards the door.

"Ready folks? Let's book," Mat said, and away they went to take a guided tour of some of the money-spinning enterprises engaged in by the Vancouver chapter of the Kings Crew.

CHAPTER 37

AT 9:00 A.M. sharp Mat and company pulled up to Dominic Hall's temporary offices in a rented Jeep Grand Cherokee, large enough to comfortably transport its four occupants for the day.

Mat turned and reiterated his instructions. "Remember everyone, I'll do the talking, unless you're asked a direct question. And if you are, keep your answers brief. We're dealing with a bad bunch here – career criminals, so be careful how you conduct yourselves. I'm not sure what we're going to see today, so be prepared for anything and let's be professional. When we're finished, and by ourselves, you can air whatever's on your mind, but keep it under your hat until then. Don't show your cards."

"Gotcha, boss," Foley replied on everyone's behalf.

They walked into the reception area of *Hall and Barlow,* and a flippant young girl from the temp agency welcomed them.

"Ya, hi there. What can I do ya for?"

What a piece of work this one is, Mat thought to himself. *Dom must have hired the cheapest one available. Minimum wage, likely.*

"Yes, good morning. We're here to see —"

"Mat, cut the formalities. C'mon in here, for Christ's sake," a voice boomed from the adjoining office. It was Dom Hall.

Mat nodded to his three companions to follow and the four of them filed into Dom's makeshift office. He was sitting behind a large wooden desk that must have come from a used furniture store by the looks of it. Atop the desk was a cup of Tim Hortons double-double, and a box of Timbits. Dom's cheek was bulging on one side with doughnut and coffee.

"Hey, Dom, how's everything today? I brought along some company. Hope you don't mind," Mat tried to make light of the change in plans.

Dom sat without responding, chewing. Finally he said, "Well, you, and Foley, and Adriana I know, but who may I ask is this?" gesturing towards Crystal.

"This is Crystal Waters. She joined us a while back to help out in a variety of ways with our *special projects*," meaning *money laundering*, without actually saying it. Dom understood and smiled, nodding. Foley noticed him looking at her breasts, like every other man who first meets her, and clenched his teeth. *Bloody, boob-staring pervert,* he thought quietly.

Dom wanted to entice Mat into joining the Kings Crew as an exclusive money launderer for the broad base of operations that drove their revenues. He would hardly make an issue of a few extras along for the ride on that basis. It was his intent to make Mat feel welcomed, comfortable, a contributor at a senior level, so he took on an accommodating posture.

"Hell no, I don't mind. We're all family here, far as I'm concerned. But let's not waste time socializing. We've got ground to cover today, so we better get a move on. I'm gonna show ya how we make a lotta dough, under the radar. Let's go, kids!"

The party bustled out the front door like out of town buyers going to look at houses with an eager realtor. Mat and Dominic jumped in together in his luxury Lexus ISF 10. The others boarded the rented Jeep and followed along behind.

Proceeding down the road, Dom commented, "This baby hauls, puts out four hundred and sixteen horses. It's got a five liter V8 and does zero to sixty in four and a half seconds. One of many perks of the job. It could be yours, free, by Monday, plus the million, if we come to an agreement," Dom said, smiling and looking momentarily at Mat.

"I'll keep that in mind," Mat replied. "How many cup holders does it have?"

Dom's head turned around from watching the road ahead, and the two laughed together. "Good one!"

"Where we goin' first?" Mat continued.

"We're gonna start small and work our way up to the real money-makers. Relax, in a few minutes I'll show you one of our *hobbies*."

Mat agreed and tried to do just that — relax. He was on this trip to observe, learn, and keep an open mind. They stopped at a red light and a police cruiser pulled up in the lane beside them. Two young officers sat in the front seat and mouthed words that couldn't be heard. One of them spoke into a radio mic with a coiled cord leading to the dash. Mat wondered whether they'd been made already and the cops were running license plates or something else through their data base. Moments later, the light turned green, and both cars pulled away without incident. Mat breathed out heavily.

Dom pulled into the parking lot of an industrial building several blocks later. He stopped at the front door and said, "Let's go. Here's where we start." Both men exited the vehicle, as the Jeep behind them parked at a nearby stall.

"What's this? The Kings Crew have taken up bingo?" Foley asked looking up at the sign — *Lighthouse Bowling and Bingo*.

Dom looked back at him, then at Mat, and said, "Dogs."

Dom, Mat, Foley, and the two girls proceeded in through the front door and past the attendants at the cash window, who paid them no mind once they saw Dominic. The echo of bowling balls crashing into the pins reverberated through the building and excited youngsters and other patrons ran about the food court and lobby in high spirits. Piped in music was annoyingly loud, unless you were a giddy kid at a birthday-bowling party, or some other such reveler. *What a noisy, bloody, racket,* Mat thought.

"Follow me," Dom said, going to the far side of the building and opening a remote door with a key from his pocket.

The first thing Mat noticed, and every one else upon entering the room, was the smell. It stunk. It smelled like a combination butcher shop, raw meat odor, and the distinctive dog shit smell of the holding kennels at the SPCA. The second thing he noticed was the incessant yelping of hundreds, maybe thousands of puppies. It was a chorus of young dogs, frantically barking and howling in unison.

"This, my friend, is a nice little money tree, plus it's kinda fun," Dom said to Mat. "Let's look around."

The room they had entered was actually at least half of the total floor space of the building. The bowling and bingo was just a cover, a ruse to throw off suspicion by anyone as to what else might be going on here. The sound of the bowling lanes and the rock music blasting through the overhead speakers easily masked the muffled howls of the rack after rack of puppies in the kennels next door.

Rubber hoses stretched across the concrete floor at every angle. Attendants in stained white aprons and face masks shuffled around with dog food dishes and hypodermic needles, busily performing clean up and ghoulish tasks on the animals. The city zoo couldn't have been better organized. Overhead fans sucked out foul air and added to the drone of the hellish sound of enslaved, helpless animals, used for *God knows what.*

Mat and Foley looked around, in wonder. The ladies were aghast. Nobody was sure what, if anything, to say. Thousands of dogs — in a warehouse. Where do you start?

"This fuckin' thing makes us twenty-five grand a month, minimum," Dominic boasted. "Great walkin' around money. People love dogs, *and blood*."

"How so?" was all Mat could respond.

"Dom started walking slowly through the building and explained, "Ever heard of a puppy mill? This one is the mother of all puppy mills in British Columbia. We have at least one like it in every province across Canada. Dogs are bred here en masse and shipped off to buyers and pet stores across North America. Even a worthless mongrel will fetch upwards of three hundred bucks if it's marketed right."

"What kind of marketing do you do?" Mat asked.

"Well, we supply pet stores all over the continent with whatever they order. When people buy puppies or kittens from those stores, they have no idea that most of them come from a place like this — a pet factory. We also run ads on websites like Kijiji, Craigslist, others, with pictures of puppies. We give them cutsie, breed names, like *Shnoodle*, or *Cocka-Poo*. In reality, we have no idea what breed they are. Pure bred mongrels, mostly — Heinz 57, *sooner hounds*. Phony papers are drawn up to falsify their shots and immunization. When people want to see them, we arrange to meet them some place like a parking lot and we bring the dogs to them."

Mat was curious. "Why do you do that?"

"So people can't track us down when something goes wrong with the dog after the sale. In a breeding facility like this, it's almost impossible to control all the diseases that dogs pass around. Parvovirus and distemper are common, and usually fatal. All sales are final. Follow?"

By now, Mat's group and Dom had crossed the building and the kennels here were larger, containing bigger dogs, many of them full grown.

"These are our real money-makers," Dom said proudly. "These bad boys are used in the ring. They're Pit Bulls, Bull Terriers, and Bull Mastiffs, or some combination of the three for the most part, and they can fight like Tasmanian Devils! They'll tear the hide off of each other in minutes, sometimes to the death."

"You sell them too?" Mat asked.

"You bet. Send them all over the continent. Dog fighting is a huge underground business. We make money from stud fees, admission fees, and gambling. Oh, and we always make sure a surplus of our best hookers are on hand after the show's over.

"A champion ring dog will sell for a thousand dollars, easy, then he'll win his price tag back three fold every time he's put in the pit. But the real money comes after he's proven to be unbeatable — after he's killed or maimed perhaps a dozen other top dogs." Dom smiled as he explained the process.

"The *real* money? What are you saying?" Mat asked with a W5 reporter's curiosity.

Dom went on, "It's easy. You prove that the dog is the Mike Tyson of the dog fighting ring, and contenders line up to put another animal up against it. A while back someone put a wolf in the ring with this guy, double his weight," he said, stopping at the cage of a large pit bull with chewed off ears and scars covering his head, neck, chest and legs. Poor thing.

The dog looked up at them with surprisingly docile large brown eyes. Under other circumstances, he might have made a good pet. Now, all he knew was *kill.*

Without much pause, Dom carried on, "The wolf got carried out after the fight. Anyways, once a dog is an established champion, you run the odds up astronomically against the underdog, because everybody knows that the challenger's going to lose. Then you bet heavily on the should-be loser, and on the day of the fight we dope the champion, withhold food and water, or sometimes we drain about thirty percent of his blood to slow him down, make him lethargic. Not enough for anyone to notice, but enough to shift the advantage to the other dog. The champ goes down to a mutt in a death grip at his throat, and we win our bet at ten-to-one odds or better."

Mat was stunned at the cruelty. "But you lose your champion," he reasoned.

"Don't matter. He's served his purpose, and by that point the dog is getting worn down. Look at this guy. He won't live another year if we never put him in the ring again. Killed probably two dozen fighting dogs, maybe more. He fought a wolf and won. Think he didn't sustain any injuries along the way? He lived a warrior and should die, proudly."

Mat couldn't contain himself any longer. "You'll understand my concern if I point out that this whole operation is unbelievably inhumane. This is animal cruelty at its worst!"

Dom shrugged it off. "Ya, at face value I can see how someone would arrive at that view. But in the context of the tens of thousands, millions even, of chickens, cattle, and pigs that go to slaughter every day, how are dogs any different, really? What? Chickens only cluck and peck the ground, but dogs lie in your lap and fetch sticks? They're animals. How would you like to be a force-fed, cage-raised turkey around Christmas or Thanksgiving?" and he laughed at his own sick humor.

"Have you ever watched a rodeo, and considered what they do to those animals in the name of wild-west entertainment and competition? A calf bursts out of a gate, running in full, bewildered panic, and a two hundred pound cowboy on a quarter horse runs him down, ropes him by the neck, jerks him right off his feet, throws him on his back, and ties three legs together, three seconds, flat. Wow, there's a show. What a contest!

"They harness beautiful Arabian horses to chuck wagons and roar around a dirt track, and it's commonplace for horrific crashes to happen, killing magnificent animals and *ah shucks*, cowboys, so dumb when you hear them talk, it's embarrassing.

"I watched a video a while back of a thoroughbred horse race in the States that took place in muddy, sloppy conditions.

One horse slipped and fell on the greasy track and the jockey was thrown. The horse got up and started running in the wrong direction. As the rest of the riders rounded a turn, mud and water spraying with blinding force, the stray horse ran straight into an oncoming mount — both traveling at some forty miles an hour. They hit like colliding freight trains, killing each other instantly, and sending the jockey twenty feet skyward. Five years later, when the documentary was filmed, the brain damaged jockey still looked and sounded like she had cerebral palsy, but was grateful to be alive. Two majestic Arabians dead and one person ruined for life — I ask you, if you're concerned about animal welfare, should rodeos or horse racing in rainy, muddy conditions be allowed?

"Dog fighting is cruel, but the mistreatment of livestock and thoroughbreds is wholesome, western entertainment. How does that make sense?

"Look what we do, under government sanction, at the yearly seal hunt. Hundreds of thousands of them clubbed or shot to death, for their fur... *for fur!* It's the largest annual slaughter of marine mammals in the world. Makes you proud to be a Canadian, don't it? They're just dogs, folks, *not pets.* They're working animals, and expendable in the end. Shit happens."

Dom continued walking along, then looked down abruptly. "Ah Christ, now look — *I'll say* shit happens! And I just bought these shoes last week." He'd stepped in dog crap and an expensive pair of Gucci wingtips with fancy gold buckles had been fouled. Everyone looked at his soiled, fancy shoes, but nobody spoke. Dom wiped at his shoe with an empty burlap sack, cursing under his breath.

The group stood silent, watched these wretched animals, listened to the wails of thousands of puppies, gagged at the putrid smell, and cringed at the thought of their fate. Crystal dabbed her eye with a tissue. Adriana's lips were pursed tightly. Foley looked on, stone faced.

Dom continued, "At $300,000 to $400,000 a year, and growing, this is one more source of funds that we need to put though the laundering process. Right now, we handle it mainly as cash, but it's getting too unwieldy to manage. If we had someone like you, we could control it, invest, expand operations, and you'd make a *shit load*. C'mon, let's move on to some more of our other enterprises." He led the group out the back door and around to the parking area.

Numbly, they all climbed in the two vehicles and drove off. Dom turned on the radio and cheerfully cranked it up like he was in a great mood today. Mat was at a loss for words, and wondered what they'd be seeing next.

CHAPTER 38

THE EXPENSIVE LEXUS rolled smoothly down the road and soon Jay-Z and Alicia Keys were performing 'Empire State of Mind', reverberating hypnotically on the 13 speaker Premium Sound System with the bad boy rapper *tellin' it like it i*s to the rest of society, like we didn't get the memo.

Dom turned and sweet-talked Mat, "Listen to the quality of this stereo. You wouldn't get better sound at a live concert. Its got USB ports for a Bluetooth, MP3 and an iPod. This is a *fine automobile* and it should be yours, in my opinion. Whadda ya say?"

Mat replied, "Well, she gets you there and back, I suppose. Hip Hop isn't really my thing. You got any George Strait or Brooks and Dunn? "

Dom laughed and changed the station to something more subdued. "They say money and sex make the world go 'round. Ever hear that?" he asked.

"Ya, but there's been some dispute over which one comes first in priority," Mat said.

"*I hear ya, bro.* After you see this next business, I think you'll know the answer to that question." He drove on, accelerating the powerful Lexus as he merged into traffic onto the busy highway.

Behind, the rented Jeep with Foley and the two ladies struggled to keep up.

Soon they were in front of a three story building located in Vancouver's squalid area of the downtown eastside. The place was fairly non-descript. Weathered white stucco, fifty years old, at least, darkened windows with protective iron bars, heavy, steel front doors with an intercom at the side. They parked curbside, exited their vehicles and walked towards the structure.

At the side of the building sat a group of Vancouver's homeless people, dressed in rags, filthy, unshaven, hung over, and in the worst of health. The unmistakable stench of marijuana wafted through the air. An empty bottle of Jack Daniels was propped up against the building beside them. Stolen shopping carts from Walmart and garbage bags full of drug paraphernalia, cans, and bottles were horded at their side, ready for drop off later that day for a handful of change at some recycling facility. They looked at the party approaching with curiosity and despair in their faces. What terrible events had occurred in their lives to bring them to a fate like this? How would anyone dig themselves out of a hole like the one they were in now? Like lepers in medieval times, they were outcast, and had no hope or desire of reintegration into society. They'd given up long ago and were on the road to self destruction — a welcome relief from where they were now.

"Should we be sorry for them?" Mat asked, looking at them. "This is mostly of their own doing."

Adriana responded animatedly, and without hesitation. "Yes, we should. They're human, and they've made some mistakes in life, like all of us… Maybe started out with nothing, and went downhill from there. Do we only forgive the small errors people make? They deserve assistance and love. What if it was you? It's harder to forgive than condemn, don't you think? Someone should help them get back on their feet."

"You could have left it at 'yes'," Mat replied. "I get the rest."

Mat and his party climbed a short flight of stairs at the entryway, stepping around a semi-dried puddle of vomit kindly left earlier that night by some drunken bum. The ladies looked down at it and locked eyes communicating disgust, without words.

Dom pressed the buzzer for entry.

"Ya, who's there?" came the reply through a fuzzy speaker.

"Dominic Hall. Open up."

At the rude sound of a '*ZZZZT*', the lock released and Dom pulled the heavy door open. The party entered the building. They proceeded down a long hall to the back of the building and through another set of doors to an office area, where a large man sat at a desk. He would easily fall into the category of *morbidly obese*, and the office was littered with empty coke cans and junk food wrappers – cheezies, chips, twinkies, chocolate bars, wagon wheels, pure junk.

This guy is a health food fanatic, Mat's inner companion said. A television was on at the far side of the room and Regis and Kelly were carrying on about some joke that came up concerning Viagra and older men. Regis laughed, a little too enthusiastically, and Kelly made some acerbic comment about men over twenty five, and their flagging sexuality.

At the far side of the room sat three girls – cheap tarts, made up to the nines, in leather, fishnet stockings, and stilettos, on a worn out sofa, chewing gum and flipping through magazines. They looked like they might be on the farm team for the Bunny Ranch in Reno, Nevada. Prostitutes, without question.

"Hey Dom, how's every little thing?" the rotund hood greeted the accountant.

"I can't complain — wouldn't do any good if I did," Dom replied. "How's tricks? How many skanks out today?"

"I got twenty five on the street right now, with another eighteen coming in after six. So forty three till they start coming back around midnight," the big man reported. And these three are *on call* for the phone-ins, nodding to the sluts on the sofa.

Dom considered the info. "Not bad, I guess. We need to start ramping up the talent pool, so we're ready for the 2010 Winter Olympics. Demand from the outta town Johns will be through the roof. Step up the recruitment efforts, okay?"

"Will do. I'll put the word out right away," replied the fatso.

Dom turned to Mat and Foley. "Each of these hookers will pull in five hundred bucks a day, minimum. We should have twenty, twenty-five thousand by tomorrow morning. After we piece off the girls for their services, with some walkin' around money and *coke or meth*, we'll still have ninety percent of the take, for a day's work, and we'll need every cent of it."

"Why?" Mat asked reflexively.

"To fund our movie production business." Dom looked at his guests and winked. "Come with me. *This business* nets us around two mil a year, and it's growing like wild fire."

Dom led his entourage to an elevator and pushed the up arrow. As they waited, Dom said, "Now you're going to see one of our more artistic endeavors. You like movies?" he asked, his eyes narrowing to slits, directing the question towards Adriana and Crystal. They both looked at him stoically, but neither answered.

The elevator doors parted and Dom led his party to a production studio where perhaps a half dozen camera men and microphone boom operators were hovering over two girls and a guy, all naked, writhing like fish in a net, on a set designed to look like an expensive hotel room. They were fornicating like breeding dogs, with one girl performing as a dominatrix with a riding crop. She was watching and smacking their asses, demanding, *'faster, faster!'* while she rubbed her crotch feverishly with her other hand.

Another girl was off camera making moaning and groaning sounds for the benefit of the sound track. Bright lights were strategically placed to provide perfect illumination for the shoot. A camera man was focusing his lens, inches away from the performers' crotches, fully engaged with each other, pumping and humping like mad. There was a dildo and a vibrator on the coffee table in front. It was hardcore pornography in the making. Mat noticed that the room kind of *smelled*.

"Step right up, now. This is always fun," Dom encouraged his friends. "Ever seen a dong like that?" pointing at the young, stud actor with a cock that looked like it might have been transplanted from a horse, as he turned the girl over to do her, *doggy*.

Foley and Mat stared, open mouthed, and the two ladies turned away, in disgust.

After a minute or so of *action*, the director yelled, "Cut!" and the one female uncorked herself from the male, while the other set down her whip.

"Fluffer, take over," yelled the director, and a third girl appeared out of the shadows and proceeded to have sex with the randy young male, at a reduced level of intensity, to keep him aroused between takes. Other crew members adjusted the props and set, and touched up the two actresses lipstick and hair, getting ready for the next scene. This was just another day at the office, for them. Probably shot a thousand other scenes like this one.

"Jesus Christ, and I went into accounting," Dom said looking at the blissful young actor, now receiving an attentive round of felatio from his assistant. The two naked females sat fully exposed, at the side of the set, nonchalantly receiving touch ups from the makeup department.

"Okay, we get it," Mat said. "Now let's get outta here!"

Dom looked at him and laughed. "What do ya say boys, now there's a job with benefits, right?" still admiring the exceptional support the leading man was receiving from his *fluffer.* "I'm doin' well to get my sexytary to bring me coffee."

Mat didn't respond to the comment, but redirected, "You said this thing drives around two million a year?"

Dom nodded agreement. "This here today, is pretty much bread and butter porn — be on the internet by tomorrow, but the real cash cows are the movies with kids in them. *Vids with kids,* we call them. Pervs will pay triple to see that twisted shit.

"We haven't even scratched the surface of this market. Nothin' but upside to this business. I don't have to tell ya how that speaks to our money laundering needs — and *your* potential for profit."

Mat and Foley just looked at each other... *Vids with kids?*

"Let's go back downstairs, and I'll let you in on some of the other things we organize from this building," Dom said, leading the party out of the room and back towards the elevator.

As they left the room the director called out, "Action!" and the moaning started up again.

"There's almost nothing beyond our ability to get involved with, if we feel there's sufficient profit in it. And bear in mind, the only criteria we need to meet is that whatever we do, it has to churn money, and lots of it," Dom explained as they walked along. "Just like corporate America, without the lies, hypocrisy and pretense," he mocked.

Mat was starting to feel ill at what he'd seen so far. "I for one, am thoroughly convinced, let me assure you," he replied.

"Good, then we're moving in the right direction." Dom opened the door to the office and gestured for everyone to enter. He led them back to a second office, and they crossed the room past the fat, junk food, hooker boss. Mat noticed that two of the whores on the couch were now missing — *out on call,* and the last one waited patiently for her next phone-in. No doubt, she'd be on her way to some hotel room before long. A hundred bucks, for a quick sucky-fucky with some outta town business man, who'd be back home with boring Betty in a day or two.

Mat and Adriana sat down at a table in the office while Foley and Crystal pulled up two wingback chairs. They all seemed stunned by the things they'd seen today. Nobody spoke. Dom sat on the lip of a desk in the corner and faced them all.

"Alright now, I know some of this might be a little hard to digest, but like I said before, we don't make any pretense about what we do in the world. Our goal is to make money and avoid the law. It's a cruel world, but it's not our job to fix it.

"Dog fighting, prostitution, pornography... It'll always go on, whether we participate in it or not. Mankind relishes violence and depravity, always has. The Romans used to make gladiators hack each other to pieces, and now we read about it and watch movies that glorify it. How many young men and women have been killed or crippled in all the wars around the globe in the last hundred years — and for what? So pompous politicians can play chess with the lives of citizens? Or control the world's oil reserves, perhaps?

"Now we've got guys on the UFC — *ultimate fighters*, they call themselves, that pound the life out of each other on TV in a barbaric, anything-goes, hand-to-hand, fight to the finish... *Mano-a-mano*, and people love it. What about sex? The internet is flooded with porn and dating websites and they attract millions of hits every day. How many celebrities are caught in sex scandals? I couldn't *begin* to start naming them all, and they're just the ones that *got caught!* Ah, this is the world we live in... *Trouble in paradise.* We're just *soldiers of fortune* out to make a living in an imperfect world."

The room was silent. If Dom's four observers disagreed with his philosophy they were in no mood to dispute the point. Cruelty, unfairness, brutality, hypocrisy, depravity. Everyone knows these things exist, but that doesn't mean you need to be an advocate, in the name of profit. Putting up an argument to that effect to Dominic Hall would surely fall on deaf ears. The point of today's exercise was to have an open-minded look and then, in all likelihood, decline any further involvement.

Finally, Mat said, "Dom, when you said you had some other business ventures that you wanted to show us, I never would have dreamed that *these* are the kind of things you guys do to make money, that's all. You can understand our concern."

"No, no, *I do* understand. But what kind of things did you think we'd be involved with. Neighborhood bottle drives? Bake sales? Flea markets? Car washes by girls in bikinis?" Dom asked, laughing as he spoke.

"Of course not, but you indicated before that you've infiltrated mainstream business and industry. I guess I expected to see something along those lines," Mat came back.

"That's true. We have insiders in places where a little influence can go a long way when it comes to awarding contracts in the bid process. In other cases, we bribe decision makers when we need to, and if that doesn't work, we threaten them, or their families, and if none of that works, we're not above contract murder. When one of your friends or colleagues gets killed *in some accident,* for not cooperating, it provides a definite incentive when a favor is asked of you. Action talks, bullshit walks," he said, as poetically as his crude language could express.

"I see," Mat said.

Adriana had held her tongue as long as she could. She wanted to know what other things these hoods were involved with.

"Mr. Hall, you said there's other things you organize from this building. I take it you don't just peddle women and make movies here? What else are we looking at, exactly?"

Dom smiled. "Oh, how right you are, my dear. And I believe we have a legal councilor that could coach *you too* into participating in our affairs for mutual gain, right Mat? From these humble surroundings, we organize such exploits as robbery, auto theft, loan sharking, kidnapping, credit and debit card fraud, identity theft, blackmail… I could go on. Point is, we make money, and a hell of a lot of it, tax free."

Then Dom turned his attention back to Mathew. "And if you can climb down from your lofty ideals as to what constitutes *ethical crime*, you'll see that there's more money to be made here than you could muster in ten careers within the law. Once you decide to make your living outside the law, your options really aren't restricted as to what you can do, at all. Crime is crime. There isn't good crime or bad crime. It's *beautiful* in its simplicity. And Mathew, my friend, *you* have a place in our organization that will make you a *very, very rich man.* It can be done on a handshake."

The room was quiet while everyone tried to comprehend the conversation. Mat shifted in his chair. Foley stared ahead, dead serious, his blood boiling. Crystal looked like she was about to cry. Adriana put her arm around her, like a big sister, and held her close.

Dom paused and looked around, pleased with his performance, thus far. "I've got one more thing I'd like to show you, then we'll break for the day. I said I was going to take you on a tour of some of our more interesting business ventures and I'm not going to disappoint you now. I hope you see that we try to be creative in how we drive our revenues, and this is one that I'm particularly proud of. I've been saving it for last."

He smiled like Tony Soprano, and held out an open palm to the door way.

"Won't you join me?"

With some hesitation, everyone stood, touched each other's backs affectionately, and walked back to the cars.

If they had been shocked by what they'd seen so far, they were about to bear witness to something that nobody would have guessed was possible in a civilized, western country.

And yet, it's commonplace *and happening,* right here at home.

CHAPTER 39

THIS TIME THE entourage made their way out of Vancouver on a series of streets and freeways, eventually taking 99 south to White Rock, a whisker north of the Canada-U.S. border. Perhaps it was by design, or maybe it was just a fortuitous circumstance that Mat rode again with Dominic, because if he had been with Foley, it's likely that they would have turned around and just gone straight home.

The vehicles arrived at a building that looked somewhat like a neighborhood community hall, but it was really just a big, very old, ramshackled house in an area of the city near the Semiahmoo Bay. There wasn't much else in the area by way of housing and commercial property and traffic was sparse, hardly noticeable. To the side of the building in a large, covered carport of sorts stood several Harley choppers, polished and lined up like they were for sale — beautiful machines, really, collectively valued in the hundreds of thousands of dollars.

"You know why they call this place White Rock?" Dom said as everyone stepped out of the vehicles.

Adriana responded, "Of course. Anyone from these parts knows it's because of that big bolder down near the ocean. This is a tourist destination where locals from the lower mainland like to spend a day at the beach, or shopping, or dining out. Nice little place, this," she said, looking around.

Dom pressed on. "Ya, but it's not called *Big Bolder* or *Nice Little Place.* It's called *White Rock?* Do you know why?"

Adriana paused. "I give up. Lead on Mister Tour Guide."

"Because that big, fuckin' rock on the beach, near the promenade is a *glacial erratic* from the last ice age, and it's white because it's covered in *bird shit* from the sea gulls, not counting the graffiti."

"Jesus Christ, but you're a profane son-of-a-bitch," Foley put in.

Adriana added, "What a fascinating and delightfully recounted piece of trivia."

"Ya, really," Dom went on. "It's been there for twenty thousand years, since the last ice age. It rode in on a massive sheet of ice, that melted and dropped it right where it stands today. By the time Jesus was born, it had already been there for eighteen thousand years, covered in bird shit. They should have named this place *Bird Shit, BC.* How many birds do you think have lit on that rock since the ice age? A million? A hundred million? A billion? What do you think the average inhabitant of this area looked like that first laid eyes on it? I bet they weren't six feet tall, with blonde hair and blue eyes, with a BlackBerry in their pocket," he said, looking at Foley.

Foley said, "That's a pretty safe bet. You've given this rock a lot of thought, I see, and it's a flip phone, though I doubt they had that either."

Dom laughed. "*A lot of thought?* Not really. My mind just wanders off sometimes. I mean think about it. It's been here for twenty thousand years. Do you think it'll still be here that long into the future? And do you think mankind will still be here by then? If we are, do you think we'll still celebrate Christmas, or believe in God, or do you think *science* will be the new god, having explained *everything* in the universe? What happens when there's no more mystery, *no more questions,* and no need of blind belief, or faith? Science has nailed it all. At the rate technology is advancing, *we'll* be God, by then. Considering how far we've come in *two* thousand years, where do you think we'll be in *twenty*?

"What if we've annihilated ourselves somehow before then, or an airborne virus or some other pathogen evolves, maybe like MRSA, only ten times worse, that is one hundred percent fatal and highly contagious among humans? Or an asteroid hits the earth like the one that hit the Yucatan Peninsula sixty-five million years ago in Mexico and turned this place into a clouded, burning hell for a hundred years afterward and wiped out the dinosaurs, and most everything else? That must have been some event, not just a popcorn fart like the explosion of Mount Krakatoa, one of the biggest geothermal events in recorded history!"

Crystal elbowed Adriana discreetly, and whispered, "*This guy's crazy*, if you ask me." Adriana rolled her eyes in agreement.

Foley was listening to all this and added, "For an accountant, you've got an awfully vivid imagination, my friend."

Dom replied, "Well, it's because I have an interest in history and astronomy. I like to think I'm a *big picture* thinker. We all have interests and think about other things than what we do for a living.

"I know a guy who lives in Vancouver and has a cottage near Vernon on Lake Okanagan. His pastime is rowing. Goes out on the lake, early in the morning, and rows a boat around in the mist all by himself, facing backwards, for hours. You'd think that after about ten pulls on the oars, that'd get old, but he loves it. I wonder why. My theory? It's because he's not thinking about rowing a boat out there. He's in perfect solitude, in harmony with nature and himself, and it puts his head somewhere else that just feels good. It connects him in with his inner self and it's euphoric, nirvana. It's his private drug of choice that opens up his mind and it gives him insight, and the escape that's a rush of sorts. Good for him, I say — follow your passion, *if you can find it*. He's found his.

"Here's another one. I have two young daughters at home, twins. One watches animal shows on TV — Discovery, Animal Planet, that crocodile hunter in Australia that bought it from a sting ray last year. She's mesmerized by that stuff. Sits glued to the TV all day, if you'll let her. Doesn't even talk. Her mind is tuned out. The other will stand at an art easel for hours at a stretch, painting pictures, completely lost in herself. What do you suppose she's thinking about while she's creating those pictures? I look at them and marvel at their budding interests in life.

"*We all* think outside the box, when no one's looking. The trick is to capture it, and put it to use. It's the essence of human creativity. That's why you're good at what you do, isn't it, Mat?"

Mat said, "I *live* outside the box, Mr. Hall."

Adriana added, "So tell us, why are we *here*, today?"

Dom pointed with his index finger out to the ocean and continued, "Just out there are the Southern Gulf Islands in the Gulf of Georgia. One of them is called Gabriola Island. There are literally *hundreds* of other islands out there that are part of a larger archipelago that also includes the San Juan Islands of Washington State. It's important you keep that in your pretty little head. I'll explain why later.

"It's an odd place, this White Rock," he continued. "Airplane pilots are known to call it *the hole in the sky*. Know why that is, Adriana?" Dom asked, teasing.

She played along. "Well, in my *pretty little head*, I'm still trying to believe you know a word as big as *archipelago*, but I'll take a guess that it's 'cause there's a hole in the sky up above?"

"Yes, exactly! For some strange reason, the sky above White Rock is often sunny and clear, while the rest of the lower mainland is rainy and overcast. Meteorologists are baffled by it. It's like a Bermuda triangle thing. How fucked up is that?"

Foley wondered out loud. "And what's the draw? Are there any puppy mills and porn studios here? Or are we down to stealing babies from the hospital to sell on eBay?"

Dom laughed, "Oh, I'm sure all that goes on, probably worse, but that's not our line of work down here, my friend. We're into something much, much more lucrative. Follow me, I'll show you."

The five participants rounded the corner of the building to the front door and Dom knocked twice slowly, then three times in rapid succession. The door opened and just inside stood three heavy set biker types, lookin' meaner than hell. One stepped forward and he and Dom did the three stage, soul brother handshake — *one, two, three.*

"Hey man, been expectin' ya," the biker said. His upper lip was an ugly, twisted rope of scarred flesh, poorly healed after some earlier traumatic injury, camouflaged under a thick, graying moustache. His thinning hair was pulled back into a *man ponytail,* and he wore a dark sleeveless tank top that exposed his arms, tattooed and well muscled.

"Everything cool, bro?" Dom replied. "Got a little tour thing goin' down here."

The biker surveyed the group warily. "Just business as usual upstairs. We've got another boatload coming in late tonight, after midnight probably."

"Where from?" Dom asked.

"Sri Lanka. Mostly men this time, but we can put 'em to work right away," the big hood replied.

Dom seemed pleased. "'kay, let's pay 'em out at ten cents on the dollar this time. Give 'em a good long time to work it off."

"You got it, boss."

413

Dom turned to his guests, "Come with me, folks, and I'll show you around."

He led them up a set of stairs and through another door. Inside was a large room, sparsely furnished, with plain overhead lighting, venetian blinds — pulled shut, a kitchenette, littered with empty soup cans and plastic bread bags, and a filthy bathroom. There were men, women and children, numbering perhaps thirty, sitting around on stackable chairs, a couple of sofas that looked like they might have been rescued from the dump, and more people on the floor with their backs to the wall. They looked bored, hungry, dirty. One lady was openly breast feeding an infant, her exposed tit, no cause for concern. Most looked to be Indian, Arab, African, Asian, and the only thing they seemed to have in common was that they looked to be refugees in the throes of dire straits.

Foley looked around the room and asked, "What are these people, prisoners?"

"Not exactly," Dom replied. "They're aliens from overseas, homeless people now, looking for a better life. Boat people, some."

Mat added, "This doesn't look much like a *better life*, to me. How did you come to be involved with them?"

"We've got contacts in various parts of the world where the locals live in terrible poverty or suppression by corrupt, military regimes," Dom explained in a serious tone. He walked over to a black family huddled together on the floor, dressed in rags, dirty, two parents, no more than thirty years of age, and two small girls, perhaps aged six or seven, all of them, skinny and desperate with hunger — perfect subjects for a World Vision Canada charity telethon. They looked up at the party with desperation, dread, and a plea for help on their faces. The young girls clung to their mother's side like they feared for their lives. They did, certainly.

"This lucky family comes from Nyala in Darfur, Sudan. They were driven by armed soldiers, hell bent on murder and rape, to a refugee camp while many others of their relatives and friends weren't so lucky — dead, slaughtered like cattle. Take my word for it, they're a blood-thirsty bunch of sons-a-bitches over there and as sorrowful as they look now, they'd be worse off in their homeland.

"*Hundreds of thousands* of their countrymen have been killed over the last few years in what amounts to genocide — people are being wiped out by the thousands on ethnic grounds, a *holocaust* in Africa. We gave them a chance at living in a free land. They'll eventually apply for landed immigrant status as refugees, but first they'll have to work off their debt to us for getting them out. We'll house, clothe and feed them, and ensure that they're employed at one of our operations, until that day."

Adriana spoke up. "Mister Hall, that amounts to *human trafficking.* You're taking advantage of people who are in a disastrous predicament of one sort or another, and transporting them around the globe, enslaving them to your operations. It's beyond criminal. *These are people.*"

Dom stifled a laugh. "*Semantics,* my dear. Faced with a life here in Canada with a roof over your head, food and employment, or living in squalor, starving in open-air, refugee camps, patrolled by guards armed with guns and machetes in North Africa, which would you choose?

She looked again at the poor souls cowering on the floor, but couldn't answer.

Mat asked, "And how much is the debt they owe to you for this humanitarian act of *rescue* you've provided?"

"Well, let's put it this way, they won't be making any plans for at least three to five years. We'll keep 'em busy. Don't worry about them. If they ever become landed immigrants or citizens, they'll most likely live on social assistance for the rest of their lives, and make babies. Christ, we should be so lucky!"

Mat continued, "And what kind of *employment* do you provide them with?"

"The kind where you don't pay taxes, eh?" Dom answered and laughed with gusto.

Mat noticed four young girls down a row of lost souls, dark hair and skin, possibly from India, Afghanistan, or Pakistan, no more than pubescent, budding teenagers, dressed in rags and sitting together on a couch. Their simple, desperate parents might have been duped into selling them to some lying serpent, in hopes of finding a better life for them away from the oppression of the Taliban or Al-Qaeda, and away from the ravages of poverty and war in their homeland. Were they not so filthy and disheveled, they might have been pretty. They looked innocent, and scared, and they were.

"What about them?" he gestured, raising his chin to the girls.

Dom looked over and smiled. "2010 Olympics are just around the corner," and he winked. "We'll clean 'em up and find *something* for them to do... *brown sugar.*"

Mat instantly recalled Dom's instruction to the fat, hooker guy to step up recruiting efforts for more girls to service the outta town Johns at the Olympics. *Vids with Kids,* rang back through his head.

The group looked around the room at each cluster of refugees, and wondered what story lay behind their journey from poverty and despair to this desolate room, as illegal aliens, now under a burden of debt to a Vancouver biker gang. It was simultaneously sad, and sickening.

Dom continued to explain, "We bring in all these derelicts from one shit hole or another in foreign countries where dogs on the street live better than people. Convincing them to come here isn't usually very hard because their lives there are basically hopeless, and worthless. Living in Siberia would be preferable to where they come from. They board any number of freighters that we control through our influence at Port Metro Vancouver and we drop them at Gabriola Island, or one of a hundred others — out there," he said pointing out to the Gulf.

"They're warehoused there until we can put 'em to use here on the mainland at one of our grow ops, or factories, or something else. Sometimes we either sub-hire them out, or sell them outright, to other businesses that may have severe labor shortages. And for the right price, some of them will even be used for organ donation."

"What!" Mat said, astonished. "You harvest their organs?"

Dom was resolute. "Damn straight! A liver or heart can fetch over a hundred grand on the open market, and that doesn't include the medical team's fees. For some rich fat cat who doesn't have time to wait on some list of eligible recipients, the cost is not even a consideration. You think someone like Conrad Black, or a hundred others, is gonna wait in line if he needs a heart, or kidney, or a *hair cut*, urgently? They don't exactly fall into the *take a number* demographic of our proud country.

"It's an unfortunate reality that these poor buggers are expendable when it's necessary to save someone else who ranks a little higher on the *all men are created equal* bell curve. It don't matter on a large scale, they're breedin' like grasshoppers in Saskatchewan over there. There's over a billion people in India. China has even more. What about Indonesia? More, still! Christ, they'll overtake the world soon with hordes of bare foot, starving, fornicating baby factories, all praising Allah, or Buddha, or Jesus, or someone else draped in robes, watching over mankind with impossible expectations from some white cloud in the sky. These few that get culled for an organ, here or there, are insignificant. Call it their destiny, their *raison d'être*. It's just business, and it's growing fast. Can you *imagine* the money you stand to make?"

As the conversation proceeded, there was a sudden commotion at the front door, with bikers yelling, slamming doors, and firing guns. Something was happening outside, and it wasn't good. *What's going on now?* everyone wondered. It sounded like they were under siege by the U.S. army — guns and grenades booming and exploding, destruction unfolding in the yard and at the door, personnel running every direction, taking evasive maneuvers. One thing was certain, something major was going down.

Dom looked shocked, as did everyone else, and they ran back to the room's entryway and down the stairs to the front door. Outside, a group of Asians, perhaps twenty strong, were smashing away at the motor cycles with metal baseball bats and crowbars. Others were pinning down the bikers with gun fire, preventing them from exiting the building to intervene. Mirrors and chrome fittings flew off the bikes, others fell over, crashed to the ground and caught fire from gasoline seeping out of the tanks. The vandals were destroying the bikers' pride and joy — their beloved Harley choppers. It was sheer panic, like a scene out of Michael Bay's *Pearl Harbor.* Sorry, no Ben Affleck or leading lady in this version of combat mayhem, just outright demolition and carnage between two west-coast criminal gangs.

It was Jimmy Yang, and his cohorts — the Red Sun Boys. "Get ready for hell," Jimmy had mouthed earlier in the mirror to the Kings Crew, after they stole back their shipment of drugs. *This was it.*

First, the bikers had stolen their shipment of cocaine, then they had the audacity to infringe on a business of their specialty. The Red Sun Boys were human traffickers, or *Snakeheads,* as they liked to call themselves, and now the Kings Crew were meddling in that business too! The Red Sun Boys had been insulted and dishonored. This would not be tolerated. The bikers' headquarters for smuggling, enslaving, and selling illegal aliens had been discovered through shrewd reconnaissance, and it was high-time for payback of the most severe degree.

Mat called to Adriana, "Stay by me, keep your head down!" She held close to his side and they pressed against the back wall together, trying to stay out of harm's way. Mat's gun was in his hand but, in truth, he had no real opportunity to use it. They clung tightly to one another and feared their luck had finally run out. *God, not now, not here, not with Adriana!* Mat thought to himself.

Foley had wrapped his arms around Crystal and put his back to the action volunteering himself as a human shield, should any incoming gunfire find its way to them. She cried out in panic, "What's happening? Who are they? They're shooting at us. Let's get outta here!"

Foley barked back, "Stay put, Darlin'. Now's not the time for anything heroic. We've gotta just wait this one out and hope for the best. Close your eyes and hope we see tomorrow!"

As the bikers and Mat's party watched the chaos going on, they couldn't open the door more than a crack or they'd draw gunfire from the gang outside. Bullets from machine guns *pinged* in rapid succession through the door and smashed into the walls, leaving a line of holes ripped through the drywall inside. Bikers tried to return fire with hand guns but couldn't get a clear shot away. One man already lay dead on the floor, with a bloody hole through his cheek, just under his eye, that passed out the back of his head. People were shouting, cursing, running for cover, and they were pinned down like marines storming a beach. The adage *there are no atheists in a foxhole,* certainly held true here, in this makeshift, hold-out today.

Dom shouted, "Mickey and Bruno, go downstairs and get the hardware, then go around back and see if you can get out the other door! Me and Eddie will stay right here in front 'til you give the signal... *Hurry!*"

Then Dom said to Mat and his group, "*You bunch...* If you wanna live, go with these guys and remain downstairs. There's no time for discussion. Go... *Now!*"

Mat and Foley each had their piece in their hand, but with Adriana and Crystal along, the first priority had to be their protection. This gun battle was intensifying fast and the boys followed Dom's advice.

"This way," Foley said, following along behind the bikers down a stairwell to the basement.

Bikers from other parts of the building were assembling now in the front corridor and hasty plans were being drawn up about mounting a defense. Within minutes, a half dozen or more bikers were heading to other exits and windows to return fire on the Red Sun Boys. The room full of refugees was in chaos with people screaming, crying, and shouting out in several different languages. Window glass was shattering and falling to the floor from stray bullets whizzing in all directions.

In the basement, the two biker hoods opened a locked cabinet and took out a G36 machine gun and a 10 gauge sawed off shot gun loaded with buckshot, both devastating weapons in close range combat. Other bikers soon descended the stairwell and also took out an assortment of rifles and handguns, then pounded back up the stairs to join the action. Upstairs, gun fire continued to sound, and now the bikers were returning fire from windows throughout the building.

Soon the sound of Mickey's machine gun was heard along with the distinctive, explosive blasts from Bruno's shot gun. Asians were scattering in all directions. Their stronghold had been disrupted and bikers flooded out the building, mounting a vicious defense.

From the far side of the parking lot, a member of the Red Sun Gang raised a shoulder mounted RPG7 rocket launcher, kneeling on one knee. He took careful aim with the horrifying weapon at the front door of the building, and squeezed the trigger. This was a specialized assault weapon designed to take out tanks in battle fields such as Afghanistan or Iraq, and when the projectile found its mark, the front of the building disintegrated in a fiery cloud of red flame and smoke. The concussion of the blast sent bricks, glass, metal and mortar flying through the air like fireworks on the 4th of July. The foundation of the structure shuddered is if an earthquake like the one that hit Haiti had just occurred. As follow up, a bunch of Asian gangsters rushed the building with semi-automatic guns drawn, firing at anything that moved, and made their way to take control of the building. It was bloody hell, sheer bedlam, and victims were falling to gunfire like characters on an XBOX 360 video war game.

Downstairs, dust, debris and tiles from the ceiling reigned down on the Bull Dog Security group and Crystal screamed out in terror, while Foley held her in his arms. Mat and Adriana hit the floor face down, with their arms covering their heads.

"Jesus Murphy, what the hell is happening up there?" Mat called out. "We have to do something!"

"Like what? Run up there and get killed?" Foley replied.

Moments later and the Asians had taken control of the building. The bikers were mostly in the yard now, trading pop shots with their adversaries from behind dumpsters and parked vehicles. Ten or twelve Asians made their way through the structure, guns drawn, wary of everything. Most went upstairs to the main area, two others went downstairs, to the basement.

Foley, and the others heard footsteps coming down the stairs and assumed, quite reasonably, that it might not be company they wanted to entertain. Foley jumped to his feet and ran to the door, hiding behind it to jump whoever might be entering.

The door opened and in walked one man holding a gun, then another. Foley immediately punched him hard in the side of his face, sending him to the ground, and snatched the gun from his hand. He tucked it into his belt.

Mat raised his gun on the other man and said, "Drop it, pal, or you're history." Foley too, trained his pistol on the second man.

The first guy recovered from the punch after a moment, and rose to his feet. The men hesitated, then, realizing they were trapped, the second hood's weapon was surrendered as instructed.

"Over here," Foley demanded, gesturing towards a concrete wall where they could be guarded safely.

Crystal was watching intently, and finally she rose to her feet, her eyes fixed on the two captives.

"*Give me that gun*," she said to Foley. Suddenly, all eyes in the room were on her. She looked single-minded. "Give it to me, *now!*"

CHAPTER 40

FOLEY WAS A little taken aback by Crystal's request, as was everyone else in the room. As far as he knew, she'd never held a fire arm in her life. He couldn't imagine why she'd want to start now.

"Crystal, what's gotten into you?" he asked.

The question should have been, *Who's* gotten into you? "They have," she answered. "We know each other, don't we boys?"

One hood spoke up, with an accent, "What she talk about? We don' know her."

"Liar!" Crystal shrieked out. "These are the pigs that raped me at Jack Kincaid's business a few weeks back. I'll *never* forget your faces. Give me that damn gun!"

Foley said, "Li'l darlin'… let's not be hasty. *Are you sure?* You were pretty banged up, as I recall."

"Am I sure? I'm absolutely, positively, totally, one hundred percent sure! This is the animal that bit my breast — there's still a mark on it. And both of them *ffff…*" She hesitated, despite her rage, to use improper language.

"*Had their way* with me," she continued. "You said we'd kill them if we ever caught up with them. You promised to *put a slug in them* if we ever found them. You gave me *your word,* remember?"

Foley *did* remember and he regretted making such a promise under the duress of trying to calm her down right after her ordeal. Still, if these really were the culprits responsible for raping and beating her to within an inch of her life, it wouldn't take much convincing for him to keep true to his word, and snuff 'em both, right here and now.

"*The gun!*" Crystal held out her hand to Foley, who was looking at the hoods, trying in vain, to recall their faces from the brief moments he saw them before.

Mat joined the exchange. "She sounds pretty certain, Fole. If these are the guys, they deserve what they got coming."

"Mathew!" Adriana interrupted. "Don't encourage her. She just wants revenge."

Mat responded, "You're a lawyer. It's called *justice,* something we rarely see handed out fairly and promptly in our society any more."

The room was filled with tension. The two hoods had a look of horror on their faces that they were finally going to pay for their crimes. Both Foley and Mat held their guns on each of them, aimed squarely at center mass.

Foley handed his gun to Crystal, then removed the one tucked into his belt and held the hood at bay with his own gun.

Foley said, "You guys have any last words? Now's your time to atone. It'll give ya some release, boys, for unforgiveable crimes." Considering the treatment Foley had been given recently by the Red Sun Gang, he didn't have a lot of compassion for them.

"Mistah, *please...* Don' let her do dis," one of them pleaded. "It all *his* idea — I only tag along 'cause I a'scared he kill me I try stop him."

The other hood looked incensed at the accusation. "*You lie!* You da one dat cut off her bra to get whole ting started!"

"No, no... He make me do it, I swear! *Kill him, kill him,* and make him pay! I tell others he killed in gun battle wit' bikers."

Crystal stepped in, "Shut up, both of you! In case you've forgotten, I was there. I know exactly what happened and you're *both* responsible. Your boss told you to leave me alone and keep quiet. Instead you wrapped a dish towel around my mouth and forced yourselves upon me — first one, then the other. You're sadists and cowards and your judgment day has arrived. On your knees, both of you!" She held out the pistol menacingly, with a straight arm. Both hoods complied with her demand and dropped to their knees. Their execution was at hand.

Foley had a look of torment on his face. He was actually scared of what events lay ahead. Only now, was he beginning to understand the outrage she carried for what these monsters had done to her. This was a side of Crystal he never would have dreamed of seeing. Was he about to actually witness his girlfriend execute her assailants? Did he just hand her his gun, lending his complicity to the act? The Red Sun hoods knelt before her and cowered together on the cold floor. One was starting to cry like a frightened child. The other was so terrified that the corners of his mouth grimaced wide like Jack Nicholson as the Joker.

Crystal stepped forward and pointed the pistol at the terrified one's head. She looked at him with zero sympathy in her eyes. Her hand was steady. The second hood wept openly, knowing his turn would be next. Both of them now pleading and kneeling before a woman they once beat and defiled like a captive animal, they remembered all too well now. How the tables had turned. Mat and Adriana stepped back and held on tightly to each other. This kind of justice wasn't pretty. The gun was now six inches away from the hood's forehead.

"*Nooo... Please,*" he begged. He pinched his eyes tightly shut, waiting for the end. A few moments seemed like an eternity.

Crystal stood before him, resolute. The gun shot that would spray his brains all over the wall behind him was imminent.

Finally, he started gasping for air, his diaphragm spasmically overriding his will to breath. He fell forward onto the concrete floor and wailed like a Syrian torture victim. He didn't just piss his pants, or maybe he did, but more to everyone's attention, he'd soiled himself, and the room now stunk of diarrhea.

As if sidetracked by the first one's antics, she then trained the gun on the second hood. To everyone's shock, she fired the weapon, and its report made a deafening bang in the confines of the small room. Whether deliberate or not, she'd missed his head by scant inches, and he cried out in horror, tears, snot and spit bubbling disgracefully out of his face. He couldn't take another moment of this and he pitifully held up his hands in front of his face and cowered behind them, as if he might stop a bullet in his palms. He fell back against the wall, bawling shamefully, more like a little girl, than a man. Both hoodlums were now undignified and bereft of all pride and composure. It was ugly.

"*Please, don'. I do anyting...*" They were reduced to begging, wretched curs, utterly defeated before the woman they had brutalized without sympathy, and now they plead for her mercy. Killing them would provide no more retribution.

Crystal stepped back and lowered the gun. Her eyes welled up with tears.

Mat came forward to console her, but Foley put his hand on his arm, and whispered, "No, this has to be *all her.*"

She spoke. "*Well... well... well.* So now we see what kind of men you really are. Brought to your knees by a *woman.* The woman you beat and raped, together. You'll carry a shame around in your hearts for the rest of your miserable lives, and one day someone probably *will* shoot you, and you'll deserve it. From this day forward, whenever you look in a mirror, remember what you did to me, and how you begged me for your life today, and that I gave it to you. I'm better than both of you cowards — don't ever forget it. Get out of here, you miserable, pathetic pigs, and damn your souls to hell!"

For the second time in Crystal and Foley's presence, the two *sewer rats* scrambled to their feet and shuffled to the door to make a narrow escape from death with their tails between their legs. The sound of them stumbling up the stairs, each trying to get out first, was the last thing everyone heard.

A stillness came over the room. The gun fire outside had subsided now, and the sounds of the battle had ceased. Like lucky survivors emerging from a subterranean bomb shelter after a horrific battle, Mat and his group brushed themselves off and made their way back up the stairwell to the entryway at ground level. There was smoke in the air from the explosion at the front door, and fires kindled where lumber was exposed from the blast. The refugees had scattered, and what bikers remained were distracted and mourning over their destroyed choppers. Dominic Hall was nowhere to be seen.

It was like the dreadful, but brief storm of a tornado had passed over, and now everything was returning to calm.

"*Jesus Christ,*" was all Mat could muster, looking at the carnage.

"I'll second that," Foley said.

Mat turned to Adriana, "And you wonder why I drink?"

Foley said decisively, "To tell you the truth, I haven't really liked any of the guys we've come across on this assignment, not one."

Adriana added, "*There's* insight. I think it's safe to say Crystal feels the same way."

Crystal said, "*I got them...* I got those bastards," and she started crying, softly.

Foley agreed, "You sure did. You got them good! But folks, we gotta move, and I mean fast. This place is gonna be crawlin' with cops in minutes, if it isn't already. I'd just as soon not be around having to answer a bunch of nosey questions."

With haste and trepidation, they all approached what was left of the door way — a twenty foot, gaping hole in the wall of blown up, burned rubble. A bulldozer couldn't have done more damage in the length of time the battle lasted. The air was smoky and smelled of gunpowder. Beams of sunlight streamed in from outside. The wounded were moaning pitifully and struggling to stay alive. Dead bodies from the bomb's blast and the gun fight were scattered everywhere. Other injured parties to the battle staggered around and lay at random all over the property. The choppers were smashed to pieces, some burning in puddles of spilled gasoline and oil. Black smoke billowed into the air. The wrath of God had surely been visited upon this place. Looking around, aghast at the bloodbath, Mat's team couldn't help being shocked.

Adriana was last to leave the building and suddenly she called out, "Mat... here, *quick!*"

Mat and Foley turned around and paced quickly back to the building. Adriana pointed her finger and said, "Look."

At the far side of the blast zone inside the building, lay a body, or what was left of it, virtually severed from the waist up. They walked over for a closer look. He must have been very close and taken a direct hit when the RPG grenade detonated at the front of the building. All that remained were the mangled remains of a burned, unrecognizable upper body, head and arms mostly gone, and legs with shoes still on — *Dominic Hall's* gold buckled wingtips. He was killed, good and dead, never knew what hit him.

They all looked at the grisly scene in horror and silence — fresh blood, burned flesh and exposed entrails, strewn bricks and lumber, conduit hanging from shattered walls, dead bodies, and the dismembered, incinerated body of Dominic Hall laying at their feet, shoes intact. Crystal put her hand to her mouth to avoid being sick and ran outside.

428

Foley caught up and subdued her, and they all hurried back to their vehicle. Once everyone was inside, Foley floored it, and as they turned the corner, a block away, four police cruisers with lights flashing and sirens screaming passed them going the other direction. Soon, *Bird Shit, BC* was zooming out in the rear view mirror. They didn't know whether to be happy or sad at the day's events, but they'd seen enough crime and corruption to do them a life time, and they luckily dodged the police at the end of it all. Now they were on the move again, unwilling criminals, all of them.

On the ride back to Vancouver everybody seemed a little numbed by what they'd seen and experienced. It was like it was all still sinking in. Nobody spoke.

Finally, Mat decided that nothing good was going to come of this group, the way they were, and piped up, "Well, I'd say we've got one hell of an opportunity here. There's a boat load of money to be made with these guys if we jump in and join the pool party. How 'bout we give it some thought?"

Simultaneously, the other three heads in the SUV spun around and looked at him, sitting in the back seat. If Foley hadn't been driving, he might have turned and given Mat a slap on the back of his head. Crystal's mouth and eyes were wide open, literally.

Adriana said, "Are you out of your ever-lovin' mind? Have you completely taken leave of your senses? Did you take a bump on your head back there?"

Foley joined in, "She's right, Buck. I wouldn't join up with that outfit if they offered me the lead role in all their movies for the next year. And if you're calculating on takin' any more work from them, I'll shoot you in the leg myself, first!"

Mat put his head back and laughed. "Geeze, you guys. Can't you take a little joke? I just thought I'd try and wake you all up and get you guys out of the dumps. I know we saw some heavy shit today, but life goes on. Anyone would think we've just been to a funeral."

"We have," Crystal said. "Or maybe a *slaughter* is a better description. And how long do you think some of those illegal refugees that we saw will last here in a foreign land. Winter's coming soon — they're from Africa. And what about the ones being *warehoused* on Gabriola island? From what I've seen, I hate to imagine what the conditions are out there. They've got nothin' to their names... *nothin' at all.*"

Adriana added, "And those young girls that were being hired out by that perverted slob. It was sickening. They're being coerced into prostitution and controlled by crystal meth, cocaine, heroine, and God knows, what else. They're unwitting slaves. And the ones that think they've hit the red carpet are fornicating on camera with men they met ten minutes ago and being paid *by the scene.*"

Foley put in his two cents. "And the dogs..."

Mat cut him off, "And worse, *Vids with kids.* Child pornography!"

Foley added, "Don't think we saw even the tip of the ice berg here today. This was a teaser. I can just about guarantee you that these boys are into stuff that goes far beyond dogs, tarts, and refugees. They've got their claws into government, law enforcement, gambling, big business, international trade, immigration, you name it. And now they've got our number — *money laundering,* and we're caught by a bunch of hoods and gangsters like hooked fish behind a trawler."

Mat added, "Well, they won't have our number for long, 'cause I'm making some changes to this little sideline of ours and bringin' down the curtain. *That's all folks. Elvis has left the building.*"

Adriana's eyes lit up. "You're getting out? Quitting the money laundering game altogether?"

"Call it retiring — *semi*-retiring, for now. And you and I have some talking to do, *one on one.*"

Foley spoke up, "*Ahhhhh,* now don't be shy, son. You can propose to her in front of us. We're all family, here."

"I propose you hurry the hell up and get us back to Vancouver. Driver, *step on it!* And put a hat on when you're the chauffeur, damn it. Can't get *good help* any more."

They all laughed, and Foley picked up the pace on Highway 99 back into the city. Mat had succeeded in bringing his party back to reality and putting them in a talkative mood. There was still work to be done, however. It was time now to bring this thing to a close.

He had been contriving a master plan, and now he had to pull it all together.

CHAPTER 41

BACK IN THE city, the party disbanded with Foley and Crystal going inside Bull dog Security. It was close to quitting time and as usual, Danielle was busy handling day to day issues and dispatching service personnel around the city on various technical calls. The place looked good, Foley noticed. Business was buzzing and, despite the economic recession of the last year or more, this place was a going concern. The in-trays of service work orders, and inquiries regarding new business were overflowing.

"Hi, Foley, Crystal. How's your day been?" Danielle asked, enthusiastically.

Foley and Crystal exchanged an *if you only knew* look, then Foley said, "We've had a busy day — a real eye opener! Took in some interesting sights. Anything I should know about happening here today?"

She shook her head. "Same ol', same ol'. Mat coming back here too?" she asked.

"No, he and Adriana took off together. Got a feelin' he'll have something to announce next time we see him," he replied, as he and Crystal walked down the hall to his office.

Danielle looked puzzled. Mat hadn't quite been himself lately and she hoped there wasn't anything wrong. "Wait and see, I guess," she mumbled to herself.

Across the city, Mat's BMW rolled to a stop in front of Adriana's house and he killed the ignition. The two of them looked across the plush leather, bucket seats at each other and she said to him, "What is it? There's something on your mind."

"Yes, there is. Let's go inside. I need a drink." He smiled subtly, knowing she'd disapprove.

Once inside, they said hello to Mina and asked Manuel how his day had been at school. He answered with enthusiasm and showed obvious delight at seeing his new friend again. Then Adriana shooed him down to his bedroom to do his homework.

It was still a warm, summer day, with the sun just starting to set in the western horizon. Adriana poured them each a cold glass of wine and they went out to the back yard to a gazebo with comfortable, rattan furniture and a glass-topped table. It was a tranquil setting, a little piece of nature, with large trees swaying in the breeze, birds and squirrels chattering, a babbling fountain running into a pond with goldfish, and a picturesque, tangerine skyline just before dusk. They sat back together and exhaled a sigh of relief. *Did all that really happen today?*

Mat said, "Quite a show, *quite a show, yes siree.* I feel like I'm going to wake up any minute and it was all just a dream. A tour of the Kings Crew's ventures in trade and commerce, gang wars, Crystal's little performance…"

Adriana interrupted him, "Quit *pussy footin' around* — to quote your pal Foley, and tell me what's on your mind? I don't need a re-hash of today's events. I was there too, remember? Speak up, Mister Crawford!" She looked damn serious.

Mat paused, then continued, "Okay. I said I was getting out of the business and I meant it. You know, I always thought that as the money guy, I was sort of insulated from the crime that generated the cash. At arm's length, so to speak. I didn't actually rob the diamond mine. I didn't embezzle funds from the corporation. I didn't buy or sell the cocaine that produced buckets of cash for a notorious biker gang. *They* did the crimes, I just did some financial tricks with the loot and turned it back into legitimate capital, and got paid rather well for my services."

"A court of law would view it differently," the lawyer interjected.

"Yes, and now I do too."

"How so?"

"Dom said I was hypocritical in looking for only *ethical* crimes to get involved with. 'Crime is crime. There isn't good crime or bad crime,' he said. I realized that even someone as crooked as Dominic Hall can deliver words of wisdom on occasion."

Adriana said, "But crimes do vary in degree and consequence. Shoplifting a pack of gum from Costco is not as severe as committing arson at a retirement home, for example."

"Didn't you call that *reduction to the ridiculous,* before?"

"Sorry. Go on," she said.

"My point is, if you participate in the underworld of crimes that generate large sums of money, and we're talking *very severe* crimes now, in most cases, then *you are* a party to it, no excuses. You may not directly commit the crime, but you condone it. You're a part of an evil plan, a conspirator, and if you have any principles, it can eat away at you from the inside out, even while you're in denial. There are good, honest, hard working people, and then there's you."

"True enough. I follow completely," Adriana agreed.

"If I launder the Kings Crew's coke money, then I'm contributing to the drug addicted hooker's dilemma of doing something immoral, irresponsible, and illegal, just so she can score another hit. And I'm a party to the married man's infidelity, who's paying a street walker for sex, then bringing a disease home to his wife, who passes it on to his best friend."

"You paint a lovely picture," she said, and took a liberal swallow of her wine.

"And I'm contributing to the pushers who try and hook young kids — not much older than Hannah or Manuel, with cheap drugs, so they can get them addicted and ensure a steady supply of future, desperate customers. And when they're hopelessly and hideously addicted, and there's no turning back, I'm aiding and abetting in the murder of the convenience store clerk who gets robbed for a hundred measly bucks in the till, so they can buy one more hit of meth, or coke, or some other poison.

"Then there's the matter of corruption within the government, police services, and our courts of law who compromise the system, or look the other way in a myriad of criminal matters, through bribery, or coercion. I'm a part of that too. It just grows, mutates and evolves like an unstoppable disease, and it's sickening.

"Gangs, mafia, unions, business, industry, police, judiciary, government. All mocking each other's authority, pushing the envelope of what they can get away with, and pointing fingers at someone else... it never ends. It's like an infinitely expanding network of criminal honeycomb, multiplying, feeding on itself, and permeating the whole global village. In the worldwide effort to fight and counteract it, like the war against drug trafficking in Brazil, it's an admirable gesture, but we're failing — miserably, perhaps.

"And in the big picture, I'm a small cog in a big wheel, but nonetheless, a part of a global conspiracy that commits untold crimes against good people and bad, all in the name of drug trafficking.

"And God forbid, if I got lured into an involvement with any of the debauchery we witnessed today, I wouldn't be able to look in a mirror again for the rest of my life. Dogs, hookers, pornography, human trafficking, murder, gang warfare, and no doubt there's much, much more, and worse going on out there. It's a cancer in society that's eating away at everything that's good and worthwhile in the world, and you can submit to the sole temptation it offers — dirty money, or you can walk away from it."

Adriana gripped her wine glass and said, "I feel like I'm back in a law school lecture hall. Where is all this going, Professor?"

"Where it's going is that I've done a lot of things that fall to the left side of the line between right and wrong, and I've had my fill of it. Getting fired unfairly at the bank years ago put a demon in my head and bent my thinking and actions in a wrong direction. I'm not proud of my past, and I've paid a price for it in my personal life and in my self esteem now. And God knows, it's just blind luck that I haven't been killed or arrested."

"*Yet*," Adriana added.

"I want to move on, put it all behind me, and make contributions to things that are constructive, that will make me, and others, proud, for a change. I'll never be perfect, but from now on, I'm gonna stand on this side of the line, so when someone like Captain Toromenta asks me what I do for a living, I won't have to evade the question. I'll be able to look him in the eye and give a straight answer, and a truthful one."

Adriana's eyes widened. "And just when are you going to turn over this new leaf of morality and good citizenship?"

Mat set down his wine glass and turned towards her in his chair. "Tomorrow, and I'd like you to come with me. I'm going back to Panama."

She stared at him speechless, although a thousand thoughts were racing through her head. He returned her gaze with optimism and anticipation.

Five... ten... fifteen seconds... finally she said, "Do you mean you're *going for good?*"

Mat replied, "I'm going to live there. I'll buy some real estate, something nice — I've got the money. I'll get a working visa and set up another branch of our company, then travel back and forth between Panama and Canada a couple, three, four times a year. I've researched it at length. It's the perfect solution… *if you'll join me.*"

Adriana was thunderstruck. "What about my law practice? My house? My life?"

"You'll have a *new life* in a beautiful, modern, affluent country, with me. We can learn to speak Spanish, together. You can get your legal accreditations down there if you want to keep working, though I don't know why you'd want to… We'll be millionaires, many times over."

Adriana tripped up on that last comment. "What? Where's all this money going to come from?"

Mat was on a roll and looked at her like he was selling a dream. "First, I have money squirreled away in overseas accounts in several countries. I can pull it all in and put it in the *Empressa* in Guatemala. Together with the money that's already there, we'll have eight million. And there's still another three million in transit. That's eleven million and change, securely hidden in the Empressa's accounts. I'll make sure Foley's set up for life, then we'll have the rest. We can get by on several million, for a year or two."

Adriana looked astonished and said, "But *most* of that money belongs to the Kings Crew. They'll be looking for it. They'll kill if they have to, to get it back."

Mat knew something that she didn't from his conversation with Dom Hall and Jesse Novak. The only one left alive who knew anything about the money was Jesse, and he wouldn't be mounting a world wide search for Mathew Crawford — money launderer, or for a parcel of loot that was basically *found money*… It was from the theft of drugs that someone else had paid for, the Red Sun Boys. 'You never take unnecessary chances, or put yourself in jeopardy, over money,' he had once lectured Mathew.

He explained, "Look, nobody but you and I know where the money is — securely hidden in a protected account in a Guatemalan bank. Even Foley thinks it's somewhere in Panama, although I never meant to keep secrets from him. The only ones in on the caper from the start, I learned, were the two accountants and their crooked counselor, Jesse Novak. Both the accountants are dead, and Novak may well be a slippery, corrupt, double dealing lawyer, but he protects himself by staying out of the limelight of criminal affairs. I'm thinking I might just *keep it all.* Send Novak a clear message that if he comes looking for me, or the money, I'll see to it that he's exposed as a thief and a traitor amongst the Kings Crew. He'll be lucky if they don't lynch him, or just cut him in half with a chain saw.

"I've been doing this long enough to know how these types work. He won't come after it because it would put him in danger — he'd be exposed. If the other bikers found out they'd been duped out of the action to the tune of millions, and that he was a party to the deception, he'd turn up in a slaughter house, disemboweled on a meat hook with his nuts in his mouth."

Adriana looked aghast. "*Mathew, please.*"

"If the Red Sun Boys caught wind that he was in on it, he'd wind up sporting a bolt from a crossbow in the lapel of his Harry Rosen suit, like Jack Kincaid. If the cops got onto him, he'd be linked to untold files in the cold case department. And he knows all that. He's crooked as a dog's hind leg, but he's not stupid, and self preservation is number one on his list."

Adriana listened attentively and said, "You seem to have this all figured out. What if something goes wrong. You can't plan for everything."

"Planning for everything is *what I do.* On the long shot that Novak really does get ambitious and decides to mount a pursuit, I'll have Foley get involved. Novak's a dirty lawyer, out of control, but Foley can be a *lethal killer,* under control. Novak would disappear from the social pages of Vancouver's polite society over the course of a weekend, I'm confidant."

Adriana swallowed hard, and said, "I thought you wanted to walk the straight and narrow. What happened to standing on the right side of the line between right and wrong?"

"I'm trying to fight my way out of this mess. You don't come to a knife fight empty handed. If I have to take down a rat like Novak to get out of all this, I'll just add that to the long list of sins I'm already guilty of next time I'm in the confessional booth. Once this is all finished though, I guarantee I'll never look back, probably," Mat replied, without really noticing the contradiction in his last statement.

Adriana noticed, however, and laughed quietly. Then she said, "Alright lover, I'll be at your side, whatever you decide to do. But there will be a lot of preparations to make. You don't just move to another country, like you move across town. I know. I've done it before."

Mat nodded and pointed out, "I'm a detail guy, by nature. I've researched it and getting a visa to enter the country is not that difficult, especially if you're bringing over some wealth and buying real estate. I'll contact our lawyer friend, Marcos Del Rio, and get all the details about what's required. Compared to what we've been doing, this will be a walk in Stanley Park."

Adriana was excited by their budding plans, but scared too about the prospects of taking such a bold step. She was on board with her man, but also practical minded about making everything work.

She sipped the last of her wine and said, "Here's what I suggest... You go to Panama and make the arrangements on that end. I'll stay here, and close off everything I can — transfer client files, put my house and car up for sale, pay any bills and start closing out accounts, that sort of thing. I'll make a list for you to do too, when you're back. Then, we'll go together, and start over." It was done. Mat had convinced her, and they were on their way down the road of new beginnings and adventure.

Mat nodded and looked at her almost in disbelief of what was happening. He felt like the luckiest guy in the world. He was breaking free of the world of criminality. The girl of his dreams had just agreed to stand at his side. He would always love Hannah and he planned to visit her often. Now, however, he would also have Manuel — his new little pal. He was excited about starting up his company in Panama, especially since the business here in Vancouver was doing so well, and with Foley and Danielle, it would remain in good hands. Best of all, he was going to be living the good life, in a beautiful, sunny, warm country with enough wealth to never worry again.

Mat stood up and took Adriana by the hand, raising her out of her chair. He put his arms around her and held her tightly. "*Thank you*," he said. "And this time I mean it!" They both laughed and hugged like newlyweds.

"It's nice to hear your gratitude, darl," she replied. "But this is a big step for me... *for us*. I don't mind telling you, I'm scared!"

Mat felt the same, but moreover he felt something else and wanted to share it with her. In fact, he wanted to share it more than anything else in the world, right now. He released her from his hug and held her hands in his.

"There's something else you should know. It's important," he said sternly.

"There's more? What now?"

"Just a detail, really, but one I think you'll want to hear. I've come down a long road to get where I'm standing today, and I've got some scars on my face to show for it, but there's a few things I know for certain now and one of them is... *I love you, Adriana*, with all my heart, and I never, *ever* want to be without you again. I want us to grow old together, and have each other for the rest of our lives. We're meant to be together."

Adriana's eyes welled up, and a tear rolled down her cheek. *At last!*

Mat looked on, surprised actually, at how easy that was to say to her. He meant every word of it, and had to stop himself from going on and on and sounding melodramatic, like some syrupy *B-actor* in a daytime soap opera.

"Geeze… I thought you'd be happy. How come you're crying?" he quipped.

"Oh, Mat, just *shut up* for once and let me enjoy the moment. *I love you too*, you fool. Haven't you known it from the start?" and she pressed her head to his shoulder.

"Stop it before I start crying too," he replied. The emotion of the moment was thick in the air, as they both shared powerful feelings. With one hand, he turned her head from his shoulder toward his face, and kissed her lips tenderly. Her tears were salty and sweet on his tongue, and he relished the taste, and smell, and sight, and feel of her in his arms. He drank her in and never wanted to let her go.

So Mat's master plan was on the table. Now they just had to make it happen.

CHAPTER 42

BY NEXT MORNING, Mat was sitting in the passenger seat of Adriana's car, destined for Vancouver International Airport. His luggage was packed for a stay of perhaps a week, and his open-ended plane ticket was waiting for pick up at Air Canada. Long enough to meet with the lawyer, to pick up government applications for visas and any other requirements, and to look around at possible places to buy a house.

Adriana would lay low back in Vancouver, not taking any chances on running into trouble with criminals and gangs. Foley was charged with watching over her like a Secret Security agent assigned to the President. Everything was set. She pulled into to the departures drop off area and the two lovers kissed once before parting.

On cue, just like before, they spoke to each other at exactly the same time.

"Call me?" she said.

"I'll call you," he promised, over top of her.

They laughed like infatuated teenagers, as he leant in the car window and pecked her once more on the cheek. Reluctantly, she put the shift in D and waived goodbye, merging into airport traffic.

Mat walked into the busy terminal where other travelers were milling about in every direction. He approached the counter under a sign that read *Air Canada Customer Service,* where his ticket would be waiting. *Now there's an oxymoron, if I've ever heard one,* he said to himself. After a short wait, he stepped up to an official looking, uniformed young woman who looked *pissed off* about something, and in a terrible hurry.

"Hello. Mathew Crawford... There's a ticket here for me, I believe?"

"Put your luggage here," she snapped, nodding towards the scale. "Any carry on?"

As the ticketing agent tapped away on her keyboard, Mat felt a hand on his shoulder from behind. He turned around. It was detective Jerome Lundgren. *Ah Christ, now what?*

"Mr. Crawford, going somewhere?" the Inspector asked with condescension. His steely blue eyes were piercing into Mat. Behind him stood two burly young men in police uniforms, complete with black leather gloves, shoulder mics, hand cuffs, night sticks, and holstered hand guns.

Mat's heart nearly jumped out of his chest. "Inspector, what are you doing here?" he said.

Lundgren replied, "I thought we agreed that you wouldn't be leaving the country, without notifying my office? You're a *person of interest* in a police matter, did you forget?"

"Well, this is a business trip and I'm running a business. Did *you* forget? "

Lundgren looked directly at Mat, a sly smile cleverly turning up the corners of his mouth now.

"And would that business have anything to do with a stolen shipment of cocaine from China? A murdered ship's captain? A vicious rivalry between two of our city's most violent gangs? A human trafficking operation? And money laundering? I could continue, but is it safe to say, I'm on the right track?"

Mat was caught. The cop knew everything, he was certain. In moments he would be wearing hand cuffs, being Mirandized, then led out of the terminal by the two uniforms. *So close, and now this.* Everything Christine had predicted about his eventual downfall would now come true — arrested, tried, convicted, property and assets seized, incarcerated, ruined.

"I'm not saying another word without a lawyer!" Mat said emphatically.

Lundgren looked unimpressed. "God, I wish I had a dollar for every time I've heard that from someone about to take a fall."

He gestured to the Tim Hortons down the way and said, "Relax, let's get a coffee and have a little chat. Shall we?"

Now Mat was really confused. This cop appeared to have the whole story. Why was he now turning this into a social call?

"Alright, of course," Mat said, as if he had a choice. Away they went like two friends getting together for a *'chat'*.

They each bought a regular coffee and sat down together at a table for two. The uniformed police officers waited at the far side of the corridor like guards at Buckingham Palace.

Lundgren said, "I hear that location is everything with these Tim's franchises. In a busy airport like this, it's gotta be a real money maker. But in some of the outlying areas, you can lose a fortune trying to keep it alive, until you're finally broke. You can lose your life savings."

"I suppose," Mat added, weakly.

Lundgren continued, "My brother bought into a franchise. His take on it after three years of blood, sweat, and tears?" Mat looked on but made no comment. "Franchises are designed to make money for the *franchisor.* They're like pimps taking money from hookers. Bleed ya dry, 'til you're used up, done, and buried. *Franchisees* die a cruel, agonizing death, more often than not. Says he wouldn't go into one of those again if you held a gun to his head."

Mat was in agony. "Did we come here to talk about franchises, and your brother?"

"Oh, I'm sorry. You're still thinking about our little exchange back at the Air Canada check in, I take it," Lundgren said.

"Ya, it's sort of on my mind."

The detective took a sip from his coffee and made a face. "Damn, too much sugar, again. My doc says I gotta start cuttin' back on sugar and salt. The stuff will kill you. It's basically just super-refined poison, and it's added to almost all processed foods. It can put your blood pressure and blood sugars way outta whack. But then I always said, 'If you live long enough, something's gonna kill you.'" He grinned widely and chuckled.

"Listen — here's where we're at. I put a police order into the airline to flag your name, for any ticket purchases. Last night we got a call that you're planning a little trip to the Republic of Panama... on business. *Ya right.* So I ask myself, should I spring the trap on everything I know about this guy's activities, bust him, and throw the book at him? And I've been a cop, a good one, for twenty years next month, so I'm predisposed to putting the bad guys away whenever I can. You follow me so far?"

"I'm trying my best to keep up, ya."

"Then I say to myself, 'But why would I pull the rug out from under a guy that could do more harm to the real criminals *inside* their own organization, than we have for years with all our badges, resources, money and authority, from the *outside?*' Maybe I'm getting old, but I'm starting to believe that winning the war against these guys is more important than adhering to the strict letter of the law. Dominic Hall, Carlos Garcia, The Kings Crew, The Red Sun Boys, others... We know 'em all. That's the business we're in.

"See, they've infiltrated us, we're aware, but that door swings both ways. We've got guys on the inside of their operations too. Our own little paparazzi spying on every piece of dirt they can find. God, this game's getting old. Sometimes I wonder why we bother. When's it ever gonna change anything? I bust my ass to put 'em away, and some slippery lawyer gets them off on a technicality, or plea bargains for a slap on the wrist."

Inspector Lundgren took a swallow of coffee and continued, "We know about the stolen shipment of cocaine, the murder of Captain Montgomery Furlong, your contract to money launder the proceeds of the drug sales, and that 'hick up' at the end where those little, Asian ferrets stole back their treasure of *white death*. Who expected that?

"We even had a good officer stumble across them when they were loading and transporting it out of a facility in Burnaby. Poor bugger got gagged and tied up with mover's tape in a warehouse for his trouble. How's your coffee? You don't seem to be drinking it."

Mat lifted the paper cup to his lips and pulled in a mouthful. "It's fine. Go on."

"'kay, anyways, now some wise guy approaches me with my kid at a Canucks game, and starts makin' small talk. Turns out he knows my name, and my kid, and my wife, and where I live... *without* my telling him. Says he wants to make a deal with me. *Suggests* it would be in my family's best interests to cooperate. It goes like this.

"First, he says we're being watched, so if I try anything cute there's someone close by who will put a hole in my head with a .22 caliber zip gun. He says he represents a major crime syndicate in Vancouver and they want an inside man working in the Vancouver Police Department, homicide division. Next he tells me they've got a million bucks, cash, for me in exchange for my cooperation and collaboration from inside the cop shop. They've even got a guy who can launder it, so I can put it to use when I'm ready."

Mat interrupted, "And you agreed? You accepted a bribe?"

"I didn't say 'yes'. I didn't say 'no'. I said, 'I'm listening'. Then he says he's got all the dirt on the Furlong murder and a drug heist that went along with it. He lays out the whole story including your involvement as the money launderer."

"That son of a bitch!" Mat cursed. "I've got a pretty good idea who was behind that scheme, and I'll bet he's a dirty lawyer with expensive suits and the ethics of a pit viper. Did you get any names in this offer to make *you* a dirty cop and *me* a captive slave to their organization?"

"Patience, my friend. Anyways, the *deal* goes like this. They've dropped their pants and shown you their whole operation trying to entice you to be their full time employee, as the money guy, only you're playing hard to get. Seems you might want to go your own separate way after the drug deal is finished. They can't let that happen. With what you know, you could bring down their whole operation.

"So, if you don't cooperate and agree to work for them, full time, then I approach you and tell you that I got all the evidence I need to bust your ass and throw you in the slammer until roughly this date in the next century — *unless* you take the job like a good boy and work for the Kings Crew. And I can go after the Red Sun Boys, who I now know have millions of dollars worth of cocaine, that they'll be selling on the street.

"If, on the other hand, you take the job without any coercion and become their exclusive money launderer, I turn a blind eye, take my million dollars, and walk away. And down the line there'll be plenty more inducements of a similar nature for me, as their inside guy on the Vancouver Police Department.

"Gotta tell ya, it's a tempting offer. Five more years, and I retire — either a very rich man, or one who's gonna just get by on a policeman's pension." The detective finished off the last of his coffee, then crushed the cup in his hand.

Mat tried to summarize the deal as he understood it. "They want to pay you to threaten me with arrest if I don't agree to join their organization, full time. Or if I do join of my own accord, they want to pay you to look the other way, and collude with them on future crimes, for additional bribes."

Detective Lindgren smiled. "That's pretty much it. Now, I wonder which solution I should opt for? I'm here now, with two young bulls that would be happy to walk you to my car. Or I could let you get on that plane and probably never see you again. With the flip of a coin, it could go either way. *You tell me,* what would you do in my shoes?"

Mat could feel himself sweating under his arms. This was either the *luckiest* day of his life, or the *unluckiest.* "I guess I'm about to find out," he replied.

The detective looked Mat in the eye and said, "Now I'm gonna make *you* a deal. I'm not sure how many millions of dollars from that bunch of hoodlums you've got transferring around the world from one account to another, but I'm confident, it's a *lot.* I don't want five cents of that money to *ever* wind up back in their hands. I don't care how you do it, but you keep that money out of Vancouver and away from these creeps, for good.

"If you're as good as they tell me you are, you'll find a way to put millions of dollars out of their reach, and that's good enough to earn you your freedom today... deal? We've got moles inside their walls and if that money surfaces here again, we'll find out about it, and hunt you down like *the hounds from hell.* You follow?"

"Ya, I follow. So that's the *deal?* You let me go free if I promise to bury the treasure?"

Lundgren paused then said, "Against my better judgment, you get on that plane, 'cause now *you do* have business to take care of, and when you do, you better change your name and keep a low profile for a long, long time. They'll be looking for you."

Mat understood only too well. "I can tell you right now that I have *no plans* of doing any more business with that outfit, and I certainly won't ever be their full time employee. If you don't arrest me, they'll want an explanation."

"I'll say you gave me the slip at the airport. You wouldn't be the first criminal that got away," Lundgren said.

Mat wondered about the rest of the offer. "And what about you? Will you take the million dollars, cooperate with them on future deals, and accept other bribes? Be *their man* on the inside of the VPD homicide unit?"

Lundgren looked at Mat and winked. "*That's* the sixty-four-dollar question. They've threatened my family, and *money talks...* You better move along. It's last call for boarding. Don't wanna miss that flight now."

Mat didn't wait around for the man to change his mind. He stood and walked away, straight towards the departure gates.

"Oh, and Crawford..." Detective Lundgren called out.

"Ya?" Mat replied.

"Remember that Sorentino guy that got knifed at The Sutton Place Hotel a few months back?"

"Ya, what about him?" Mat said, hurrying to catch his flight.

Lundgren smiled, held up his hand with index finger and thumb, and shot Mat with a mock gun. 'Gotcha!' he might have said.

Mat realized, *that fast*, that he just admitted he *knew* the MO, and that the victim was a man — named Sorentino. And that Lundgren just caught him red handed. He may as well have made a full confession. He stopped dead in his tracks and looked back, a *deer in the headlights*.

"Get the hell outta here," Lundgren said. "Diamond smugglers deserve what they get."

Mat gathered himself, practically sprinted down the hall to his departure gate and was the last passenger to board the plane, before the door slammed shut. He took off his jacket before sitting down in window seat 6A and realized he was practically steaming with perspiration. He twisted the little air jet above to cool himself off.

An elderly lady with blue-grey hair sat beside him and said, "Well, here we go. At the other end, we'll be different people after this trip."

"Different?" Mat repeated.

"Oh, yes, dear. Life is a journey that changes you from one stop to the next, isn't it? It's the journey that makes us who we are." She smiled sweetly.

The large airliner taxied down the runway, then gave a mighty roar on take off, becoming miraculously airborne within seconds. Mat watched the ground below trail away and was overcome with a sense of relief, new beginnings, and incredible good fortune.

After hearing the safety regulations, first in English, then in French, and watching a live demonstration of how a seat belt buckle works, Mat put his head back trying to comprehend all that had happened. *Life certainly is a journey,* he thought, *and you do change along the way.*

An attractive young lady came around offering refreshments. "Some OJ and Champagne for you, sir?" she said.

"Sure, fill 'er up," he responded, eagerly. Then he thought, *No time like the present to start becoming a better man.* "Just OJ for me, thanks... Hold the Champagne." She topped him up as requested and moved on to other passengers. He held up his drink and, looking out the window below, smiled and sent a mental message to Adriana. *Here's to you, girlfriend. Love ya, darling.*

✳ ✳ ✳

451

Heading home on Marine Drive, Adriana felt an unexplained sense of connection and delight as the image of Mat's affectionate smile danced across her mind's eye, like warm sunshine on her face. For the first time in a long while she felt happy, relaxed, and just *good* inside, as if he was still with her, right now. Everything was going to be alright, she realized.

She looked skyward, and watched a distant, silver airliner sparkling in the sun, leaving vapor trails as it disappeared across the Rocky Mountains. With hardly a sound, she whispered, "*Love you, Mister.*"

AUTHOR'S ACKNOWLEDGMENTS

Writing a work of fiction reminds me of the old riddle, "How do you eat an elephant? One bite at a time, of course." That's what writing a first novel is like. The idea for this novel came to me after reading an article in a local newspaper about the criminal activity central to this book. It occurred to me that, like many things in life, good people can easily get led down the road to doing bad things, and like a trap, it's usually easier to get into trouble, than out. On a whim, I sat down and hammered out the first chapter in one sitting, with no real plans for doing anything further, sort of an experiment in creativity. I liked it, and my imagination ran wild with where the story could go from there. I was hooked.

The first person I sought a second opinion from was my most trusted friend, and confidant. I'm talking, of course, about my wife, **Pamela**. Thanks, so much Pam, for your love, support, feedback, brilliant ideas, and encouragement to continue working on bringing this crazy project to conclusion. With you, ever at my side, I am always confident that I can accomplish life's challenges, big or small.

It also has to be added here, that our lovely daughters, **Sydney and Taylor**, provide inspiration and entertainment daily ("How many pages is it now, Dad?") that make everything I do in life, including composing this novel, worthwhile and fun. Thanks, girls, for standing behind me and making me proud every day as I watch you grow, learn, and develop into lovely, talented, and intelligent young ladies. I truly am a lucky man, just to be your dad.

Douglas Hutton, President of **King Motion Picture Corporation**, you were a great sounding board on a number of issues I came across in creating this story. I made the changes you suggested, as we traded numerous emails and phone calls, and I hope you spotted them as you read the book. I sure appreciate the interest you showed in discussing the story and raising the finished work to the high quality of the many projects you have worked on over your colorful career in music, TV and film production, the arts, and literature. Those who have listened to the historical odyssey of your recently acclaimed, musical production, *This is My America*, or browsed through your television programs as part of the series, *This Living World*, will know that your standards of artistic excellence are a hard act to follow. Thanks Doug, for your encouragement to press on, your leadership in how to tackle a difficult project, develop it to its full potential, and see it through to its final and best fruition. "Go hard, or go home!" I hear you my friend, loud and clear."

A special thank you goes out also to **Jim and Mildred Flewitt**, maternal grandparents to our daughters, and the keystone of an extended family clan. The generosity and true warmth you have extended us, and others, over the years has been greatly appreciated and under acknowledged. Please know that your love and support has provided an enormous part of the fabric that has knit our family together and contributed to what we are today. Thank you for more things than could ever be listed here.

Thanks also to **Andy Van Ruyven** and **Rick Noelte** whose sincere, unexpected interest and encouragement to complete this project didn't go unnoticed. Sometimes you meet people on the road of life whom you don't initially, expect to become close to, but they soon distinguish themselves as very special people, with insight, ideas, and unique aspirations of their own. From those qualities you watch, and are vaulted to greater efforts and higher ambitions in an endeavor just to keep up. Thanks, guys, for raising the bar and letting me know that your expectations of me were to complete this book and to do it first class. *No pressure.* Hope I didn't disappoint you! Also, I wouldn't normally admit this to another man, but my wife loves you guys, both of you, and you know that. Thanks for all your support and genuine friendship to our family going back many, many years.

A while back, Ringo Starr sang *With a little help from my friends,* and without the encouragement of so many of my friends, often veiled behind jokes, playful ridicule, and teasing, I might not have put my head down with dogged determination and completed this novel, just to prove I could do it, and avoid another roasting by you bunch! For all the party animals we chum around with at our cottage at Fairmont, BC (*'A Hemingway walks among us!'*), too numerous to mention, thanks for just being friends, last year especially. Your kind support, compassion, and the numerous, thoughtful discussions we shared together really were, and are, appreciated.

George & Maddy Jenkins, you stand in a category by yourselves as family friends and surrogate grandparents to our girls. Your support, and endless, warm hospitality, stretching back many years around the dinner table, on the deck, or in the yard, will never be forgotten. Thanks for becoming more family, than friends, taking a keen interest in everything we do, smiling always, and believing in us. That kind of support would go a long way towards helping anyone prevail through challenging times. You're first class friends, and people! Thank you for inspiring me to think, and write about good people.

Mel Haughton, my lady friend in Hickory Creek, Texas. I owe you a *thank you* around the size of a Texas-Mickey! They say everything happens for a reason. If I hadn't bumped into you and your husband Lee in the hot springs of Fairmont, BC, I wouldn't have developed the sections you helped me with to near their potential. Funny, how a casual conversation can turn into an eye-opening and enlightening session with so much personal relevance. Thanks Mel, for trading numerous emails with me, and editing some sections of the manuscript that you had a lot more expertise in than I did, clearly. You set me straight on a few things that I didn't really know what I was talking about, and it improved the work substantially. Thank you, my friend. P.S. You're pretty darn close to my character, Adriana Santos!

In writing this first-time novel, I almost couldn't believe it when I actually finished it, or so I thought it was finished. This acknowledgment goes out squarely to my editor and friend, **Ann Westlake**, of **Writer's Cramp Editing Consultants** in Delta, BC. One lesson I learned through this process is that a good editor will take a rough diamond and turn it into a polished gem. I had pondered and developed the manuscript to the best of my ability and sent it off to you with the expectation that you might be stumped to find many errors in punctuation, grammar, plot, description, character development, pace, voice, and a hundred other issues. To my humbling surprise, it came back with enough red ink to wear out two Bic Roller Balls. And when I looked at your corrections and ideas, I realized, you were right. As an author, there is a line where your own objectivity stalls in reviewing your own work, and a second set of qualified eyes becomes necessary. Thanks, Ann, for your eagle eye, creative suggestions, and kid gloves in turning me around and pointing me in a better direction. You made it fun, and I look forward to working together again.

Most importantly, I'd like to send out a special thanks to **my readers** who place their faith in me to take them on a thrilling adventure of action, intrigue, and romance. I know that there is no shortage of other places where you can spend your entertainment budget and I sincerely hope you are happy with your decision to embrace my novel. I'm proud of it. I wrote it for you. It's been challenging and enjoyable completing this work, and I hope your experience in turning the pages has been as rewarding and enlightening as mine was in creating it.

On a closing note, I want to send a heart felt acknowledgment to someone whom I miss and think about almost daily as a source of inspiration, belief, and eternal encouragement, my late father, **Lloyd Gordon Sr.** Here was a man that could make you really believe you could accomplish anything in the world that you set your dreams upon, because he believed it for you. Dad never lectured, but he sure listened, then offered sound advice with practical, common sense. We shared many laughs together that I'll never forget. He was a *gentleman* by definition — a truly, gentle man; perceptive, kind, tolerant, and wise. For a long time, I had wanted to write a good novel. "It does your heart good, to *want* something," he once told me, and I'll remember those words, and others, all my life. His understanding and prudent counsel in all my life choices, good and bad, guided me through my earlier years, and taught me things I didn't even realize I had learned, until after he was gone. Dad, thanks. What I'd give to go fishing with you one more time, to talk, laugh, and hang out together, like before. I sure miss you.

Once more, a big, hearty *Thank You,* to everyone mentioned above! Let's do this again some time, shall we?

AUTHOR BIOGRAPHY

Lloyd Gordon, a Canadian, worked most of his career in the lease financing business in Toronto, Ontario and Calgary, Alberta. Reading and writing have always been high among his passions as well as fitness and exercise activities. Before relocating to the Okanagan Valley of British Columbia in 2008, a region known for its beautiful vineyards, fruit orchards, and wineries he owned his own business in Calgary. Now, with wife of twenty years and twin daughters, he and his family enjoy the four seasons of Canada, the warm, sunny summers, picturesque lakes, abundant outdoor activities, and relaxed lifestyle of the BC Interior. It was here that Gordon applied himself to the creation of his first full length novel, The Dirty Money Trap. Other projects are already underway.

Made in the USA
Charleston, SC
23 May 2010